"*Hot Summer* is the perfect summer beach read, the perfect escape, and the perfect reality every romantic deserves—a book to make you believe in happily ever after. Cas and Ada's chemistry sizzles and their love and tenderness could melt the hardest heart. If I hadn't already been a hopeless romantic, *Hot Summer* would have made me one. Absolutely, hands down, one of the best romances I've read."

—Karelia Stetz-Waters, author of *Satisfaction Guaranteed*

"Everhart's sophomore endeavor sizzles with will-they-or-won't-they chemistry. The scorching slow burn between Cas and Ada is so hot it nearly had me reaching for the SPF. What I loved most is that beneath the glitz and glam and cameras is a beautifully sweet story about two women learning about their own inner strength, all while going weak in the knees for each other. *Hot Summer* is a sexy and swoony sapphic spectacle—a perfect gift to all of us wishing every TV reality-dating show was a whole heckuva lot gayer."

—Andie Burke, author of *Fly with Me*

"All the fun of binge-watching your favorite reality show, wrapped up in a sexy, swoony love story. A perfect summer read!"

—Elle Gonzalez Rose, author of *Caught in a Bad Fauxmance*

PRAISE FOR *WANDERLUST*

"[A] perfect summer read—plenty of sexy enemies-to-lovers tension and enough immersive travel descriptions to feel like you got a whirlwind vacation, too." —*Reader's Digest*

"*Wanderlust* will hit that sweet spot for those who are craving something fun with some more profound moments and a slow-burn romance that will have you wanting until the very last page. . . . [A] fun romp for those looking to travel within their book." —*Culturess*

"Debut writer Everhart crafts complex characters with well-developed backgrounds and plenty of entertaining banter. . . . Set against the backdrop of gorgeous international locales, this slow-burn rom-com will appeal to fans of travel and social media story lines as well as the forced proximity trope." —*Library Journal* (starred review)

"[A] sparkling debut . . . Everhart's layered characters leap off the page, and the no-nonsense approach to both Dylan's abortion and her sexuality is refreshing. Far-flung backdrops—including Marrakech, Reykjavík, and Tokyo—add to the fun. Everhart is a writer to watch." —*Publishers Weekly*

"From the first page, I was all in for this thoughtful, thrilling, and romantic trip around the world. Everhart's writing is both light and cinematic, tying the reader's heartbeat to every moment of Dylan and Jack's love story."

—Annabel Monaghan, author of *Nora Goes Off Script*

"*Wanderlust* is an absolutely stunning rom-com debut! Elle Everhart masterfully crafts a heartfelt and adorable love story while also delving into complex family relationships and seriously relatable real-life issues. On top of characters I immediately fell in love with, the book takes us on a gorgeous trip around the world—I was left with major travel envy! This romance had me smiling the entire time, even through my tears. Elle Everhart is a writer to watch!"

—Falon Ballard, author of *Just My Type*

"Elle Everhart more than delivers with a sparkling voice, mastery of craft, and character chemistry that sizzles off the page, all while unpacking the timely and critical topic of reproductive justice. Carefree yet complex Dylan and adorably uptight cinnamon roll Jack stole my heart and swept me around the world in this cinematic, immersive, steamy dream of a ride!"

—Courtney Kae, author of *In the Event of Love*

"Elle Everhart's debut is laugh-out-loud funny, sizzling hot, and full of heart. Jack and Dylan are undeniable proof that opposites do attract, and following them around the world is the great escape we all need right now!"

—Jenny L. Howe, author of *The Make-Up Test* and
On the Plus Side

"Elle Everhart's *Wanderlust* is perfect for anyone who's longed to travel the globe seeking love, adventure, and even themselves. This is a soaring escapist romance that unpacks timely real-life issues and reminds us that trusting your own heart can lead to destinations unknown and unforgettable, that going away means coming back, and that the best journeys are in memories, not miles. *Wanderlust* is a book to be whisked away and enjoyed in a sun-drenched somewhere."

—Lillie Vale, author of *The Decoy Girlfriend* and
The Shaadi Set-Up

ALSO BY ELLE EVERHART

Wanderlust

HOT SUMMER

A Novel

ELLE EVERHART

G. P. PUTNAM'S SONS
NEW YORK

PUTNAM
— EST. 1838 —
G. P. PUTNAM'S SONS
Publishers Since 1838
An imprint of Penguin Random House LLC
penguinrandomhouse.com

Library of Congress Cataloging-in-Publication Data

Names: Everhart, Elle, author.
Title: Hot summer : a novel / Elle Everhart.
Description: New York : G. P. Putnam's Sons, 2024.
Identifiers: LCCN 2023055412 (print) | LCCN 2023055413 (ebook) |
ISBN 9780593545126 (trade paperback) | ISBN 9780593545133 (e-pub)
Subjects: LCGFT: Queer fiction. | Romance fiction. | Humorous fiction. | Novels.
Classification: LCC PR6105.V476 H68 2024 (print) |
LCC PR6105.V476 (ebook) | DDC 823/.92—dc23/eng/20231204
LC record available at https://lccn.loc.gov/2023055412
LC ebook record available at https://lccn.loc.gov/2023055413

Printed in the United States of America
1st Printing

Interior art: Heart float © BudOlga / Shutterstock
Book design by Alison Cnockaert

To Emmet, whom I love more than anything.

And to you—thank you for reading. x

It's hard here in paradise.

—"Sideways," Carly Rae Jepsen

THERE WAS NOTHING quite like stumbling into the office still half-drunk from the night before.

Cas had chewed an entire pack of gum on the way in that morning but, as a quick breath test in the lift up to her office confirmed, last night's gin was still very much present on her breath. And coupled with the, well, artful way her eyeliner was smudged under her eyes, she looked like she'd rolled out of the sewer before dragging herself to work.

In her defense, this wasn't Cas's usual commute. It was rare that she had to be in this early after a late-night event, and Cas would never have let herself drink so much if she'd known she was going to have to be here at this ungodly hour. And she especially wouldn't have drunk so much if she'd known she was going to be in a meeting with their chief marketing officer. In typical Robert fashion, though, he'd only felt the need to text her and request this god-awful eight A.M. meeting at nine last night when she was already five drinks deep.

Because he was nothing if not considerate.

And, all right, she shouldn't be drinking that heavily on the job, but it was the only thing that helped her pretend these dating events for Friday, the premier dating-app company she worked for, had anything to offer her these days. She could only host awkward singles mixers and talk to the same carbon-copy people about their very particular interests for so many nights in a row before she wanted to go lie down in the middle of the motorway and hope for the best.

Cas leaned forward and examined her reflection in the lift doors. She'd genuinely tried to make herself look presentable this morning, had even borrowed some of her roommate Aisha's vitamin C serum in a last-ditch attempt to brighten things up, but you would never know it by looking at her now. Her skin was sallow, dry; her mascara and eyeliner had refused to come off when she'd cleansed, hence the smudging; and her eyes looked like they were trying to retreat into her skull. She'd chugged a sports drink on the tube, but she was also halfway through an iced coffee, which was probably not doing anything to help her debilitating dehydration.

"Fuck," Cas muttered. She might have just been happy that she was able to show up here so early in the first place (gin stench, dry mouth, and all), but there had been something . . . suspicious about Robert's message after she agreed to the meeting. Something that told Cas she needed her wits about her this morning.

21:34

Robert: Great! If you could refrain from mentioning the meeting to anyone, I'd appreciate it. Talk tomorrow.

The fact that he had asked her not to let *anyone* know, not even her direct supervisor, had set off immediate alarm bells in Cas's head. She'd had to order herself another gin to keep from immediately texting Skye, her closest friend at work and her second roommate, to overanalyze it. The only solution, at that point, had been to hope she'd drink so much that she'd forget.

A solution she was clearly regretting now.

Cas scrubbed some eyeliner off with her index finger before slashing open the zipper on her crossbody bag. She unearthed her lip balm and swiped a thick coat across her lips as the lift floated to a stop on the ninth floor.

The lift opened onto a small lobby, little more than a reception desk and a pair of armchairs in Friday's signature purple. They'd left the standard concrete on the floor—seemingly an aesthetic choice, although Cas couldn't imagine that Friday would have been able to afford anything other than the bare minimum in the early days—but there had been concerted efforts to warm it up since they'd moved into this space six years ago. Cas hadn't been here then, they'd moved into this building about a year before she joined and started running their live events, but she could only imagine what this place must have looked like without all the rugs and plants and soft touches their receptionist and general genius, Jana, had added.

Jana smiled as Cas stepped off the lift. "Morning, Cas." Her gaze flicked quickly over Cas, probably taking in the way she was practically dragging her body behind her as she walked. "Looks like you had fun last night."

Cas laughed, though it sounded more like someone had

thrown gravel into a blender. "You know how much I love First Date, Speed Date night."

"I need to go to one of those at some point," Jana said. The phone started ringing and she turned toward it slowly. "My single life is, like, fucking tragic." Jana paused. "Thank you for calling Friday, how may I direct your call?"

"That makes two of us," Cas whispered as she unearthed her ID card and tapped it onto the reader on Jana's desk to sign in for the day. Jana turned her head away from the receiver to laugh.

"Of course. Hold, please." She clicked a few buttons on the phone before dropping the receiver back onto the base. "Don't talk to me about tragic," Jana said, rolling her eyes. "You've got a new person on your arm every week."

Cas attempted a smile, but the tightening around her eyes made her feel like her gesture probably looked less amused and more . . . unsafe to be around.

"Well, someone's got to make sure the scrubs we recruit are worth our time."

Jana barked a laugh and lifted her mug off her desk with a flourish. "You're too much."

"That's what they tell me. Hey, do you know if Robert is in his office?"

"Haven't seen him this morning, but let me check the system," Jana said. "Sometimes he likes to sneak in."

She took a sip of her tea and started rapidly tapping her mouse with her free hand, her eyes scanning the screen for a few seconds before she clicked her tongue. "Yup. He's here—must have shown up while I was putting the kettle on."

"Perfect." The sooner she got this meeting over with, the better. "Thanks, Jana."

"Of course." Jana flashed a wink. "I hope the meeting goes well."

"I— What do you know?"

"Nothing you won't know in about ten minutes. Now go, you're going to be late."

There was no sense pressing Jana for more. Cas had worked with her long enough to know that Jana said exactly as much or as little as she was ever going to. Cas half waved and walked off into the office, slinging her ID badge around her neck as she went.

The office was quiet for eight in the morning—most of the events team tended to arrive around eleven or even later if they were out on location organizing some details for whatever they had going on that evening, but the day staff were numerous, about a half dozen other departments in all. It was still a little before eight, so Cas supposed most people would be rolling in over the next hour or so, but it was almost apocalyptic, how silent the office was at the moment. The few people she did see were wearing large over-ear headphones and typing quietly on their keyboards, and honestly, Cas was jealous of them, in spite of the early hour.

She'd do anything to hide in her music and clack away on her keyboard every day and get paid for it. Her eardrums would certainly thank her if she started spending less time a meter away from pub speakers, and it would be nice, for once, to switch off. To work without having to plaster some big smile on her face and act like the sun shone out her arse.

Where most everyone at Friday worked at long, open tables, the executive offices were private, tucked away in the corner and lined with gorgeous windows. A few years back, they'd built a partial brick wall to separate the executive suites from the main floor, and it deadened whatever sound there was as Cas walked into the assistant bay outside the offices.

Robert's assistant, Colby, was sitting, as he always was, at his desk, and he smiled perfunctorily as he finished typing. "Go on through. I've let Robert know you're here."

"Thanks." Cas took another long, bracing sip of her iced coffee and opened Robert's door. And promptly squinted into the too-bright sunlight shining through his windows. It felt like someone was pointing a laser directly into her retinas.

"Ah, Cas." Robert was smiling, but there was no trace of warmth in his voice. "Good morning. I hope the hour isn't too early for you."

"No, not at all." They both knew Cas was lying through her teeth but neither of them challenged it.

"Well, good," Robert said, his eyes still on his computer screen as Cas sat down on the hard purple chair opposite his desk. "Because there are some big things I'd like to talk with you about."

That couldn't be good.

"Oh?"

Robert turned in his chair so he was finally facing her. "I have a proposition for you."

Robert tented his long fingers in front of his face, his glasses halfway down his nose so he could stare at Cas over the rims, the way he always did when he was trying to be particularly scary at their all-team marketing meetings.

It was an expression that was, unfortunately, highly effective. Robert's blue eyes were famously like ice. Sharp and unfeeling and deadly, like those meter-long icicles that fell off roofs in Norway and impaled people.

"Okay?" Cas had long since learned not to try to anticipate where things were going where Robert was concerned. He often had very different ideas about what was reasonable or, hell, even feasible.

"You may have already heard, but the exec team has recently been talking about developing . . . closer ties with some big media properties."

She had heard, funnily enough. Not a lot, just a passing comment one of the higher-up assistants made in the break room, about how much work scheduling was "now that we're trying to get TV execs on board." Cas hadn't really thought anything about it at the time; these things hardly ever mattered to events. They were much lower in the office hierarchy despite the fact that their work was what kept the lights on.

"I've heard whispers," Cas admitted.

Robert nodded sagely. "I figured. Though I'm sure those whispers were far from thorough, so for clarity's sake . . ." Robert grabbed a stack of papers from the corner of his desk and flipped it around with a flourish. There was a flow chart—no, an organizational chart—for some new marketing integration division and . . . holy hell.

"I'm on here." Cas pointed at her name, there at the top of the page. With more than a dozen people reporting to her.

"You are." Robert sounded like he might've been talking to a child, but Cas couldn't bring herself to be bothered about his tone. "We've seen the work you've been doing in events and we've been impressed. We all agreed that it's about time we give you a new challenge."

In a million years, Cas would never have expected to hear these words out of Robert's mouth. She knew that she was working hard—she advertised the hell out of every single dating event she ran—but it was always thankless. Something she was expected to do, not something she was going to be celebrated for. And certainly not rewarded.

All the rejected internal job applications she'd put through over the years were more than enough evidence of that.

"So, I—" She felt like her brain was short-circuiting. "I would report to you?"

"As CMO, yes. You'd be the direct line to the executive level from this new office along with Kaya—it's not quite reflected here, but we're merging print with digital, so Kaya will still have control of that side of things." Robert was studying her carefully, reading every micro-reaction on Cas's face. She should probably try to contain her excitement—she was certain this offer must have a thousand strings tied to it—but she was too tired. Too hungover.

"We're still working on the final org chart, so if you've got feedback on that, we'd love to hear it."

"Of course." Cas unzipped her bag and extracted a pen from the depths, and wrote a small note, *feedback*, with a tick box at the very top of the page.

"Before we get too far ahead of ourselves, though, we should talk about one more thing."

Cas's pen froze. "Okay."

"Broadcast is an entirely new venture for us. We want to make sure that we move seamlessly into that space." Robert grabbed another packet of papers off his desk and handed it to Cas. "And we thought it would make perfect sense to start with one of the most popular properties on television."

Hot Summer was scrawled across the top of the packet in big bold letters, and Cas's brows furrowed.

"The dating show? Is the idea that people watch *Hot Summer*, get depressed with their own tragic lives, and then download our app?" She chuckled—it was absurd, surely not their plan, but—

Robert laughed, the sound needles on Cas's skin. "In essence. But we thought, for this first year, we could get a little more . . . creative. See what we could do with these new broadcast partnerships."

Ominous.

"Meaning?"

"We want to send one of the Friday staff onto the show this year," Robert said. "Test out a more organic marketing opportunity. And we think you're the perfect candidate."

Cas heard Robert perfectly clearly. Technically understood the words as soon as he said them. But still, something wasn't clicking. Surely he wasn't saying what she thought he was saying.

"What?"

"For starters, I know you're a fan of the program. That sort of familiarity will serve you well. But more important, you've spent the last five years running a majority of our late-night dating events. You've been in more social scenes than I think most people will be in their entire lives. And I get glowing review after glowing review from clients who tell me you made their night memorable, and they're excited about their future romantic prospects."

Cas might've been happy to hear the compliment if it wasn't so easy to impress people on these nights out. They were drunk for one thing, giddy from spending time with people who might be interested in having sex with them for another, and even if all that failed, Cas knew she could be incredibly charming. She'd spent years cultivating the perfect persona—not-so-affectionately labeled Friday Cas among her friends—to ensure that everyone had a good time at these events. Friday Cas was bubbly, fun, always ordering drinks for the table, and the first to propose a scheme that was equal parts sexy and playful. She was seemingly open in a way that got other people to talk to one another, and she was an expert at spotting chemistry. At convincing people to give someone a shot, to see what happened, to *let love take them.*

Cas raised an eyebrow. "Yeah, but that doesn't mean I'll want to explore my *own* romantic prospects. And especially not on live television."

Frankly, an extended event she could do—send her off on a weekend somewhere, she'd be able to swing it—but the live television piece was immediately more nerve-wracking than Cas would ever be willing to admit. She was obsessed with *Hot Summer.* She watched it every year and wasn't the least bit embarrassed about how she followed the ups and downs of the relationships, the wild highs and lows that this type of program loved. She knew all too well the way that the show twisted people around. Made perfectly happy people unravel for the entire country to see.

It was excellent television, but not exactly something Cas wanted to subject herself to.

"You don't have to make a genuine romantic connection,"

Robert said, dismissing her concerns with a wave. "I know you haven't exactly been interested in getting seriously involved with anyone, so we're not going to pressure you on that front."

Cas's brows furrowed. "How do you know that?"

Robert leaned back in his chair, his imperious expression slightly hampered by the feeble creak of the springs as he tilted too far back and swiftly tried to right himself. "I've heard whispers."

Oh Christ. Cas could only imagine the things he'd heard over the years. Especially because, once she and Skye became friends, Cas tended to care more about the entertainment value of her storytelling than whether anyone was listening in.

She crossed her arms. "And these whispers were enough to convince you that I should spend all summer lounging around a villa in a bikini?"

"These whispers were enough to convince me that you had the right skills for the job."

"I—"

"If you flip to page three, you'll see a more detailed outline of our proposal. Take some time to read it, but do it quickly." Robert flipped through his own packet and jabbed his index finger at the page. "If you agree to go on as a contestant, you'll be installed as the new head of our marketing integration division when you're back at the end of the summer. In return, we expect that you maintain a professional image as much as possible—we've outlined specific lines in the contract, I know there's quite a bit of . . . suggestive behavior on the show, so we've been flexible in our expectations. We want future partnering between the show and Friday to feel natural, so become someone that the viewers like, that they trust—and, of course, make it to the show's finale."

"The *finale*?"

Fucking hell. He was trying to make this impossible.

"The research we've done has shown that people who make it to the *Hot Summer* finals bring with them huge opportunities for brand integration. You've already cultivated a social media following—albeit, a modest one—and we think that that, coupled with the following you'd get from a successful run on *Hot Summer,* will make you an ideal candidate for brand opportunities. You can leverage those connections to help grow this new division *and* use your new following to advertise Friday's services. A win-win."

Cas was loath to admit it, but it actually made some sense the more she thought about it. People lucky enough to be well-liked on this show saw an absolute explosion in their social media by the time they walked out of the villa, enough that they were able to coast on the collaborations with fast-fashion brands and protein-shake companies for at least a few years afterward. Those who really leveraged it were able to completely turn their lives around and build a career, but with this job Robert was practically handing her? She wouldn't even have to worry about turning her following into an income stream. Not in the same desperate way as everyone else.

"Yeah, okay." Fuck it. She wanted something new, and this was certainly that. "I'll review everything and get back to you, but let's do it."

~~~

A month later, after several interviews, planning meetings, and one very long psych evaluation, Cas got the final email confirmation from *Hot Summer*'s production team. She was officially in.

Hot Summer 2024 Cast:
Meet the lovers who are going to keep this summer SCORCHING

By Liliana Yu

The official *Hot Summer* cast lineup is here and holy HELL. This summer is looking even hotter than ever. With the lovers set to storm into the villa on Sunday night, this year in gorgeous Cyprus, let's get to know who we'll be watching get down and dirty all summer long.

ADA HALL

Age: 28
Hometown: Brighton
Occupation: Small Business Owner
@adahall

Why she's looking for a Hot Summer: "I'm ready to have some fun this summer. And if I meet 'the one' along the way, that's even better!"

CAS MORGAN

Age: 29
Hometown: London
Occupation: Event Planner
@casmorgan

Why she's looking for a Hot Summer: "I've been dating pretty casually for a few years, but it's time

I settle down. No better way to do that than spending time in a gorgeous villa for eight weeks!"

LEXI YOUNG
Age: 21
Hometown: Essex
Occupation: Influencer
@lexxxiyoung

Why she's looking for a Hot Summer: "I'm fun and flirty, and I'm very down for a super hot summer!"

MADDISON FULLER
Age: 23
Hometown: Newcastle
Occupation: Bar Staff
@maddifulls

Why she's looking for a Hot Summer: "My dating history is actually embarrassing, so when I got the chance to have a great time and possibly find love? I knew I had to go."

SIENNA BRICE
Age: 26
Hometown: London
Occupation: Case Worker
@siennabricex

Why she's looking for a Hot Summer: "My job can have its serious moments, and I'm looking to let loose! I also haven't had a proper boyfriend in ages, so . . ."

BRAD STANNARD

Age: 23
Hometown: Leeds
Occupation: Estate Agent
@bradstantheman

Why he's looking for a Hot Summer: "I'm single, so I figured why not? You're only young once, right? Plus, girls love me, so I don't think I can go wrong here."

CHARLIE SIMS

Age: 25
Hometown: Hull
Occupation: Scaffolder
@charlie.sims

Why he's looking for a Hot Summer: "I'm trying to be more open to different experiences, and this is definitely a really different experience!"

FEMI ABIOLA

Age: 27
Hometown: Birmingham

Occupation: Pharmacist

@femiabiola

Why he's looking for a Hot Summer: "I want to find my soulmate. That probably sounds foolish, but I am *so* ready for love."

JAYDEN CHAMBERS

Age: 20

Hometown: Manchester

Occupation: Electrician

@jaydenxchambers

Why he's looking for a Hot Summer: "I'm searching for that special spark."

REECE SIMMONS

Age: 21

Hometown: Essex

Occupation: Footballer

@reecesimmonsofficial

Why he's looking for a Hot Summer: "I'm hoping to meet a girl I can bring home to Mum, but, if nothing else, I'm hoping I'll have a good time."

We've got a really exciting mix this summer—even with a few older cast members than we've had in previous series. Maybe the producers are finally hearing our cries?? (Though, next summer, get us at least two older men!) Fingers crossed everyone on this summer's cast manages to find their perfect One . . . and that they bring us all the drama along the way!

Hot Summer premieres on RealTV on June 10 at 9 P.M.

CAS'S ARSE WAS going to be stuck to this leather seat. Probably permanently.

It was (arguably) her fault for deciding to wear bikini bottoms that covered absolutely nothing, but she'd also been asked to take off her shorts the moment she'd gotten into the car.

As though her denim shorts were going to be visible to the audience while she was sitting in the back seat.

The driver currently navigating along the steep, gravel-strewn road that wound up to the Cypriot villa where Cas and at least nine other strangers would be living this summer had spent the last ten minutes ignoring Cas's pointed questions about the decision to have her half-naked in the back of the Jeep (*unprotected*, as she'd last put it, *from the stray pebbles flying in through the open top*). She was starting to think he was hoping she would just stop asking.

"My arse is going to be so red," Cas said, the words almost a threat. She tipped her hips to one side, the sticky sound of her skin separating from the hot leather filling the silence.

The driver sighed, his hands skimming over the wheel as

he guided them into another turn. Cas waited for a minute, two, but the driver remained silent.

He should consider a job for MI6. He was probably very good at keeping secrets.

The car began to slow as it crested the hill, a few hundred meters away from the enormous modern villa that was Cas's new home. The front of the villa was lined with windows that reflected bright blue sky, and the winding tan gravel path gave way to a low-lying wooden walkway lined with fairy lights. Cas had just opened her mouth to ask why they were stopping when the front passenger door opened and Chloe, the show's main producer, climbed in.

Chloe's long blond hair was pulled up into a ponytail that rivaled Ariana Grande's. She was wearing a slightly too dark shock of blush across her cheeks and the bridge of her nose, and her lips were shiny and plump with gloss. She reminded Cas of the girls she'd picked up off the floor of the Spoons bathroom at her final Friday event last week before jetting off.

"Okay." Chloe popped her gum, eyes scanning her clipboard. "Cassandra, right?"

"Cas," Cas said automatically.

"Right." Chloe scratched out *Cassandra* on her clipboard and wrote *Cas* in large loopy letters. "In a few minutes, we're going to film the first few shots—you'll be walking in with Ada"—Chloe pointed with her pen out the back window—"in the Jeep behind us."

Cas turned quickly in her seat, eyes straining as though she would reasonably get a glimpse of this "Ada" in the Jeep still trundling up the road.

"Are we first in?"

She hadn't seen any cars ahead of them, but it was always a good few minutes between the arrivals. Though, if Cas's memory was correct, only the first two lovers walked in together.

"First in," Chloe confirmed.

Cas barely held back her celebration—this was exactly what she'd been hoping for when she'd gotten into the car this morning, the only thought that kept her going at half past five, jet-lagged, eyes barely open.

She'd spent the better part of the last few weeks thinking through every possible step of her strategy to meet Robert's demand of making the finals, but she'd known that so much of her actual experience once she got to the villa would be out of her hands, down to luck. Cas could have made it work no matter what order she came in—if she was coming in last, she'd have to command more attention, make sure she got a few good comments in—but this made everything significantly easier.

The girls in first, on average, had a much deeper connection with the audience, especially early in the summer.

Even with her attempts to suppress her joy, the smile was evident in Cas's voice. "Great."

Chloe looked at Cas for a long moment, her expression shrewd, before her gaze flicked down to scan over Cas's outfit. Cas had gone a bit over the top with the bikini she'd chosen for today, but if she wanted to make an impression, this bikini was *the one*.

The bottoms were nothing to write home about—simple, tie-waist bottoms that weren't quite a thong but still left most of her arse exposed—but the top?

The top was the stuff of Cas's dreams.

It followed the same shape of a typical triangle bikini, but the fabric itself was barely large enough to cover her. There was a thin line of black that ran underneath her breasts and tied behind her back, and there were more thin black strips of fabric straining up across her chest and tying behind her neck. It almost looked like a harness, but an incredibly fragile one, like the tiniest slip of the finger could send the entire thing tumbling to the floor. The top also left every single one of her tattoos visible, which she loved. The full sleeve, to be fair, was hard to hide, but she even got to show off the words on her ribs—PROPHET OF LIES in serif font—and those almost never saw the light of day.

She'd spent a long time looking at herself in the bathroom mirror that morning before she left the holding hotel, partially to come to terms with what she was about to experience, but largely because she couldn't get over her reflection. Her short brown hair, sleek and skimming her shoulders that shimmered with body highlighter, the shock of her tattoos and bikini against her pale skin, and *fuck*. Cas was turning herself on so much, she didn't think any of the people in this villa stood a goddamn chance. She'd spent weeks spiraling out, coming up with a plan to meet Robert's ridiculous expectations, but maybe this summer wouldn't be as tough as she thought.

Chloe briefly met Cas's gaze again before returning to her clipboard.

"Once you're inside the villa, you and Ada are to go straight through the house and immediately out into the back garden. The other women are going to arrive and then our host, Mila, will be there to start the matching process."

Cas nodded blankly. "Will we be getting phones like in previous years?"

The phones didn't seem *that* useful—they were basically jail-broken iPhones with, like, four apps, none of which were the internet—but she needed all the information she could get.

Chloe was scribbling something on her clipboard. "Your phones will be on your bedside tables after you're partnered up. It'll have a case with your name on it, but there are obviously limitations. You can take pictures, receive texts, but that's about it."

Chloe finished writing, and after a quick scan over her notes, she looked up at Cas. "When I get out of the car, Joe is going to lock the doors, but that's to serve as a signal for when you should get out of the car at the top of the hill. We'll have you standing up through the open top, so hold there"—Chloe pointed her pen at the roll bars above them—"and we'll be filming as you approach, so make sure your face is right."

That comment felt more barbed than necessary.

"Once we're set up to film your exit, Joe will unlock the car doors. The moment you hear it unlock, open your door and step out. There will be a camera right there, and it will follow you as you turn back toward Ada's car to greet her. You have to collect Ada before you make your way into the villa.

"The drive up will have a voice-over from your initial interview, but if you want to shout excitedly or something, we can cut that in." Chloe said it like she thought the last thing Cas would do was shout excitedly while she was sticking out of the roof of a car, and while she wasn't *wrong,* Cas wanted to prove the point now.

"Hmm." Cas tilted her head to the side, reveling in the feeling of her hair skirting across her shoulders.

"Okay." Chloe's voice was short, clearly getting tired of what must be her first of many of these conversations. "Now, unless you have questions, I need to go run Ada through this."

"No questions," Cas said, though her confirmation didn't appear to matter because Chloe had already opened the car door before Cas could even finish.

The silence hung heavy in the car for a beat before Joe locked the doors, the mechanical clicking so loud that Cas almost physically startled. They sat in silence for fifteen minutes before Joe finally glanced back at her.

"Here." Joe smacked his palm against the back of the center console. "Stand right up against the front seats."

It took a bit of maneuvering, but Cas managed to slot herself through the roof, her palms curling over the roll bars as she scanned around. There were people dotted along the road, all of them currently pointing massive cameras in her direction. Her grip tightened on the bar, her knuckles going white.

Cas was just about to slap on her best camera smile when she felt fingers skate across her skin to the mic pack on a belt around her middle. She jolted and found Joe's hand in the air in a *whoa* gesture.

"Just turning your mic on," Joe said.

Cas glared at him. "You could have asked."

"I'm sorry," Joe said, and he genuinely looked it. "Normally the contestants don't mind it."

"Well, I do."

The surprise touch was way too reminiscent of the bad

Friday nights, the ones that left her feeling a little slimy in her own skin and with a mountain of paperwork to complete to make sure that person was never invited back again. The bad nights were less frequent these days, but someone still tried to put their hands on her every few months, thinking her laughing and talking and smiling was some kind of invitation.

It was a major part of why she needed to get the hell out of events.

Cas exhaled softly as she cast her gaze back out to the scene in front of her. She rolled her shoulders discreetly before tilting her head to the left, then the right, a repeat of the little ritual she did before every one of her Friday hosting nights back home. She'd long since lost her actual nerves before these things, but there was something to the practice that helped her feel that much more grounded and ready for whatever was going to come.

The car started slowly up the drive, enough that Cas's hair began gently flowing in the wind. As they drove, the camera crew along the road took swift steps backward, careful to keep pace with the car without tripping. In the final edit, Cas knew they'd be playing her interview with a bright pop backing track, and the contrast with her reality, the crunch of the gravel and muffled conversation from the crew and the wind in her ears, made Cas laugh out loud.

It was natural and unexpected and, *god*, she knew it would look glorious in the final cut.

The moment the car stopped at the top of the hill, Cas dropped through the sunroof, careful to avoid knocking the front seats with her elbows, and positioned herself at the back door. The windows were heavily tinted, but she could just see the rush of the camera crew along the pavement as they positioned themselves at their next marks.

"I'm going to unlock in five," Joe said, eyes trained forward on the producer he could see through the windscreen. "Remember, there's going to be a camera right in your face when you open the door."

"So make sure my face is right," Cas said, echoing Chloe from earlier.

"I'm sure your face will be right," Joe said absently before he flicked the locks and Cas immediately opened the door. Just as Joe promised, the camera was almost directly in front of her, but Cas smiled naturally, casting her gaze off to the trees in the distance. She stepped out carefully onto the gravel, positioning her foot just right so that her stiletto didn't slip over the irregular stones.

It was warm outside, but the soft breeze now blowing against Cas's skin was a welcome change to the stuffy heat inside the car. The wind was brushing her hair back across her shoulders, and as the camera very obviously scanned over the length of her—catching the bounce of her breasts as she stepped out, the tantalizing press of the ties across her body, the miles and miles of perfectly highlighted skin—Cas felt a knowing smile tug up at the corner of her lips.

It was tricky business, letting the camera consume her like this, but Cas would do anything if it meant she got through the next eight weeks unscathed.

Following Chloe's instruction, Cas started making her way toward the Jeep parked a few meters behind her own. The car door was opening as Cas approached, but then the woman—Ada—shut the door and Cas felt her heart stutter in her chest.

Ada was *gorgeous*.

Cas had known she would be—everyone on this fucking show was stunning—but Ada . . . Ada was exactly Cas's type of girl.

Her long red hair was shining with gold in the sun, the loose waves curling over her white, freckled shoulders and tickling the middle of her back. She was already smiling as she turned around, but it seemed genuine, not at all crafted for the cameras. Even at a distance, Cas could see the way the warmth reached her dark eyes. Her face was coated in freckles that Cas was sure would only darken as the summer progressed, and she had the softest dimple in her right cheek.

Automatically, Cas felt her gaze drag down over the rest of Ada's body. She had full, round hips and the bright red, high-cut bikini she was wearing was a brilliant shock of color against her pale skin. Her top was strapless, the cups gathered at the center around a gold heart-shaped ring that held the top together. It was the perfect bikini to premiere for this show.

As per the show's expectation, Ada was also wearing heels, though she seemed less comfortable in hers than Cas was. Ada had opted for a platform sandal-style heel in a soft cream that was just a shade lighter than her skin. The platform should have made them easier to walk in, but Ada's foot slipped slightly as she took a step toward Cas, and her left hand immediately shot out to brace herself against the car.

Cas's smile widened automatically and she took a few quick steps toward Ada.

"Hi," Cas said, injecting her voice with as much bubblegum warmth as possible. She was Friday Cas on steroids. "I'm Cas!

It's so nice to meet you!" She almost said *Welcome to Friday Date Night* but caught herself at the last second.

Cas held out her arms as she approached, and Ada stepped into her embrace, rocking them both side to side.

"I'm Ada," she said into Cas's hair before she pulled away, her palms coming to rest on Cas's elbows. "I'm so happy to meet you, too!"

This close, Cas could see that her eyes were molten brown with flecks of gold and forest green in the center.

Cas swallowed. "Ready to go inside?"

"Only if I can hold your hand." Ada's cheeks were red, though from embarrassment or the heat, Cas wasn't sure. "I'm going to face-plant in this gravel otherwise."

Her smile was bright, her eyes shining with amusement at her predicament and a genuine warmth that matched the tone in her voice. It was one moment, but there was something just . . . *real* about her, and Cas knew Ada was, in all likelihood, going to be a public favorite. One to beat if she was going to make the finals.

Cas laughed and immediately took Ada's hand. "Of course. I need it, too, or I'm going to break an ankle in these."

She lifted up her shoe, turning her foot to the side so Ada could see the four-inch stiletto she'd paired with her bikini.

Ada's eyes went wide. "How the hell are you walking in those?"

Together, they started down the drive, the gravel crunching underfoot. Hand in hand with Ada, it was almost possible to ignore the camerapeople walking alongside them, Steadicams strapped to their chests.

Cas winked. "Lots and lots of practice."

WITH ALL HER "research" (i.e., watching *Hot Summer* every single summer for the last nine years like the incredibly well-adjusted person she was), Cas had thought she'd be prepared for the villa. Thought she'd known what to expect. Wouldn't be surprised by the grandeur of it all.

But no amount of seeing these things on television compared to the feeling of walking up to an enormous mansion knowing that this was where she was going to spend most of her summer.

The modern design of the exterior continued inside: Every wall was a crisp white, and there was a thin metal railing that wound up the stairs to the upper floor. There was a single pendant light hanging from the high ceiling, though it was high enough that it probably wasn't going to feature in any shots of the entry.

From the front door, Cas could see at least three neon signs, one of which read *smooches* in *Hot Summer*'s signature pink and bubbly script font. There were decals of mouths all over the walls—mouths licking lips, licking ice cream, sucking on lollipops—and every piece of furniture Cas could see was in an electric shade of either pink, green, blue, or yellow.

It shouldn't have surprised her. This was the exact color scheme the producers went for every season. But seeing it *in person* . . .

"Holy hell."

A shock of laughter rolled through Ada as she took in their surroundings, and it was only then that Cas realized she was still holding Ada's hand. Cas felt her cheeks heat slightly and she loosened her grip. She'd meant to do it subtly, but Ada must have felt it because she instantly dropped Cas's hand.

Cas cleared her throat. She was calm. Cool. Incredibly collected. "I feel like I blacked out and woke up in the middle of Amnesia or something."

Ada's brow furrowed and Cas hastened to clarify. "It's a club in Ibiza." She rolled her eyes. "Lots of neon."

"Oh." Ada nodded slowly as she took a step forward, leading them out of the entry and into the lounge room. When they made eye contact again, this time over Ada's shoulder, there was something almost withdrawn about Ada's expression, uncertain. Awkward. "Is that your usual scene, then?"

The lounge room was smaller than Cas had expected. There was a white L-shaped sofa covered in pillows in the corner and a television hanging on the wall opposite, though Cas couldn't imagine why they'd bothered installing it. One of *Hot Summer*'s strictest rules was that the lovers be isolated from any and all contact with the outside world save for the very select times the producers allowed them access to public

opinion. It was, apparently, a way to keep the contestants honest and prevent them from playing to the camera, but frankly,
Cas thought they did it just to make everyone feel a little bit
unhinged.

People tended to make more dramatic decisions that way.

Cas realized what Ada was implying and laughed, though
it sounded a little more like a snort. "Absolutely not. My clients
talk about it a lot, though, so I'm forced to hear about it via
exposure."

"Oh?" Ada's eyes lit up. "What do you do, then?"

"I work for F—" But, thankfully, Cas caught herself.

On the surface, the question was innocent. *What do you
do?*, aka where do you work? The NDA Cas had signed was
fairly ironclad, even down to the fact that it barred her from
mentioning her employer. They hadn't wanted to risk talking
about her affiliation with Friday in case it set anyone snoop-
ing, and they'd taken great care to wipe any and all photos of
Cas off their social media. But they'd known this question was
coming, and Cas and Robert had spent an unnecessarily long
meeting coming up with what she said next.

"I'm an event planner." She subtly shook her hair out and
brightened her smile. "I do parties and club nights and things
back home in London. It's fun, but it's nonstop. Especially in
the summer."

That, at least, was an easy truth. She'd rather be most
places than sweating it out in some pub while she watched
single people drool all over one another. Yet another reason
she'd agreed to this plan in the first place, the promise of a way
out of all those sticky nights.

But Cas didn't need to invite any more questions; it was time to do what she did best. Pivot.

"What do you do?"

"I'm a small business owner," Ada said. "I do, like, stationery, stickers, things like that."

"Do you design your own stuff, then?"

Ada nodded. "I studied graphic design in uni, and I started it then as a little side project. I got really lucky pretty quickly and it grew enough that I ran with it after I graduated." Ada turned on her heel to follow Cas down the corridor, and immediately wobbled a little.

Cas's hand shot out to grasp her elbow.

"We need to get you out of these shoes," Cas said, laughing.

"It's only a matter of time before I crack my head on this tile," Ada agreed, tapping her heel against it.

They walked quietly for a few steps, a million questions on Cas's tongue. It wasn't normally this hard—or this awkward—having conversations with people, but she was suddenly viscerally aware of every single word coming out of her mouth. Whether it was the way Ada kept smiling at her or the gazes of people who, in less than twenty-four hours' time, would be picking apart every word she said, Cas couldn't be sure.

It was certainly easier to blame the faceless thousands for the reason her tongue was tied.

Cas peeked her head around the corner before hitching her thumb over her shoulder. "The bedroom is that way if you want to have a look."

"Are we supposed to?" Ada's bottom lip was between her teeth, and it was almost endearing how nervous she seemed.

Cas shrugged, but before she could speak, a deep voice boomed through the villa.

"Cas and Ada. Please proceed through the bedroom and into the back garden."

Ada nearly jumped out of her shoes. "What the fuck was that?" Her hand was pressed to her chest, her eyes wide, and Cas couldn't help but smile.

"Voice of God," Cas said. They used this every summer as a way to redirect people when they weren't doing what the producers wanted. They cut it out of the actual episodes so the audience never heard it, but every lover talked about it in their post-show interviews.

And Cas had spent *hours* watching said interviews and reading every online forum she could find.

There wasn't going to be a lot of direct producer involvement this summer—in fact, there wasn't likely to be *any* as long as nothing catastrophic happened. *Hot Summer* was pretty unique in that all of the lovers were more or less sent into the villa and let loose for an entire summer with very little to do besides making out with one another. Sure, they'd get called in for the occasional interview, had scheduled (and highly structured and unaired) mealtimes, and a series of embarrassing challenges to break up the days, but for the most part, they were left to their own devices.

"I guess we're not moving fast enough," Cas continued.

It was a short walk down a narrow corridor from the lounge to the bedroom. There was a small step down into the bedroom and Cas was sure someone was going to wind up tripping up before the summer was out.

The bedroom was classic *Hot Summer*—five crisp white

Ikea beds with various neon accent pillows and throws—and yet another neon sign that Cas just glanced at before Ada opened the sliding glass door that led out into the garden.

The heat was intense as they stepped outside, especially after the short time spent indoors. It wasn't the thick, sopping wet heat of London summer, but it still felt like Cas had opened an oven door directly into her face.

She scanned the garden as they walked along the short, trellised path that ran past the outdoor kitchen and down to the stairs into the garden. Cas's eye was immediately drawn to the tiered deck stretching across the garden and sparkling blue water in the infinity pool that, even from this angle, seemed to touch the horizon. There was a fire pit with a curved sofa in the far corner opposite the pool—the place, Cas knew, where they'd hold all their formal ceremonies—and a gym tucked away beside the hedges at the edge of the house. There were places to gather in every corner—daybeds and beanbags and stacks of pillows scattered throughout that invited you to grab them and make yourself at home.

It was a master class in bringing people together and making them feel like they could relax.

But just as she thought it, Cas also started noticing the cameras hidden across almost every inch of the exterior. They were tucked in corners in the kitchen, hanging from trees, nestled in the hedges that lined the back of the property and shielded the villa from prying eyes. Cas was sure there were a thousand more that she wasn't seeing, but the microphone she had around her waist suddenly felt that much heavier.

"I think we're supposed to go down there," Ada said, pointing to one of the high-top tables just off the pool deck. There were a few stools around the table and, on top, an ice bucket with a bottle of cheap champagne waiting for them.

Cas grinned, a thin attempt at hiding the nerves now swirling through her stomach. "What makes you think that?"

"Just a hunch," Ada said. She was smiling again, the right side of her mouth hitched up just a touch higher than the left.

They uncorked the champagne, and Cas poured two generous glasses into the white plastic flutes stacked in the center of the table. Her contract had been very clear that they were only going to get a few drinks a day—one this morning and then two, maximum, at the first-night party later—and Cas needed every ounce of alcohol she could get to soothe the anxiety twisting itself up in her chest.

It wasn't that she was nervous. Not in the way the others might be. She wasn't hinging her romantic future on this show, she wasn't a fool, but she could feel the tension in the air all the same, thick around her. She needed this show, needed to be liked, needed to get to the finale.

"So." Cas swallowed a sip of champagne, blinking through the rush of bubbles in her nose. "What's your dating situation been like?"

Ada laughed and immediately raised her glass to her lips. "Not great." She took a sip, and when she lowered her flute, her expression was soft, almost sad. "I just got out of a long-term thing a few months ago."

"Oh no." Cas moved her hand to rest briefly on top of Ada's. A show of solidarity without being too over the top. "I'm sorry."

"Yeah, she wasn't ready to commit, and I don't know." Ada shrugged. "I'm ready for something serious, you know? That's why I'm here."

She.

"Are you bi, then?" Cas tried to ask it casually, like she had absolutely no interest in the response.

Ada nodded. "I kind of flick between using 'bi' and 'pan.' I'm not sure which fits best."

Oh my *god*.

"Me, too," Cas said. She was genuinely excited for the first time, and she could feel it coating her words. "I usually use bi, but I think that's more because I like the memes."

Ada snorted. "Fair enough. I'm so glad there's another queer person on this show. I was worried I'd be the only one."

"No, god, me, too."

Hot Summer had long since touted itself as the show where *anyone can date anyone,* but in practice, it was still one of the straightest dating shows on television. They'd had a few (read: *very* few) queer couples over the years, but the show rarely broke the hetero mold.

Cas quickly ticked through her mental roster. There were Tess and Sarah in Season 2, who coupled up for approximately four days before Tess broke it off to get back together with some toxic meathead. Alex and Max in Season 4; Cas remembered that they coupled up during Bombshell Week and lasted until about a week before the series end. Season 5 had Poppy and Niamh, but they were partnered up so briefly that, as far as Cas was concerned, it barely even counted. The show had let them get together for a day and a half before putting them through a public vote that ultimately sent Poppy home. It was tragic.

Every year, Cas watched, desperate for a Hot Gay Summer, and every year, she was disappointed.

"My mates are going to lose it when they find out about this," Ada mused, a soft smile curving at the corners of her lips. She then tipped her head back toward the sky and shouted, "Hear that, Shan? This *isn't* the straightest show on telly this summer!"

Cas couldn't help the laugh that escaped and held up her glass. "Cheers to that."

They clinked glasses, the dull thud of the plastic a sad substitute for the bright tinkling of glass.

"Anyway," Ada said, "what about you? How was your romantic life before this?"

It was an innocent question, and one she'd get a million times before the summer was out, but Cas needed to hedge her bets. If she had any hope of being liked, she knew she couldn't give the full answer. And even though Ada seemed lovely and sure to like pretty much anyone, Cas weirdly cared about what she would think. A lot.

So, a glossed-over version of reality it was.

"I haven't dated anyone seriously in a while," Cas said. An understatement by massive proportions, if her hookup count could be believed. "I haven't found the right person worth settling down for, you know?" Another lie. But then again, the person she *had* settled down for had up and left her, so that wasn't exactly Cas's fault.

"Ah." Ada twirled her champagne in her hands. "You're more of a 'let's go on a few dates and see what happens' type of girl, then?"

More like a one-night-stand sort of girl.

"Usually, yeah. I'm hoping I find someone here. It's a bit lonely, only going on first dates all the time."

It was a lie, her hope of finding someone, but it rang suspiciously true, that comment about her loneliness. It was uncomfortable to think about, too much to unpack right now, and Cas felt herself start to get nervous as Ada opened her mouth to reply. Luckily, before Ada could say anything, they heard a loud shout from the villa.

"Hi, girls!" There was a woman standing at the very end of the walkway near the outdoor kitchen, and she threw her arms up into the air when Cas and Ada spun round to look at her. She'd already been grinning, but her smile only grew as she sprinted across the deck toward them. "I'm Sienna. Look at you two, you're gorgeous!"

"Please," Ada said, giving Sienna a squeeze. "You're stunning!"

Sienna's dark brown skin was perfectly highlighted, shimmers of gold on her shoulders, across her collarbone, and on the high points of her cheeks. She was wearing an electric blue bikini that complemented the neon orange eyeliner she had swiped across her lids, and her hair was slicked back into a perfect high-top ponytail that swung as she walked.

"These men better be worth it, I'm telling you," Cas said, handing Sienna a glass of champagne. "We're tens, so if these men are threes . . ."

Sienna laughed and knocked her elbow playfully against Cas's. "That's exactly what dating in London is like, so at least I'll be used to it." Cas was thrilled to have another Londoner about, someone to talk to if she found herself missing home.

Maddison came through next, pausing for a moment at the top of the stairs, hands on her hips, like she was waiting for the camera to finish catching all her angles. She seemed nice enough, if a bit aloof, but Cas supposed she could be forgiven for that given the oddness of their situation.

Lexi was last through, and despite the volume of the group's conversation, they could hear her cheer before she even stepped out into the garden. From the moment she opened the door, Lexi was screaming, her Essex accent thick as anything.

"Oh my god, the pillows! The lights! Oh my god, it's fucking gorge!"

Cas choked, and Ada started patting her on the back in concern. "Are you okay?"

"I think so." Cas sounded like she'd swallowed a handful of gravel. "Or maybe I'm dying. Unclear."

"Pretty sure our contracts prohibit dying," Sienna said quietly, and that just made Cas choke all over again.

Lexi practically danced down the stairs, talking at lightning speed about everything she saw, and grabbed them all in enthusiastic hugs when she made her way to the table. Her dirty blond hair was perfectly curled, and she was wearing a white thong bikini that showed off her slightly orange self-tan. "I can't believe we're here, girls, we're going to have the best summer of our lives! You're all *so* lovely, truly, I can't wait to get to know you all, like, ah! Girl gang, right? Morning chats, coffee, all that!"

Cas felt like she was going to have a cognitive-overload-induced aneurysm.

"Amazing," Maddison agreed, and she handed Lexi the final glass of champagne. "Save some of that energy for the boys, though, eh, Lex?"

Lexi laughed loudly, the sound echoing through the garden. "I might kill those boys if I bring this energy."

"I'll cheers to that," Sienna said, raising her glass. "Who needs boys?"

"To killing boys and having the hottest summer of our lives," Cas said, raising her glass and meeting Sienna's in the middle.

Soon, with Lexi whooping loud enough that Cas was pretty sure her right eardrum had burst, everyone's flutes were in the center, and together, they clinked their glasses.

"To the hottest summer of our lives!"

4

THEY'D BARELY FINISHED their champagne when someone shouted from inside the house.

"Ladies! Are you ready to have a hot summer?"

The whole table fell quiet for a flash of a moment before the excited whispering began.

"Is that . . ."

"Mila?"

"Oh my god."

The first person round the corner, though, was not Mila Sexton, the longtime host of *Hot Summer,* but a cameraperson. Then, barely visible behind the camera, Mila herself.

Even over all the whispering, Cas could hear the sound of Mila's heels on the stone tiles, her solid, sure footsteps a death knell that they'd amp up a hundred decibels and synchronize with a steamy dance track in the final edit. The moment Mila stepped to the top of the stairs, her long brown hair blowing gently in a breeze that Cas would've sworn wasn't there a second before, everyone at the table started screaming.

"Oh my god, Mila! You're gorgeous!" Lexi, predictably, was the first one off her stool, and she ran screaming to the bottom of the stairs to watch Mila descend.

Mila was immaculate—her cheeks were a soft, perfect rose, her skin glowing with summer bronze, and her cherry red lips were shining with gloss that perfectly matched her tiny bodycon dress.

"Come on, girls." Mila's Scouse accent was extra thick, a kind of performance in itself. "Let's get you some men!"

She held her pose at the top of the stairs for a long beat before the cameraperson stepped back and Mila made her way carefully down the stairs, making sure not to spike her stiletto through the decking.

"Okay." Mila's voice softened as she approached the table, her smile present but not quite reaching her eyes as the cameras turned away. "Here's the deal. There are bits of tape hidden in the grass." Mila pointed to the stretch of lawn between the pool deck and the fire pit. "Doesn't matter what order you're in, just find a mark and stand on it. You're not to move from that mark unless you're going to step forward, and then you only move one full step"—Mila demonstrated, exaggerating for effect—"to show interest. Then move back to your mark."

Mila paused for a moment as though she was expecting questions before she clapped her hands. "Okay, great. So get to your marks, we're going to film some close-ups, and then the boys will start to arrive!"

And this was the moment. The first big test.

Cas had been thinking a lot about this initial partnering,

trying to sort through as many of the details as she could without knowing any of the people she was going to be in the villa with.

She had long since decided that she didn't want to get romantically involved with anyone this summer. It was too messy, too emotional, and a riskier bet, tying yourself to someone that the public might not like. Once you were in a couple, you were either saved or eliminated as a couple. And Cas would not get her heart tied to a sinking ship.

If she wanted to make it to the finals, she knew she would need to find a "romantic" connection at *some* point, but the real way to get herself through the summer?

A solid friendship couple.

It didn't matter what kind of friendship couple you were talking—it could be a will they / won't they, a pair of unlucky-in-love chronic singles, anything. A friendship couple was almost always the safest route if you wanted to make it to at *least* week five without any real difficulty.

Her concentration broke when Sienna grabbed Ada's hand and pulled her along as they walked out from behind the table.

"Come on, babes," Sienna said, smile warm. "Let's get some boys."

One by one, they lined up on the tiny dots of yellow tape. Cas stood at the far end, Ada on her right side. Sienna, Lexi, and Maddison, respectively, across the rest of the row on the small section of grass.

The cameraperson—Omer, apparently—took his time getting close-up shots of each of them. They didn't have to move much, just stand on their marks, look off into the distance, and smile, but Cas was certain she looked less glamorous and more pained.

A great way to make an audience impression if there ever was one.

As soon as he finished filming, Omer ran to the top of the stairs, and Cas felt the butterflies start up in her stomach again. She only had to wait two seconds, though, before Mila plastered on her bright grin, waved her arm toward the stairs, and said, "This is Jayden."

Cas knew that the *Hot Summer* producers spent the year scouring the country for the hottest people imaginable, but seeing Jayden make his way down the stairs was like something out of a film about, like, gods. Jayden was wearing bright blue trunks that popped beautifully against his light brown skin, and he had tattoos that danced along his arms and across his chest, a few of which seemed to match the tattoos Cas had down her own right arm. Even from here, Cas could see the muscles that cut into his skin—his biceps alone were probably bigger than her head. He was wearing simple white high-top trainers and he bounced on his toes in excitement as he came to a stop at the bottom of the stairs, his gaze lingering over the line of women opposite him before he turned to smile at Mila.

Sienna and Maddison immediately stepped forward and Mila laughed. "You're keen, aren't you?"

"Uh, yeah," Maddison said, her head tilting to the side so her ponytail swept over her shoulders.

Mila laughed again. "Well, Jayden, Sienna and Maddison have stepped forward for you. That must feel nice?"

Jayden smiled down at the grass for a moment. "Yeah, it definitely does."

"I'll bet. Sienna"—Mila pivoted on her heel to face them—"why did you step forward for Jayden?"

Sienna cocked an eyebrow and drew a short line in the air in front of her. "Look at him."

Jayden laughed and ducked his head, his right hand coming up automatically to skim over his close-cropped hair.

Mila grinned. "Well, of course. Did anything else draw you to him?"

"Not that I'm going to tell him right now," Sienna said. It was the perfect response—teasing and flirty, but still not giving anything away. The exact kind of quip Cas needed if she had any hopes of coming out of this first partnership ceremony as someone memorable. Sienna, definitely, was going to be a standout—between the comment and her expression, the slightest smirk tugging up the right corner of her mouth, her eyebrow still cocked in a challenge, she was a perfect picture.

If Jayden's expression was to be believed, he very much agreed.

"Now, Jayden." Mila paused for a long moment, first looking at Jayden then scanning across the women opposite. "You can choose to partner up with either of the girls who stepped forward for you, or you can choose someone who didn't step forward. The choice is down to you."

Jayden didn't even hesitate. "Maddison, you're lovely, but I'd like to partner up with Sienna."

Maddison shrugged a little before she stepped back in line, and the smile that spread across Sienna's face was immediate, impossible to miss for its brightness. Jayden made his way to her in a half dozen long strides, and after she greeted him with a kiss on the cheek, he wrapped her in a firm hug, crushing her to him.

"Uh." Even from this distance, Cas could hear the air being crushed out of Sienna's lungs. "Jayden, don't kill me, please."

The next few boys who trotted through were similarly attractive, though Cas hadn't yet felt pulled to step forward for any of them. They were fine—handsome, even—but if Cas was going to spend weeks sharing a bed with this guy, she at least wanted to feel *something*. Or be able to pretend that she felt something.

A young guy named Reece coupled up with Maddison, and a tall, admittedly lovely man, Femi, coupled up with Lexi (though there were a few glances from Sienna that suggested that she, too, had been thinking of stepping forward), until, finally, it was just Cas and Ada left to be coupled up.

"Cas and Ada!" Mila was smiling, but there was a slight frustration in her voice. "Why do you think you haven't stepped forward yet?"

Fuck. Did she look picky? Standoffish?

"I can't possibly compete with these girls," Ada said, gesturing down the line. "I want them to get their first choices, you know? Who am I to swoop in and steal someone off them?"

"Definitely," Cas agreed. She held Ada's gaze for a long beat before she turned to look at Mila. "It's over for Ada, though, if I'm into the next guy that comes down those stairs."

Ada laughed from beside her, and Cas was drawn back to her. Ada's smile took over her whole face, was shining in her eyes, and Cas couldn't help but match her expression.

"Well, then I hope this next lad is your type, Cas. Please welcome Brad to the villa!"

Brad was the traditional *Hot Summer* blond blockhead, in that he was blond and had a head shaped like a literal block of cement. He had an okay smile and a strong jawline, but it just . . .

It felt like a shrug, looking at Brad.

But maybe there was more to him underneath it all. There probably wasn't, but maybe Cas was just being . . . judgmental.

Until Ada stepped forward, the only one to do so, and Cas whipped her head round in incredulity.

She was going to step forward for *Brad*? Brad, of all people?

Mila beamed. "Ada! Brad tickled your fancy, huh?"

Ada nodded mutely, and Brad's smile widened.

"Well, Brad, as you can see, Ada has stepped forward— you're the only one she's stepped forward for. How does that make you feel?"

"Quite special, Mila."

Oh god. He was posh. His slicked-back hair and now this accent? He was probably, like, an estate agent or something, too. The worst people she'd ever met in her life were estate agents.

Almost like her thoughts summoned him, Brad's eyes flicked to Cas. His head tilted just slightly, his left eye narrowing as his gaze swept over Cas.

It took everything Cas had to keep the scowl off her face.

"You can choose to partner up with Ada or you can choose any of the other girls in front of you, even if they're already coupled up." Mila paused for a long moment before she continued, and Brad's eyes finally snapped away from Cas. "So, Brad, who do you think you're going to choose?"

Brad pointed at Ada floundering in the middle of the grass. "Beautiful Ada, of course."

Mila looked delighted, beaming at him as if Brad had just revealed he'd cured cancer. "Get on over there, then! Introducing your fourth couple, Brad and Ada!"

Brad seemed to be walking in slow motion as he made his way over to her, like he was intentionally slowing his pace so the cameras had to linger on him for as long as humanly possible. He ran his hand through his hair as he walked across the grass, an almost shy smile on his face as he looked at Ada from underneath his lashes.

There was no way that softness was genuine.

Brad touched his fingers to the outside of Ada's arm before leaning down to kiss her cheek. "Nice to meet you."

Ada pressed up onto her toes and, before he could pull back, kissed his cheek. "Nice to meet you, too."

A wave of nerves—quite different from before—swept low in Cas's belly.

Charlie was last down the stairs, and though Cas already knew she was going to have to step up for him, Lexi practically threw herself forward the moment Charlie stopped walking. Charlie, apparently unable to resist that kind of enthusiasm, decided to go with her, sending her former partner, Femi, over to Cas's side to round out the final couples.

Femi smiled as he approached, his expression bright despite the incredibly brutal way Lexi had just cast him off.

"Rejects club, eh?" He leaned down and pressed a kiss to her cheek, and Cas laughed, her hands landing on his firm biceps.

"My usual club, to be fair."

"Please." Femi settled beside her, close but not so close that he was crowding her. "I bet you're fighting people off twenty-four seven."

Cas grinned, something a little mischievous in her smile. "Well, people don't tend to keep me around for long."

Or, rather, *she* didn't stick around.

Mila clapped her hands together, an enormous smile on her bright red lips. "We now have five gorgeous couples. Sienna and Jayden, Maddison and Reece, Lexi and Charlie, Cas and Femi, and Ada and Brad. You're all going to spend time as couples, getting to know one another, competing in challenges, sharing a bed . . ." Mila waggled her eyebrows because apparently her suggestive tone wasn't enough to communicate her meaning.

"And as you spend the summer together, the public is going to make their judgments on your relationships and you'll have to decide: Is true love worth more than public opinion?"

Cas tilted her head, her brows pinching together slightly as she processed Mila's words. They were vague—probably intentionally so—but they were also *new*. In all her summers spent watching this show, Cas had never heard anything like it before.

Her thoughts started racing. There were always moments in past years when the public was able to influence the dumpings, or a challenge pulled in social media reactions. But the public was never acknowledged so outright before.

This . . . sounded like something different.

And it was going to profoundly fuck Cas's plan if she couldn't figure out what it was.

"In eight weeks, the public will vote for their favorite couple, and that couple stands to win a huge hundred-thousand-pound prize. But remember . . ." Mila let that sit heavily in the air for a moment, taking the time to look at each of them in turn. "This is *Hot Summer*, and the path to true love rarely goes the way you expect."

Ada shifted beside her and Cas glanced her way. Ada's arm was wrapped loosely around Brad's waist, and though her expression seemed carefully blank, Ada's smile brightened as their eyes caught and she flashed Cas a wink.

Cas straightened her shoulders, tipping her chin up just a bit before turning and meeting Femi's eyes. Neither of them had chosen the other, but that could be exactly the recipe for success.

Two scorned lovers, united by friendship. Perpetual wing-people.

"I'm going to leave you to get to know each other, but I'll be back very soon."

The words were innocent, but there was something threatening about the way Mila said them.

Omer took a few close-up shots of each of the couples before he left and then, finally, they were on their own.

They all stood stock-still for a full minute, staring round at one another, before Femi clapped his hands together in a way that was scarily reminiscent of Mila.

"Well, lovers, shall we get to know each other?"

NO SOONER HAD Femi finished his sentence than the Voice of God rang out over the hidden speakers. "Lovers— everyone should report to the bedroom now and collect their phones. They're on your beside tables and can only be used for photos and receiving texts from production."

Jayden took the stairs two at a time, and Charlie and Brad jostled each other as they ran, Brad knocking into Charlie's shoulder so hard Charlie tripped over a stray flowerpot near the kitchen. It was absurd, and absolutely the sort of thing that would make it into the show, or the weekly Missed Moments episode at the very least. These early moments were key in building out each lover's personality, and Cas realized she should probably say something. Stand out a little.

"If I'd known we were going to be running, I'd have worn a different bikini." She pressed her hands to her chest as she jumped over Charlie's leg dangling out in the walkway, and Ada laughed.

"You think you're having regrets." She nodded down toward

her own chest, her hands doing their best to press her breasts flat. "These things are no joke."

One of the phones was beeping when they made it into the bedroom, and Femi dove across two beds to snatch it off the bedside table.

"'Lovers! Welcome to *Hot Summer!*'" It was almost impossible to understand Femi through the laughter in his voice, but it was also endearing, his excitement. It softened him, made him seem real. A far cry from the chiseled model who'd walked through the door half an hour earlier. "You are free to get to know one another for the rest of the afternoon. Dinner will arrive in a few hours and will be announced by text. Until then, have fun."

You would've thought they were in some kind of Olympic sprinting competition to get back to the garden. Sienna paused only long enough to kick her shoes off—"I'm going to trip and die if I keep running in these things"—and the other girls followed suit, shoes flying wildly across the bedroom as they stumbled toward their phones. Ada managed to get her shoes off first and grabbed her phone and Cas's off the bedside table separating their beds. Ada tossed the phone to Cas, howling with laughter as Cas shrieked and turned away, her phone falling with a clatter to the floor.

"You're such a baby," Ada said as she slid past Cas toward the garden door. "It's a phone, not a spider."

"I've never been good at having things fly toward my face," Cas said, snatching her phone off the ground.

"Good luck on this show then, mate."

Things were still high energy when Cas and Ada made

their way back into the garden. A few of the boys were jostling each other in the grass, kicking around some ball one of them had found, and Sienna and Femi were sitting on the pool deck, laughing their heads off about something. At the sound of their footsteps, Sienna turned around, her smile growing when she spotted Cas and Ada on the stairs.

"Hey!" She patted the edge of the chair she was sharing with Femi. "Come sit with us!"

Cas grabbed a seat on the pool lounger next to Sienna and Femi, careful to leave enough space for Ada to join her.

"We were talking about what we want in a relationship," Sienna said.

Femi raised an eyebrow. "Were we?"

"We were about to be," Sienna said. She smiled at Femi, and the corner of his lip twitched.

"Okay, then. What are you looking for?"

"I want something serious," Sienna said. "I want to be able to have fun with them, I want us to have the same goals, and they need to be someone I can introduce to my mum. And they should be someone she actually *likes* this time . . . haven't been great on that front."

Cas and Ada laughed, but there was a new softness in Femi's expression that hadn't been there a few moments before. "That's what I want, too. Someone who makes me laugh and that I can bring home to my mum and sisters."

Christ, she was going to sound like such a monster compared to these people.

It wasn't that Cas hadn't dreamed—once—of meeting someone who she could introduce to her friends, who were her true family by any meaningful definition of the word. She just knew well enough now that that introduction wasn't going to make someone stick around if they didn't want to.

"I want a laugh and everything, but really, I want someone that I can trust," Ada said. She turned and looked at Cas as she said it, and there it was again, that rush that ran straight through Cas's middle. "And someone who cares enough to notice things, you know? There's been a serious lack of both in my last few relationships and it's getting exhausting."

Cas knew she was supposed to speak up next, but there was no way for her to answer this question honestly and not seem like a complete arsehole. *I'm not looking for anything serious* was the truest answer, but to say that out loud? She might as well sign her death warrant with the public herself.

"I . . ." Cas shifted so she could lean back on her hands, startling when she realized her hand had brushed up against Ada's hip. Ada muttered a little "sorry" and Cas looked up to tell her she didn't need to apologize, when their gazes caught.

"I guess, I want trust, too." Cas was speaking to the group, but her eyes were locked with Ada's. Focused on the way Ada's dark brown eyes seemed liquid, golden in the sunshine. "Trust is hard to come by, you know, I've—"

She barely caught the words before they came tumbling out of her mouth. She wasn't ready to reveal all this, not until she could find a way to talk about it that didn't make it sound like she was still desperately recovering from the one time that she'd fallen in love. She supposed that there was no way to make it sound "not sad," because it was, in fact, incredibly sad that she was still recovering after someone broke her heart so many years ago.

It wasn't that she was still in love with Saoirse. Cas didn't even spend any time thinking about her. They'd broken up years ago; Cas had long since moved on, because there was no other choice when Saoirse had decided to move, permanently, back to Ireland. It was just that if Cas believed that you learn lessons from every relationship—and Cas did believe that—it made sense that the lesson she learned had stuck with her.

That getting attached to people before you knew that they were going to stick around was dangerous. And you could never predict, even when you'd made a commitment, that anyone *would* stick around, so what was the point in getting attached at all?

Her friends thought it was a desperately sad way to live, but Cas had a good time. She had a lot of great sex, had some really amazing first dates, and she hadn't had her heart broken once in the last four years.

She could feel the words on the tip of her tongue, begging to be said. It would be good to let the audience see this about her. They'd feel like they knew her better, like they had something to root for. Cas finally "overcoming" her trust issues, finally "finding love" . . . it would be a story for the ages.

But she couldn't talk about it yet. It was too much, too messy, and to excavate it now . . .

The silence sat, thick, between them all for a beat before Ada turned to look at Sienna.

"I'm really hoping that I find someone here," Ada continued easily, as though Cas's almost confession had never happened. "I love the success stories."

Finally, something Cas could talk about without putting her foot in her mouth.

"The Yousefs and Amanis," Cas said, and Ada nodded.

"They never would have met if it weren't for this show, and there's something about that that I think is really just . . . maybe 'magical' is dramatic, but really nice."

"I know what you mean," Cas said, though, in her heart of hearts, she was having a hard time believing it. Not believing that Ada truly wanted those things—she seemed like she was being genuine—but that those things could happen for people who weren't like Amani and Yousef. That any random person could just come on this show and find someone that they clicked with, someone that they wanted to build a life with.

Ada shrugged, her smile soft. "I'm a catching-feelings type, I guess."

"Uh-oh. I better watch out, then."

Cas barely had time to register that it was Brad speaking when he sandwiched himself in on Ada's left side, taking up the rest of the chair. He wasn't paying attention to the fact that he was now squishing Cas and Ada together, Cas's elbow stabbing into Ada's hip, and was, instead, too busy laughing at something Charlie was shouting at him from across the garden. His laugh was too loud, too in-your-face, and it set off actual fight-or-flight signals in Cas's brain.

She'd heard that exact laugh from these exact kinds of men on way too many nights out. Had had to suffer through their excruciating conversation more times than she could count.

She supposed she should thank him, though (however begrudgingly), for saving her from having to navigate the minefield that was their topic of conversation.

"Hey"—Brad finally spared a glance for Ada—"can you slide over a bit? I'm hanging off here." He gestured down at his leg which, sure, was hanging off the edge of the chair, but there wasn't any room for them to move.

"You should just sit there." Cas pointed toward the chair behind them. He could also leave. Whichever.

Brad leaned forward, angling his head so that it was directly in Cas's line of vision. Cas raised an eyebrow at him. A challenge.

"Cas, right?" Cas nodded, and Brad's smile widened. "How have you found it in the villa so far?"

"Well, I've only been here for about ten more minutes than you have, so . . ." Cas thought the eye roll was more than obvious in her tone, but Brad either didn't hear it or was choosing to ignore it.

Brad laughed and knocked her thigh with the back of his hand. "Fair enough. Anyway, I was thinking we should play a little game."

"You can go back to playing football and leave us to our conversation." It might have sounded like a suggestion, but the instruction was clear in Sienna's voice. And, god, Cas loved her for it.

Brad just laughed again and spun, his shoulder knocking into Ada's. "Jay! Come get your girl!"

Sienna scoffed. "Excuse me?"

Brad, though, ignored her, and continued shouting to the villa at large. "Guys! Come to the pool, we're going to play Never Have I Ever!"

"Brad." Ada turned toward him in a failed attempt to catch

his eye. "We were having a conversation, we weren't looking to play a game."

"Nah, come on, a game'll be jokes! We've got nothing else on anyway."

"We were having a chat, mate," Femi said, watching as everyone else came running from their corners of the garden and grabbed seats on the pool deck. "Next time just ask, yeah?"

But Brad was too focused on the gathering crowd to acknowledge Femi. "Okay, guys, sit down! We haven't got drinks, so let's, like, raise hands if we've done it. I'll start first and then we'll go round."

There were only four deck chairs, but Jayden grabbed a few beanbags from the grass and tossed them over onto the deck for people to sit on. Lexi and Maddison perched on the end of the pool, their feet dangling in the water, and once everyone was settled, Brad clapped his hands, a shit-eating grin on his face.

"Never have I ever kissed someone of the same gender."

And fucking hell. Of course he'd started with this. He was already leering around at them all, practically salivating.

Cas refused to bend to his gaze as she, along with all the other girls and Jayden, raised their hands.

"Okay," Cas said, jumping in to take control before Brad could say something else stupid. This was a hell of a lot more people than she expected, and she needed to know the lay of the land. "Were we just experimenting or are we queer?"

"Experimenting," Maddison and Lexi said at the same time.

Sienna rocked her hand back and forth in a so-so gesture.

"Experimenting at the time, but possibly? I'm still sorting it out to be honest."

"Same," Jayden agreed. "Though I had a boyfriend last year," he continued, laughing awkwardly, "so maybe I've figured it out."

Cas grinned and tapped her toe to the outside of Jayden's trainer. "Yeah, maybe. I'm very bisexual, though I've dated more women, if that means anything?" Cas flicked her gaze to Ada, who was nodding.

"Yeah, me, too."

Brad pumped his fist. "Score."

If Cas made it through this summer without killing Brad, she should be awarded a Nobel Peace Prize.

Femi frowned at him. "Mate. Don't be gross."

Brad had just opened his mouth to reply when, thankfully, Sienna swept in.

"Okay, never have I ever had a successful date off a dating app."

"Wait, what about that app, uh . . ." Lexi was clicking her fingers together, trying to come up with the name she was missing. "That one where you go to live parties and stuff instead of swiping. Does that count?"

As soon as Lexi said it, Cas felt everything go still. Like she was an antelope, praying that the lion hiding in the grass wouldn't see her.

"Friday," Charlie said. "I went to one of their things once. I'd say it counts—it's basically like live swiping, some of those events."

Brad laughed. "Brutal."

One by one, most everyone in the group raised their hands, and Cas had half a second, maybe less, to decide where she was going to fall. Her arm twitched at her side, almost rising, but it was dancing too close to the truth for Cas's liking, the conversation. She didn't want to get herself into a situation that she couldn't get out of, didn't want to accidentally cross the line in her ironclad NDA without realizing it. It hadn't exactly forebade her from admitting that she used dating apps, but any and all suggestion that she was on the show because of her affiliation with Friday was expressly forbidden and this conversation . . .

It felt like a slippery slope that led straight to the courthouse.

Besides, she wasn't technically using the app to meet people anyway—she was running the fucking events—so it wasn't really a lie.

In the end, Cas was the only one who didn't raise her hand.

Shit.

She'd miscalculated.

Lexi was the first to start shouting. "Never?!"

Cas half laughed, half shrugged, a piss-poor attempt at covering her arse. "I just prefer to meet people out, I guess."

"It's actually impressive, if you've just been dating casually," Ada said. She laid a hand on Cas's thigh, a simple gesture that made Cas feel like she was melting straight through the chair. "Are you a fairly outgoing person?"

Friday Cas was.

Cas nodded. "Yeah, I'd say so! I like being able to go up to people and, like, immediately read their energy, you know? You can't do that as easily from a text conversation."

"No, oh my god, I get that," Sienna said. "I once had a guy off Hive take me to a cemetery on a date."

Ada's laugh shot out of her. "What?!"

Sienna was grinning, barely containing her laughter. "Yeah. He just sent me the address, and it looked like some kind of park when I googled it, so I didn't know until I got there. And then he asked if he could have some of my blood for some ritual he was doing."

And even though she should still be trying to read everyone's reactions, decide if they believed her story about *energy*, all Cas could think about was the press of Ada's fingertips into her thigh as she laughed, the brush of Ada's hair against Cas's biceps. Cas drew in a breath, and it was Ada's perfume, peach and citrus and something almost smoky, blended perfectly with the warm sun and thick salty air.

"Jesus Christ," Femi said, and Sienna dropped her hand onto his thigh, her own laugh finally rocking through her.

"Yeah, I definitely needed Jesus that day."

#HotSummer—Live Updates

@HotSummer ✅: the summer's first couples are OFFICIAL and they are looking 🔥

@fionamccarthy: everyone except Brad who looks like a sentient bit of pavement

@niamhmurray: as;ldkfj STOP

@cararyan: Femi is so cute I love him

@sadeadegbite: frrrrrr if he doesn't come out partnered up with anyone, he can partner up with me

@dylancoughlan ✅: can we talk about Sienna because like . . . holy hell she's STUNNING

@katewalsh: I know, she's gorgeous

@aoifebyrne: they really DID IT when they cast Sienna because she is on a whole other level

@steffancherry ✅: my official #HotSummer rankings, as always, ladies first: lexi is lowkey annoying, I already know I'm going to hate her by like episode 3

@steffancherry ✅: maddison . . . irrelevant

@steffancherry ✅: Sienna is a goddess, no one can touch her, if they eliminate her, I'm not watching anymore

@steffancherry ✅: ada is tbd, she seems kind of bland, but I'm a sucker for a redhead so idk

@steffancherry ✅: cas thinks she's a gift to mankind but defo has a big storm coming

@jamiedoyle: . . . Why did Cas say she's never used a dating app???

@ronanflynn: what do you mean?

@jamiedoyle: i swear she works for friday, that hybrid in-person/app company

@jamiedoyle: I've been to a few of their events and she's always there hosting

@ronanflynn: wtf that's . . . so weird?????

@moonlighthiker: wait . . .

@averyart: there's actually no reason to be lying about this . . . v sus

6

THE LIGHTS WERE on far too early the next morning.

They didn't even have the decency to turn them on gradually, just flicked them on all at once so the only thing Cas could do to protect her retinas from disintegrating was to throw her arm over her head and start groping for a pillow to hide under.

"Oh no." Cas felt more than heard Femi start laughing beside her. "You're not a morning person, are you?"

"No, I'm fucking not," Cas muttered, her head now firmly planted under the pillow. "And I'm telling you now, I will fight you if you laugh in my face before I've had coffee, something to eat, and, like, an hour to come to terms with being alive."

Femi laughed again, this time loudly enough that Cas could definitely hear it.

"Well, let me go get you a coffee, then. How do you take it?"

She loved him.

"Black. Iced. Please."

"Got it." Femi flung the duvet off and Cas shivered against the gust of freezing air that hit her legs. She was ready to yell at him, when he tucked the duvet back over her, taking extra care to wrap it in tightly around her so she was insulated.

Satisfied with his work, Femi shouted to the rest of the room, "Anyone else like a coffee?"

Cas snuggled back under the duvet as everyone else started shuffling off, her eyes falling closed again until, a few minutes later, the edge of the bed dipped followed by the sound of something being set onto the bedside table.

"Coffee's on the side table," Femi said, patting the lump of duvet that roughly aligned with Cas's right shoulder. "I've also got you a pastry. There were pain au chocolats in the cupboard."

Cas peeked out from underneath the duvet.

"Thank you." She tried to smile at him, but she was mostly squinting into the overhead lights.

"No problem." Femi patted her shoulder once more before he stood up again. "I'll see you outside in a few."

"Doubt it." Cas snaked her hand out and grabbed her coffee. Femi laughed before walking back outside.

Cas sipped at her coffee and picked flakes off her pastry for the next few minutes, all the while trying her best to listen to what everyone was talking about outside.

She should probably just get up, see what they were all on about, but the idea of leaving this bed . . .

Ada slid open the garden door, her face splitting into a grin when she saw Cas still snuggled under the duvet.

"How have you not gotten shouted at yet?"

Cas shrugged. "I'm awake. What else do they want from me?"

"I'd venture that they want you to get out of bed and join the rest of us in the land of the living."

"Overrated."

Ada snorted. "Okay."

And she dropped down on the end of Cas's bed. She watched as Cas tore a chunk off her pain au chocolat and stuffed it into her mouth.

"How did you sleep?"

Cas hummed and lifted her hand to cover her mouth. "Okay. It was weird being in a room with, like, nine other people, though."

She'd really only thought about how awkward it would be once people started hooking up in the bedroom, but it was weird full stop. Every exhale, rustle of the sheets, stray snore, was a reminder that Cas wasn't in her own bedroom in London anymore.

"No, yeah, that was weird," Ada said. She sounded contemplative, a little distant, like she was mulling something over. "How did you find sharing a bed with Femi?"

"Yeah, it was good," Cas said. "He didn't hog the duvet or kick me, so . . ." She shrugged. "Success."

"Hmm." Ada nodded absently, and Cas raised an eyebrow over another sip of coffee.

"How was sharing a bed with Brad?"

"It was okay," Ada said slowly, her eyes moving from Cas over to the garden door. "I felt like he was trying to, like . . . brush up against me, though."

Cas frowned. "What do you mean?"

"Like he was really close to me all night," Ada said. "And maybe that's just how he sleeps, but it was like . . . mate, we've literally just met, give me a bit of space."

Cas couldn't say that she was entirely surprised, especially given his behavior yesterday. Brad seemed like he was the kind of person who felt he was entitled to whatever he wanted. Attention, affection, you name it.

Still, she wanted to be careful how she worded this. She didn't want to upset Ada if she could avoid it.

"Do you feel like he was, like . . . trying something?"

"No, it didn't feel like that," Ada said. Her gaze drifted off over Cas's left shoulder, looking toward the bed that she and Brad had vacated half an hour before. "More like he doesn't have proper respect for boundaries. Like he expected that, just because we're sharing a bed, I was going to be all right with him trying to put his arms around me."

"No, yeah, in no way are those two things the same," Cas said. "Did he ask?"

Ada shook her head. "When I brushed him off and shifted away, he seemed to take it fine. He didn't try it again."

"But you felt like he was there the whole night."

"Yeah." Ada chewed on the inside of her lip, her gaze locked on the garden door. She didn't make eye contact with Cas for a long moment, but when she did, she plastered on a smile.

"I don't know, maybe it's fine. He was telling me about how much he liked me already and all that, like, how he feels like we have this great connection, so." She shrugged.

"Yeah, but this early? Like, less than one day in?"

Cas should probably try to keep the skepticism out of her voice, but honestly.

Ada leaned forward and dropped her voice to a conspiratorial whisper. "That's what I was thinking, like . . . Is it weird that he's acting like this already or am I just in my head?

Because, like, Sienna and Jayden seem into each other and even Charlie and Lexi—"

"Yeah, but that's clearly mutual attraction," Cas said. "Are you even into him?"

She definitely didn't seem like she was—or, if she had been, she'd gotten the ick at lightning speed—but it was probably best to keep that thought in her own head.

Ada's cheeks reddened slightly. "No, I'm— I *could* like him, maybe."

"So, you're not into him," Cas said flatly.

"I could be," Ada said. "If I gave it time."

"Do you want to have to force it, though?" She wanted to say, *Do you really want to "give it time" with someone like Brad?* but that felt a touch too aggressive.

"I don't feel like it's forcing it. More like giving it time to blossom."

It took everything Cas had not to roll her eyes.

"I don't know, maybe I'm just overreacting," Ada said before Cas could reply. "Like maybe he's just being weird because he's getting used to being here and I'm too in my head about things."

No way was that true.

Cas nodded. "Yeah, maybe."

Ada was quiet for a beat before she flashed Cas another forced smile and popped up off the end of the bed.

"I'm going to go back outside. Come with?"

Ada held out her hand. And Cas was torn.

She could say something, keep them talking about Brad, keep them inside and away from everyone else. It was easy to convince herself that she just wanted some more time away from the action, away from the conversation, but Ada was clearly ready to move on, to stop talking about this, and Cas didn't want to force Ada into a discussion she plainly didn't want.

But Cas also didn't want Ada leaving this conversation thinking that anything about Brad was going to change. He could surprise them, sure, but he probably wasn't going to.

Ada wiggled her fingers, inviting, and Cas sighed.

"Yeah, all right. But I'm not going to like it."

Cas took her hand and let Ada drag her to her feet, groaning theatrically about how cold the air-con was all the way.

Once they were outside, Ada lifted her hand to cover her own eyes. "Do you want to grab a seat under one of the umbrellas?"

Cas nodded, and after waving at the crowd in the kitchen, they started walking down to the pool deck.

They dropped all their things onto the chairs, and the moment they sat down, Ada started slathering a thick coat of sun cream over her legs.

"Can you get my back?" Ada held out the bottle, already pulling her hair over her right shoulder.

Cas stared at the bottle for a long moment, her eyes trained on but not really reading the label. She waited for a beat longer than was normal before she reached out to take the bottle.

This wasn't actually that deep. She'd put sun cream on people before. Loads of people.

"You're probably burning already, so." Her voice was thick. *God.* "Sure."

Ada's laugh was loud, louder than Cas expected for her terrible joke. "My best friends said the same thing to me before I left. And they're running my social media now, so I'm sure they have, like, a daily Ada Burn Watch they're posting about."

Cas snorted, grateful for the distraction she could latch on to. "Oh god. Mine are running my social media, too. Don't give them any ideas."

As happy as it made her to think about them, mentioning her friends made Cas feel strangely . . . sad.

She hadn't been away from Aisha and Skye in this long in, god, *years*. She'd known the deal coming into the villa, but now that she was actually here, the idea that she wasn't going to be able to talk to them for two whole months made her feel a little sick.

Who knew she was such a melt?

Ada turned her head a little so she was slightly facing Cas. "I'd love to meet them when we leave."

Cas squirted more sun cream onto her fingertips and, very gingerly, lifted the middle strap of Ada's bikini top. "Are you from London, too, then?"

"Brighton originally. But I moved up for university, and once I got to London I just . . . never wanted to go back."

Cas hummed softly. "Do you think you ever will?"

"Probably one day," Ada said. "I loved walking along the beach every morning, going for long kayaks on the water." She was quiet for a second, and Cas felt the weight of Ada's thoughts between them. All the ideas Ada had for a future that would someday come to pass. "I don't know when I'll be ready to move back, so I'm just enjoying London for now."

Cas nodded and put a final bit of sun cream on her hands. She shifted away, just far enough that she had a clear view of Ada's lower back.

"The idea that you love the place where you grew up is so bizarre to me," Cas said quietly. She was usually much more guarded about her home life—and a little voice in the back of her mind reminded her she shouldn't trust anyone a hundred percent in this game, but there was something about Ada that just seemed honest. Plus, moments of vulnerability never hurt with the viewers.

"Where did you grow up?"

"Surrey." It tasted bitter in Cas's mouth. "In some tiny village you've hopefully never heard of."

"Why 'hopefully'?"

"It's, like, two shops and a bunch of posh arseholes."

"That explains your accent, then," Ada said, laughing.

Cas would've snapped at anyone else, but then Ada looked at Cas over her shoulder, her lips turned up in a cheeky smile, and, well . . .

"It also explains why I have a horrible name like *Cassandra*." She emphasized the vowels extra hard, and Ada laughed again, her shoulders shaking.

"Why do you hate it so much?"

Cas was quiet for a long moment, just watching as the last of the sun cream disappeared into Ada's skin. She capped the bottle, handed it over Ada's shoulder, and then leaned back against the seat of Ada's chair to indicate that she was still mulling over Ada's question. A big part of her wanted to ignore this question, shrug it off, say it was too long or too formal or some other vague approximation of the truth, but then Ada turned slowly, her eyes trailing along Cas's legs before flicking up abruptly and meeting her eyes.

"I think I just never felt like it fit me," Cas said finally. The words felt like they were tripping thoughtlessly from her lips, but Ada's little hum of understanding made it worth it. "I felt like my parents gave it to me because they imagined that I was someone I was never going to be."

Ada shifted closer, close enough that their legs touched, Ada's knee to the outside of Cas's thigh. The whole of Cas's attention felt like it zeroed in on that one spot where she and Ada were connected.

"That makes sense."

Cas breathed something like a laugh. Which was ridiculous, she shouldn't be feeling whatever was going on in her chest about something that didn't even matter anyway. But Ada was just . . . she had affirmed Cas so easily. So simply. No questions, no need to discuss it, just this was Cas's story and Ada was nodding along, accepting it.

Cas shrugged and slid her gaze to the gym where Lexi was throwing weights around with the boys. They kept shouting, shocked, because she was lifting heavy and somehow managing it without her tiny arms falling off. And that reminder of where they were, of the microphone around her neck and the cameras in the shrubs, was like a jolt to the system.

Cas leaned down and grabbed her water bottle from the ground, taking a drink to avoid saying anything more. Ada took her cue and grabbed her own water and took a hearty drink, seemingly nonplussed at Cas's evasion.

At that moment, someone screamed—*screamed*—from the gym. Lexi was shaking her phone in the air, weights long forgotten.

"I've got a text! Guys, I've got a text!"

Lexi jumped up onto the bench press and read the message at the top of her voice.

"'Lovers! It's time for your first challenge!'" Lexi's words were almost impossible to understand, she was so giddy. "'Get ready to break the ice! #ColdFoamWarmHearts #SlidingInto Feelings!'"

THE OUTFITS THAT the producers left out for them in the dressing room were, without a doubt, the most ridiculous things that Cas had ever seen in her life. They were giving Lara Croft if you put all her clothes through a woodchipper—a lot of clingy spandex and tiny, *tiny* pieces of fabric.

Ada saw Cas's expression and laughed. "I know. Even *my* arse is going to be out in these, and it's concave."

Sienna snorted and then immediately covered her mouth. "Sorry—"

"Don't be." Ada waved her hand. "It's true."

One of the boys whistled as the girls filed into the entry, and a quick glance around revealed it to be Brad. He wrapped his arm possessively around Ada when she walked over, and he said loudly enough for everyone to hear, "Damn, babe, you look *fine*."

If Cas wanted to elbow him in the nose, well, that was her business.

On TV, it always looked like the challenges were held in some grand arena, but in reality, the challenge spot was a large square platform in the middle of a dusty field behind the villa. They'd trooped through the gate hidden in the hedge fence surrounding the villa, all of them talking and laughing in anticipation, but with every step, Cas was dreaming of going back and lying by the pool.

It would certainly be more fun than standing here doing . . . whatever the hell they were about to be doing.

There were cameras set up along the railing lining the platform and a few more on posts around the perimeter and, most likely, several hidden within the challenge space itself. There was one foam-covered slide running down the center of the platform toward a tower of inflatable rectangles that were painted to look like blocks of ice and, at the top of the slide, a stool with a plastic box full of cards.

Cas knew that *Hot Summer* wasn't exactly known for the most intricate challenges—they were mostly about getting lovers soaking wet and grinding on one another—but there was something particularly tragic about the challenges in real life. Especially because they'd be spending half the challenge time building the towers back up so they could get destroyed again.

Maddison's phone dinged as they climbed into the arena and she scanned her screen before flashing a bright grin at them. "'Welcome, lovers, to the first *Hot Summer* challenge!'"

Everyone applauded, Cas the most enthusiastically of them all. She would rather have put her head in the way of a cricket mallet than do this, but she absolutely could not show it.

"'Today,'" Maddison continued, "'you're going to be competing in a little game called Break the Ice! You'll each choose a statement from the box'"—she slapped her palm down onto the box—"'and then you'll slide down the luge into the blocks of ice at the end. After you've broken the ice, you'll kiss the person you think the statement is about!'" Maddison's excitement increased as she read, so she was practically squealing by the time she reached the end. She beamed up at all of them. "'Now, who's ready to Break the Ice?!'"

Everyone on the deck cheered, and, thus, the game began.

Charlie bounded up first and grabbed a card from the box without much fanfare. "Who says that they've had sex in at least three different outdoor spots?"

It seemed a little perilous when Charlie sent himself barreling down the waterslide into the inflatable ice blocks, especially because they were all standing there waiting at the end, in the direct line of fire. He was dripping with foam as he popped to his feet, neither he nor Lexi seemed to mind as he pressed her back into the railing and planted a snog on her that even Cas felt a little uncomfortable watching.

She hooted right along with the rest of them, but this definitely felt more like something they should be doing on their own, rather than in front of nearly a dozen other people and as many cameras.

Lexi was panting as Charlie pulled away, and he grinned as he tugged the card from the waistband of his shorts, waving it teasingly in the air.

"Okay, let's see if I was right . . ." He peeled the sticker off the card and revealed *Lexi* written at the very bottom.

"You're a bit of an exhibitionist, then, Lex," Maddison said, her words barely audible over Charlie's celebration.

"Not on purpose," Lexi said. "I just get, like, really horny outside for some reason, I don't know."

"Remind me to take you on lots of hikes when we get home," Charlie said.

Femi ran up next, and he made a big show of swirling his hand around in the box. "Ohhh, let's see . . ."

"Just pick one, you arsehole," Sienna shouted, and Femi flashed her a bright grin.

"All right." He plucked a card out and flicked it upright in his fingers. "This one says, 'Kiss one of the *four* lovers who say they've kissed more than two people in one night.'"

As soon as Cas heard it, she knew it was about her.

And three other people, but still. *Her.*

Femi seemed to hit every pile of foam Charlie missed on his trip down the slide, so he was covered from head to toe by the time he reached the end. Despite his rapid blinking and the rushed way he was trying to wipe the soap off his face, he was grinning from ear to ear as he popped to his feet.

"We need one of these in the garden," Femi said, coming to stand in front of Cas. He'd worked out she was one of the names, then.

"You guys would smash your heads in."

"It'd be worth it," Femi said, grinning at her. "Ready for this kiss?"

Cas rolled her eyes, smiled. "Sure."

Femi's touch was tentative, his eyes on hers all the time as though he was gauging her reaction. She decided to make it easier for him and leaned forward, closing the distance between them.

His lips were soft and the scratch of his stubble against her skin wasn't unpleasant. His lips parted slightly and the taste of him, warm mint, was nice. She'd had a thousand kisses like it in her life—a good time, something she could lose herself in if she really tried, but lacking that spark, that *thing* that made her feel like she was crumbling in their hands.

There was enough there that Cas knew she could lean in to it if Femi was interested, but judging by the few quick, largely closed-mouth passes of his lips over hers before he pulled back, she would bargain that they were on the same page.

Femi smiled gently, awkwardly at her as he stepped back, his hand falling away, and Cas couldn't help but smile. "Thanks."

Femi laughed and wrapped his arm around Cas's shoulders. It was an easy gesture, a warm one, and it settled the anxiety in Cas's stomach. "'Thanks.' Careful with those compliments, they'll start to go to my head."

And then he peeled the sticker off the card, and sure enough, there it was.

Cas. Alongside *Maddison, Charlie, and Brad.*

Which was fucking great. Of course she somehow had something in common with *Brad.*

"Okay," Charlie said, raising his hand. "Who's done more than two? I'm just two."

And Cas knew exactly how this moment would be played out on TV: Brad, leaning back against the railing, arm around Ada, smug smile that would paint him immediately as a lad about town, a scoundrel who you couldn't quite help love (or undress for) anyway. He'd be their Tom from Season 6, the one everyone loved to hate so much that he made it to the finals, especially once he appeared to "reform" in his final couple with Crystal.

It was a stark contrast to the way Maddison was presenting

herself—pink in the cheeks, downturned eyes. She was shy, playing at ashamed. A reformed party girl here to find love.

And then there was Cas. Unapologetic. She could almost hear the slut-shaming posts.

"In my defense," Cas said, "mine was a speed-dating event my friends dragged me to. You had to kiss everyone when your time was up to check for chemistry."

"I've got no defense but tequila," Maddison said with a little self-conscious laugh. The rest of the group joined her laughter and Cas could kick herself. Yet another moment she'd let herself get outshined.

Brad was actually jumping up and down when it was his turn. He was stretching out his arms like he was getting ready to fight a bear rather than rush down a water slide and then kiss someone.

"'Who went viral on TikTok after a breakup with their ex?'"

Brad flung himself down the slide and, without even stopping to check that she was ready, pressed Ada back into the railing and smashed his mouth against hers. Ada let out a squeak, whether in surprise or in protest, Cas wasn't sure, but her arms remained by her sides rather than wrapping around Brad's waist in an attempt to pull him closer.

Brad still had Ada's head in a vise grip, his mouth moving very aggressively over hers, when Sienna grabbed the card from Brad's waistband and peeled off the paper.

"That's correct!" Sienna said.

Brad's mouth popped off Ada's like a suction cup yanked off tile.

"Holy shit, really?"

Ada's cheeks were blood red. "Yeah." She tucked a piece

of stray hair behind her ears and very discreetly wiped her mouth. "I made a video about some when-you-break-up-with-your-partner stationery I carry and apparently it struck a chord."

Brad nodded absently, clearly only half listening, and Cas knocked her elbow lightly against Ada's.

"That's cool. You'll have to tell me more about it later."

Though the challenge had felt like little more than a chore for the first few rounds—especially when it came to setting up the "ice towers" again and again—things rapidly devolved as more and more of them were covered in foam and slip-sliding across the platform.

Something that, of course, didn't stop them deciding to race and see who could build their section of the wall first.

"Holy fuck!" Cas slid into a near split, sending her blocks flying out of her arms. Sienna had just caught her around the waist, but Cas's momentum sent the pair of them flying into Ada and, most tragically, back into the stack of ice they'd spent the last few minutes building.

"Ha!" Femi leaped over them, catching himself on the railing to keep from falling over, the final block for his section of the wall in his hands.

Reece had just announced the final question when someone else, someone new, spoke from behind them.

"Got room for one more?"

A petite brunette jumped up onto the challenge platform, her crop top barely covering her breasts, the spandex shorts tight against her perfectly full thighs. Her T-shirt featured a bomb emoji, and it only took a fraction of a second for Cas to figure out what was going on.

Everyone else, meanwhile, was still screaming.

It was rare that they brought a bombshell in this early—it was normally a few days, a week, before they threw everyone into chaos. If the producers were doing this this early, the summer was probably going to be a lot more dramatic than usual. And a lot more difficult to survive.

The brunette walked over to Reece and handed him a card. Her steps were lithe, longer than you would have expected for someone her height. There was a grace about the way she moved, like she was dancing across the stage rather than simply walking.

Reece traced his eyes over her for a long beat before he cleared his throat and looked down at the card she'd handed him.

"'Last question. Bombshell Tia will kiss the person she thinks matches the statement. Tia . . .'" Reece flicked his gaze to her again. It was clearly meant to be brief, but their eyes caught and held for a long moment before Reece turned back to the card again. Maddison shifted her weight awkwardly.

"'Tia,'" Reece continued. "'Who do you think brags that he's slept with more than three hundred women?'"

Cas felt her stomach turn. Not about the number, she didn't give a shit about the number, but bragging about it? Childish.

Tia hummed thoughtfully, her hand even coming up to her chin to complete the perfect image of *woman in thought*. She walked along the line of people in front of her, her eyes raking over every single man as she walked past. When she reached Brad at the end of the line, he was physically vibrating, clearly desperate to be the one to get to kiss her. Tia either noticed his excitement and wanted to play into it or just felt like he was the

most attractive (wrong, but Cas supposed everyone was entitled to their own opinion) because she slid her hand up his
forearm and immediately stepped in for her kiss.

But Brad, apparently, wasn't ready to let Tia control the
pace. He swept down and crashed his mouth to hers so forcefully that Cas was pretty sure she heard the sound of their
teeth smashing together.

Even standing at the opposite end of the line, Cas could
hear how wet the kiss was. That seemed to be Brad's style, and
though the thought definitely made Cas ill, she could only
imagine what it must sound like to the people standing closer,
or, god, to Ada, who was standing on Brad's right side, just
trying to pretend it wasn't happening.

Brad didn't pay the slightest bit of attention to the way that
Ada was now staring at her feet. Instead, he added salt to the
wound as he disconnected from Tia and shouted, "Best kiss
all day!"

SIENNA WAS AT Ada's side as they left the challenge platform, and Cas jogged up right behind them. It probably looked a bit silly, running after them like she was in school, but she needed to make sure Ada was okay.

She hadn't reacted, she had just stood there, blank-faced, until Reece's phone pinged and announced the end of the challenge, but the small sigh she'd let out as she climbed underneath the railing and dropped into the dust . . .

"It's okay," Sienna was saying, her voice low and her mouth nearly pressed against Ada's ear in an attempt to prevent her comment from carrying. "Come on, babe, let's go talk. You're okay."

"I know." Ada's voice was thick, though whether with tears or suppressed anger or something else, Cas didn't know. She didn't have tears in her eyes, but maybe she was phenomenally good at controlling them. "Let's just get back into the villa and then I'll talk to you."

Sienna steered Ada into the back garden, her steps remarkably quick now that she wasn't wearing towering high heels. Cas could hear everyone else starting up behind them, the sound of their laughter ringing through the air, but Sienna wasn't distracted in the least. She led the three of them down to a small seating area off in the far corner, well out of the way from the center of the action.

Sienna eased her arm from Ada's as they approached the sofa and guided her gently to a seat in the middle of the curved white couch. Sienna and Cas sat down on either side and Ada exhaled a rough laugh.

"This feels very dramatic."

"We just want to make sure you're okay," Sienna said.

Cas nodded. "It's fine to take a minute to be upset."

Even if Brad was disgusting and offensive on about a thousand levels, it was still callous, shouting about someone else like that in front of your partner.

"I'm not upset. I'm pissed off." With the way she was cutting the words out on her teeth, she certainly sounded like it. "Yesterday, he comes storming in and interrupts us; last night, he's all over me; today, he's going feral over getting to kiss some girl right in front of the *other* girl"—she jabbed a finger into her chest—"he's partnered up with!"

"He was practically frothing at the mouth," Cas said. It was probably the wrong thing to say, but—

Ada laughed, her whole body shaking a little with the effort. "Right? He looked like he was gluing himself to her."

"If it makes you feel better, I don't think Tia enjoyed it," Sienna said. "She was wiping her mouth when he finally pulled away."

"That doesn't surprise me," Ada said. "I had to, too."

"I'm not surprised," Cas said. "It sounded like you were making out with a waterfall."

Ada snorted and dropped one of her hands so it came to rest on Cas's thigh. The contact was sharp, instant, and it sent a pulse of want through Cas. Even through the sticky foam coating her skin.

Ada left her hand there for a long second before she pulled away and sighed again.

"Honestly, he's just fucking rude and careless, and it's pissed me off."

"And now you have to share a bed with him and not smother him in his sleep," Sienna said.

Ada groaned. "I'm sleeping on the couch tonight."

"You can bunk with me," Cas said. "Femi won't mind."

Ada laughed. "I'm sure he wouldn't, two gorgeous girls snuggled up on either side of him."

"That'd probably be his dream," Sienna said.

"Attention, lovers." The speaker was directly next to them in the garden, and the voice was *loud*. Sienna screamed. "One by one, you're going to make your way into the confession hut and share your thoughts about today's challenge. No one is permitted to shower until after their confessional has been recorded."

The groan that went through the villa was palpable.

~~~

Cas had just finished settling into the round rattan chair when a speaker on the wall opposite crackled to life. "Hey, Cas, it's Chloe. Are you ready to talk about the challenge?"

"Yeah." Cas crossed her arms, tucked one foot up underneath her. It was unsettling, talking to someone you couldn't see. "Definitely."

"Perfect." Cas could hear the rustling of papers over the line. "So what did you think of the challenge today?"

Seeing as she was still covered in a layer of grime so thick Cas was sure she'd need a chisel to get it off, she wasn't thrilled about it.

"It was really fun!" She smiled at the camera and hoped the truth wasn't etched into her face. "It was great getting to know everyone; I think it really helped us bond."

"Did you learn anything surprising about your fellow lovers?"

Cas thought for a moment before she barked a laugh, falling back into her chair. "I was surprised that Reece has had a foursome."

"Why was that surprising?"

"He just seems so . . . innocent." It was the nicest way to say that Reece seemed like he still curled up with a stuffed animal every night. "I didn't expect it of him."

"What did you think about Brad's kiss with Tia?" Chloe was quiet for a long minute, but when Cas didn't speak, she clarified. "Did you think that Tia chose Brad on purpose?"

"Well, she had to guess who she thought fitted just like the rest of us. And Brad defo seems like he'd brag about sleeping with people, so I can't say I was surprised she thought it was him."

"You looked annoyed during the challenge, though, would you say that's fair?"

Fuck, had she? She needed to control her damn face.

She paused for a long moment, weighing her words carefully before she spoke. "I . . . was just more concerned about how Ada was feeling."

"How is she feeling?"

Cas grit her teeth together. "I think that's more for her to say. I don't want to speak for her."

Chloe hummed and there was more rustling of papers over the line. "Is it fair to say that you and Ada have bonded quite a bit already?"

"I think that's fair."

"Do you think it was okay for Brad to kiss Tia, then?"

There were so many layers to this question. It seemed so simple on the surface—did she think that Brad was within his rights to kiss Tia or not—but the more Cas thought about it, the more she realized that there was no clear way to answer this, at least not within the social guidelines of the show.

"I think that everyone is well within their rights to get to know whoever they want. That's the entire point of being here, right?" She pressed her lips together as she tried to formulate her next sentence. "My issue with the whole thing, though, comes from the fact that Brad was talking to Ada like she was the sun itself since they were partnered up yesterday afternoon and then he turned around and literally tried to inhale Tia.

"If he wanted to be open to knowing people and exploring and whatever, that's fine, but he should have made that clear to her. He should have said that he thought she was cool or whatever the hell he thinks about her, but he also should have said that he wanted to get to know other people. Though, honestly—"

She knew she was spiraling a little out of control, but she was getting carried away by her frustration now.

"I actually think that so many men come on this show and do exactly what Brad just did. They act like the woman they're partnered up with, whoever she is, is the best thing that ever happened to them, only to turn around and snog the hell out of the next person they see that even remotely takes their fancy. They talk about finding a connection, but none of them actually make a real effort. You're not making an effort if you're going around snogging everyone.

"I know they like to talk about it like it's some *test*"—she did the world's most sarcastic set of air quotes—"but that's—I'm sorry, that's bollocks. You know how you feel or you don't, you don't need to shove your tongue down someone else's throat to figure it out. And if you do, maybe you need help, I don't know."

She stopped abruptly, nearly swallowing her own tongue in her haste. She was angry, yes, but there was no reason for her to let it all loose like this. Not in the second episode. Not before people really knew who she was.

She exhaled sharply and with such force she was surprised she didn't fog up the lens of the camera.

"I don't know. Whatever. Anyway, I think he just needs to have a conversation with her."

Chloe was quiet for a long moment, so long that Cas actually started to think that Chloe had either left or was dismissing her without so much as a goodbye. Finally, the speaker clicked on and Chloe's voice spilled into the confession hut.

"Fair enough. Thanks, Cas, that's all we need from you today. Can you send in Sienna, please?"

Cas struggled to her feet and, with a perfunctory wave at the camera, made her way out of the confessional.

9

AT THE START of the week, Friday had seemed like a thousand years away. And there were definitely moments that dragged, but for the most part?

It was blink and you miss it, that first week.

It was a quick study in getting to learn one another's habits, too. How Femi rolled out of bed and ran to the kitchen to put the kettle on before anyone else was awake, how Jayden tended to steal all the pillows in the bedroom to make a stack he could lean on while he and Sienna had their morning conversation. The way Maddison sang to herself as she put on hand cream, how Tia came skipping in every morning from the extra bed in the living room and dove into bed next to Sienna.

The way Ada would lie, stretched out, duvet kicked off, staring at the ceiling for the first few minutes after she opened her eyes.

Cas had expected it would be strange, sharing a house with nine, then ten, other people, and in a lot of ways, it was. No matter where she was, no matter what time of day, Cas was either sitting with someone or she could hear shouting and laughter and conversation all across the house. It was impossible to sit alone with your thoughts in a space like this, surrounded constantly, talking constantly, being drawn into the beach hut constantly to dissect your feelings, real or otherwise, with the producers.

There were only two toilets, too, and it was humbling, having to lift your microphone and whisper that you needed to use the toilet so they could unlock the door for you. It was nice that there weren't cameras in that part of the bathroom, but *god,* she hated having to ask like she was three years old.

But it was remarkably easy to get used to, sharing this space with so many people. Even the worst parts, like fighting it out every night to get a shower (because if you were any later than, like, fourth, you were guaranteed cold water), weren't so bad.

It was the parties, though, that were the biggest shock of the season so far. She'd always thought these parties looked fun, like they stretched out all evening, but in reality, they all met their two-drink maximum about thirty minutes in, the dance sequence lasted for four songs and four songs *only,* and then they all floated around the garden until the Voice of God told them they were allowed to go to bed at some ungodly hour of the morning. It was quite the opposite of the sort of events she was used to.

Her favorite part about being here, by far, was the morning, when the boys brought their coffees up to the change room off the bathroom and the girls had a gossip while getting ready for the day. Cas was usually still waking up, and thus, silent, but she liked how giggly and chatty everyone was in the morning, liked the little antics they planned for their day. One such antic: Femi plopping down in front of Sienna that morning and declaring that he was going to try to do her makeup.

Sienna eyed Femi suspiciously as he pumped a deep pool of foundation onto the back of his hand. "You better not make me look like a fucking clown."

"I've got three sisters," Femi said. "I know how to put makeup on."

"Having sisters doesn't mean you automatically know how to do makeup," Ada said. She was smearing a heavy layer of sun cream into her cheeks, her freckles cast white as she attempted to blend it all into her skin. "My brother doesn't have the first clue about makeup."

"I actually do, though." Femi dotted the foundation brush into the product and started swiping it across Sienna's cheeks. "My sisters used to make me model for them, like, *regularly*. I was their little doll."

His technique wasn't perfect, but Sienna ended up with an actually decent face of makeup after about half an hour's work.

"See, I told you," Femi said, admiring his handiwork as Sienna examined her face in the mirror. "You look hot."

"I always look hot," Sienna said. "But, yeah, you did all right."

In spite of those bright moments, by Friday evening, Cas felt like she understood how people eventually started going a bit mad in this place. She'd always thought that those conversations on the Missed Moments episodes were fabricated (because, surely, no one would invent a game like the infamous Banana Toes from Season 3 unless the producers put them up to it), but they'd spent so many hours staring at one another over the last few days that Cas had found herself thinking that, really, you could turn anything into a game if you were bored enough.

Cas was just about to roll off the deck chair and suggest a Banana Toes reprise (she was pretty sure she'd seen a few bunches of bananas in the kitchen) when Brad shouted from across the garden.

"Text!"

Cas sat straight up at Brad's announcement, her mind already flying through the possible things that could be on that text message.

A date. A new arrival. A challenge.

It probably wasn't a new arrival—Tia was still settling in, and though Reece was trailing after her like a puppy, they hadn't yet had a partnership ceremony to cement any changes. And, oh god, it wasn't Saturday yet, but it could be a partnering. It was close enough to the regular schedule, since partnerings happened on a weekly basis, but just different enough that they'd be surprised. Here they were all lying around comfortably and thinking they had twenty-four more hours before everything went to hell. Suckers.

Cas really needed to pull Femi aside now that she was thinking about it. Figure out what their plan was.

She'd enjoyed spending time with him, but it was painfully obvious to her that there wasn't any sexual chemistry between them. Still, they got on, and it probably wouldn't be too hard to convince him to stay in a friendship couple with her. Especially because neither of them seemed that interested in anyone else.

Or, well, Cas wasn't. Cas had definitely seen Femi's eye wandering in a specific direction this week, but she didn't think he was quite ready to act on it yet.

"'Lovers.'" Brad was reading in his best announcer voice

and it made Cas want to punch him. "'Please gather around the fire pit for an announcement.'"

"Oh fuck."

Cas hadn't meant to say it so loudly, but there it was.

Ada laughed, but there was a tightness to her expression that belied the sound. "It's probably fine. Maybe there's a DJ coming tomorrow or something."

She didn't sound convinced.

The mood was appropriately somber as they made their way across the garden, all eleven of them flocking from the corners they'd scattered to in an attempt to find something like privacy. They settled automatically into their couples, Tia sandwiched uncomfortably between Reece and Jayden.

Cas dropped down on Ada's right side, leaving just enough space at the end of the bench for Femi. Or, at least, she thought she had. When he sat down, his thigh was hanging off the edge of the bench, and Cas swore quietly.

"Sorry, sorry." She shifted to the left and her thigh immediately rubbed up against Ada's. Cas jolted. "Fuck, sorry." Cas pressed her thighs together, trying for even a half centimeter's worth of space, but she could still feel the heat of Ada's thigh along the outside of her leg.

Ada just smiled. "No worries."

Charlie's phone beeped the second everyone was finished getting settled.

"'Lovers,'" Charlie read, his words slow and careful, like he was defusing a bomb rather than reading a text, "'this summer, we've decided to do things a little differently.'"

Maddison's phone chimed.

"'In previous summers, you've had to wait until the public

nominations in week seven to find out what the British public think of you.'"

Maddison stared at her phone for a long second after she finished reading, the blue light illuminating her face eerily.

Cas's phone.

She almost didn't think it was hers at first. It had to be Ada's, Femi's, maybe even Brad's. But Ada's head whipped round at the sound, and Cas had no choice but to accept that she needed to tug her phone out from the strap of her mic belt.

To find three little words written on her screen.

"'But this summer . . .'"

They were really trying to stretch this out for all that it was worth, weren't they?

After a long, weighted beat, her phone beeped again.

"'We've decided to keep you a little more up to date.'"

The words themselves didn't actually say that much. Didn't even mean anything. But Cas's brain was spinning with options.

Were they going to be put to the public vote earlier? They already had people vote for their favorite couples to eliminate people as they moved into the final weeks, but maybe they were going to have people voting earlier. More often. Fuck, was this what Mila was alluding to on their first day? Maybe it was individuals instead of couples this year.

In a way, that could make her strategy easier, especially if she managed to make herself even passably likable, but there was something to be said about the protection a couple could provide. If the person you were partnered up with was popular, that went a long way in terms of saving your skin, even if people didn't love you.

Cas had seen it plenty of times on previous seasons. It was the reason that Adam—a literal cardboard cutout of a man—made it to the top two in Season 7.

Sienna's phone pinged.

"'This summer, the public is going to be voting for you—individually—every week . . . and your rankings will be posted on the television in the living room for all to see.'"

What. The. Fuck.

"They're going to *rank us*? Weekly?" Lexi's jaw was hanging open.

Before anyone could say anything else, though, Reece's phone beeped, shattering the silence and immediately ratcheting Cas's heart rate up to fifteen thousand.

"'The first ranking was completed last night. . . . So let's find out if you made a good first impression.'"

"*Now?*" Femi's eyes were blown wide, disbelief all over his face.

"I guess we better hope we got a good edit," Sienna said.

Cas felt like she was going to be sick.

Brad's phone beeped.

"Go to the lounge for your first rankings ceremony now."

The screen was already lit up when everyone walked into the lounge room, the *Hot Summer* banner with two numbered lists titled "Boys" and "Girls" underneath. The numbers themselves were blank, but even seeing them there was enough of a reminder of what was to come to make Cas's palms sweat.

She knew that this night was being intentionally crafted for drama on the show, but Cas hadn't anticipated how stressful it would feel to actually be living this in the moment. Separated from the dramatic music and the jump cuts between shocked faces, it could have felt like any other activity they had done so far. But the looming presence of the screen on the wall, the promise that her name was there, somewhere on the board . . .

She hadn't had enough time. Hadn't done enough. Hadn't given the viewers enough of a reason to love her. Or, at least, to like her enough to keep her around until she found her "match" so she could sail into the finals.

They had barely finished getting settled on the sofa inside when Maddison's phone beeped.

"'Welcome to your first ranking. These ranks will not affect your couples.'" Maddison's voice was shaking. "'Only you can decide if your partner's ranking matters. . . . Tomorrow night, you'll be forced to decide whether you stick with your partner or, if they're ranked low, twist and re-partner with someone else.'"

Cas could feel her heartbeat in her throat, her pulse hammering violently in a way that made it hard to breathe.

Ada's phone.

Her hands were trembling as she lifted her phone off her lap, the light noticeably flickering across her face as she read. "'The girls are going to learn their rankings first. Rankings will be revealed one at a time, starting with the girl in first place.'"

Ada swallowed hard, and after a glance at Cas, and then Sienna, she set her phone back down in her lap.

Despite the speed of the introduction messages, everything was almost eerily silent as they waited for the first ranking to be revealed. In spite of herself, Cas could hear the music they'd play over this moment in the edit, could almost see the way that they'd be jumping from face to face, desperate to get the most dramatic series of reaction shots possible.

Charlie's phone beeped.

"'The most popular girl this week, and first in the rankings is . . .'" He stared at his screen for a long second, his brow furrowing. "There's no name here."

Cas exhaled. Tried to sound calm. "They'll send it to you."

Sure enough, his phone went off half a second later.

"'Sienna.'"

A little cheer went up around the living room as her photo popped up on the television. Jayden pressed a kiss to Sienna's temple; Ada wrapped her arms around Sienna's neck in a swift, fierce hug; and Cas, leaning over Ada so she could reach, tapped the outside of Sienna's knee. Cas moved to straighten up when she felt Femi leaning in from behind her, his arm stretching along the back of the sofa so he could reach Sienna.

He brushed his fingertips lightly along the outside of her shoulder, and, though everyone in the room was trying to congratulate her, when Sienna turned, she only had eyes for Femi.

"Congratulations."

Sienna was beaming, the relief written all over her face. "Thanks."

Reece revealed that Ada was second, and they all celebrated again. Ada had thrown her arms around Sienna so easily, but Cas kept hesitating, unsure. She wanted to give Ada a hug—it was nothing, a hug—but would it be too much?

Not as a gesture, but too much for Cas to handle?

Cas was still arguing with herself when Ada turned, an electric smile lighting up her face.

"Congrats," Cas said. She leaned forward without thinking now, her arms winding around Ada's neck. "You deserve it."

Ada laughed, and the brush of her breath against Cas's neck made her shiver.

Ada pulled back a little, brow creased with concern. "Are you cold?"

Cas had goose bumps down her arms.

She shook her head. "No, I'm all right."

The emotional high of the first two reveals didn't last as they continued into third place. With each text, the tension in the room ratcheted higher, especially after Tia, surprisingly, snagged the third place spot.

Cas, Maddison, and Lexi were left, until Brad announced that Lexi had swung fourth.

Cas hadn't expected she'd be in first or second, she'd been hoping for third, thought fourth was a solid bet, but now, here she was, staring down the barrel of last place, her heart so massive in her throat that it was impossible to breathe.

She couldn't be last place. Not if she wanted any real hope of staying to the end.

Last place would be the nail in her coffin. The final straw that kept her in hot, sweaty pubs getting pawed at by strangers until the end of time.

Femi's phone pinged.

His movements were sure, steady. He wrapped his arm around Cas before he even moved to pick up the phone, squeezing her briefly against him in one last show of solidarity.

She had never adored him more than she did in that moment.

"'The final two positions will be revealed at the same time. . . .'" Femi trailed off appropriately, staring at his screen for a few beats longer than necessary before he dropped his phone back down into his lap. Everyone was completely silent as they waited, the tension so thick Cas could feel it, choking her, squeezing her, until, finally—

Beep.

Femi stared down at his screen and Cas knew what he was going to say before he even said it from the way his fingers twitched on her shoulder.

"'In fifth place, we have Maddison.'"

Beep.

"'And, in last place . . . Cas.'"

Both of their photos now joined the others on the television screen. Cas pressed her lips together into a fine line, determined to keep her expression neutral, but she was sure that she looked just as angry and confused as she felt. Was sure that everything was written all over her face for the entire fucking country to see.

Femi squeezed her shoulder and leaned over to whisper into her ear. "Are you okay?"

Cas nodded mutely, her gaze frozen dead ahead. Femi squeezed her shoulder again, leaning into her so she could feel the heat of him directly against her side.

"I adore you no matter what," Femi whispered. "And the public's wrong. People don't know you like I do."

Cas nodded again, though his words barely registered.

Last place.

Last fucking place.

She needed to get her game together.

And fast.

CAS HARDLY PAID attention to the rest of the rankings—was only aware of the fact that, on the boy's side, Femi scored the top spot, despite being shackled to someone as desperately unlikable as Cas.

The only moment of vindication she received was the fact that Brad was also ranked last on the boys' side. But even that relief was short-lived when her brain whispered that that meant she and Brad were liked an equal amount by the British public.

Cas thought that was going to be it for the evening, but then, just as she was getting ready to bolt, Tia got a text. Luckily for Cas, it was harmless.

"'Lovers! To celebrate your first successful ranking, the top two lovers are going out on a date! Sienna and Femi, please get ready to leave the villa now.'"

The girls ran up the stairs, and Cas mustered every ounce of energy she could. She was excited about this for Sienna and Femi, she was, but the urge to sit in a corner and sulk was almost overwhelming. Still, Cas worked diligently, dragging outfits out of the wardrobe alongside everyone else as soon as they got to the change room, taking direction from Sienna as she adjusted her makeup.

"I think I want to wear something pink," she said, "or no, oh my god. *Red*. Ades—" Sienna turned around, still wiping lip balm off her lips. "Can you get that red jumpsuit?"

"The one with the ribbon top?"

"Yes." Sienna whirled around in her seat and started rummaging through the lipstick container. "I don't know how I'll do the top yet, but I'm thinking crossed straps, around the neck?"

Cas started pulling shoe options from the wardrobe by the door. "Gorge."

Sienna didn't do much to her makeup—just freshened up her concealer in a few spots, swiped on shimmery eyeshadow, and applied lashes before deciding she wanted to add a light lip stain before her lip gloss. She was standing in the mirror trying to sort out how to tie the top when Femi shouted from downstairs.

"Sienna!"

Cas stuck her head out of the change room and gazed down over the balcony to the entryway. Femi stood there, black trousers and socks on, shirtless, several button-ups in hand.

"Where's Sienna?"

"Getting ready. She's trying to look hot for you."

Sienna laughed from inside the change room. "I am not!" She shouted it loudly enough that Femi could hear, and he smiled, his nose wrinkling a little with the gesture.

"What color are we wearing, Si?" He raised his voice so she could hear him, and without hesitation, Sienna responded.

"Red!"

Femi glanced down at the shirts in his hands—yellow, green palm leaf, pink, blue—and swore softly enough that only Cas could hear him, before turning on his heel.

"All right, lads, anyone got a red shirt I can borrow?"

Sienna had just finished adding the final touches to her outfit when her phone beeped to let her know that it was time to leave. She examined herself one last time in the mirror, turning to admire the long line of her legs in those trousers, accentuated by the black, strappy pumps she'd chosen, before walking out the door.

And the look on Femi's face when he saw her.

Cas was glad, for the first time, that she was living in a house with a thousand cameras, because it meant that that expression was captured from at least a dozen angles.

He'd been smiling a moment before, laughing with the boys about something as they waited in the entry, but as soon as he heard Sienna's heels on the balcony, he glanced up, his whole body freezing in place when he spotted her. Cas could see it, the way that his entire world had just spun on its axis, reoriented itself so that it was about Sienna, only and always Sienna.

Cas had never seen someone look at someone else like that. So raw and open and real, their feelings written all over their face, not a care in the world about who saw them. About whether people knew how you really felt.

Femi had his heart in his eyes, and it softened his smile, and though it was small and gentle and easy, there was an immensity to the look all the same. A comfort, a warmth that was all-encompassing.

Sienna pressed her lips together in a failed attempt to hide her own smile, her eyes sliding shyly toward the floor as she made her way down the stairs. Femi's arms were around her the moment she reached the landing.

He whispered something to her, loudly enough that the mic was surely going to capture it, but not loudly enough that Cas could hear it. Whatever it was, though, it made Sienna smile at him, and in that moment, Cas felt like she saw everything laid out between the two of them. All the possibility and potential of what they could be.

Cas glanced to Jayden, leaning up against the wall by the corridor into the lounge. His hands were in his pockets and though he wasn't smiling, there was an ease about his expression all the same. An acceptance.

Cas walked over and mirrored Jayden's stance. "You okay?"

Jayden was still looking at Femi and Sienna, separated now, taking in each other's outfits. "I let him borrow my shirt."

"That's nice of you."

Jayden shrugged. "He should look nice for her."

They all cheered as Sienna and Femi made their way out the door, but the moment the door closed, Cas walked silently upstairs on her own.

No one tried to stop Cas on her way out—they either knew she needed the time alone or didn't care enough to intervene. After a few seconds, she heard the garden door slide open, a loud shock of laughter as she walked into the bathroom.

That should be her. Out there grabbing the camera's attention.

At least she was still likely getting enough screen time—they'd probably edit this together in some pathetic montage. Dramatic cuts between Cas sitting alone in the bathroom, red-faced and covered in mascara and tears, and the lively party out in the back garden.

Maybe people would feel bad for her. Hate her less.

It was Cas's worst habit, the way she liked to hide away to lick her wounds. She could hear Aisha in her head as she dropped down onto the ground, back pressing firmly into the side of the bathtub—*You have to start talking about your feelings, Cas, or you're going to combust*—and the laugh that burst out of Cas now was thick, wet, depressing.

It was definitely better to be hiding away if that was what she was going to be laughing like.

The idea that she was going to talk about her feelings here? That would only make things worse.

Cas groaned softly and dropped her head to her knees.

"Bad time?"

Cas looked up at the sound of Ada's voice, surprised because she hadn't heard Ada approach. A feat that should have been impossible in the shoes she was wearing that night.

And something that was explained when Cas noticed said shoes dangling from Ada's right hand.

"No." Cas straightened her legs out in front of her, tried to subtly brush away the moisture under her eyes. "I just needed a minute. I'll be down in a second."

"No, you won't," Ada said simply. In one fluid motion, she sat on the floor next to Cas, her legs stretched out. She was the perfect mirror to Cas except her legs were about five inches shorter.

Cas stared at them for a long beat, and Ada laughed, knocked her left foot against the side of Cas's calf. "Shut up."

Cas pressed her lips together in an attempt to hide her smile. "I didn't say anything."

"You were thinking something," Ada said, and when she turned, her eyes were bright, despite the concern that creased her features. There were only a few inches between them, and Cas was surprised to see that Ada's gaze was set an inch above her own.

"How are you taller than me right now?"

Cas straightened her posture, squared her shoulders, but still, Ada was a little bit taller.

Ada laughed and straightened up, giving herself another centimeter. "I have a long torso."

"Okay, brag."

Ada rolled her eyes and knocked her shoulder lightly against Cas's. "It's hardly a brag when I'm in the store trying to find anything that fits me properly."

"You're telling me." Cas smacked her thighs with her palms. "It's impossible to find trousers that don't make me look like I'm about to go wading into the Thames and tried to dress accordingly."

Ada snorted. "My dad always called those floods. When I was twelve and, like, really growing, he'd just look at me and go, 'Oh hey, Noah, ready for the flood?' I *hated* it."

Cas had never had anything like that with her family. Her parents said more than their fair share of things that she hated, sure, but she never had that nostalgic tone in her voice when she talked about it.

Ada was watching her. Cas could feel her gaze like a physical touch on her skin, could follow it as it moved from her cheek, down her neck, along her shoulder.

"Are you okay?"

"Yeah." The word was out of her mouth automatically, but the way it broke at the end probably wasn't doing Cas any favors.

"I can't imagine how you must be feeling right now," Ada said softly.

"Not great," Cas admitted. Her tone was still defensive, the exact kind of thing Aisha would be chastising her for as she watched this play out on television tomorrow night.

It was just stupid, reacting like this, stupid that she cared, because she hadn't come on this show for herself and who cared about a stupid marketing job at Friday anyway, but that almost made the whole thing worse. With all the effort she'd been putting in—how she'd been editing herself and making sure she said the exact right thing and trying to keep her face in check so she couldn't be misconstrued—even then, people still didn't like her.

She'd been walking around this house all week, playing through scenarios in her head like some kind of *Hot Summer* expert, and now she looked like a clown.

"It's kind of sick, how they're going to have the public ranking us every week." Ada started fiddling with a long fray hanging off the end of her shorts. "It's hard enough being in here, you know? Being watched every minute of the day. No access to our friends and family."

"I'm not surprised they're doing it, though," Cas said. The move had been unexpected, sure, but the decision to rank them, to make them hyperaware of their place in the villa? It added a whole hell of a lot of drama, and that was all the producers ever wanted off this show.

Cas was almost positive the viewers would go feral over it.

"I know, but, like . . ." Ada shook her head, drew in a deep breath. "I hate that you're feeling like this right now. They're judging you off some highly edited, picked and chosen pieces of your life here. They have no idea who you really are."

Ada probably hadn't intended for it to, but the comment made Cas laugh a little. Because that was exactly her strategy—she *knew* that she'd be edited, that she'd be picked apart, and she'd tried to position herself as someone anyone could like anyway. She'd known that she hadn't been going out of her way to stand out. That she'd been sitting on the sidelines more than was reasonable, but last place? The least liked girl in the villa when, technically, she was one of the girls who had been there the longest?

By only about fifteen minutes or so, but still.

Tia had moved in on Reece within half a second of being here. Lexi shrieked, like, *constantly.* And she was *fourth.*

"I hope you know—no, that you really *feel*—that this isn't a judgment on you."

"Isn't it, though?" Cas hadn't meant to sound so tragic, but there it was.

"No! They don't *know* you. I know you. Femi knows you. Sienna knows you. We all love you. These people"—she gestured widely, waving her hand toward the invisible crowd watching this moment—"don't know you. They don't get to have an opinion on you."

"Well, apparently, they do," Cas muttered. She tucked her knees up into her chest, and though she wanted to wrap her arms around her shins, hide her face away, she resisted the urge.

"But they don't get to have an opinion that has any effect on what you think about yourself," Ada said fiercely.

For someone as soft, as easy as Ada, there was something almost menacing about her expression now. The firm set of her jaw, the square of her shoulders, the blazing look in her eyes like she'd uppercut anyone who stepped even a toe out of line.

It was a good look on her.

"You look like you could kill someone right now," Cas said.

"I feel like I could kill someone right now," Ada said. "I hate that you're up here, hiding in the bathroom, because some strangers didn't like your bikini or something this week. I guarantee that's what they've based this on, something so incredibly stupid."

"Honestly," Cas said, and it was a bold choice of words for someone who couldn't be completely honest, "I think it's because I've just, like . . . stayed out of everything this week. Just sat there and probably made my little faces." She made one of them now, all pinched eyebrows and turned-down corners of the mouth. "Apparently, I have a serious resting bitch face. I'm sure that didn't endear me to people."

She'd have to smile more. Laugh more. And, Christ, she hated, viscerally fucking hated, that she was giving in to an entire country that was telling her she looked so much nicer when she smiled.

"I swear, sometimes it feels like no matter what you do, people are going to have something to say about it. I'm in the top with Sienna right now, but who's to say that won't change next week? That I might do my hair differently or laugh too much or laugh too little or say something to piss off Brad and then he's running around talking shit about me all week and then that's me, hanging out in the bottom with you." She cringed as soon as the words left her mouth. "Sorry. No offense."

"None taken." And really, there wasn't. "You better partner up with someone else tomorrow, though. Brad sucks." She knew she was trying to pivot the conversation away from herself, but it also needed to be said. Ada needed to get the hell away from that relationship.

"It won't be up to me tomorrow," Ada said. And it wouldn't—with more girls than boys in the villa, the boys would get to choose whom they wanted to partner with. The girls were completely at their mercy.

"See if you can pull someone in twenty-four hours," Cas said, smiling. "I'm sure you can manage it. Look at you."

Ada exhaled a laugh and rolled her eyes. "I'm not going to try and steal someone. I'd rather, like, recouple with you, but maybe it's too early for Hot Gay Summer."

It was a little throwaway joke. But it still made Cas's heart start racing in her chest.

"Femi, though," Cas said. She tried to say it dramatically, like all would be lost for Femi, but her voice sounded raw. "I couldn't abandon him yet."

"I don't think you'll need to worry about Femi for much longer," Ada said.

"What do you mean?"

Ada shrugged, her eyes sparkling. "Sienna."

"You noticed that, too?"

"It'd be impossible not to," Ada said. "You saw them tonight."

She had.

Cas was surprised to note that she, too, was yearning to feel something like it. To look at someone the way that Femi was looking at Sienna.

"She's still considering Jayden, though, right?"

Ada shook her head. "She says she can't figure him out. He's on the quieter side and spends all day with the boys like he's trying to avoid her or something."

"We have to get her together with Femi, then," Cas said.

"I don't even think it'll be that hard, to be honest. They just need a little nudge." She punctuated it with a tap of her shoulder against Cas's, a brief moment of contact that Cas felt, electric, down her spine. "If tonight doesn't seal the deal for them, then maybe we can make that our mission. Get your mind off these pointless rankings and get our lovebirds together."

Cas couldn't afford to forget the *pointless rankings* entirely, not with everything she had at stake, but she could pretend. Could spend a little more time trying to relax and actually enjoy her time here.

It might even help her if she could figure out how to do it right.

"I think that sounds like a plan."

#HotSummer—Live Updates

@moonlighthiker: it'll be real interesting to see if this changes anyones game

@averyart: you mean like if people recouple based on weekly rankings and stuff?

@moonlighthiker: yeah . . . like . . . I bet it's going to happen at LEAST a few times

@dayla14: how would they think they'd get away with that though? Like obvs we're all going to be watching for it

@tiffstuff: . . . you're acting like they bring rocket scientists onto this show

@tiffstuff: there was a boy who couldn't find Spain on a map two years ago

@dayla14: lolololol fair enough

@gracekellylol: not surprised Sienna is at the top! She better coast to the finale in the top spot or I stg

@mayashah02: I felt kind of bad for the people at the bottom

@lorrylorna: ok but . . . BRAD????

@mayashah02: lolol true. And CAS lol
ok nvm

@alexeiiiii93: she's crying about being last. Stop scowling at everyone and maybe we wouldn't hate you

@cerifrancs: no ok but. That bathroom scene with Cas and Ada??? I'm actually . . . liking Cas?????

@rorykavanagh: no omg seriously. Like the other day when they were talking outside, too. One of her best moments!

@cerifrancs: YES! We were just talking about that. Idk why she's so quiet the rest of the time, it's annoying

@rorykavanagh: honestly if she would just open up we'd hate her at least 30% less

@fionahughes: tbh I know Ada was joking about Hot Gay Summer but like . . . 👀👀👀

THE NEXT TWENTY-FOUR hours seemed to pass by in a blink.

Cas was consumed—all night, all morning, all afternoon—with worry about the partnering ceremony that evening. About what Femi would do, what he *should* do, now that the rankings were in.

How long would people continue to like him, think good things about him, if he stayed associated with her? He was clearly well-liked, and short of, like, actively fighting one of them, that probably wouldn't change overnight. But people would start to question him—his integrity, his judgment—if he continued to be Cas's partner, especially given his clear feelings for Sienna.

As easy as it was to fall down that spiral, it was just as simple to examine the alternative. To see this as an opportunity. A lifeline. Because how long could she stay at the bottom if she was tied to someone like Femi? If the public had such a strong positive feeling about him, surely it must say something about her if he was actively choosing to associate himself with her.

And even more broadly, if she continued to spend time with Sienna and Ada. Yes, Cas was in the bottom, but she was surrounded by the most well-liked people in the villa. Surely, *surely*, that had to count for something.

It made her feel a little sticky thinking about it, but maybe, if they refused to cave to the public pressure, the audience would reevaluate their ideas of her.

Cas kept hoping that Femi would come and find her at some point during the day, but he was never around anytime Cas looked for him. He still brought her a coffee in the morning, still flashed her the same grin he gave to Ada and Sienna before he ran outside into the sunshine, but by the time Cas's brain had switched on for the morning?

He was playing two a side with Reece, Jayden, and Charlie, then he was in the gym, and then he was just . . . gone.

No matter how much Cas tried to play it cool, she was definitely starting to stress as the sun dipped lower and lower. As her moment of fate crept ever closer. She could have gone to talk to him about it, but she didn't want to feel like she was pressuring him. Last place, least liked as she was, it would have been painfully obvious to her, to Femi, to everyone, exactly what she was after. The smooth rocking of her pool float in the water was the only thing keeping Cas from giving away the very last shred of her dignity and begging Femi to keep her.

Cas was lucky enough to grab the first shower that evening, so she had more time than usual to choose her outfit. Cas thumbed through the wardrobe, considering each bodycon dress and micromini with an intensity that far exceeded the actual severity of the situation. She eventually decided on a mostly sheer bustier top that hugged her curves and a white faux leather skirt with a slit that exposed most of her right thigh. It was a very different style from what she usually wore, but she liked the contrast in the fabric, and even more, she liked the way that it felt when she put it on.

She was sitting at the vanity blending foundation down her neck when Ada walked in, hair dripping, and made her way to the wardrobe.

Cas was not at all watching the path of the water droplets over her collarbone.

"I thought you weren't going to wash your hair."

"The boys let me get into the outside shower before them if I promised to make them coffee tomorrow morning," she said.

"They should have let you in for nothing," Cas said, tilting her head back to check that she'd blended her makeup well enough. "It's not like they take more than two seconds to shower."

"Whatever." Ada grabbed a halter dress out of the wardrobe and examined it before putting it back. "I'd get up tomorrow and make myself coffee anyway, so it's just a few more mugs."

"Fair enough."

Neither of them spoke as Ada continued searching through the wardrobe, though Cas felt her eyes drawn to Ada over and over again as she held out her options. Each one—a tiny dress that was more cutouts than dress, a skirt set that looked barely bigger than a postage stamp—made Cas feel like she could hear her heartbeat against the inside of her chest.

The most recent selection, a royal blue bandage skirt and a halter top with a cutout across the chest, appeared to have Ada somewhat mesmerized. She tilted her head to the side, considering it, and Cas tried to distract herself by applying bronzer to her skin to stop herself imagining Ada in it.

Or, god, imagining peeling Ada out of it. A thought that hit Cas like a ton of bricks.

She'd known, from the first moment she'd walked into the villa, that she found Ada attractive, but it was unavoidable now. Undeniable in a way that was really going to be a problem if Ada didn't feel the same way.

Though it might be an even bigger problem if Ada *did* feel the same way.

Because Ada was genuine. Looking for a connection with someone that transcended whatever time she was going to spend with them in the villa. Cas had no interest in anything lasting beyond the second she stepped out that front door.

Ada scraped her lip over her bottom teeth and locked eyes with Cas in the mirror. "What do you think about this?"

Cas thought far too many things about that little skirt. And only about three of them were possible to share at the moment.

"You should wear that," Cas said. She grabbed her sponge off the table and started diffusing the blush across her cheeks. "You'll look hot in it."

"Do you think?"

"Yeah." Cas grabbed an eyeshadow brush and a random palette. Started very casually doing her eyes.

The other girls, thankfully, started filing in over the next few minutes, the laughter and conversation the perfect distraction from everything going on in her head.

Cas had just finished putting the final touches on her

lipstick—a bright, almost electric red that looked like poison against her lips—when Femi appeared in the doorway.

"You all are looking lovely."

"Thank you," Sienna said. She had just emerged from the wardrobe, a set of Barbie-pink separates in her hand. "You're looking decent yourself."

Femi was wearing a soft pastel striped shirt, but the lines were abstract, curving and waving around the top instead of forming straight lines. The pink, yellow, green, and blue popped beautifully against his dark brown skin and the faded black jeans he'd paired with them for the night. He'd left a few of the top buttons undone, and Cas watched Sienna's eyes drift over the exposed planes of Femi's chest.

Femi, though, was twisting his fingers together and staring at Cas. "Cas, have you got a second?"

Cas flashed him a smile, though the anxiety was swirling wildly in her gut now. "Of course."

Her feet were remarkably steady as she stood, her fingers relaxed as she set her lipstick back in the tray on the vanity. No one spoke as she made her way to the balcony door, but Ada caught her hand as she passed, a quick squeeze and a glance that gave Cas the last bit of confidence she needed to walk outside.

The balcony was small, little more than a tiny two-seater bench, a few potted plants, and a string of fairy lights. It was a nice space, seemingly private, but the door into the change room and the fencing, both, were glass.

Cas sat very carefully on the bench, tugging the hem of her skirt down with so much force she might have ripped it in half.

Femi kept his eyes on hers. "Sorry I didn't come find you

earlier today. I was in the beach hut for . . . a while this afternoon."

Ah. So, the producers made sure that Cas and Femi weren't having this conversation until now.

"How are you feeling about tonight?" Femi asked.

Cas exhaled, the sound shaky and almost a laugh. "Honestly?"

His expression softened into a smile. "Honestly."

"Horrible," Cas admitted. "I feel like I should have spent the night packing my bags."

"Really?"

She nodded. "Not because I think you'd— Not because of you. Just . . . I don't know. I'm last. Why would anyone keep me round?"

Femi hummed absently. Didn't contradict her. He leaned back against the glass, crossed one leg over the other. He wasn't looking at her, was watching the girls as they finished putting their makeup on, though, Cas noticed his gaze catching on Sienna. Admiring her as she checked her outfit in the mirror, smiling, just a little, when she threw a cotton pad at Ada's head. Exhaling gently as she laughed at something Tia said.

Finally, he drew in a deep breath. Turned back to Cas.

"You're my best friend in here, you know," Femi said quietly. He sounded almost awed, like he couldn't quite believe it.

"Try not to sound so surprised."

He nudged her lightly with his shoulder. "It's just easy to talk to you. I like our little debriefs in bed at night."

From anyone else in any other context, it might have sounded suggestive, but Cas knew exactly what Femi meant. Those moments at night, lights out, neither of them tired enough to actually sleep. They always stayed up a little longer to recap everything that happened that day, making little jokes or observations about whatever ridiculous thing occurred. Plus, the chats helped to drown out the soft moans and sound of smacking lips from Lexi and Charlie's bed at the other end of the room.

"Me, too," she agreed.

"It's important to me that I'm partnered up with someone I trust. I feel like I trust you. And, thinking about tonight . . ." Femi said. "Would you be willing to stay in a friendship couple?"

Cas was nodding before Femi even finished asking. This was everything she wanted. Right here on a silver platter.

"I'd stay in a friendship couple with you until the very end if you'd let me. But . . ." She took a deep breath. This could fuck everything up. "What about Sienna?"

Femi half shrugged, half shook his head. "Jayden's going to choose her tonight. He was talking about it downstairs." He was quiet for a moment before he rallied, smiled. "Besides, I'm going to worry about saving you first, always. I can't imagine being in this villa without you."

"Me, either."

The sense of relief was immense, overwhelming. After the stress of the day, the feeling of having the weight lifted off her shoulders nearly brought tears to her eyes.

They were quiet for a beat before Cas glanced at him. "I'm so glad that Lexi cast you off onto me."

Femi laughed, and Cas loved the sound of it, how big and round and loose it was. Like he was full of so much joy, it was positively spilling out of him.

"Me, too." He stood and extended his hand. "Now, let's go partner up."

"I hope you have a big, soppy speech about me," Cas said.

"Oh, you know I do. If you don't cry, this partnership is over."

"I'll have to make sure I grab my eye drops on the way out, then."

Femi laughed and wrapped his arm around her shoulders, jostling her as he tugged her into his side. "I hate you."

Cas rolled her eyes and turned the door handle. "Liar."

CAS HAD JUST opened the door when she heard someone scream from the back garden. Lexi, if she had to put
money on it. Cas had to admit . . . Lexi's volume was helpful
sometimes.

"Text!"

"Here we go." Femi put his hand on Cas's shoulder, gave it
a gentle squeeze. "You ready?"

"As I'll ever be."

The girls lined up, a foot between each of them, and after
taking her mark, Cas stared across at the boys sitting anxiously
on the bench. Reece's leg was bouncing and his hands kept
moving restlessly from his mic belt to his knee and back again.
Even Brad was sizing them up, gaze flicking around like he
couldn't decide where to look. Cas felt like she was vibrating
out of her own skin, but Femi was calm, easy, and he winked
when their eyes met.

And then Jayden's phone beeped.

"'Welcome, lovers. Tonight, you're going to have your first
partnership ceremony. One at a time, the boys will choose

who they would like to partner up with. The girl not chosen will be sent home from *Hot Summer*.'"

Even though Cas knew she was safe, that Femi would choose her, the words still sent a chill down Cas's spine. Someone grabbed her hand, and Cas looked down to see Ada's fingers wrapped around her own.

When Cas looked at Ada, her eyes, big and warm and brown, were glowing in the golden light. Ada squeezed Cas's hand, and without thinking, Cas stepped closer. They weren't close enough that their bodies were touching, but it was enough that, even in the humid night air, Cas could feel the echo of Ada's body in the space between.

Jayden's phone beeped again. "'Jayden, it's time for your selection.'"

Jayden pressed his palm into the bench as he stood, and before he tucked his hands behind his back, Cas noticed they were shaking. In her peripheral vision, Cas saw Ada turn toward Sienna slightly and give her arm a little nudge.

"He's so nervous. It's nice," Ada whispered.

It would have been a sweet moment if Sienna had responded in kind. Instead, there was an almost vacant look to Sienna's expression, like she was too far gone in her own thoughts to really hear anything happening around her.

"I've decided to partner up with this girl because," Jayden began, pausing briefly to clear his throat as his voice broke, "I've really enjoyed getting to know her this week. And I'm hoping to spend many more weeks getting to know her."

Cas should have been watching Jayden, but she couldn't take her eyes off Sienna. She seemed to have frozen to the spot.

"I think she's really funny and interesting and I can't wait to learn more about her. So, the girl I'd like to partner up with is . . ." Jayden waited the obligatory five seconds before he said, "Sienna."

As much as she looked like she was lost inside her own head, Sienna was remarkably good at rallying. She smiled as soon as Jayden said her name and made her way to him in short, sure strides. Their hug was quick, even on Jayden's end, like neither one of them wanted to get too close.

Sienna looked over to Femi as she sat, and she smiled as he mouthed something to her. It was a softer smile than the one she just had, easier at the edges.

Charlie was next, and his speech to Lexi was short and sweet and clearly everything that Lexi had been hoping to hear. With the obvious couples out of the way, it was a toss-up, in Cas's mind, who would go next. It could be either Femi or Reece last—Reece was probably going to change partners and Cas was the least popular girl in the villa at the minute, so either choice would be dramatic for the audience—so it would likely be Brad next. A safe middle choice, but you never could quite predict Brad, either. Especially with the way he'd acted since Tia had arrived.

Almost as though she'd summoned it into existence, Brad's phone beeped next.

Brad cleared his throat. "I'd like to partner up with this person because I think that we've had a really nice start to our time in the villa together. I think that she's smoking hot, I mean, obviously, she's right fit, and I'd love to continue to share a bed with her."

He laughed congenially, but Cas felt something twist in her stomach at his words.

This—*this*—was all he could think to say about Ada? That he thought she was sexy and he wanted to keep rubbing up against her under their duvet?

It's understandably a part of his attraction to her, sure, but it didn't need to be the reason that he told everyone he wanted to stay partnered up with her. It shouldn't be the *only* reason that he had when Ada was clearly so much more.

"I think that I'm going to have a great time if we stay partnered up together, so for that reason, the person that I'd like to partner up with is . . ."

Brad waited for the allotted five seconds even though, from his wording, it was immediately clear who he was going to be partnering with.

He smiled at Ada like he'd just put fifteen lightbulbs in his mouth. "Ada."

Brad wrapped his arms around Ada's waist when she reached him and pressed her against him, their chests smashing together with the force. She huffed out a puff of air, and Brad just laughed and whispered something into her ear.

Ada flashed him a cursory smile as she pulled away, but rolled her eyes at Cas as she sat down.

It was three of them left now. Two choices, one of them on their way out the door.

In five minutes, they'd know. Cas would know.

Just as Cas expected, Reece's turn was next, and in a twist that surprised no one, he decided to re-partner with Tia, leaving Maddison vulnerable. His speech was heartfelt, warm, and when they sat down on the bench, they were snuggled close, practically tangled together.

And then, finally, it was the moment Cas was waiting for.

Femi's phone beeped. He stood.

Cas's hands were trembling and she smoothed them down her thighs. She knew Femi was taking a risk, tying himself to her for another week, but if she could turn it around, it would be a risk that paid off. If Femi and Sienna couldn't work it out, this partnership could take them both to the finals. It would change both their lives.

Cas flicked her gaze to Ada, sitting there on the bench, right next to the empty space where Cas would hopefully be in ninety seconds' time. Ada had her legs crossed, toe pointed toward the fire, as many inches as was socially acceptable between her body and Brad's. As they made eye contact, Ada nodded once and drew in a deep, exaggerated breath. It took Cas a second, her lungs kept starting and stopping, but she matched Ada's breath. The left corner of Ada's mouth lifted ever so slightly and she snuck Cas a wink.

It was captured on about a dozen cameras, but in that moment, it felt like it was just the two of them.

Femi cleared his throat and Cas found his gaze again. The moment their eyes locked, his smile widened.

"I've decided to partner up with this person because every single time I talk to her, she makes me laugh. She's my best friend in this villa, and I know that the public has a different opinion about her, but, I have to say, they're wildly misinformed."

Oh Christ.

"I don't know what they think they've seen of her, but I can tell you that I've only ever seen a friend. Someone who cares about the people in this villa, who wants us to have a good time and loves making us laugh. Yeah, she's covered in tattoos and loves to scowl, but trust me, that's more appearances than anything. She's really soft on the inside. This person also always shares the duvet and has only thrown a pillow at my head once even though there's been plenty of moments where I've deserved it in the morning."

Cas laughed, shaking her head.

"I'm always going to partner up with her, no matter how low the public ranks her. The person I'd like to partner up with is . . . Cas."

And it should have felt good—*I'm always going to partner up with her, no matter how low the public ranks her*. That was it, her saving grace, her promise that she'd be in this villa as long as Femi was, and unless people turned against him in a drastic fashion after this speech, he was going to be here for a long time. Instead, Cas felt a sinking guilt in her stomach threatening to suck her straight into the earth.

Cas's legs shook as she made her way across the grass. Femi smiled at her, expression steady, and wrapped his arms around her the moment she reached him. There wasn't a hint of hesitation about him, he just pulled her in and gave her a deep squeeze that Cas felt all the way down to her toes.

"Thanks." She said it quietly, but she was sure her microphone had picked it up. Those things were supersonic.

"Of course," Femi whispered. He pulled back, held her at arm's length, pressing his fingers into her elbows like he wanted to keep her there. "You're not going anywhere without me."

As she sat, Ada reached over and gave Cas's leg a meaningful squeeze, and without thinking, Cas moved her hand so it rested on top of Ada's. It wasn't much, just the press of Ada's palm against her skin, but it sent pins and needles zinging straight to Cas's stomach.

Finally, Maddison's phone dinged.

"'Maddison,'" Maddison read, her voice appropriately somber. "'As you haven't been chosen, your hot summer has, unfortunately, come to an end. It's time to say your goodbyes.'"

Maddison was shifting her weight back and forth on her heels, but as soon as she finished reading, she lifted her gaze. Even from this distance, Cas could see the tears shining in Maddison's eyes.

"It's been an amazing journey," Maddison said, "if a short one. Reece . . ." She trailed off, shook her head, started again. "I don't have any ill feelings. I really do wish you and Tia the best of luck."

Reece touched his hand gently to his chest, and then, as one, everyone rose from the bench to envelope Maddison in a hug.

THEY'D JUST FINISHED seeing Maddison off through the front door when Cas's phone pinged.

Because of *course* it was Cas's phone.

"'Lovers,'" Cas said, and despite the fact that her hands were still trembly, her voice, at least, was steady. "'It's time to get ready for bed. Lights out in one hour.'"

Most everyone lingered in the entry, but Cas turned the moment she finished reading the text and made her way upstairs. She should have stayed, talked more about Maddison, strained her ears to hear the sound of the Jeep that was going to take her away, or whatever it was they were doing downstairs, but she needed to get out of there.

Needed to go feel guilty on her own.

She was able to remove all her makeup and wash her face before anyone made their way to the bathroom, but she heard the top step creak as she was patting her face dry and then a whisper that made her entire body go cold.

"It should've been Cas."

It was Lexi, standing outside of the bathroom.

"What?" Charlie, it sounded like.

"She's least popular," Lexi whispered. There was a soft thud, like someone leaning up against the wall. "Why is she allowed to stay and Maddison wasn't?"

"Well, but it was Femi's choice, wasn't it?" Charlie said. He could not have sounded less interested, but Cas tried not to let that go to her head. It was less an endorsement for Cas's continued time in the villa and more a reflection of how little Charlie seemed to care about anything.

"They should've sent home the least popular people this week," Lexi said. "If they're going to bother ranking us this summer."

Charlie just hummed vaguely, and Lexi huffed. "Whatever."

And then Lexi walked into the bathroom, Charlie at her heels, and froze.

This was a crossroads moment. Cas could confront her, make her own up to what she said. It would bring the drama the producers and audience loved, would show that Cas wasn't going to take any shit, but it could also be too confrontational. Too much.

But if she ignored it, pretended she hadn't heard anything, then she was too passive. A doormat. Someone the audience didn't need to respect.

And, in that moment, Cas wanted respect more than anything. The Cas she was outside the villa wouldn't leave this unaddressed, so why should Cas in the villa let it lie?

Cas tossed her face cloth into the washing basket and dotted some moisturizer onto her face. "You could have said that to my face, Lex."

Lexi's cheeks were blood red. "I . . ."

Cas waited, smoothing moisturizer into her skin, but that was apparently all Lexi had to say.

"Right." Cas put toothpaste on her toothbrush but didn't start brushing right away. "Look. I know Maddison is your friend and you're probably not trying to be rude. But I'm here. She isn't. Get over it."

"I'm just saying that it's not fair," Lexi started, and Cas scoffed.

"It's not fair that Femi wanted to stay partnered up with me? That he decided to stick with me, despite what the public had to say?"

"It's not fair that you got to stay and she didn't." Lexi shrugged. "I just think the people in last place should've gone home."

"Well, they didn't. And you don't get to decide whether Femi's choice was the right one—he did what was best for him, and I'm grateful to him for it. I'd also appreciate, in future"—Cas switched on the water and wet her toothbrush—"if you showed me some actual respect and said this to my face instead of chatting shit to Charlie behind my back."

Charlie raised his hands in a faux-innocence gesture—because of course he was going to leave Lexi out to dry—and Cas rolled her eyes before popping her toothbrush into her mouth.

~~~

Cas was still fuming when she made her way down to the bedroom a few minutes later.

She'd tried to remain calm while she was in the bathroom, especially because Lexi and Charlie had continued going about their own nighttime routines, albeit more awkwardly than usual. The second she walked into the bedroom, though, she huffed angrily and dropped down onto the bed.

Reece and Tia were lying on their new, now shared bed at the other end of the room, Tia's leg threaded through Reece's. She rolled halfway onto her back as Cas arrived, brow furrowed. "You okay?"

Cas nodded and tugged the duvet down before wiggling herself underneath. "Yeah. Just tired."

"Yeah, same." And Tia rolled back toward Reece.

It had been a nice distraction, that little disagreement with Lexi upstairs, from her anxiety. But she needed to tread with caution, couldn't let herself get carried away—the public wasn't exactly looking for reasons to like her, but people would pounce on anything she did that solidified their opinion that she was the worst.

Though, maybe, this was exactly what she needed. Friday Cas clearly hadn't impressed them, so maybe it was time for real Cas, the one who would never stand for this passive-aggressive shit, to make an appearance.

She was lying on her back staring at the ceiling as, one by one, more of the lovers started returning to the bedroom. It sounded like a few of the boys had made their way back out to the kitchen—Cas could definitely pick out Femi's and Jayden's voices, and she assumed Brad must be there, too, because she hadn't seen him since they'd left Maddison at the door. She'd just closed her eyes when someone picked up the duvet and slid in underneath.

Cas didn't even need to open her eyes to know who it was. She caught the sweet smell of Ada's perfume again, peach and smoke and a little bit of salt air. It should have been light now, faded after hours of wear, but the scent seemed to cling to her skin.

"Hi, Ada."

Ada huffed, and when Cas looked, she was frowning. "How'd you know it was me?"

She'd done her hair in a plait, and it fell loosely over one shoulder. She wasn't wearing anything special—an oversized cropped T-shirt with strawberries on it and a pair of matching sleep shorts—but something about it made Cas's heart molten in her chest.

It was strange, an uncomfortable feeling, one she swallowed down.

Cas rolled onto her side so she and Ada were facing each other. "Your perfume. What is it? It smells so nice."

Ada's cheeks flushed the slightest pink and she tugged the duvet a little higher up over her shoulders. "It's not my usual perfume."

"What is it?"

"It's . . ." She looked down at the microphone hanging around her neck, her fingers tracing the cord in a way that might have appeared absent to anyone not two inches away from her.

"Oh god. Is it Claire's body spray or something?"

Ada laughed. "No, god. It's just expensive, that's why I'm embarrassed."

"Oh, so it's Tom Ford or Chanel or something."

"Tom Ford," Ada confirmed. She still wasn't meeting Cas's eyes. "I splurged on it when I found out I got onto this show. Scent memory is apparently one of our strongest senses and . . . I don't know." She flicked her gaze up so that her eyes found Cas's. "I wanted to remember this place."

"I personally can't imagine wanting to remember this place right now, but I hear you."

"Fair enough." Ada's fingers moved to the end of her plait and she started brushing them through the loose strands. "My best friends were completely taking the piss out of me about it. A lot of 'why would you want to remember men gyrating at you all summer?'"

Cas laughed. "They're right, though."

"Oh god, please don't tell them you said that," Ada said. Her eyes were shining with amusement, the gold vibrant against the dark brown of her irises.

Cas pointed to one of the five cameras hanging from the ceiling in the bedroom. "That ship has sailed, love."

Ada flicked her gaze to Cas's again. Her eyes seemed to darken, and Cas would have sworn, *sworn*, that she felt the featherlight touch of Ada's fingertips against her thigh.

"But, I don't know." Ada tucked her right arm underneath the pillow. "I just felt like this was going to be a big summer, you know? Like, looking back, it was going to be something I wanted to remember. Anyway." Ada exhaled, her mint breath on Cas's neck. "I wanted to check on you. You disappeared pretty quickly earlier."

"I needed a second," Cas said. "I was feeling a bit overwhelmed."

"You do that a lot," Ada said. When Cas's brow furrowed, she clarified. "Take time on your own when you need to process something."

Cas looked down, watched her index finger trace a tight circle on the sheets so she didn't have to look Ada in the eyes. "It's one of the worst things about me. My best friend Aisha's been trying to coach me out of it for years."

"I mean, yeah, you can't disappear every time something doesn't go your way, but it can be helpful to take space sometimes. Get your head together before you do something you regret."

That was the excuse Cas always used—she was trying to avoid making a mistake, was trying to be careful—but she knew, deep down, that she was running away before things got too hard. Before she felt vulnerable.

"I do hide out too often, though," Cas admitted quietly. "I hate confrontation and it's easier to just . . . disappear."

Ada hummed again, thoughtfully this time, her eyes searching Cas's face. "Why do you think that is?"

"God, I don't know. Too much confrontation growing up, probably. As soon as I realized I could just leave the house, I never looked back." She wasn't smiling now, could feel emotion pricking in the corners of her eyes. She swallowed hard, tried to bury it, but it cracked her voice all the same. "Probably didn't set me up with the best coping mechanisms."

Lexi and Charlie walked into the bedroom then, Lexi swinging her water bottle so, every once in a while, it smacked Charlie in the side of the leg. Lexi made eye contact with Cas for half a second before she looked away, but neither of them said anything.

"I did make a nice step forward tonight, though," Cas said, lowering her voice to a whisper. She slid a little closer to Ada in hopes they wouldn't be overheard. If she was really lucky, even her mic wouldn't pick it up. "Lexi was chatting shit about how I'm still here when we were upstairs."

Ada's expression was immediately outraged, an echo of the one from last night in the bathroom. "What the fuck?"

Cas waved her off. "It's fine. I talked to her. I'm sure it'll pass in a few days and we'll be back to orbiting around each other like we have been all week."

"Still," Ada said, and Cas watched as her gaze flicked over to Lexi and Charlie's bed. "If she tries anything again . . ."

Cas laughed. "I'll let you know."

"It's probably good that this happened here. Not that she said anything rude about you, I mean," Ada said, "but that it happened while we're all trapped in this house. You've got to deal with it. No running away."

Before Cas could reply, Femi walked in and immediately dropped his hands playfully onto his hips at the sight of them. "Now, where am I going to sleep?"

"You can go sleep in Sienna's bed," Ada said, her eyes flicking to Cas for the briefest moment, the flash of a grin on her face. "I'm sure she won't mind."

Femi raised an eyebrow. "And then where will Jayden sleep?"

"With Brad, I guess," Ada said. "Or we can make Brad sleep outside and Jayden can have my bed all to himself."

"Who's to say I don't want a bed all to myself?"

Cas rolled her eyes. "Femi, please."

"What?"

She stared at him for a long moment. It didn't seem like he was trying to draw her out, he seemed genuinely confused. Like he hadn't the slightest idea what she was talking about.

And she was not about to get into it in front of the bedroom, even if half of the lovers were still wandering around somewhere.

Cas sighed. "We'll talk about this tomorrow. We can have pool float breakfast."

They'd gotten told off by the Voice of God the last time they'd tried to have pool float breakfast, but as long as Cas didn't drop a croissant into the water again, they'd probably be able to get away with it.

"Sounds like a plan," Ada said. "Now, good night, we're going to sleep." And with that, Ada whipped the duvet over her and Cas's heads.

It was dark, warm underneath the duvet. Despite how close they were, Cas could just barely see the outline of Ada's features, lit up by the tiny slice of light where the blanket wasn't quite tucked in all the way.

Femi scoffed lightly. "Oh, I don't think so."

And then he dove into the space between them and wrapped his arms around them both, trapping them under the duvet, and Cas was lost in the sound of her and Ada's shrieking laughter.

A FEW DAYS later, the entire bedroom was woken before dawn.

Two phones—one on the bedside table to Cas's left and one a few beds away—were beeping every thirty seconds, each time angrier than before as their owners continued to ignore them.

Cas groaned and stuffed her head under the pillow, but Femi rolled over toward the bedside table, and half a second later, Cas heard the sound of plastic scraping against wood.

"Ades." Femi's throat was raw and it was the first time that Cas had heard even the slightest hint of sleep in his voice. "I think that's your phone."

Ada huffed from the next bed, and through her pillow, Cas heard the smack of Ada's palm against the bedside table. And, a few seconds later, the sound of a duvet being thrown back and Brad groaning in protest as Ada climbed out of their bed.

Cas slid her head out from under the pillow.

The lights in the bedroom were still off, but Ada's phone screen was lit up, her face glowing from underneath. Her strawberry shirt was hanging off one shoulder and a few strands of hair had come loose from her braid in the night and were now hanging around her face.

Cas could hear Charlie starting to roll around a few beds away, trying to grab his own beeping phone, but her eyes were on Ada.

"What's it say?" She tried to whisper, but her voice came out louder than she'd intended and cracked in the middle.

"It's a date," Ada said. She was already sounding more awake. "Apparently someone called Leo has chosen me for an early morning walk on the beach."

"What?" Brad's voice. He sat straight up in bed, and even in the darkness, Cas could see the shock on his face.

Ada just shrugged, didn't answer him.

"Charlie, are you ready?"

"Yeah, give me a second." Charlie had thrown off the duvet and was lying there, staring at the ceiling. Lexi hadn't made a sound, so she was either quietly pouting or was somehow still asleep.

"Who's your date with?" Jayden's voice.

"Some girl named Delilah," Charlie said. He pushed up off the bed and stretched, his T-shirt sliding halfway up his stomach.

"Hope she's cute," Jayden said.

Charlie turned quickly over his shoulder to look back at Lexi before he whispered, "Yeah, me, too," and went to get ready.

Cas had hoped that she would fall back asleep once they left, but after what felt like an hour's worth of tossing and turning, she decided to give it up for lost. She kicked off the duvet, frustrated, and Femi turned his head on the pillow, already grinning at her.

"Giving up?"

"Shut up," she muttered.

That just made him chuckle. "Do you want coffee?"

"Yes, please." The sun was out for the first time in days, shining underneath the blackout curtains. Cas turned her head and stared at Ada's empty spot in bed.

It was selfish, but Cas hoped Ada wasn't being blown away on this date. That this "Leo" was nice, but not *the one*.

"Well, I was promised pool breakfast *days* ago, so why don't you get up and come help me, then?"

"It was too cloudy and cold for pool breakfast," Cas said evasively.

"Well, the sun's out now." Femi grabbed her hand and dragged her up to sitting. "Come on."

The air was cooler than Cas had expected, but the decking was already warm from the sunshine. She grabbed a fistful of pain au chocolats from the cupboard while Femi got to work on the coffee machine.

She jumped up onto the island counter and took a bite of her pastry. "How warm do you think it's going to be today?"

"Probably pretty warm," Femi said. He grabbed two mugs out of the cupboard and Cas opened the cutlery drawer beside her to hand him a spoon. "Not a cloud in the sky today."

The bedroom door slid open, and Reece and Tia stepped out, Tia in Reece's jumper, the sleeves rolled several times to free her hands.

"Morning, guys," Reece said. He grabbed a banana and a

satsuma out of the fruit bowl, and handed the satsuma to Tia with a kiss.

"Morning." Femi opened the mug cupboard. "Coffee?"

"Yes, please," Tia said. She slid onto the counter beside Cas and grabbed one of the pastries from the pile before starting to work on her orange.

Sienna wandered out as Femi finished making coffee and he handed her the last mug, pressing it into her hand with a soft smile. Sienna put her hand briefly on Femi's biceps in thanks before moving to sit at the island, the legs of the stool scraping against the deck as she slid it out.

"We'll be back," Femi said. "Cas promised me pool breakfast this morning."

"Oh, nice." Sienna took a sip of her coffee and hummed her appreciation. "Anything you're hoping to talk to him about when you're floating around in the pool, Cas?"

One of the things she needed to talk about was playing out in front of her that very second.

"I've got a few talking points," Cas said. She hopped down off the counter and swept her pastries into her arms. "Now, let's get out there before they get the Voice of God to stop us."

There was a small cupboard off the kitchen where, each night, they had to drag the pool floats so they didn't blow away in the wind. There were some decorative ones—the giant flamingo, the ice cream shaped one—but Cas was partial to the enormous green and white striped one. It fit two people, was surprisingly comfortable, and had plenty of space to put snacks in the middle.

Femi carried their coffees and Cas dragged the float behind

her with one hand, trying her best to ignore the snags in the wood on her way down. When they reached the edge of the pool, she flung it into the water and, after depositing her pastries and microphone on the pool deck, stripped out of her T-shirt and threw it onto one of the lounge chairs.

The pool water was ice cold, especially in the early morning air, and Cas shrieked as she went in. She bobbed up onto her toes to avoid getting her hair wet and, as quickly as she could, dragged the float over so she could hop on.

"You should have dragged it right to the deck," Femi said. "Climbed on that way."

"All right, Mr. Know It All," Cas said. She slid to her side of the float and paddled her hands in the water so it could reach the edge. Femi set the coffees down, and once he was comfortably situated on the float, he grabbed their drinks, her microphone, and the handful of pastries before pushing off the pool wall so they floated away into the water.

"Now," Femi said, unwrapping one of the pastries and stuffing the plastic into the pocket in his swim shorts. "What was so serious we needed to have pool float breakfast to talk about it?"

"You and Sienna," Cas said simply. No sense beating around the bush.

Femi, though, was apparently going to try to play it cool. "I— What about her?"

"Anyone with eyes could see that you like her," she said. She took a long sip of her iced coffee, humming appreciatively. Femi made the *best* iced coffee. "You get this big smile on your face whenever you look at her. And you were practically glowing when you came back from that date the other day."

Femi inhaled a tiny gasp and ducked his head, suddenly shy. "It was hardly a proper date. It was just because we were ranked first—I didn't even get to ask her."

Cas laughed and unwrapped another pastry. "Would you have asked her if you were given the choice?"

"I mean . . ." Femi took an evasive sip of his coffee. "Probably, yeah. But how do you know she'd've said yes?"

Cas shot him a look. "You can't be serious."

"What do you mean?" Underneath the confusion on his face, there was an unmistakable hope.

Cas shrugged. She knew, without a doubt, that she was right, but it was hard to put it into words. To explain to Femi something so intangible, that was more about the way they moved together, the way they just *were* when the other was around. Like opposing magnets, always drawn together.

"You always have a good time together," Cas said simply. She thought back to all the afternoons she found Sienna and Femi lying on the daybed, literally rolling around with laughter. "And I feel like you have really good banter, you know? And you obviously care about each other."

Femi nodded slowly, his gaze going to the kitchen. Cas could just make out Sienna from here. She was still drinking her coffee, and she'd turned on the stool so that her legs were stretched out across the rest of the seats. Tia and Reece were still there, and Sienna was cracking up at something one of them said, slapping the island counter she was laughing so hard.

Neither of them said anything for a long moment, Femi seemingly lost in thought and Cas very content to let him think his way through whatever was going on in his head.

"She told me yesterday that she'd been hoping things would change with Jayden," Femi said.

"What did she say?"

Femi half shrugged. "That she didn't mind when he decided to partner up with her last week, but she isn't sure how he really feels about her. That he doesn't seem like he's going out of his way to find her, that he really cares about making time to talk to her every day."

"That is your relationship with her exactly," Cas said. She smiled reassuringly, trying desperately to bolster him with a little bit of confidence because he looked like he was caving in on himself. "Everything she's looking for, you're already giving her."

"Maybe." He turned to look at the pool, his eyes tracing the lines in the water. "While we're embarrassing each other . . ." Femi said, his words slow, considered, like he was examining each one before he said it. "I think there's something between you and Ada."

The laugh that rocked out of Cas was equal parts hysterical and poorly evasive. "What do you mean?"

"I mean, like, the way she looks at you." A smile curled at the corner of Femi's lips. "I think she has a thing for you. And I think you have a thing for her, too."

Cas was half shaking her head, half shrugging in the worst attempt at telling a lie in human history. "I—I mean, yeah, she's gorgeous, but, I don't— I mean, we're *friends.*"

"Are you saying you aren't interested in her?"

Cas opened another pastry, crinkling the plastic extra loudly in her palm. "I'm not saying *that*—"

"Okay, so you admit that *you*, at least, are interested in her."

"I— Ugh." Cas knocked her foot against Femi's, making him laugh. "I hate you."

"Liar."

The bedroom door slid open again and Cas's eyes snapped to it, hoping, before she even realized she was doing it, that it was Ada, returned from her date. She was profoundly disappointed to see that it was just Brad, finally deciding to grace them all with his presence.

"It's okay if you like her, you know," Femi said.

"Yeah, I know." Cas's voice was soft, soft enough that she hoped her microphone wouldn't be able to pick it up. "I just don't know if she feels that way about me."

And Ada wanted something serious. Cas . . . didn't. How could she get involved with someone knowing that they wanted different things?

She also didn't know if that was the best move for her game. If following her heart—a phrase that made her want to gag even thinking it—was worth it when she had so much on the line. This job was her chance to get out of nightlife, to move into something stable, predictable. Something that didn't end with drinking too much and trying to avoid getting "accidentally" groped by strangers.

"How do you feel when you're with her?"

The question made Cas go a little pink in the cheeks.

She knew she shouldn't be embarrassed, but the reality of actually talking about her feelings, instead of just stewing on them in her head . . .

"Embarrassing" wasn't even the right word.

Cas exhaled and dropped her hand into the water, letting her fingers trail through the ripples the wind was blowing across the surface.

"This is so ridiculous."

Femi chuckled, the sound deep and resonant and far too amused. "It's cute."

Cas nudged him with her elbow. "No, it isn't. It's tragic."

"It's not!" Femi was grinning. "It's not," he said again, more seriously this time, and Cas dropped her hand back into her lap with a sigh.

"I know you said that you think she likes me, but I don't know if we can be entirely sure that she's not just, like . . . my friend? Like, what if this is just how she shows friendship?"

Femi stared at her. "It isn't."

"It could be!" She was spiraling. "She's always hanging all over Sienna. And you!"

"Okay." Femi sounded like he was talking to a toddler. "But there's something different when she's hanging all over you."

"What's different about it?" She sounded slightly hysterical, but she was genuinely asking. She needed perspective, some-one outside herself to tell her what they were seeing, because Cas was out at sea in the middle of the night in a massive storm with no hope of finding her way back to shore.

"I can't really put my finger on it," Femi said. He leaned back into the headrest and crossed his ankles, the picture of perfect relaxation.

"You won't believe me because you're currently having a very dramatic moment, but you seem calmer when it's just the two of you. Like everything's easier."

"Easier."

Femi nodded. "Like you're thinking about everything a little less. Just letting yourself do things."

Cas hadn't thought about it like that before. But now she realized that she had been thinking about the cameras a bit less recently. Hadn't been as worried about her standing, her expressions, her words, her anything.

Honestly, she was more thinking about keeping things *off* camera.

"Just think about it," Femi said. He gave her shoulder a squeeze and Cas drew in a deep, steady breath. "If you decide you're ready to go for it, you know I've got your back. Now, can you hold this?"

He put his empty iced coffee cup into her hands and tore his microphone off, dumped them into her lap, and rolled off the float into the pool.

"Fucking hell, Femi!" He'd sent a wave of water up over the edge, completely soaking her. "I'm going to kill you for that!"

It was then that she noticed one of their pain au chocolats had escaped in the rocking, and before she could grab it, the Voice of God was there, chastising them.

"Cas and Femi, no pastries in the pool!"

"DO YOU THINK this is what actual nurses wear?" Cas asked, glancing at Ada in the mirror. They were wearing matching white bodysuits with red trim, the fabric so tight that Cas could swear it was see-through. The only nod to the fact that they were allegedly nurses was the cheap plastic stethoscopes around their necks and the floppy paper hats they'd pinned in their hair.

Ada had oscillated between tying her hair up and leaving it down, and her hair was now falling around her shoulders in loose, beach-combed waves as a result. But what was really catching Cas's attention, though, was the way Ada was essentially trying to shove her breasts inside a top that was clearly not made for anyone with actual tits.

"I hope not. I can't imagine it'd be easy to get blood out of white fabric like this."

Sienna snorted. "I'd be more concerned about being on the ward with my nipples out than trying to remove bloodstains."

After the chaos of the first week, their second and third were relatively peaceful. There was some drama going on with

Lexi and Charlie and Delilah, the new girl, but Cas had more or less been avoiding it—getting involved wasn't going to do her any favors. An approach that seemed to pay off because she and Lexi were tied for last place at the third week's rankings.

It wasn't really an improvement, but it felt like one.

In true *Hot Summer* form, though, they'd taken the first opportunity to put them all through something guaranteed to amp every single bit of drama up to eleven.

The dance challenge was notorious—every summer, they trotted the women out and got them to grind over every man in the villa in tiny outfits that aggressively threatened the possibility of a nip slip at any moment.

Gyrating in these was going to take a lot of special effort.

Ada seemed to be reading Cas's thoughts.

"I have no idea how we're supposed to dance in these."

Lexi frowned as she tied her hair up into a top knot tight enough to make a ballerina jealous. "Is dancing different in tight clothes?"

"No, I just—" Ada did an experimental body roll, and Cas watched as the top slid down, nearly causing Ada's tits to pop out.

Ada gestured down at her chest.

"I'm sure they'd blur it," Tia said.

"Yeah, but the last thing I need is Brad getting an eyeful and—"

She stopped, seeming to catch herself. No one spoke for a few heavy beats, so it was just the sound of spandex and hair spray as people didn't ask while very viscerally wanting to ask.

"He seems like he likes you," Tia said carefully.

"No, yeah," Ada said. She was nodding and agreeing, but it sounded more like an attempt to move the conversation along rather than an actual agreement. "We were talking about that in the beach hut on Saturday when I was debating partnering up with Leo. . . ." She hesitated for a long moment, and then her eyes flicked to Cas's in the mirror.

It made sense now why Ada had stayed with Brad for so long. She'd been stuck with him last week, but had still decided, for some godforsaken reason, to re-partner with him for week three. Cas hadn't understood at the time, but of course Ada was still giving him a shot when she had producers in her ear encouraging her to.

Cas shifted closer to Ada and subtly nudged her toe against the side of Ada's foot. Tried, when Ada met her gaze, to communicate that she supported her no matter what.

Ada flashed Cas a grateful smile.

"I'm kind of glad you didn't," Delilah said, laughing awkwardly as she tugged down the hem of her skirt. Cas was sure she was—being partnered up with Leo, a pairing with absolutely zero interest on either side, meant she was able to spend as much time as she wanted causing problems with Lexi and Charlie.

"Are you going to give him the cold shoulder during the competition today?" Sienna asked. She was swiping mascara onto her bottom lashes, her eyes wide and her mouth popped as she tried to get the right angle.

Ada shrugged, combing through her hair with her fingers.

"I think so. I've got to dance with him, obviously, but I don't want him thinking that it's an invitation in, like, any way, shape, or form."

"You still need to figure out how you're going to dance at

all in that thing," Lexi said. She was grinning, borderline giggling as she pointed at Ada's slowly lowering top.

"Maybe it'll have to be a lot of hip movements," Ada said. She gyrated her hips so she was almost grinding against the dressing table, sinking a little weight into her knees so she dipped a few inches in height.

Tia whooped and whistled. "Yes, girl!"

Ada's grin was immediate. Infectious.

She rolled her body again, and though the top tugged lower, it stopped just short of actually revealing full nipple, instead pressing against her breasts so that they swelled perfectly over the top.

"Holy shit." Cas hadn't meant to say it, had really only meant to think it, but the words were out of her mouth before she'd even had the ability to stop them.

And then Ada winked at her, she *winked,* and Cas was sure that she'd died and gone to sapphic heaven.

"Grind on every single one of those boys when we get to the ring," Sienna said. She rolled her own body in the chair, her hips nearly making contact with the dressing table.

"And then skip Brad and watch his head explode," Cas added.

Ada laughed and clapped Cas on the shoulder, her fingers pressing into Cas's exposed skin.

"I think we might have a plan, girls."

If Cas had thought she'd seen enough when they'd been practicing, it was nothing to the actual competition. It was more awkward than Cas had anticipated, largely because, despite the music they always played over these scenes in the edit, there was absolutely no music playing during the competition itself, but there was still something almost unbearably sexy about it, especially once they all got over the awkwardness of dancing around without any music on.

Cas's approach hadn't been well thought out—she skimmed her body across each of the boys, traced her tongue down a few throats, but with each turn she took, with each pass of her hips, she felt herself leaning into it just enough that she knew she'd get away with having a passable performance on social media.

Or, at least she hoped she would.

Where the real joy came, though, was watching the other girls dance. And Ada in particular.

Watching Ada's body move as she glided over the boys who couldn't keep their eyes off her.

Cas felt herself getting drawn further and further in. She was mesmerized by the curves of Ada's body, by the slow, sinuous way she moved. She looked so sweet and innocent most of the time, and the contrast was making Cas's pulse skyrocket.

Ada took extra time with Leo, like she knew that that was the perfect way to set Brad's teeth on edge. Cas was torn between watching Ada grinding on Leo and watching the way that Brad's body very intensely began to betray him, from the firm set of his feet on the ground to his crossed arms and furrowed brow that gave away every single thought in his head.

Ada had just skimmed her hands along the inside of Leo's thigh, eliciting a sharp, thrilled laugh from his mouth, when Brad huffed and pushed himself to his feet.

Standing there, a few feet away, it felt like watching a car crash in slow motion.

Ada didn't notice at first, just leaned down and ghosted her lips over Leo's before moving to plant a kiss on his jaw at the last second, laughing as he came forward to chase her for an actual snog.

For that flash of a moment, there was an unbeatable power on Ada's face. An awareness of her raw sexuality, of her *appeal*. She could have everyone in this villa chasing after her if she wanted. It wasn't a look Cas had ever seen on Ada's face, and it was like a wire had sparked to life under her skin.

As Ada straightened, she realized just how pissed off Brad was. Cas expected her to speak to him, to ask him what was going on or otherwise give him a platform to vent his grievances, but Ada just raised her eyebrows, impatient and almost amused, like he was a toddler throwing a fit in the middle of Sainsbury's. In response, Brad huffed angrily, said, "Fuck this," and stormed off.

Ada's face was a perfect mask of indifference as Brad jumped over the rope surrounding the platform and stalked off toward the villa. Cas was sure that, before long, producers would be calling out to him through the Voice of God to convince him to get back into the ring.

Or maybe they wouldn't. This was, after all, the exact kind of drama that they lived for.

As soon as Brad disappeared, a slow smile stretched across Ada's face.

"Well, I was due to give one more lap dance, so . . ." She held her hand out to Cas who was standing closest to the end of the bench where the boys were sitting.

"Cas, would you like to be my guest of honor?"

Cas didn't know what to say. Couldn't have said anything

anyway because she felt like she'd swallowed her tongue. She half shrugged, half nodded, a very poor attempt at a casual response, and Ada's smile gleamed, her teeth flashing in the sun. Cas's attraction to Ada had never been sharper than it was in that moment. She felt it viscerally against her skin, the way it was tearing through her veins, the way it multiplied and twisted over itself as Cas placed her palm on Ada's.

For all Ada's talk about not being able to manage this challenge gracefully, the way she spun Cas into her seat was the very picture of ease. Cas fell back against the bench with a heavy thud, and though Cas heard everyone shouting gleefully (Femi was wolf whistling like his life depended on it), it was almost as if she was underwater as Ada approached her, her steps slow and deliberate, something almost predatory in her gaze. Ada streaked her tongue along her bottom lip, and Cas felt a spike of desire through her gut. She pressed her palms into the bench, her fingers curling over the edge, her knuckles white with the effort of restraining herself.

Cas's legs parted with each step Ada took toward her, like the steps themselves were a tether pulling at Cas's knees. Ada swept forward, her hair sliding over her shoulder and tickling Cas's arm, which jerked with the effort of keeping still. She longed to bring her hands up to Ada's waist, to press her fingers into Ada's skin and mold herself to Ada's curves.

Ada slid her stethoscope along Cas's collarbone, the pressure so light that Cas could barely feel the cool plastic against her skin. It was a simple move, but more than enough to put Cas at the brink, her flesh breaking out in goose bumps as Ada teased her.

"Well," Ada muttered, her head tilting curiously to the side. "You have a racing heart, Ms. Morgan."

Ada pressed the disk to Cas's chest and Cas had to physically bite back a moan.

"Hmm." Cas felt more than heard Ada's disapproving hum. "I don't like the sound of that at all. I'm going to need to give you a more thorough examination."

As she said it, her free hand skirted over the outside of Cas's left thigh, her fingertips catching on the hem of her shorts. Cas arched her body toward Ada, desperate and needy and out of her mind. Ada's hand curved around Cas's hip, and just when Cas thought she was going to draw their bodies together, Ada pressed her back down into the bench.

Ada leaned down and whispered into Cas's ear, drowning out the sounds of the boys oohing and whistling beside her. "Stay still."

Cas swallowed, her mouth stone dry, and nodded.

Cas was just aware enough of everyone else to keep a lid on her real reactions. She knew the boys were watching her, she knew she was being recorded on a dozen hidden cameras that would later be edited together and sent out for a million people to see.

It was enough self-awareness that she managed to maintain some sense of her dignity, but inside her head, Cas felt like she was melting down.

There was no denying that there was real chemistry between them. Cas couldn't be imagining it, couldn't be making it up, because it seemed like it was written all over Ada's face. Like she was just as into this as Cas was.

Half of Cas's mind told her she was delusional, but if she compared this moment to the way Ada had danced with the boys, there was a real energy to her movements that had been missing before. It was the gentle way that she traced her hands over Cas's body, the way she teased her, and the way she smiled, all cheeky and proud and victorious, whenever Cas exhaled shakily or shifted in her seat, desperate for some actual contact.

Ada snaked her body over Cas's in a final move, their whole bodies flush together for the first time, and the heat of it made Cas feel like she was going to explode. She could feel Ada's breath on her neck, her lips ghosting over Cas's skin, and before she could stop herself, Cas moved her hands to Ada's hips, holding their bodies together for a beat that was simultaneously far too long and far too short.

At that moment, the bell rang, signaling the end of Ada's turn. Ada laughed brightly, her grin all over her face, and reached down to take Cas's hand. Cas followed easily, her body jelly, as Ada lifted her to her feet. She nearly wobbled as she settled her weight onto her heels again, but she had just enough dignity left to keep from going face-first onto the decking.

Ada dropped her hand as she turned back toward the girls who were all hooting and shouting and carrying on. Cas watched as Ada skipped back to the queue—literally skipped—like she didn't have a single care in the entire world.

DESPITE ADA'S EASE at the end of her turn, she grew stiff as the rest of the challenge passed by.

The sun was just starting to dip below the horizon as they all walked back up to the house, most everyone laughing and dissecting the challenge. Ada had won the sexiest dancer on the girls' side, and she was twirling the plastic medal they'd given her between her fingers as they walked, her eyes trained on the ground.

Brad never returned after his tantrum, and while it was hilarious to witness, even Cas couldn't deny that there was probably quite the storm waiting for them when they got back to the villa.

Ada slowed and Cas, unwilling to let her fall behind, matched her pace. After a few seconds, she and Ada were a few meters behind everyone else, the sounds of their conversations already getting carried away on the wind.

"I hope it was okay that I recruited you for the dance," Ada said suddenly. Cas must have visibly blanched, because Ada grimaced. "Or, okay, if it wasn't, I hope we can make up?"

"No, no, it was okay." It was more than okay. Cas would be thinking about it for at *least* the next fifteen years. "You're a great dancer. Put the rest of us to shame."

Ada's cheeks flushed. "Thanks. I was on the dance team at school."

"I hope you weren't dancing like that at school."

Ada laughed softly, the sound subdued. "No. Well, not at official dance team events anyway."

They were quiet for a beat. Cas had half a mind to leave the Brad situation alone, to let Ada bring it up if she wanted to, but then she was trying to avoid . . . well, avoiding things.

"Are you going to go talk to him?"

Cas couldn't decide if it was better for Ada to completely ignore him or for her to squash this then and there. On the one hand, squashing it meant that they might be able to get along somewhat civilly for . . . however long they had to wait until the next partnering ceremony, but he had also seemed really, *really* pissed when he'd stalked off.

Ada sighed. "I guess I have to, don't I?"

"Probably," Cas said. "It'll take years off your life, I'm sure, but it seems best to get it over with."

Ada let out a small laugh, her eyes dipping down toward her shoes. "I don't feel like I have many years left at this point, so I hope not."

Cas knocked her elbow lightly against Ada's. "Come on, you can do it. Go tear him a new arsehole."

Cas had spent half her life running away from confrontation and now here she was, actively encouraging Ada to go challenge Brad to a fight in the back garden.

Ada groaned—a sad, miserable sound, very reminiscent of

a kicked puppy. "Are we sure it has to be me? I bet we could get Femi to tell him. Or Leo. Either of them seem like they'd be up to the job."

"I'm sure they would be," Cas agreed. Femi looked like he wanted to rip Brad's throat out when he stormed off. "But he probably needs to hear it from you."

"I doubt he's going to listen."

"I mean, yeah, I'm sure he's far too much of a misogynist to hear what you're actually saying. But that doesn't mean you don't deserve to demand that he hear you."

"No, yeah."

Ada didn't move, so Cas stepped forward and flipped the latch, pushing it open just enough that they could slip inside the back gate.

Brad was sitting at the fire pit, head bent, and even though a chill ran down her spine at the sight of him, she tried to smile encouragingly to Ada.

"Go now. And then it's over." Ada hummed evasively, and Cas raised her eyebrows. "You can't avoid it forever."

"Rich, coming from you," Ada muttered, and Cas just laughed.

"Yeah. So if I'm telling you you need to go talk to someone, you *really* have to go talk to them."

Ada huffed. "Fine."

Cas grabbed a spot on the pool deck and kept a careful eye on their conversation, but she had to remind herself, again and again as Ada's gestures grew wilder and angrier, that this was Ada's situation to handle.

A few of the boys were in the gym area nearby, Femi, Jayden, and Leo all laughing among themselves as they swapped turns on the bench press. They appeared not to notice the conversation happening at the fire pit, but every now and again, Cas saw Femi look up, his eyes studying Brad and Ada, checking to make sure everything was all right.

Cas couldn't hear what either of them were saying, but she could just make out Brad's face from her spot by the pool. His expression, at first, was passive, dismissive, but the more Ada talked, the redder he got until he was standing, shouting. Damn near in her face.

"If you hadn't acted like such a fucking whore, Ada, then I wouldn't be angry!"

Femi, Jayden, and Leo were all instantly on their feet, their weights long since forgotten, and Cas was already halfway across the grass when the Voice of God crackled to life.

"Brad—report to the beach hut immediately."

"Fuck!" Brad walked past Ada, nearly knocking into her with his shoulder and, for good measure, kicked a beanbag into the pool on his way back inside.

"Hey!" Femi shouted. "Brad!"

Cas quickly shook her head at him. "Femi, let him go."

He needed to stay right where he was. The producers could deal with Brad; he didn't need to get involved. Didn't need to get himself kicked out, too.

Femi pressed his lips together, but he nodded. "Let me know if you need anything."

The only thing Cas needed right now was to talk to Ada.

Ada didn't move as Cas approached, just kept her gaze trained on the horizon. She looked like she was a thousand miles away, lost inside her own head, and a spike of anger shot through Cas's chest.

"Hey," Cas said, her voice gentle. "Are you okay?"

Ada nodded but didn't make eye contact.

Cas frowned and shifted closer, her hand resting lightly on Ada's upper arm. "You don't seem okay."

"No, I'm—" Ada sighed, one hand moving to comb through her hair and sending a few wayward locks falling across her face. She was quiet for a long moment before she finally looked at Cas.

"He was being such an arsehole," Ada said. "You should have heard some of the shit he was saying to me."

What he'd said loudly enough for the entire villa to hear was bad enough; she couldn't imagine him saying anything worse.

She was going to kill Brad. Fucking kill him.

But it was Ada in front of her now. Ada who needed her.

Cas opened her arms, and without even a moment's hesitation, Ada stepped into them.

Her arms went around Ada's shoulders as Ada's slid around her waist, her hands balled into fists at the base of Cas's spine. She buried her face in Cas's neck, her red hair spilling down Cas's back, and she took a deep, trembling inhale.

Cas squeezed her tighter, tried to press every good feeling she could into the hug. "I'm sorry," she whispered. "I'm so, so sorry."

It wasn't enough, wasn't anywhere near enough. But then, what could Cas say that would erase the last few minutes from Ada's memory?

"I wish I could fix this," she said. She smoothed Ada's hair down her back, her fingers threading loosely through the strands. It was a nicer version of what she wanted to say—because she *wanted* to say she would run Brad over with a car the minute they got out of here—but the sentiment remained the same. She wanted to do something that would make this better. Would make Ada feel better.

"You don't have to fix it," Ada said. She hadn't picked her head up, so Cas could feel Ada's breath against her neck as she spoke. "You're here. That's enough."

It didn't feel like enough. It wouldn't feel like enough until Ada was smiling again, until she was light and easy and laughing.

"I can't even believe it," Ada said. She pulled back slightly so she could look Cas in the eyes, her arms still tight around Cas's waist. "After everything—and I didn't even want to be with him! I was only still partnered with him because they told me I *should give him a chance*—"

The words were barely out of Ada's mouth when the Voice of God spoke again. And, unfortunately, they weren't announcing Brad's immediate removal from the villa.

"Ada—please report to the beach hut."

~~~

All told, Ada was probably only gone for a few minutes, but it was long enough that Cas managed to turn over her last few words about fifteen thousand times.

Ada had admitted that she wasn't with Brad by choice. It wasn't because she had any sort of lingering attraction or wanted to give him the benefit of the doubt. Instead, production had explicitly told her to stick with him.

They *must* have seen what kind of guy Brad was. Must have seen the kind of reactions that he was drawing out of Ada, even when she wasn't into him. The idea that they would have willingly kept him around, that they would have put her through that?

Cas thought she knew this game when she'd agreed to this whole scheme, but week after week, Cas was learning that she didn't know a damn thing about what she'd signed up for. What the reality was like behind the screen.

In spite of her better judgment, Cas had hoped that Ada would seem relieved, or at the very least less anxious, when she walked out of the beach hut, but she was pale as a ghost when she came back outside.

Cas scrambled down off the kitchen counter as soon as she saw her. "What did they say?"

Ada exhaled shakily. "He's been taken out front to cool down. He has to talk to someone, a production therapist or something, but he'll be back in an hour or so."

"They're not kicking him out?!"

Ada shook her head. "They said he didn't actually hurt anyone, so they didn't think it fair to remove him. Apparently he's 'extremely remorseful.'"

"That's bullshit." Cas knew this conversation was safe from being aired—they never showed it when people talked about the show like this—and they'd probably call her into the beach hut anyway, but Cas didn't care. She needed the producers to hear it. She needed to say it. "He was in your face! Who knows what he could've done if they hadn't called him away."

Or if he hadn't listened. Even thinking it made Cas feel sick.

Ada shrugged, defeated, and Cas could feel herself twisting angrily against the restraints of this feeling.

"This is fucked up."

"Yeah." Ada half laughed. "I told them the same thing about a thousand times in there, but they weren't budging."

"So he's just going to come back in after having some little chat and then what? We're supposed to go about the rest of the night as usual?"

"They're canceling the night-filming session tonight. After dinner, we're supposed to go straight to bed."

"And where are you supposed to sleep? Where is *he* sleeping?" Ada just stared at her, and, *god,* Cas hated that she knew the answer. "You can't be serious."

"The idea of him sleeping next to me . . ." Ada shivered, a look of disgust on her face. "It actually makes me feel sick."

"Sleep outside," Cas said. The words were out of her mouth before she even considered them, but she knew it was the best suggestion. "I'll stay out here with you if you want."

Ada's brow furrowed. "Doesn't production want us sleeping in the living room if we're not sleeping in our own beds?"

Cas had to admit that that sounded vaguely like a rule they were supposed to follow, but she couldn't be bothered to actually ask anyone about it or even consider following it right now.

If they weren't going to kick Brad out for the way he'd treated Ada, then they could fucking choke.

Cas shrugged. "Who cares? We're still sleeping in a public space; it's not like we're hiding from the cameras or something."

Ada nodded absently, her gaze trailing over to the large circular bed.

"Okay," she finally said, her voice getting stronger, surer, as she continued. "Yeah, let's do it."

"Great. As soon as dinner's over, I'll steal the duvet off your bed." Cas extended her hand, holding it there for a long beat before Ada took it and Cas lifted her to her feet.

"Don't steal the duvet." Ada's lips were twitching a little. "Brad'll need it, he's right next to the air-con unit."

"That's a him problem," Cas said. She turned round as they walked so she was facing Ada, her own smile growing as Ada's expression lightened. She didn't look completely like herself yet, but she was a lot closer to the version of her that Cas knew.

"Well, I guess he'll have the top sheet," Ada said. She was biting back a smile now and Cas's whole face exploded with her own.

TRUE TO HER word, the moment dinner was over, Cas ran inside and tugged the duvet off Ada and Brad's bed, tucking it up under her arm (in spite of Ada's laughing protests) and dragging it behind her as they went to the dressing room to change into their pajamas. She cast her gaze back over her shoulder, her eyes snagging on Ada's, which were shining with amusement, their gold centers sparking, and, fucking hell, Cas couldn't breathe.

It was tragic, *tragic*, standing here feeling like this and pretending she was feeling anything otherwise. Very out of Cas's usual wheelhouse, if she was being honest.

Once freshened up, Cas and Ada made their way back outside. Brad was sitting on the duvet-less bed, arms crossed, staring daggers at them when they walked into the bedroom, but Cas just rolled her eyes, took Ada's hand, and together, they went back outside.

They walked with slow steps toward the daybed tucked away in the far corner. The idea of sleeping outside together had seemed simple enough. Casual enough. Friendly enough.

But now, every step Cas took felt like one more nail in her own coffin. Her heart was in her throat, stuttering as they approached. The pillows were scattered all over the bed from earlier that afternoon, and Ada swept them up to the head of the bed with one swift motion of her arm.

"What side do you fancy?" Ada asked.

"I—uh— Any. Whatever one you don't want is fine."

Outside of the villa, she tended to gravitate more toward the side of the bed her phone was charging on, but she had a three-meter charging cord, so she didn't even need to be that wedded to it if she didn't want to be.

"Really," Cas said in response to Ada's arched eyebrow. "I'm not picky."

Ada tugged down the right side of the duvet before climbing into bed. "You know. I don't think I really thanked you for this afternoon."

Cas couldn't meet Ada's gaze as she slid into the left side of the bed. "Why would you need to thank me?"

"You looked like you were about to tear Brad apart before the Voice of God got to him."

"It's what anyone would have done—"

"Cas." Ada brought her hand down onto Cas's thigh under the duvet. The small motion felt like a cannonball through Cas's ribs. "Let me thank you."

"You don't—" Ada raised a stern eyebrow and Cas changed course. "You're welcome."

Ada patted Cas's thigh gently, clearly glad she'd gotten Cas to bend.

"Seriously," Ada said. "I don't think I would have made it through today without you."

"You would've," Cas said. Ada clicked her tongue at her, but Cas was quick to clarify. "No, you would've. Sienna's a great friend, she would have happily coached you through."

Ada laughed softly. "That's true." She was quiet for a beat, the silence thick, as if there was something hovering just between them. Finally, Ada drew in a gentle breath. "I was especially grateful for you, though."

Their eyes met and Cas felt it pin her to the spot.

As thrilled as the sentiment made her feel, it was uncomfortable, the faith Ada so obviously had in her. Did Cas deserve it? Had she earned it?

"You still would've survived it," Cas said. She slid a little farther under the duvet. Her voice was thick, not at all casual like she'd been trying for. She swallowed. Tried again. "It just would've been less fun."

Ada rolled her eyes, but the smile tugging at the corner of her lips was everything. She shifted until she was lying down, her red hair splaying out across the pillow.

It was a visual that immediately conjured another context, made Cas think of things she definitely shouldn't be. She couldn't give Ada what she wanted—she repeated it in her head like a mantra.

Ada was quiet for a long moment, only the sound of the breeze in the tree above them breaking the silence.

"You know, I should have known it was going to be bad when Brad picked me," Ada said finally, her fingers playing absently with her microphone wire. "Who the fuck saunters over like that, like he thought he was walking a runway or something?"

"Arseholes," Cas said, her tone matter-of-fact. She hadn't

meant it to be a joke, but it drew another laugh out of Ada, and Cas warmed.

Cas had noticed Ada sneaking glances at her, but now her gaze was trained on the sky. The fairy lights above cast dots of light across her freckled skin, and she finally looked at peace for the first time in days. She was the most beautiful person Cas had ever seen.

This, this was the sort of thing Brad should have been talking about in his stupid re-partnering speech. Not just that Ada was attractive, but the impossible softness of her skin. How the smattering of freckles across her chest looked like constellations, the way her copper hair skimmed across her shoulders. Just a few of the thousands of things someone could love about Ada.

Like.

Like about Ada.

"Tell me something I don't know about you."

Ada turned her head on her pillow, her shoulders shifting slightly as if she was about to roll over but decided against it. "Like what?" Ada's eyes were impossibly beautiful in the dark. "My favorite color?"

Cas snorted, a valiant but failed attempt to stop her heart racing.

"Please, I already know your favorite color."

"What is it, then?"

"Blue," Cas said simply. "You wear blue almost every day."

A parade of Ada's blue bikinis, dresses, tops, adorable pajamas, floated through her mind. Her favorite, without a doubt, was the two-toned strappy bikini Ada'd worn earlier that week, but even the ratty tie-dyed jumper Ada was currently wearing had its merits.

Cas reached out gingerly and fingered the tattered cuff of Ada's sleeve, her index finger sliding against the hole torn in the seam. Cas watched the way the loose threads caught on her skin before she looked up. She'd intended to meet Ada's gaze, but found Ada's eyes trained on the soft circles Cas was dragging along her sleeve.

She watched Ada watching her for a long beat before she swallowed and pulled her hand away. "Anyway, yeah, it's blue. What do you think my favorite color is?"

"If we're just going off clothes, it's black," Ada said flatly, and Cas had to laugh.

"Okay, you're not wrong. Though, I'm also partial to a nice lavender."

"Are you?"

"You seem surprised."

"I am," Ada said, rolling onto her side now and tucking her right arm up underneath her head. "I didn't picture you as a pastels girl."

Cas opened her mouth to argue the point, but there was no point. "Fair enough."

Neither of them said anything for a few long moments. The silence would have been easy if they weren't both lying on their sides, facing each other. In this position, it felt like there was a tether pulled tight between them. The anticipation of something building, tugging behind Cas's gut, pulling her forward . . .

Ada smiled. "But okay, if you already know my favorite color, what do you want to know?"

"Anything." Every piece of information Cas learned about Ada felt like she was getting something special. Precious. Cas was hoarding them, very Gollum and that ring, and it was sort of embarrassing but she also couldn't quite help it. "Something I don't know."

Ada hummed softly and rolled onto her back, revealing a stretch of her bare stomach. Cas skipped her eyes across it before drawing in a deep breath and mirroring the position.

"I can start if you want," Cas said quietly.

"Okay."

There were a million things that Cas could've told her. Millions of things that Ada didn't know. But Cas wanted to tell her the big thing, the thing she hadn't talked about with anyone but Aisha and Skye in the days after it all fell apart. It terrified her, the impulse to open up about this, but she *wanted to,* wanted Ada to know this about her. To understand her.

"I was engaged once. A few years ago." A long exhale, a weight being lifted off her shoulders. "It was the last real relationship I had."

Ada's expression blossomed with understanding. "Oh."

"Yeah. We were a few weeks away from our wedding when she called it off. She wanted to move back home and she didn't want me to come with her."

Said like that, it was almost simple. Almost erased all the pain and desperation and god-awful heartbreak Cas had barely survived after Saoirse left. It made it seem inevitable, like Cas was always going to be leaving tragic, rambling messages on Saoirse's voicemail and then sobbing in the shower.

"That's really horrible," Ada said. She took Cas's hand, their fingers weaving together. "I'm so sorry."

Cas looked down, watched the smooth progress of Ada's thumb along the side of her index finger. It was the first time they'd held hands like this. Close, the soft touch of the duvet, the brush of the breeze on their exposed skin. It was intimate, something that was just theirs.

"It hit me like a fucking train." She'd meant to laugh it off, but it came out thick, choked. "One day, I'm getting final fittings done, and the next, she's standing at our door with all her shit packed."

How empty her flat looked without all Saoirse's color in it. How the sheets still smelled like her, no matter how many times Cas washed them.

"I felt like my heart was getting ripped out of my chest," Cas whispered. She could still feel the echo of that pain, not the full brunt of it, but the memory. Cas knew, now, that their relationship had been crumbling for months, that Cas was hastily holding it together with whatever she could while Saoirse already had one foot out the door. But Cas's heart still broke a little for her past self. For all the ways she'd tried to heal herself from something that had torn her apart so completely.

"No wonder you haven't wanted to get close to anyone since."

"I didn't even know how to. Now . . ." She shook her head. "Now I think it's just easier, you know? Keeping to myself."

Even as she said it, though, there was a quiet whisper in the back of her mind questioning it. Was it easier to keep to herself? Had she ever really been happier this way?

"Or you're just hiding," Ada said gently.

Leave it to Ada to cut right to the heart of things.

"I . . . yeah," Cas admitted. "I've just always felt like . . . you know, you can't predict if anyone's going to stay. Even with a commitment. So what's the point in getting attached in the first place?"

The words sounded hollow even to her own ears. But she'd clung to them for years, had believed them wholeheartedly. She'd shaped her entire world around them.

"I get that. But . . . you've got to take a risk, haven't you? Being vulnerable and really knowing someone . . ." Ada half shrugged. "There's nothing better than that."

Friday Cas would've said that hundreds of things were better than that. A drink or four, a dance with a stranger, a challenge that got everyone around her laughing.

But there was a reason she wanted to leave that life. Leave that version of herself behind. It was empty, never-ending, chaos in its purest form. She was never able to settle on those nights, couldn't relax, and, *god,* she wanted that. She wanted to relax. To settle into something.

They were quiet for a beat before Ada whispered, "Can I tell you something?"

"Of course you can."

"My mum left when I was six." Ada's voice was remarkably steady, as if she was stating the plainest fact in the world. "I don't remember much about her, but I remember feeling like she never wanted anything to do with us. Like she was always waiting for me and my brother to go pester someone else."

Ada was quiet for a beat.

"My brother, Alfie, had it worse," Ada finally said. "He was eight when she left, so he remembers her a bit more than I do. To me, it felt that she was someone I imagined rather than my real mum."

"Have you had any contact with her?"

Ada shook her head. "Haven't spoken to her since she left. I've got no idea where she's living now." Ada laughed a little, but there was a hollowness to it. "She could be dead and I wouldn't have a clue."

"Well, that's dark."

Ada shrugged. "It's true. And if she didn't think it was worth sticking around when we were small, I don't see why I'd have to care if she was or wasn't. It doesn't make a difference to me either way."

"No, I know what you mean." Cas gave Ada's hand a gentle squeeze. "My situation definitely isn't the same, but I think I kind of feel similarly about my parents. Kind of feels awful to say it but . . ." She shrugged.

"It doesn't have to be awful if that's how you feel," Ada said simply. "People spend so much time talking about how, just because someone is related to you by blood, you have to be willing to let them stomp all over you or abandon you or treat you like utter shite and then you always let them back in your life. Blood relation doesn't have anything to do with it. If people are dicks, you don't need to let them take up that space in your life."

"I feel like that's maybe just a queer person thing."

Ada hummed. "Maybe. But honestly, I was so much happier the moment that I finally cracked that with my therapist—like, I don't actually have to stay hung up on my mum. I don't have to wonder what she's doing, I don't have to care about her, I don't have to think that her leaving was some kind of commentary on me, because it wasn't. It was completely about her and how selfish she is, and it's probably for the best that she left."

Ada's words seemed to roll over Cas one at a time, an emotional steamroller, crushing her ribs, her lungs, her heart, pressing each and every spot where Cas had hidden feelings exactly like the ones Ada had articulated.

Deep down, she had always worried it was her. That if she'd been different—more serious, more reserved, more . . . *less*—maybe then she wouldn't have been ignored.

Maybe then she would have been enough.

"I spent my whole life running away from things," Cas said quietly. "From the way they made me feel, from how I thought they felt about me . . . You ran right toward those feelings, and I have no idea how you did it."

"A lot of starts and stops," Ada said. "I spent the whole of my early twenties sorting it out. It wasn't a simple visit to my therapist and I was healed."

Cas chuckled. "No, yeah, I figured. I just . . . That takes a lot of bravery. I don't know if I have that."

Ada didn't even hesitate. "You have that."

Cas didn't let go of Ada's hand, but instead shifted her grip so that their fingers could slide together. "I hope you're right."

Ada waited a long beat before she looked up, her eyes instantly finding Cas's.

There was something almost heated in her gaze—not quite a full blaze, but the still-smoldering embers of a fire long buried. "I know how brave you are, Cas."

Ada's palm pulsed against her own, emphasizing her words, and Cas felt the pressure run straight through her.

"Thank you," Cas finally said. She'd unfurled herself almost completely tonight. She could see the raw edges of her heart, frayed and dangling in the wind, but it had been terrifyingly easy, giving Ada these pieces of her. She let her thanks linger for a fraction, before flashing a cheeky smile. "Now, we should get to sleep. This might be the only time all summer we get an uninterrupted eight hours."

Ada laughed easily, her hand sliding away from Cas's and tugging the duvet over her shoulders.

Cas watched as Ada snuggled into her pillow, her long red hair falling in pieces over her freckled shoulder. The feeling in her chest was so immense, so intense, that the only hope she had of containing it was closing her eyes and hoping the feeling disintegrated by morning.

#HotSummer—Live Updates

@zainisms: brad is FUCKING TOXIC can the #hotsummer producers get him off this show pls????

    @ibistorm: ada babes dump brad and get with Leo he's fine

    @callumbryant ✓: Brad is SO LUCKY #TheLads and I aren't on this season because this would not fly with us

    @aidanshaw ✓: bro absolutely. This man really thinks he can just treat women like that???

@aleenadevlin: he actually should be removed from the show I'm not even kidding

@jardsgotjokes: . . . for what? He literally just left the game like?? It's not like he did something ACTUALLY awful

@aleenadevlin: ???? He almost slammed into Ada in the villa! That man is a series of walking red flags

@jardsgotjokes: you're just making assumptions about him based on his edit

@aleenadevlin: and you're a fucking clown mate

@cerifrancs: brad sucks ok but more importantly!! Cas and Ada sleeping on the daybed together???? 🫠

@faisaaaal: brad is irrelevant can we talk about CADA???!!!!!

@lorrylorna: aklsjfd cas and ada look so hot together 🫥

@xena__: PLS I SHIP IT SO HARD

@faisaaaal: no ok but actually like. Ever since Cas and Ada have been spending all this time together, I'm actually like . . . liking Cas?????

@airjordyyyn: no but like . . . Me too???? What's happening

@jackwilliams95: Cas is ONLY likable when she's around Ada

@steffancherry ✅**:** is public opinion shifting on @casmorgan? How do you feel about Cas now?

❑ Love her!
❑ Like her
❑ Indifferent
❑ Dislike/hate her

@samera.1: if these two don't get together I SWEAR TO GOD I'll never watch hot summer again

18

BECAUSE SHE WAS sleeping outside, and thus at the mercy of the sunrise, Cas was awake far earlier than usual the next morning.

The daybed was shaded by a few trees that hung overhead, but the slant of the light in the early morning, and the reflection of it off the pool, sent a streak of sun across the bed. Cas's legs were tangled in the duvet, one of her arms buried underneath the pillow, and she turned onto her side before opening her eyes, soaking in one more moment of the sound of the birds chirping in the distance and the soft rustle of the wind through the trees.

She had known that Ada was in bed beside her, but Cas was still surprised at how close they were when she opened her eyes.

Ada was lying on the edge of her pillow, their faces nearly touching now that Cas had rolled onto her side. Ada's head was turned toward Cas and she was curled up into a small ball, her knees tucked into her chest and her arms folded across her stomach. It was an innocent position, vulnerable.

If Cas hadn't already been angry about the way Brad had been treating Ada, this would have done it. Seeing how, even in sleep, she'd felt the need to protect herself.

Cas knew she should roll away, find her mic, maybe get up, start the day, but she couldn't bring herself to move. Not yet.

Instead, she followed the trail of sunlight across Ada's skin. Counted each and every new freckle that revealed itself across the bridge of Ada's nose. Traced the curve of Ada's lower lip and thought, for just a moment, about what it would feel like to have Ada's lips pressed against her skin.

The confessions from the night before had replayed in Cas's mind as she'd drifted off to sleep, and she felt them again now, lying here and looking at Ada. Cas marveled at Ada's strength, her willpower. At Ada's belief that, somewhere, Cas had a similar kind of bravery inside herself.

It was hard to believe it, especially when Cas thought about what she'd let her life become, but she wanted to believe it. Wanted to believe that she could open herself up to more without getting hurt again.

She let herself look for a moment longer before finally accepting that she wasn't going to fall back asleep—especially not with the bird in the tree directly overhead that had decided to start a full concert. Cas grabbed her microphone from the ground beside the bed before slipping carefully out from under the duvet.

In spite of the early hour, it was nice, being up before everyone else in the villa. She hadn't experienced this much actual silence in this house since she came here a few weeks ago, and she hadn't realized how much she'd missed it until she was standing at the kitchen island alone, cup of fresh coffee in her hand, only the sounds of the birds to keep her company.

Cas was no stranger to chaos. Her entire life was spent in every rowdy "night out" place London had to offer, and she'd long since perfected the ability to carve out a space of her own just to breathe. Her independence gave her the ability to separate herself from everything going on.

It was the one thing that was probably keeping her sane in this house that was practically bursting at the seams. But it was also probably the very thing that was keeping her at the bottom of the list in terms of likability. She'd managed fifth *once*, but it was a tie and, therefore, barely counted.

Though, it had been nearly a week since they'd gotten updated rankings. It was very possible that things had changed in that time.

She'd find out tonight. But even as she thought it, there was a little part of her brain that whispered . . . *Who cares?*

Ada and Femi were right—she wasn't going to be able to control the way people responded to her, couldn't make people understand who she was through a television screen. She was putting all this pressure on herself to conform to this ideal of what she thought a *Hot Summer* woman should be and the plan was actively blowing up in her face.

Why should she bother caring anymore? Bother trying to change herself or edit herself anymore?

She wasn't ready to give up on the job—she'd spent years applying to jobs only for this opportunity to finally, *finally* fall into her lap. The promise of a life lived during daylight hours, a life that didn't involve shouting over heavy bass, was too much to give up on, but maybe she should give up on the tactics she'd been deploying to try to win it. They weren't working anyway, and, sure, changing things up could potentially have zero impact, but it couldn't make things *worse*.

People already hated her. What did she have to lose?

Cas was midway through a sip of her coffee when she felt someone's arms wrap around her middle. She started, nearly sloshing her coffee down her chest. Cas felt the softest tickle of long red hair against her upper arm.

"Hi," Ada said, her voice in Cas's ear. She gave Cas a soft squeeze and then she leaned forward and pressed a kiss to the hinge of Cas's jaw. It was probably meant as a friendly cheek kiss, but it was so close to the tender skin of Cas's neck that she shivered before she could even think to stop herself. "How are you up this early?"

"That fucking bird woke me up," Cas grumbled.

Ada hummed, and as close as they were, Cas felt more than heard it, Ada's chest vibrating against Cas's shoulder blades. "He woke me up, too."

Cas was still wearing her pajamas, a long Ramones T-shirt that skimmed her thighs and a pair of bike shorts, and even though it was more than she normally wore around the villa, there was something almost too sexy about it. The scene was so domestic it was nearly indecent.

Cas never would have thought that a tattered jumper and frilly shorts were her thing, but she was very, *very* wrong.

Cas lifted her coffee to her lips again and realized that her hands were shaking.

Jesus Christ, she really needed to get it together.

Ada gave her one final squeeze before she stepped away, her fingers trailing across Cas's hips as she moved. Cas buried her shaky breath in another rushed sip of her coffee.

The morning went, more or less, the same as every single morning had since they'd arrived in the villa, with the added benefit of Cas helping Ada avoid Brad at every turn. If the producers weren't going to do anything about it, Cas sure as shit was, and to her delight, most of the boys were more than happy to help.

Femi, Leo, and even Reece, after a bit of roasting from Tia, volunteered to serve as "bouncers," and they guarded the dressing room door as the girls got ready that morning. They'd rigged fake earpieces out of their microphone wires, and spent their time pretending to talk to one another over them as Leo did the morning coffee and pastry run. For an extra bit of flair, he'd delivered the coffees on a platter with a towel draped over his arm and, after Sienna requested it, had hastily drawn on a mustache with an eyeliner he snatched off the vanity.

It was ridiculous, very over the top, but each and every antic was bringing a smile to Ada's face. And Cas knew then that she'd happily orchestrate a thousand stupid activities if it meant that Ada kept smiling like that.

Once the girls were done getting ready, the boys formed a tight circle around Ada so they could escort her into the garden, the four of them talking in code into their earpieces.

"The eagle needs the pool lounger," Leo said, complete with fake walkie-talkie feedback sounds. "I repeat, the eagle needs the pool lounger *stat*."

They spent the afternoon alternating between lounging in

the sun, floating in the pool, and playing the new game Reece had invented to pass the time, Beanbag Ball, the rules of which involved the beanbags, a ball launcher made out of two T-shirts Reece and Jayden had tied together, and the bowl of the fire pit. Jayden was keeping a strange distance from Sienna, but neither of them commented on it. Cas kept thinking she should bring it up, but she couldn't find the words to address it and so decided to leave well enough alone.

She could probably guess what was going on there anyway.

The score was a nail-biting 4–4 when Delilah's phone pinged.

"Oh god," Delilah mumbled, feeling around on the grass for her phone. "Guys, I've got a text!"

Shouts of "A text?" "Oh my god!" and "Read it out!" came from across the villa.

"'Lovers,'" Delilah said, reading the text in a loud, clear voice. "'Tonight you're going to find out this week's public rankings. You're halfway through, so we thought it was time to shake things up a bit: The least popular boy and the least popular girl will be immediately removed from the villa. If they are not from the same partnership, their partners will be single. #BuckleUp #TheresBeenALotOfMovement.'"

And there went Cas's peaceful afternoon.

~~~

The dressing room was uncharacteristically quiet as they got ready that evening.

There were a few comments—"Do you think I should wear this dress or this one?" "How much time do we have left?"— but the energy had been completely sapped out of the room.

This was the first time all summer that multiple people were going home.

If things continued the way they had been, in a few short hours, she'd find herself on a plane back to England. And because Robert was nothing if not shameless, she was sure she'd be in a nightclub not too long after that, passing out shots and dancing around trying to get people to make out again.

And what's more, if she left now, she'd miss the friends she made here and . . . whatever it was that was stirring between her and Ada.

Their conversation last night and Femi's words the other morning during their pool float breakfast had been swimming around in her head all day. Cas could still feel the memory of Ada's arms around her waist, of Ada's lips on her jaw, and that, along with the way they'd spent the entire day lounging together in the sun?

It was making it really hard to convince herself that keeping her emotional distance was a good idea.

The boys were already in the lounge when the girls made their way down the stairs, the silence stretched so taut between them that Cas could feel it, tight against her throat, as she walked over to the sofa. Femi had his arm stretched out over the back of the couch and he grinned at Cas and patted the cushion beside him as she approached. He'd left just enough room for her to join him, but as she sat down, Cas felt someone else sliding in beside her.

"Hey." Ada shifted uncomfortably, tugging her dress down the backs of her thighs to avoid flashing the camera as she crossed her legs. "Do you mind if I sit with you guys?"

Cas choked out something like a response, and luckily, Femi swept in.

"No, 'course not." He reached across the back of the sofa, leaning a little into Cas, so that he could touch his fingertips to Ada's shoulder. "You're always welcome to join us."

Brad was sitting on the far left side of the sofa, hatred written all over his face. Ada must have felt his gaze on her, but she refused to look over at him, to acknowledge him. Her fingers were trembling as she reached up and threaded them through her hair, smoothing out the waves over her shoulder, but otherwise, she was the perfect picture of composure.

Leo's phone pinged first, signaling the official start of the ceremony.

"'Lovers. Tonight, you're going to find out how the public has ranked you based on your time in the villa this week. As always, you are ranked individually, and not as members of your couples.'"

Leo's voice was calm, even, though there was a slightly detectable nervousness there. He'd done relatively well last week, but the threat that things had changed, that you'd somehow upset the public, was ever-present.

Brad's phone.

Brad stared down at the screen for a long moment, lips tight, before he cleared his throat and read the message.

"'As always, we'll start with the girls first.'"

The number one flashed up on the television screen, the line beside it ominously blank for half a second before—

Charlie's phone.

"'The most popular girl in the villa this week is . . . Sienna.'"

Appreciative oohs and scattered applause flared up around the sofa, and Sienna grinned at the screen before turning and smiling at Femi as he nudged her shoulder with his.

"Well done." Femi was beaming, his whole heart bare on his sleeve, and even though Sienna was sitting next to Jayden, she only had eyes for Femi.

"Thanks."

Jayden's phone pinged.

"'The second most popular girl in the villa this week is . . . Ada.'"

More applause.

It wasn't a surprise, but Cas felt her shoulders physically relax. There'd been no reason to worry that Sienna and Ada were going home, not after they'd been so popular the week before, but she knew the public was fickle. That something as little as a stray look could send people into a frenzy against you.

It made her feel better, too, that even though she was probably about to be eliminated, the two of them would continue to have each other. That, whatever happened in here, they'd be able to get through it together.

With each name read, Cas felt her heart claw higher and higher into her throat. Tia was ranked third, which wasn't a surprise since she and Reece had been solid since the moment they partnered up, but with only two safe spots left, Cas felt like she couldn't breathe.

Brad's phone.

Fuck.

"'The fourth most popular girl this week is . . . Cas'?"

Before Cas could even process it, Ada's arms were around her neck and she was exhaling hard into Cas's ear.

"Thank god," Ada whispered, her breath hot against Cas's skin. "Thank *god* you're staying."

Cas half laughed and wrapped her arms around Ada's middle. She'd intended it to be loose, a casual hug, but there was a desperate quality to it, like she was bobbing out in the middle of the sea, three seconds from drowning, and Ada was the only one with a life vest.

"I don't know that god had anything to do with it."

Ada laughed, the sound thick and a little wet. When Cas pulled away, Ada swiped the back of her hand across her cheeks, and Cas raised her eyebrows.

"Are you actually crying?"

"Yes." Ada knocked her knee against Cas's, frowning at the smile growing across Cas's face. "Shut up, I was worried. I'm not ready for you to leave me."

"I'd never leave you. Not by choice."

The words were out of her mouth before she could stop them, and Cas desperately wanted to claw them back. To pretend she hadn't basically just cracked her chest open.

Delilah was saved next, a surprising move given she was one of the newer people in the villa, which only meant one thing.

Cas slid her gaze over to Lexi, sitting stock-still in the center of the sofa. There was no love lost between the two of them, but it was still emotional, seeing the reality of Lexi's situation settle over her all at once. It was only confirmed by the message that Charlie read out—"'That means that the girl leaving the villa this week is . . . Lexi.'"

It was almost brutal how quickly they moved on. Lexi had about half a second to process the fact that she was being sent home before her phone beeped and she had to read out the boys' results. Thankfully, but not surprisingly, Femi was first, a spot he'd more than earned as the center of the villa. Reece, in all his heart-on-the-sleeve devotion to Tia, was next, followed by Leo.

Tension rose as Charlie placed fourth—officially marking him as single due to Lexi's impending departure. After a heavy silence, Cas's phone finally beeped.

"'The fifth most popular boy, and the final boy remaining in the villa this week is . . . '"

The silence seemed extra thick, a pressure that Cas could feel, physically, on her chest.

Beep.

Cas cleared her throat.

"'Jayden.'"

Reece immediately clapped Jayden on the shoulder, the relief plain on his face, but everyone else's attention was trained on Brad. He'd shifted in his seat as Jayden's name was read, pushed himself forward to the edge before stopping abruptly, his neck going red as the silence stretched.

Ada's phone beeped.

Ada grabbed Cas's hand as she lifted her phone from her lap. Her grip was tight on Cas's, their fingers wound together so fiercely you would have thought Ada was dangling over the edge of a cliff rather than reading a text message.

"'That means that the boy leaving the villa tonight is . . . Brad.'"

ADA HAD BARELY finished reading his name before Brad
was up and off the sofa.

No one moved, no one dared breathe, they just watched as
Brad stormed out of the lounge, and a few seconds later, they
heard the front door open. A million possibilities ran through
Cas's mind—Was it the producers? Was it Brad? Mila? A
bombshell?—but then the door slammed with such force the
house itself seemed to shake.

Brad, then.

Cas's arm was around Ada's shoulders before she could
even exhale. When she did, it was soft and trembling. Cas
squeezed her tighter.

"It's okay," Cas whispered, leaning forward and pressing
her forehead to Ada's temple. "He's definitely gone now."

Everything in that moment was Ada: the smell of her peach
and citrus perfume, the soft touch of her hair against Cas's
nose, the heat of her body now that she was this close. Ada
took Cas's free hand, her grip firm, like she was worried Cas
might move away, but Cas couldn't think of a single thing that

would make her move away now. That would make her want any kind of space between the two of them.

Finally, though, someone else spoke.

"Is anyone . . ." Cas sat up at the sound of Delilah's voice. "Are we supposed to go after him or something?"

Leo's phone beeped before Delilah could even finish her question. "'Lovers.'" He read so quickly, he started stumbling over the words. "'Everyone must report to the fire pit immediately. Lexi, say your goodbyes and walk to the front door. You have thirty seconds.'" Leo was up off the couch as soon as he finished reading. "Fuck. Okay, guys, let's go!"

It was insult to injury, the fact that they were forced to move on so quickly. No one had long, just stepped forward in quick succession and gave Lexi a hug goodbye. Lexi caught Cas's eyes for a brief second as Cas moved away, a sardonic smile curving at the corners of her lips.

"Karma."

Probably. But there was no sense rubbing that in now.

"Have a safe trip home," Cas said. And she walked away to make space for Charlie.

Lexi's brave exterior finally cracked as Charlie made his way forward, her arms sliding around his waist with a practiced ease. Charlie, though, was stiff, his expression distant, and even though he moved his arms around her, patted her back, Cas knew what was coming.

"Have a safe flight," Charlie said. "Maybe I'll see you when I get back."

Lexi's mouth fell open. "Are you—" She blinked. "Are you not coming with me?"

It was rare—had only happened a handful of times that

Cas could remember—but a lover could choose to leave the villa if their partner was eliminated. The only examples Cas knew of were true-love scenarios, and it was clear from one look at Charlie's face that Lexi was hoping for something she'd never get.

And then when he looked back at Delilah, who was standing, hands on her hips, surveying the scene? Well, that sealed the deal.

Lexi shoved Charlie's arms off her and she laughed harshly, wiping at the tears now spilling down her cheeks. "Wow, okay. Fuck you, then. Don't DM me when you're out."

And she stormed out of the living room.

~~~

Delilah's phone was beeping as they all made their way down to the fire pit. She stumbled as she pulled it out of her pocket, and Charlie caught her by the elbow. She smiled at him as he righted her, her fingers freezing on her screen, and Leo sighed.

"You two can flirt later. Read the text, Delilah."

"'Lovers—with so many partnerships on the rocks, we thought we'd move the re-partnering up a night. You have two minutes to decide, among yourselves, who is going to partner up. At the end of two minutes, an alarm will sound, and you'll lock in your final partnerships.'"

Everyone started talking all at once, confusion reigning, but Cas knew exactly what needed to happen. She grabbed Femi by the biceps, stopping him at the edge of the fire pit. "You need to partner with Sienna."

"I— But what about you?"

"I don't care about me," Cas said fiercely. "You have to."

"I promised I'd stay with you until you found someone."

Cas was going to shove him into the pool.

"I promised you the same thing. You just beat me to it." He started twisting his fingers together, and Cas shook his arm. "I'm serious. This is your shot. Just go fucking ask her."

"Ask her," Femi repeated.

"Ask her," Cas confirmed. She gave his biceps a firm pat and then spun him around so he was facing Sienna. "Now," she added, giving him a little shove.

Sienna was standing with Ada on the other side of the fire pit, the amber glow from the flames flickering across her skin. Femi was still anxious as he approached, but his posture relaxed when Sienna smiled at him. Femi tipped his head toward her and Cas watched as Ada pressed a quick hand to the back of Sienna's arm before walking away.

"Once we know who's partnering, sit down on the bench together," Leo said. "So we know who we have left."

No sooner had Leo finished saying it than Delilah grabbed Charlie by the hand and dragged him over to the bench. It was remarkable, how easily Charlie was able to attach himself to someone new. Made Cas feel like she'd missed a few tricks over the last few weeks.

Tia and Reece sat next, a foregone conclusion, and Cas knew that Femi and Sienna would be the next to join them. Which left herself, Ada, Jayden, and Leo.

Out of the corner of her eye, Cas saw Sienna take Femi's hand, a megawatt smile filling her entire face, and everything for Femi seemed to reduce to that singular expression, to Sienna's hand in his. It was glorious to see, a dream, and Cas couldn't help her own smile as Sienna led Femi back to the bench and, together, they sat, their bodies so close that every inch of them seemed to be touching.

"I'm obsessed with them."

Cas turned to find Ada standing there, her eyes soft as she watched Femi and Sienna whispering.

"Me, too," Cas said. She met Ada's gaze. The firelight was sparkling in her eyes, and even though Cas had thought it a million times, she was convinced, now, that Ada had never looked more beautiful.

"Cas!"

She started and looked round to find Femi staring at her with raised eyebrows. He tipped his head toward Ada, raised his eyebrows again.

And she could. Could turn to Ada right now, ask if she wanted to partner up. She didn't know how the public would take it, but the friendship-couple route had gotten her this far, surely they wouldn't begrudge her another one?

Still, she hesitated because, god, what if giving in to her real feelings was the final nail in her coffin? What if people hated it and shot her right back into last place and they sent her packing? They loved Ada, but they could resent Cas for getting close to her, could suspect that Cas was trying to latch herself to Ada's popularity—something she was saved from with Femi by being with him at the start—could think a million different things.

But then she looked at Ada again, the sprinkle of freckles across her nose, the rosy blush of her lips, the heat in her eyes, and Cas didn't know if she cared what the public would think.

She didn't know what the producers would say, didn't know how they'd sort out the fact that they'd now have two single boys in the villa, but Cas also didn't care. They could figure it out—they *had* figured it out on past seasons. It wasn't for Cas to worry about what they were going to do, not with this opportunity right here, dangling in front of her face. If only she were brave enough to reach out and take it.

The Voice of God spoke, "Ten seconds remaining!" and Leo swore.

"Okay, uh, Ada!" Leo tapped her on the shoulder, and Ada spun. "Friendship couple?"

"Uh." Ada glanced over her shoulder at Cas, a question in her eyes that Cas couldn't quite read. Whatever she saw in Cas's face, though, seemed to answer it. "Sure."

Which left . . .

"Jayden!" Cas smiled at him when he looked up at her, though his expression was vacant. Distant. He'd always been quiet, even when he was pursuing Sienna, but there was something different about him now. Something closed off. "Want to partner up? I promise I don't hog the duvet."

She'd hoped he'd smile, but she didn't even get a twitch of the lips. "All right."

The alarm sounded, and one by one, they announced their new couples for the week. No sooner had they finished declaring themselves than Ada got one last text message.

"'Lovers—to help you relax from a stressful night, we've decided to open the retreat. Choose one couple now to spend some alone time together.'"

As tempted as Cas was to choose Femi and Sienna, she knew that, really, there was one couple who deserved the time in the private bedroom more than anyone. The call for "Tia and Reece!" rang out unanimously, and Tia buried her face in

Reece's shoulder. He was all smiles as he wrapped his arm around her.

"Thanks, guys," he said, pressing a quick kiss to Tia's head. "I guess we better go get our things."

Most everyone ran back up to the villa with Tia, but Cas held back, eyes on Jayden. He hadn't moved from his spot by the fire pit and was watching the slow waving of the flames in the breeze.

"Are you okay?" Jayden shrugged. Didn't say anything. Cas waited, watched him, but he was too far gone. "Okay, well, if you need anything . . ." She turned to go and Jayden cleared his throat.

"I'm going to go to the beach hut actually," Jayden said quietly. "It's not you, genuinely. Thanks for partnering up with me. I just . . . I need some space to think."

Jayden was gone for one hour, two, and he still wasn't back when it was time for everyone to start getting ready for bed. Cas had just tucked herself underneath the duvet when her phone went off and she stared at the message on her screen.

Jayden has decided to leave the villa.

FOR THE FIRST time in a month, Cas woke up by herself in bed the next morning.

Things were subdued after Jayden's announcement last night. He had been debating leaving for a while, he said, and the re-partnering cemented it: As much as he loved them all, the format of the show just never really let him truly open up. Though Cas felt bad that he'd thought he needed to leave, she knew it was for the best and was glad for him, especially since it would be tough watching Sienna and Femi finally explore things.

She'd been enjoying all the extra bed space when Femi jumped back into bed with her.

"Good morrrrning, Cassie."

"Ugh." Cas buried her head under the pillow and shoved the duvet in Femi's general direction. "I thought I was finished with this."

"Never." Femi lifted the pillow and pressed a quick kiss to the back of her head. At least he had enough sense to dive back into his bed with Sienna before Cas lobbed the spare pillow at his head.

Sienna laughed as he bounced back onto their mattress. "One of these days, she's going to kill you and we're all going to say we told you to stop messing with her."

"She secretly likes it," Femi said. He was grinning, arms behind his head when Cas poked her head out from under the pillow. She held her middle finger up at him.

"It was hard to sleep last night," she mumbled, huffing as she gave up and pushed the duvet down completely. "*Some people* were over there grunting and moaning all night."

Femi looked down, shy, and Sienna laughed. "Please, we are *not* the worst. We're just lucky Reece and Tia were in the retreat."

"I never hear them."

"That's because you're all the way down there," Sienna said. "You should *hear* the noises coming from their bed."

"They are the worst," Leo agreed. He was sitting up, sunglasses on, duvet tucked up to his chin. "When I was over there with Delilah, I swear my sleep was cut to, like, thirty minutes a night. And I was having the *weirdest* dreams."

Ada snorted, pushing sunglasses onto her face as she propped her pillow up against the headboard.

"I bet it's a relief being down here, then. Cas is the best person to share a bed with. She's so peaceful."

"Until she tries to kill you in the morning," Femi said.

Cas glared at him, but Ada just shrugged. "She didn't try to kill me when we shared the daybed."

Femi cut his gaze to Cas's, his grin far too smug for her liking. Cas rolled her eyes and tugged the duvet back over her head.

The boys rolled out of bed and, after a few minutes, started bringing morning coffees back into the bedroom and drawing the girls out from under their duvets. Femi set a coffee by Sienna with a kiss and, blissfully, one beside Cas.

Cas wrapped both hands around her mug, smiling gratefully at Femi. "I'm still on coffee rotation?"

"You're always on coffee rotation," Femi said. Then he ripped the duvet off her legs. "Now get up and go get dressed."

Most everyone else was upstairs by the time Cas shuffled into the dressing room, and Cas sat down heavily into her chair and took a long, slow drink of her coffee.

She needed at least five more sips before she looked at herself in the mirror. Before she tried to do anything other than sit here.

"Tia got a text saying that we should get *ready* ready today," Ada said, glancing over at Cas.

Cas sighed. "Great. What's happening today, then?"

"Not a clue," Sienna said. She was fanning her face to help her sun cream dry and the errant breeze felt nice against Cas's skin.

Cas slid over to the vanity. If they needed to get *ready,* she needed to get a move on. She grabbed her SPF and started dotting it on her cheeks. "I'm glad you and Femi finally got together, by the way, Sienna."

"Yeah, oh my god." Ada started rummaging through the wardrobe, trying to find something to wear. "Did you two finally acknowledge that you're soulmates?"

Sienna laughed. "I don't know about *soulmates.*"

"Femi defo thinks you're soulmates," Cas said, raising her coffee to her lips.

"Femi's a softie," Sienna said. She was still smiling, but

there was a warmth to it that made it clear it was more than just a joke.

"You've made him even softer," Ada said.

Sienna snorted. "Girl, I fucking hope not."

Cas laughed so hard she choked on her coffee.

In spite of the banter as they got ready, there was a definite tension in the air as the morning stretched on. Cas tried to stay in the shade to keep her makeup from sweating off, and she, Ada, Sienna, and the boys floated from spot to spot around the back garden, speculating about what they were going to be in for . . . whenever they were in for it.

"Maybe we're all getting a day off," Femi said.

"Yeah." Ada unscrewed her water bottle and took a long swig. "Maybe they're taking us to the beach."

Cas peeked at Ada from over her sunglasses. "I very much doubt it."

"Let a girl dream."

It was, of course, just when Cas was starting to get comfortable that everything went completely to hell.

"Hello, lovers!"

Cas turned her head so quickly she actually cracked her neck.

Mila Sexton was standing at the top of the stairs, a smile on her face and an electric pink dress hugging her curves. This dress was more casual than the last outfit they'd seen her in, but that only made her stand out more. Only someone that gorgeous could glow in such a simple shape.

"Holy hell." Sienna's mouth was hanging open. She turned to look at Cas and Ada before turning to look back at the host. "Holy hell."

"Why's she here?" Ada said the words quietly, lips barely moving, like she thought Mila might be offended if she heard.

"Don't know," Cas said. She, too, was nearly whispering. "But it can't be good."

As soon as Cas said it, Mila started to move, and Cas could almost see the production shots coming together in her head.

Mila walking down the stairs in slow motion. Jump cuts to the faces of everyone in the villa, their jaws slack, eyes worried, some of them (Tia and, hilariously, Delilah) clutching desperately to their partners like they were already assuming the worst.

The producers of this show didn't even need to try when they were giving them content like this.

Cas could almost hear the music track they'd put over the footage when they aired it, backed by the throbbing of her heart in her throat.

There were very few reasons that Mila would be in the villa, and one of them, an elimination, had just happened the night before. She might be here to announce a twist, but they'd already thrown the rankings in this summer and Cas couldn't imagine a twist bigger than that. Which meant—

Mila reached the bottom of the stairs and threw her hands up over her head. "It's Bombshell Week!"

All the color drained out of Ada's face. "Oh god."

Her worry, though, was drowned out by the excitement across the villa.

"Hell yes!" Leo punched the air before he grabbed Femi by the shoulder. "It's time!" Leo's smile was so big, it consumed his entire face. "No offense, Ades."

Ada shook her head. Her expression was still nervous, but her words were entirely genuine. "I hope you find someone."

"Mostly she just wants her bed back," Cas said, grinning at Leo. "One night of your giant arse hogging the duvet was enough."

Leo barked a laugh and wrapped his arm around Ada's shoulders. "Are you complaining about me behind my back?"

Ada shrugged, but she turned to smirk up at Leo all the same. "I would *never*."

Leo snorted and nudged her, the action sending him and Ada careening to the side. She shrieked and smacked Leo in the chest, but Leo just laughed as he gripped her shoulder and pulled her back upright.

"All right, Leo," Mila said, holding her hand out toward their spot across the garden. "No need to dump Ada onto the ground, you can just re-partner next week."

Leo's laugh kept rolling. "Sorry, Mila, but she's proper clingy, this one."

Ada nudged him in the ribs, and Leo's breath huffed out of him.

"Okay, before these two kill each other," Mila said, laughing, "let's meet our bombshells! Everyone, come join me on the grass!"

Just like the first day in the villa, they were all directed to small dots in the grass, and rather than standing with their couples, the boys and girls were separated, a strict meter distance between the two lines, as if any closer they might just run back to their partners rather than pay attention to who was coming into the villa.

"Now," Mila said, rubbing her hands together like a movie villain, "we worked really hard this year to make sure we chose people who were a hundred percent perfect for *everyone* in the villa. Singletons are finally going to meet their match, relation-ships are going to be tested, and even the most solid couples are going to be left wondering . . . is this the right time for my head to turn?"

Cas shifted her weight anxiously. She wasn't ready for six new people to come into the villa. *Hot Summer* was notorious for its Bombshell Week, of disruption of epic proportions where the number of people suddenly doubled with new lovers. It was famed for how much chaos and confusion it brought, historically splitting up even some of the most secure couples. She figured it must have been coming soon—it was always around the midway point each season—but Cas was really looking forward to at least a few days of quiet first.

As Mila started to introduce the new bombshells, though, Cas began to feel some relief. They were hot, sure, but they were clearly intended for other people.

There was a white-blond blockhead named Ollie who looked so suspiciously like Brad that Cas would have sworn they were secretly twins. The gorgeous, tan brunette, Lucy, who made eye contact with Leo the moment she stepped onto the pool deck; he was already borderline drooling after her. A pale, freckled Ronan, who had a bright red beard like some sort of pirate, didn't seem to match anyone's taste that Cas could remember, but maybe the producers were trying to mix things up.

Cas almost felt bad for some of the people they'd brought in—the idea that Reece was going to turn his head, even for someone as pretty as Gemma, that Femi and Sienna were go-ing to pay attention to anyone but each other, was absurd. But then, that was the drama of this part of the show.

Seeing what it would take to get people to break. To do the thing they said they would never do.

"Our next bombshell comes from way up north, but, if he's to be believed, he knows what he's doing *down south,* too." Mila delivered that line with far more sincerity than it deserved. She swept her hand toward the stairs, all smiles. "Lovers, meet Freddie!"

Cas was prepared to brush him off like everyone else who had walked in so far, but the man that rounded the corner then . . . was a problem.

He was obviously gorgeous and he had a ridiculous amount of muscles, but the tragic part of this was that, at this point, in this house, that barely even registered anymore. Cas was so desensitized to attractive people that even these men who had pecs you could bounce a 5p coin off didn't stand out.

Freddie was a problem for other reasons.

Freddie was clearly sent for *her.*

It was his smile that tipped her off more than anything else. There was a wariness to it, like he'd just woken up in the Jeep they'd arrived in, had no idea where he was, and was just hoping he could get away without getting caught out. Where most everyone else—and the other men in particular—had come in, broad smiles, assets out, Cas had always been a sucker for a bit of vulnerability in a man. It was a quality she rarely mentioned as a turn-on, but at the last minute admitted to loving on the intake form at the beginning of the summer.

Ironic, that.

His dark hair was longer on top, not quite as floppy as Leo's but long enough that it ruffled gently in the breeze as he walked down the stairs. Freddie reached up as he stepped down onto the pool deck, his fingers sliding easily through the strands as his eyes skimmed down to the ground, and, fuck, it was endearing, stupidly endearing, the fact that he seemed almost shy, half naked as he was, about standing here in front of a villa full of people who were actively assessing him.

When his eyes moved up, a slow, easy, unhurried slide that made its way along everyone lined up opposite him, Cas saw that they were a bright, perfect forest green.

She bit the inside of her lip.

"Freddie," Mila said, grinning at him as he came to a stop beside her. "Welcome to Bombshell Week. How're you feeling?"

"Okay. Bit nervous, but I'm sure we'll settle in." Freddie's voice was soft, his accent thick and northern and gorgeous.

Cas was sweating.

"I'm sure you will," Mila said. She smiled before flicking her gaze to the villa cast. She didn't even bother scanning for someone, just let her eyes land squarely on Cas.

"Cas, what do you think of Freddie?"

She *knew* it.

"He seems great." She was looking at Mila, but she could feel Freddie's eyes on her as she spoke. "I'm sure we'll get to know each other." Gradually, her eyes were drawn back to Freddie's.

Even in Cas's periphery, she could see that Mila's grin was wicked and satisfied.

"I'm sure you will."

Mila introduced the last bombshell—a gorgeous, dark-skinned girl named Rita—before clapping her hands together and beaming at them.

"Now, prior to arriving, each of the bombshells chose one of the lovers they'd like to have a date with. If your name is not called for a bombshell date, you must go onto the balcony off the change room. You can observe the dates, but you cannot interact with the lovers or the bombshells!"

Great. Nothing like a little bit of torture for all involved.

"Freddie, you're up first—who would you like to have a date with this afternoon?"

Freddie ran his hand through his hair again as he stepped forward. The gesture was so annoyingly endearing, and though she wanted to write it off as a performance, a way to make himself seem soft to the audience, there was a vibe about him that made it seem entirely genuine.

Freddie looked up, his green eyes landing immediately on Cas. And she knew it, knew it before he even said it, but the thrill still ran through her all the same when—

"Cas."

ONLY ADA, DELILAH, and Femi were dateless after the bombshells announced their selections, and they were quickly sequestered on the balcony overlooking the back garden as the couples made their way to six small tables dotted along the pool deck for their dates.

They weren't much—just small, square plastic tables with two plastic chairs on either side, but the producers had put a drinks tray in the center with a small pitcher of sangria and two plastic wineglasses, so they'd at least thought to treat them to something.

There was about a meter's worth of space between each of the tables, but it wasn't enough that there would be any actual privacy while they were chatting with the new arrivals. Freddie grinned at her as they took their seats at a table at the far end, the farthest away from the people listening on the balcony.

Cas might have thought that that was the best-case scenario, but she didn't like being that far away. Didn't like how easy it would be for Ada to start inventing all kinds of things in her head about what Cas and Freddie were up to.

"They really rolled out all the stops for this date," Freddie said.

Cas immediately reached for the pitcher. "Oh, you'll be overwhelmed by luxury on this show, believe me."

She poured them each a glass of sangria, careful to avoid brushing Freddie's fingers as she passed him his drink.

"Thanks. What should we cheers to?"

"Uh—"

Freddie waited a beat, maybe hoping she would come up with something, but when she said nothing, he smiled. "What about new beginnings?"

"Yeah, sure." Cas tipped her glass toward his. "To new beginnings."

There was a lightness to the way Freddie was looking at her, an ease that was not at all reflected in Cas's own feelings about the situation.

"To new beginnings."

Cas touched her glass to his and swiftly took a drink.

Freddie leaned back in his seat, and his legs were so long that, reclined, his knees nearly touched her own under the table. "So what's it been like in here so far? I've only seen what they put on telly, but I'm sure that's not the whole story."

That brought Cas up short. "You've been watching the series?"

Freddie nodded and took another sip of his drink. "We were stuck in a hotel for about a week, but they've still been letting us watch."

Cas hummed. She hadn't heard anyone mention that they'd been allowed to do that in previous years, but that didn't necessarily mean it didn't happen. It seemed a strange choice, though, letting them watch the show after they'd been selected for Bombshell Week. They'd have a leg up on everyone else, a bird's-eye view of the villa that wasn't afforded to anyone on the actual show.

They were getting an edited version of reality, sure, but they were privy to private conversations—at least those that were aired—in a way that no one else here was.

Freddie, apparently unbothered by Cas's lack of response, leaned forward, his forearms coming to rest on the table like he was trying to block out the couple, Rita and Reece, at the table to their right.

"I did want to ask you something, actually. Before I start getting my feelings involved, you know?" He was smiling, joking, but there was something tentative in his voice.

Cas swallowed. "Okay."

"What's the deal with you and Ada? Like, are you two actually getting to know each other or are you just *really* touchy friends?"

In any other circumstance, this direct honesty was something that would have immediately endeared him to her. But, situation being what it was, Cas was less than thrilled that they were starting their conversation with the very question she was still trying to answer for herself.

"Are you asking for you or because the producers asked you to ask me?"

If Freddie was taken aback by her blunt question, he didn't show it. "Me. Though I'm sure they're curious, too. They mentioned it to me a few times after I told them I was coming into the villa for you."

Cas hummed again and raised her sangria to her lips.

On the one hand, this was her golden ticket to the next few weeks. Her chance to let someone sweep her off her feet, to transition from a heartwarming friendship couple to a heart-stopping romance. Freddie'd come in for her, had traveled all this way for her, and that would play remarkably well in any beach hut interviews she did. She could already hear the way she'd gush about it, knees tucked up into her chest, the picture of a giggling, lovestruck girl.

But even the thought of that made her skin crawl.

Coming into this, the idea that she would have to enter a fake relationship with someone at some point had been weird (especially when she thought about her boss, her colleagues, and her future professional contacts seeing her at it) but inevitable. Something she could tolerate if it meant she got what she wanted in the end. Now, though, the idea of twisting herself into someone she so obviously wasn't just felt uncomfortable.

It wasn't a matter of what would sell the audience on her anymore, it was a question of what Cas could live with. And she couldn't keep lying to everyone. Couldn't keep lying to herself.

"You don't have to tell me if you don't want to," Freddie said. "I just fancy you and think there could maybe be something here?" He laughed a little, swiped his hair off his forehead again. "I've not got an ulterior motive, I swear."

Fucking hell.

Cas exhaled. "I . . . don't know what to say because I honestly don't know what's going on with us. I mean Ada and me."

She paused, but Freddie just looked at her. Waited.

"I do have feelings for her," she admitted. She very nearly whispered it, but she swallowed down the urge at the last possible moment. Her microphone was going to capture her words no matter how she said them, so she might as well say them confidently. "But I haven't decided what to do about it. I don't know if she returns my feelings, so . . ."

"For what it's worth," Freddie said, leaning back in his chair, "I think she definitely does. Anyone watching the show can see it."

"Really?"

"Mm-hmm. You should see the online threads about it. You two got a whole hashtag and everything." He laughed and signals started lighting up in the back of Cas's brain.

Threads?

She knew there was always a bubble of interest whenever there was a queer couple on the show in the past, but she couldn't remember the last time it seemed to make it out of the smaller queer circles on the internet. Never entire threads, let alone a hashtag. And she would know. Even before agreeing to the show, she'd spent countless summers scrolling through the *Hot Summer* feeds.

She laughed awkwardly. "Oh god."

"They're supportive," Freddie said. He was studying her, reading her reactions, and Cas suppressed the impulse to squirm under his gaze. "I'm supportive, too, if that's what you want. But, cards on the table . . ."

He leaned in again, not so close that he was in her space, but close enough that he could be if she moved forward an inch.

"I am interested. If you want to be friends, I'm cool, but if you want something different . . ." He shrugged, his intention more than clear. "You know where to find me."

It would have been so easy, in that moment, to let herself

drift toward Freddie. To ignore everything she'd been feeling for Ada, all the complicated emotions that she needed to sort through. He'd been brought here with her in mind, after all, and the producers had really, for once, gotten it right.

It would have been easy.

But when she really thought about it, there was no way it could be. No way that her feelings—complicated or uncomplicated—were going away that fast. She couldn't escape Ada. Her sunny smile and easy laugh and the feel of her hand in Cas's. She couldn't escape the fact that Ada made her feel . . . safe.

It didn't matter if there was a hashtag and whether it was good or bad. Hell, at this point it didn't even matter what happened when she got back to Friday. Because, finally, Cas cared. And it was scary as hell but, fuck it, if there was one thing Ada was teaching her, it was that it was worth it, always, to be brave.

Cas drew in a deep breath. "Let's say . . . friends."

Freddie didn't hesitate. He extended his cup across the table and Cas, smiling, clinked glasses.

"Friends."

~~~

"I've got a text!"

Cas whipped around and found Lucy, one of the new girls, holding her phone high in the air. When she was sure that everyone in the villa was looking at her, she read the message. Cas had thought that they were going to be announcing the end of the dates, but Lucy apparently had something else in store for them.

"'Lovers! We're going to play a little game to help you get to know the new bombshells better. You're going to be split into two teams, and the winners will receive a party this evening. Villa boys and bombshell girls, please go to the daybed. Villa girls and bombshell boys, please go to the fire pit. #BombshellBlitz #GetReadyToGetSteamy.'"

The minute Lucy finished reading the text, both groups took off to their sides of the garden.

Freddie was up and around the table in half a second, and he extended his hand toward Cas. After a moment's hesitation, she took it. Freddie pulled her to her feet, dropping her hand before knocking his biceps lightly against her shoulder as they jogged to the fire pit.

"Ready?"

Cas laughed. "No."

Cas had never been more prophetic. Because the game was wild.

"'The tallest guy needs to snog the shortest girl for ten seconds!'"

Every time a dare was read out, the two people involved shot to their feet, the pair of them colliding in the middle. The kisses were sloppy and wet, the sounds of clashing teeth and sopping mouths drowning out even the loudest counting in the group.

"It kind of turns your stomach." Cas had leaned over and whispered it softly into Ada's ear, quietly enough that she didn't think it would get picked up on either of their microphones.

Ada let out a short laugh and nodded her agreement.

"Definitely."

Beep.

"'The boy and girl with the longest names need to get into a sex position!'"

The score was announced after each dare, and the race was neck and neck as the challenge continued. Villa boys and bombshell girls had scored first, the villa girls and bombshell boys then scored twice in a row, then they were back at a draw, and the speed picked up with each and every challenge.

It might have been uncomfortable, all of them snogging one another within the first hour of meeting, but the promise of a party that evening was more than enough to get them past most of their inhibitions. It was the perfect carrot to dangle; most of them would have done anything if it meant they got to do something a little more exciting than just lounge around.

Ollie's phone dinged and he shouted out the next dare at lightning speed.

"The person with the most tattoos should snog the person they fancy the most for ten seconds!"

Oh fuck. That was her.

"Uh!" Cas hopped instantly to her feet and spun around on the spot, looking at everyone in turn, skimming over the villa regulars and the bombshells. They didn't have time for her to sort this out, didn't have time for her to be thinking about this because they were going to lose the point and then everyone would kill her and—

Cas exhaled hard. "Fuck it."

And then she dropped back down next to Ada, put her hand on Ada's cheek. It was an invitation, a question, and normally Cas would have been panicking, convinced that her intentions weren't clear, but Ada leaned in immediately.

The kiss was rushed, hurried, little more than a frenzied

pass of their lips together as the crowd around them counted to ten.

"One!"

Even in the frenzy, though, there was a heat to this kiss that surprised her. She knew that she was attracted to Ada—it was hard for her not to realize that by now, she was borderline obsessive—but to feel her attraction so obviously reciprocated . . . It was going to Cas's head.

"Two!"

Cas couldn't put her finger on it, couldn't explain how she knew. Maybe she hoped more than anything, hoped that this wasn't one sided, that she wasn't alone in feeling this.

"Three!"

But Ada was pressing closer to her, sliding across the slick fabric of the sofa, and Cas was sure.

"Four!"

They settled into a rhythm, the breakneck speed of the kiss slowing down into something worth savoring. Ada's hand landed experimentally on Cas's hip, her fingers flexing automatically as they came in contact with skin.

"Five!"

It wasn't an immediate shift, but a subtle one, a gentle descent from the top of a cliff that, as soon as Cas slid her hand to the outside of Ada's arm, started them climbing all over again.

"Six!"

Even in the middle of the kiss, Cas was having a hard time believing it. Believing that she was here, with Ada, that Ada was kissing her back like this. She knew it was just part of a game, she *knew it*, but that didn't match up with the intensity in the way Ada was holding her, in the teasing pressure of her lips—there, but just lightly enough that Cas knew she'd pull away, leave breaths of space between them to send Cas chasing if they weren't being timed.

"Seven!"

Ada's hand slid up over Cas's biceps, curving over her shoulder before her fingertips tangled in her hair. It was a steady pressure, the kind that left Cas feeling like she was reaching for it, stretching out the boundaries of her body just to feel it.

"Eight!"

Cas needed to test the boundaries of this. Needed, more than anything, to kiss Ada properly. She swiped her tongue along Ada's lower lip and Ada's soft, shaky exhale—

"Nine!"

Cas's tongue just touched Ada's, an experiment, and, *god*—

"Ten!"

Cas pulled away then, aware that they needed to respect the game more than wanting to end the kiss. She hovered for the barest hint of a moment, her breath coming in waves, as she tried to reorient herself. Because this—whatever it was—was something massive. Something that had turned Cas completely inside out.

It was only then that she realized that Sienna and Freddie were cheering.

And then Delilah's phone beeped.

"Villa girls win the point!"

And the entire group erupted.

THE VILLA GIRLS and bombshell boys won the competition by one point.

Though they'd celebrated when the result had been announced, Cas knew that there were going to be some tense conversations later that evening about the games themselves.

Who had kissed who, who had rubbed up on who, what the status of people's relationships were now.

It was the same drama every year, and it was exactly why the producers continued doing it, but it was surprisingly awkward, living it in real life. She'd loved this drama when she was watching from home—the twists and turns of it, the intense reveals, the shouting rows—but now, it felt like an invasion, listening in whenever anyone got into a fight like that. They all sat in corners, heads ducked, pretending to be anywhere else.

She could feel Ada's eyes on her as they got dressed for the highlighter-themed party that evening, and felt her own gaze drawn to Ada's side of the room time and time again. But she knew she had to stay focused, just move through the motions. Choose her dress. Apply her makeup. Do her hair.

She knew that the other girls were watching them, but Cas couldn't pay attention to them when she couldn't even sort out her own feelings. Or, more accurately, what to do now that she'd acted on them.

Ada had come here with the express purpose of finding a relationship. Sure, she was going to get the same social media boost as everyone else, her small business would likely flourish, and she was a shoo-in for hundreds of collaboration requests. But those things hadn't been her *goal*. She'd come on *Hot Summer* because she thought it was a chance to meet someone she wanted to have an actual relationship with.

Cas's whole summer, on the other hand, was an ulterior motive. She wanted a promotion, her own office and subordinates, an escape from the endless cycle of clubs and pubs and "fun." The last thing on her mind had been finding someone to settle down with. . . .

She felt itchy just thinking about it.

She was checking herself out in the mirror once more when Ada walked over.

"You look great."

Cas had decided on a neon pink sequin two-piece dress. The cropped top had one long sleeve—the left, thankfully, so she could show off her tattoos—and the skirt was a simple high-waisted bodycon that ended about mid-thigh. The sequins scratched a little, but she loved the way they caught the light.

Cas found Ada's gaze in the mirror. She'd stuck black-light stickers down her right arm, stars and hearts and rainbows that looked plain now but would be electric once they were outside. Her dress was startlingly blue, the color so bright it was almost hard to look at, and flared out at the bottom in a way that seemed almost innocent—as long as you ignored the skintight fit and the low cut.

"Thanks. You do, too."

Ada smoothed her hands down over her dress, and Cas watched the way the hemline fluttered as her hands passed over the fabric.

"You ready to head down?"

Cas nodded. "I feel like I want one of those stickers, though." She pointed at the ones on Ada's arm, and Ada brightened.

"Oh my god, yes, wait." She darted back over to the dressing table and grabbed a sticker sheet. "Stand still."

Ada selected two stickers—a small heart and a rainbow—and stepped close, until she was barely a breath away.

"Turn this way." Ada touched her fingertips to the bottom of Cas's chin, turning her face ever so slightly to the left. It was the barest touch, but it made her breath catch. Especially when Ada's eyes found hers.

"I'm going to put the heart right next to your eye, so try not to move."

With gentle fingers, Ada placed the heart at the corner of Cas's eye, right at the edge of her makeup, the perfect accent to the glitter across her lid. She placed the rainbow on Cas's cheek, taking an extra second to smooth it down.

"Your skin is so soft," Ada said. Her words were almost a whisper, but they thundered in Cas's ear.

"Moisturizer," Cas choked.

Because Ada was asking about her fucking skin care routine.

Ada's eyes sparked with amusement. "I'll keep that in mind. Now . . ." She took a step back and admired her handiwork, though she seemed less concerned about her sticker placement and more about the fact that she'd effectively reduced Cas to a puddle. "Are you ready to go down?"

"Oh, wait, Ades." Sienna was frowning, trying to reach the zipper at the back of her dress over in her corner of the dressing room. "Can you help me first?"

"Uh, yeah, sure." Ada flicked her gaze back to Cas. "I'll see you down there. Save a drink for me."

Cas was about two steps down the corridor before someone reached out from the bathroom door and pulled her inside.

"What the— Femi!"

"I need to talk to you," Femi said. He dragged her into the toilet cubicle and shut the door behind them. "I told them I had an emergency, so we have probably, like, thirty seconds before they start yelling at us." Cas raised her eyebrows.

"You couldn't have talked to me outside?"

"I wanted to talk to you without cameras."

"We're still miked." Cas pointed at the microphone hanging around his neck, but Femi shrugged.

"I doubt they'll use it, it's just audio. Now stop wasting time, tell me what happened in your challenge."

Cas frowned. "With . . . Sienna?"

"No, she and I already talked about that." He waved his hand dismissively, clearly losing his patience. "With you and Ada. Si said you kissed her."

In spite of herself, Cas felt her cheeks heat. "Yeah."

Femi made a sound that was somewhere near a laugh and

a suppressed scream. He grabbed both her arms and shook her in his excitement, and Cas felt her own laugh tumble out.

"I guess you're excited."

"Of course I'm excited! What are you going to do now?"

His enthusiasm was contagious and impossible to ignore, especially when she was confined in such a small space with it.

"I don't know." Christ. She was giggling like a schoolgirl. "I guess we're going to have to talk about it. Figure out what our next step is going to be."

"I think we all know what it should be."

In that moment, Cas found herself wishing that she could explain the entire situation to Femi. There was a chance that he wouldn't be happy with her when she explained the original reason that she'd come on the show, but she thought that he would forgive her. Or, at least, she hoped he would.

But she knew it was impossible. She could practically feel the NDA she'd signed shoving the words back down her throat. It didn't stop her wanting to lay out every single complication to get his honest opinion on what she should do.

"You don't think . . ." She stopped, changed her mind. "Do you think she wants to partner up with me?"

"Cas." Femi squeezed her elbows, pressing his words into her skin, making sure that she couldn't forget them. "That girl is obsessed with you."

Cas groaned. "Are we *sure,* though?"

The fact that Cas was debating this, even after their kiss, must have made this the most sapphic moment in the history of *Hot Summer.* Only a moving van would make this gayer.

Femi nodded firmly and refused to let her escape his gaze even when she tried to look down at the floor. "We're sure.

Now"—he threw open the loo door—"go get her! The losers will be watching you from the balcony."

"Oh great, because having an audience will definitely make me feel less nervous," Cas said. She checked her reflection in the mirror over the sink—her heart speeding up when she noticed the stickers Ada had added. They were perfectly placed.

"That's what I figured," Femi said.

He only laughed when she held her middle finger up at him on her way out the door.

The back garden was covered in UV lights when Cas walked outside, so everything had an eerie purple glow. There were neon body-paint markers in a jar on the kitchen island, more glow-in-the-dark sticker sheets scattered around, and club music blasting over the speakers. They were small changes, but Cas felt like she'd stepped out of the villa and into a disco dream.

She grabbed one of the body-paint pens—yellow, she thought, though the light was distorting the color—and started shaking it up as she walked out to the garden. Most everyone else was already dancing around in the grass, heels kicked off onto the pool deck in favor of dancing barefoot. Freddie grinned at her, his teeth a shock of white in the black light.

He grabbed her free hand and spun her around to the beat, making sure to keep a respectful distance between them. "Nice dress."

"Thanks." She held up the paint marker and shook it. "Want some tattoos?"

He held his arm out without hesitation and Cas filled his arm with stars and swirls. They weren't perfect and definitely weren't neat, but there was a reason she wasn't an artist.

Freddie beamed at them, turning his arm so he could appreciate her designs. "Stunning. Now, let's dance!"

They were less dancing as pairs, but more as a crowd, all of them jumping and spinning and grabbing one another, letting the music take them. Ada and Sienna joined a few songs later, Sienna immediately getting swept up with Tia. Freddie had taken Ada's hand when she joined them, but had just as quickly spun her into Cas with a wink in Cas's direction. Cheeky bastard.

"He seems nice," Ada said. She was loosely moving her hips to the beat, but wasn't quite dancing.

"He is," Cas agreed.

"You going to go for it?"

If there was a moment to decide, this was it. Ada was giving her an out, a very clear choice—did she want to choose Freddie? Or, unspoken, but there in her eyes, did she want to choose Ada instead?

As if there was any question about it.

Cas put her hand on Ada's waist, stepping into her so their hips very nearly brushed.

"No."

~~~

The producers played about ten songs before they switched the music off and sent a message to Ronan, one of the new boys, that the lovers from the losing group were officially allowed to come down off their perch on the balcony and join the fun.

With the UV lights switched off, they looked absurd, like club rats blinking in the sunlight of the early morning and realizing they smelled like vodka, that their hair was sticky and they had eyeliner running down their cheeks.

They were all covered in neon paint—the designs, at first intricate, and then just lines scraped across one another's skin as they twirled by. Cas's hair had been down, but she'd borrowed a hair bauble off Tia and thrown her hair up into a ponytail at song five to stop it sticking to her neck in the heat of the evening.

Now, she had paint and glitter and stickers across her chest and along her throat to show for it.

Ada bounced over from the kitchen, her hair swinging behind her. She had two water bottles in her hand and thrust one at Cas before unscrewing the lid.

"It's a thousand degrees out tonight, I swear." She dumped a handful of water into her palm and slapped it against her neck, cooling her overheated skin. It was a simple gesture, a reasonable one given how warm it was, but the water on her skin, the droplets traveling down her chest . . .

"Yeah." Cas's throat was the Sahara. "I don't know what's going on tonight."

"Must be the dancing," Ada said. For someone who was actively killing the woman in front of her, she seemed remarkably unbothered.

"Probably," Cas agreed.

Ada poured more water into her palm and scrubbed it across the back of her neck, moaning softly at the sensation. Cas felt that sound across every single inch of her.

"Do you want to go sit somewhere?" Ada rubbed the last drops of water on her hand up her arm, smearing the paint. "I feel like we have a few things to talk about."

"Mmm, mm-hmm." Words could not be trusted right now, so animalistic grunts were apparently going to be her response of choice.

Ada grinned and took Cas's hand, winding their fingers together. It seemed so easy for her, the way she just *did it*. Didn't hesitate, didn't overthink it, didn't stop herself at the last possible second. It was simple, giving herself over to what she felt, to just doing what she wanted to without a second thought for everything that would come after.

She gave Cas's hand a little tug and Cas tripped along behind her, ready to follow her off the edge of a cliff.

Ada led them down to the daybed. They weren't completely invisible should anyone really choose to look, but it gave the illusion of privacy all the same.

Ada let go of Cas's hand as they approached the bed, immediately jumping onto the mattress and sliding so that her back was pressed up against the headboard, her legs stretched out in front of her.

Cas swallowed and sat on the edge of the bed, her feet touching the grass. "So . . ."

"So," Ada agreed. She was smiling, grinning even, and Cas was knotting her fingers together.

Cas tried her best to frown, but her own lips were betraying her, already curling up at the corners. "What are you smiling about?"

It was really inconvenient that seeing Ada made it almost impossible for Cas not to smile, especially when she was trying to be serious.

"You," Ada admitted, her smile widening. "You seem nervous."

Cas's frown deepened. All furrowed brow and everything. She was really putting on a show here, but she didn't think it was paying off one bit.

"Of course I'm nervous."

Ada raised an eyebrow. It was one of Cas's favorite expressions of hers because she could never quite get it right. Her brow was always more of a wrinkle than a raise and it was adorable. "Why?"

"I—" It was the simplest thing in the world to say: *I kissed you.* It was something she'd done millions of times, but this kiss had felt . . .

Significant.

And if she was willing to admit it to herself—and, let's be honest, she just barely was—the very thought of that terrified her. It was easier when you didn't really care about the people you were kissing, when they didn't have the power to affect you. To hurt you.

Cas was more or less willing to sit on the daybed for the rest of the evening mulling over just how bad it was that she'd snogged Ada (and that she wanted to keep snogging Ada for as long as humanly possible), when Ada spoke.

"You kissed me."

Welp, they were in it now.

"Yup." Cas put a bit of extra pop into the *p*, hoping it made her sound casual. "I was thinking, you know. It was about time."

"I thought it was about time, too," Ada said. She spun in her seat, swinging her legs around behind her so she could sit almost beside Cas. "I kept trying to drop hints, but you were *not* picking them up."

"I thought you were just being friendly."

Ada laughed and shook her head.

"Well, for future reference"—Ada leaned closer, her hair falling forward over her right shoulder, brushing up against Cas's arm—"if I'm grinding on you like that, it's definitely not friendly."

And before Cas could even catch her breath, Ada's mouth was on hers.

It felt like a jolt to Cas's entire system. Like the main power had been switched on and every single inch of her body was humming with electricity.

Where their earlier kiss had been rushed, sped up by the pressure of the game, this kiss was languid, luxurious. It was a thousand sensations all at once—the soft press of Ada's mouth against her own, the swipe of Ada's tongue along her lower lip, the brush of Ada's hair against Cas's biceps, and all of it combined with the heat of Ada's body so near her own, the way Ada was tracing her fingers oh so lightly along the back of Cas's arm . . .

Cas could have sank into this moment, lived in it for the rest of her life and been totally and completely satisfied.

Where Cas felt like she was disintegrating, Ada was unhurried, and coaxed exhales and sighs and, god, hitched groans out of Cas with ease. Cas gasped as Ada scraped her teeth along her lower lip, and the smile on Ada's lips, so knowing, made Cas hum and pull Ada closer until their chests were pressed together.

It was a little awkward given how they were sitting, but it was exactly what Cas needed. To feel Ada's body against her own, to close any distance between them, to seep into her skin. Cas shifted on the bed, moving to kiss the edge of Ada's mouth, her jaw, the very top of her throat. Ada's breath caught, her hand coming to rest on Cas's thigh.

"Fuck."

Cas grinned, beamed, and let her mouth find Ada's again.

Cas wanted to feel every single plane and curve of Ada's body, and her hands weren't shy in exploring them. Ada's dress had ridden up and Cas smoothed her hands along the outside of Ada's gorgeous thighs, squeezing lightly as her fingers traveled toward the seam of her dress. Cas traced the edge of the fabric, teasing, and with each suggestion that her hands might slip underneath, Ada exhaled hard, desperate in a way that was very much going to Cas's head.

They were probably getting a little out of hand here given that there were about a dozen cameras currently pointing at them. As soon as she remembered that, Cas slowed, moved her hand, tried to calm her breath.

Ada pulled back slightly, just enough that she could rest her forehead on Cas's. "Are my intentions clear now?"

Cas exhaled a shaky laugh. "I don't know, you might need to kiss me again. So I can be sure."

Cas felt Ada's smile against her lips and she was about to lean forward when a shout from the garden forced them both to turn round.

"Yes!" Freddie and Femi were standing up on their deck chairs, fists in the air. They high-fived, the force of their excitement causing Freddie's chair to tip and send him tumbling back into the pool.

THE BEST NIGHT of Cas's summer should have been followed up by the best morning of Cas's summer.

It was, however, unfortunately followed by an early morning text message going off in the (now very crowded) bedroom.

Cas groaned and stuffed her head under the pillow, and when the phone beeped again, she grabbed an extra pillow and slammed it on top for good measure.

Rita's voice was muffled as she read her message. "'Rita—this morning, you can choose one lover to go on a date. Choose now and get ready. You and your date will leave in ten minutes. #SkyHigh #BallooningFeelings.'" Rita was quiet for a second, considering, before she said, "Charlie—fancy going on a date?"

Cas was grateful she'd thought to put a second pillow over her head, because Charlie almost immediately tripped over one of the new beds crammed into the bedroom and swore at the top of his lungs.

Cas didn't really think anything of that first message, but then Leo got a date message of his own when they were all sitting on the pool deck eating breakfast. He'd wrapped his arm around Lucy's shoulders and, as soon as she agreed, pressed a kiss to her temple and stuffed the rest of his pastry into his mouth before jogging up to the bathroom.

"It must be date day," Cas said, watching Leo run off. They did something like this every summer, usually during Bombshell Week, a series of dates held outside of the villa for people to get to know one another better. It was an opportunity for lovers to explore a new connection with a bombshell or, if they were planning to stick with their original match, to take their partner out of the villa and spend some quality time together without the pressure of a dozen other people overhearing their conversation.

Ada tipped her sunglasses down and glanced at Cas over the rim. "Who else do you think they're going to pick?"

"Hopefully us," Cas said, laughing. "I think we could use a few hours out of the villa together."

"Oh, that'd be nice." Ada slid her glasses back up and threw her arm behind her head, stretching her body out in the sun. "What do you think they'd have us do?"

"Read each other's tarot cards or something," Cas said, and Ada barked a laugh into the sky.

"Followed by a make-your-own-pasta workshop and a six-hour-long conversation in an indie coffee shop," Ada said.

They were only kidding, but it actually sounded like Cas's perfect day. Especially the make-your-own-pasta workshop.

"If that isn't the date we get, we'll have to do that when we get back to London, then," Cas said.

"Deal."

If today followed the trajectory of *Hot Summer* series past, there would be about five date slots total. In spite of her jokes, Cas didn't think she'd be lucky enough to get one, especially with this thing between her and Ada so new, so she was genuinely surprised when her phone beeped later that afternoon as she was lying by the pool with the girls.

"'Cas, it's time for your date! Choose who you'd like to ask out . . . you leave in ten minutes! #PeachyKeen #Pick'EmWell.'" Cas looked over to Ada, now sitting up on the deck chair next to hers, the barest hint of a smile on her face. "Ada? How about a date?"

Ada leaned across the space between their deck chairs and pressed a quick kiss to Cas's lips. "See you in ten minutes."

~~~

Cas practically tore her wardrobe apart grabbing options before she was ushered into the bathroom to get ready.

She could hear Sienna and Gemma in the dressing room, talking Ada through her options, helping her pick out her makeup and do her hair, but every time Cas's attention drifted over there, Tia snapped her fingers in Cas's face.

"Focus! Stop trying to ruin the surprise!"

Cas tried on a long white pencil skirt with a crisp white crop top, a pair of denim shorts and a flowy floral blouse, but nothing seemed quite right. She didn't know what they were going to have to do—from the hashtags alone, it was probably something to do with fruit, which was a little on the nose, but it didn't tell her too much in the way of how she should dress.

If she were back home, she'd wear her usual jeans, a crop top, and her leather jacket, but the idea of wearing a leather jacket in this heat . . .

"What about this?" Delilah grabbed a set of linen separates and held them up. They were rusty orange, a deep, rich shade that would pop nicely against her tan and her brown hair. Because the fabric was light, it wouldn't be too warm, but she'd be shielded from the sun in case they were spending the afternoon somewhere without any access to shade.

"How do you think I should wear it?" Cas took the top and held it up against her chest. "Unbuttoned, obviously," she said, her fingers already working the buttons, "but what underneath?"

"Black bralette," Tia said. She rummaged around in the pile and, after a few seconds, held out three separate bralettes in Cas's direction. "I think the lace will be too much of a contrast, but you can wear this plain one. And then we'll make your hair really slick and straight . . ."

Tia was flitting around the bathroom as she talked, grabbing hair oil and a hairbrush and the hair straightener.

She'd originally planned to pair the outfit with her leather sandals but decided at the last minute to throw on a pair of crisp white trainers in case she needed to do a lot of walking. Once she was satisfied with her reflection, Tia ran to check that they were safe to leave before hurrying Cas down the stairs to the entry.

"Ada's almost done, so just wait here," Tia said. She pulled Cas into a quick hug before turning and running off toward the bedroom, followed shortly by Sienna who blew Cas a kiss as she ran down the stairs and disappeared.

It was surprisingly nerve-wracking as Cas waited in the entry. It was ridiculous—she'd already spent so much time with Ada this summer, it wasn't like they were strangers—but the nerves were swimming in her belly all the same.

She wanted this date to be perfect. *Needed* this date to be perfect.

Cas looked up as she heard the sound of Ada's footsteps in the hall and her heart stopped in her chest.

Ada looked gorgeous. Absolutely astoundingly gorgeous.

Her long red hair was done in soft, romantic waves that fell over her shoulders, and her makeup was light and dewy, a perfect sun-kissed look for the dress she was wearing. It was a simple tie-shoulder midi dress with a slit that extended to the outside of Ada's left thigh. The dress was powder blue with a white and olive floral pattern, and the fabric flowed gently as she walked down the stairs. There was a subtle glow to her skin as she moved, the barest sheen of champagne gold in the sunlight streaking through the front windows.

It was just a dress, just a date, but seeing Ada walk down the stairs, a bright smile on her face, was more than Cas could handle.

Cas took her hand as Ada came to a stop at the bottom of the stairs. "You," she said, leaning down and pressing the lightest kiss to Ada's lips to avoid ruining her lipstick, "are so beautiful."

"You are, too," Ada said, stepping back and examining Cas's outfit. "Hey," she said, her smile growing, "our shoes match."

She tapped her white trainer against Cas's, and Cas grinned. "Great minds."

There was a Jeep waiting when they walked outside, and Ada waved to the driver as she opened the back door and climbed inside.

"This feels like our first day here," Ada said, buckling her seat belt. "I was so nervous then."

"Were you?"

Ada took Cas's hand as the driver started down the hill, her thumb tracing Cas's knuckles. "Terrified. Weren't you?"

"I didn't feel that nervous," Cas said. "I felt like I had a pretty good idea of what to expect."

"I bet you spent every possible second studying this show before you arrived," Ada said, leaning back in her seat. "Party planners love details, don't they?"

"I—" Oh god. This conversation was uncomfortably close to the truth.

"Cas." Ada was grinning, her expression absolutely wicked. She clearly thought she was catching Cas out, but Cas wasn't panicking because she was afraid to admit she was an obsessive *Hot Summer* consumer.

"I actually watch this show every summer," Cas said. "It's unironically one of my favorites."

"Oh my god." Ada was smirking with something like victory in her eyes. "Are you serious?"

"Yes."

"So, you're a superfan."

"I wouldn't say *that* . . ."

"You're a superfan," Ada said. She was grinning, absolutely fucking grinning. "You are obsessed with *Hot Summer*. That's why you're really here."

"You caught me," Cas said. Her laugh was tight, but if she noticed, Ada didn't say anything.

There wasn't much to look at out the window for the first few minutes they were on the motorway, just red soil and low scrubland, but as the road curved higher up into the white hills, the bright blue sea appeared beyond the cliff's edge.

There weren't many houses visible from the road, but Cas sometimes caught glimpses of towns by the seaside or on the hills in the distance.

After thirty minutes in the car, they turned off the motorway onto a smaller side road and, five minutes later, a tan gravel drive through a wooden gate with a large hand-painted sign hanging on the beams.

FRUIT ORCHARD

"I knew it!" Ada pressed her hand into Cas's knee, leaning over her so she could stare out the window. "I knew we were going fruit picking!"

The driver stopped along the edge of the gravel car park and switched off the engine.

"Okay," the driver said, turning around, "wait here for about thirty seconds. We've got a few camerapeople at the edge of the grove"—he pointed out the window to the rows of trees that seemed to stretch out toward the horizon—"and you'll follow them into the orchard. You can also follow the yellow string they've tied at the edges of the trees. There's a picnic set up there with more instructions."

"Okay." Ada ran her free hand over her dress, smoothing it out. "Do they want us to do anything in particular, or . . ."

"Just walk, laugh, that kind of thing," the driver said. "They're going to use it for B-roll." He unlocked the door and smiled at them in the rearview. "Have a good date, you two."

Cas climbed out first and Ada took her hand as she stepped out into the car park. Their hands swung easily as they walked, and Cas was glad, as the dust kicked up, that she hadn't worn sandals today. The gravel gave way fairly quickly to grass, and with the camerapeople leading, Cas and Ada made their way through the orchard.

As much as Cas wanted to take in their surroundings, it was unsettling seeing people behind the cameras again. She had gotten so used to the mix of hidden and not-so-hidden cameras in the villa, that it was easy to forget at some points that they were being filmed. To believe that what they were experiencing was for them alone, not for a team of producers and editors, and then the hundreds of thousands of viewers.

Now, though, walking through the orchard with two guys wearing Steadicams, it was a lot more difficult to ignore the reality of their situation.

"It's so weird, seeing them. It almost feels like we're actually on TV," Ada whispered.

Frankly, the reminder of the cameras was sobering. As much as she'd been choosing to ignore it lately, all of the *real* reasons why she was here—her contract, Friday, a shiny new job—suddenly it felt overwhelming. It was becoming harder and harder to keep it from Ada.

As they continued walking, Ada took a step closer and, with a quick press up onto her toes, captured Cas's lips in a kiss. It might have been short, a peck, but Cas's free hand immediately came up to Ada's cheek and held her there.

And if Cas stumbled in a dip in the grass, it was worth it for the feeling of Ada's mouth against hers. For the smell of Ada's perfume that close.

They'd been walking for a few minutes when the

camerapeople turned down a row in the orchard, and Cas spotted the picnic set up in between the trees. There was a perfect white blanket draped across the grass, a number of orange, pink, and yellow pillows dotted around for them to lean on. There was a pair of empty baskets sitting on top of what looked like an ice chest and, beside the baskets, an empty pitcher.

Perched on one of the pillows, in a spot where they couldn't possibly miss it, was a white envelope with their names scrawled on the front in calligraphy.

Cas scooped the note off the blanket and handed it to Ada. "I'll let you do the honors."

Ada tore open the envelope and slid out a peachy pink note card.

"'Cas and Ada,'" Ada read, apparently doing her best imitation of Mila Sexton. "'Today you're going to enjoy a picnic in this beautiful orchard. There are a number of peach recipes for you to enjoy . . . but you'll have to pick your own fruit so you can finish assembling them. Take your baskets and get picking!'"

"Love a bit of manual labor on a date," Cas said, starting to roll up her sleeves. She grabbed the baskets and handed one to Ada before dropping hers onto her arm.

"How many peaches do we need?" Ada asked. She shifted the pitcher aside, looking for recipes, and opened the ice chest when she came up empty. "Oh, okay."

She lifted out a large bowl with smaller containers inside and a label—*Summer Peach Spinach Salad: 2 peaches needed*—stuck on top, as well as a bag with small bottles and chopped strawberries, labeled, *Peach and Strawberry Sangria: 2 peaches, raspberry lemonade, and wine needed.*

"So only four peaches, then," Cas said, watching as Ada put everything carefully back into the ice chest. "I think we can manage that."

"Oh no, we're not just getting four," Ada said, chuckling. "If we're picking peaches, we're picking peaches."

It was one of those moments that Cas knew would be gilded in her memory. The sun shining through the trees, the feeling of the breeze on her skin, the way Ada laughed as Cas stretched and stretched, trying to get a peach that was just out of her reach. Even if Cas caught herself sometimes paying attention to the cameras, it was easy for Ada to bring her back. For Ada to take her hand, kiss her cheek, whisper in her ear, and every time, the entirety of Cas's focus was on this incredible woman in front of her.

No amount of cameras could have distracted her.

It was a line of thought that, a few weeks ago, would have scared the shit out of Cas. Would have made her turn and run, never to look back, but maybe here, trapped in the villa, unable to leave without losing everything, maybe this was the perfect place for Cas to work on letting herself be vulnerable. Especially because Ada made it so easy to forget all the reasons she shouldn't let herself get tied down in the first place.

"What do you want your life to be like after *Hot Summer*?" Ada asked a bit later.

They were sitting on the blanket, Cas assembling the sangria while Ada carefully chopped up peaches to add to the enormous bowl of salad ingredients.

"Do you mean, like, romantically or . . . ?"

It was evasive, a question designed to buy her a few seconds, but Cas didn't miss the way Ada's right eye squinted just a little bit at the suggestion.

"Anything." Ada's voice was a little too breezy, and Cas quickly swept in to correct the misconception.

"Well, obviously, I'm hoping that we get to continue exploring this. I know that it's probably too early to put any labels on it, but . . ." She trailed off, unsure where to go from there. It was early, this thing between them, technically not even a few days old, but it felt like their relationship had been building for weeks. "I guess, professionally, I'm just going to be curious what's out there when we leave. I've been in the same job for four years and I only got into it in the first place because I needed something to distract me from everything with my ex."

"Really?"

Cas nodded. "I couldn't face those long lonely nights sobbing into my pillow. I was still violently depressed, but I was at least out and having fun and spending time with people."

Ada laughed. "That's one way to distract yourself, I guess."

"It worked at the time. But I don't know, lately . . ." She didn't want to say *unfulfilled*, even if it was true. Robert probably wasn't watching, but someone surely was, and would no doubt pass the message along if she started slagging off Friday on national television. So she decided for the most neutral option she could think of. "I feel like I'm ready for the next step in my career."

Ada grabbed the tongs and started turning the salad around in the bowl. "And what does that next step look like?"

"I don't know." And it was true. She didn't have a complete

sketch of what her responsibilities would be like in this new role, but she knew what she was hoping for. "I want something a bit more steady. With regular hours and a desk, and I want to be home for dinner every night, even if the workday is busy." Cas handed Ada a glass of sangria. "That probably sounds phenomenally boring."

"I don't think so. It sounds like you're just craving stability." Ada took a sip of the sangria, her eyes going wide at the flavor. "Wait, this is actually really good!"

"I just followed the recipe," Cas said. She started picking up the bottles strewn across the blanket, and Ada hummed happily through another sip.

"Well, you did an excellent job following the recipe."

"Thanks. Anyway"—Cas set the bottles in a neat row and poured herself a glass of sangria—"what's your big-picture dream? Like, in five years, what do you think your ideal life would look like?"

"I'd be midthirties by that point," Ada said, dishing up heaping portions of salad into the white, flower-trimmed bowls the producers had set out for the occasion, "which is kind of scary to think about. But I'd love to see my stationery business thriving—I don't quite know how much more I could grow it without hiring a team, though, so maybe that's the dream. A small team, a little office space. Maybe a physical store?"

"Where would you want the store to be?"

"In my dream of dreams, it's back home in Brighton," Ada said. Even as she said it, her voice went all wistful, eyes sparkling with hope. "I'd love to get some little storefront in the

Lanes, maybe live upstairs, and then every day after I close up, walk down and eat dinner on the beach. We used to do that a lot growing up, and the smell of the salt, the sound of the waves on the rocks . . . it was magic."

"That does sound like a dream."

From the very first time she'd stepped foot in London (at fourteen when she lied to her parents, skived off school, and caught the train because she just had to see all the "danger" they kept telling her about) she'd felt, in her heart, that she was going to live there forever. It had spoken to something in her, something that was dreadfully ignored back home in Surrey, and once she left school, she made her way to London and never looked back.

But hearing Ada talk about Brighton—the picture she painted and the love in her voice—it was making Cas wonder if it might be worth considering a few other options for her future.

"Right? I think I'll probably still be in London for another few years, but I'd really love to go back there one day."

"Anything else you see for yourself?"

"I'd like to be in a committed relationship, too. Married, I think, but I'm not dead set on it, I just want a commitment," Ada added, carefully studying Cas's reaction. "But you were engaged . . . Is that something you see for yourself?"

Cas hummed. "Honestly, that was such a weird time in my life. Obviously it didn't work out and I thought I'd never think about dating anyone seriously again and then, well . . ." She held Ada's gaze for a few moments before she looked down at her salad bowl in her lap.

"It's something I'm interested in again," Cas finally said, looking up. She found Ada still staring at her, and a small smile formed on Ada's lips as their eyes met. "A commitment."

"Here's to that, then," Ada said. She grabbed her glass and held it up. "To commitment."

"To commitment," Cas repeated.

And, gently, they clinked.

24

IT WAS ALMOST easy to forget about everything going on in the background that week.

Bombshell Week was one of the most stressful times in the villa most summers—all the lovers were on edge, watching one another like hawks, trying to determine if their partner was thinking about leaving them and re-partnering with someone else. There were clandestine conversations in hidden corners, stolen kisses on the balcony, and while Cas was certain all that must have been happening this summer, she was in her own bubble.

Holding hands with Ada across the divide when they were in bed at night, watching the boys run around in the garden in the afternoon, it was easy to let herself imagine that there was nothing she needed to be thinking about. Nothing she needed to be worrying about.

There was always the possibility, she supposed, that Ada was thinking about re-partnering with someone else, but Cas didn't know when Ada would possibly have the time to be organizing anything of the sort. They were practically glued together that week, and when they weren't, they had long, detailed debriefs about every ridiculous thing that had happened while they'd been apart.

It was a little embarrassing how heart-on-her-sleeve Cas was. Kicking her feet as she sat on the kitchen island, watching Ada make eggs for breakfast, tossing Freddie an apple with a big ol' smile on her face like a cartoon character. Laughing loudly, absurdly, as Ada, Tia, and Sienna did a "blindfold makeup challenge" with Lucy, Rita, and Gemma on a particularly slow afternoon. Cas couldn't even remember the last time she'd been like this, so giddy and excited and optimistic. Like she thought everything was working out in her favor.

She couldn't wait to re-partner on Saturday.

They'd all been lounging on the grass Friday afternoon—Charlie and Rita were off somewhere, but everyone else was playing Musical Slaps, a game Freddie had invented. There were eight of them left sitting in a circle, legs crossed, palms out on their knees, waiting patiently for the next song to begin.

"Okay." Freddie was sitting on a deck chair, his back to them so he couldn't see and unfairly bias his singing, according to Leo. "Get ready . . . set . . . go!"

Freddie burst out into a very off-key cover of Beyoncé and, one by one, each contestant in the circle slapped palms with the person next to them. They picked up speed as they went round, the hits becoming quicker, sharper the longer Freddie sang, and the four eliminated contestants ran around, causing as much distraction as humanly possible in an attempt to throw people off. Any moment Freddie was going to stop and—

Freddie abruptly stopped singing, and at the last possible

moment, Lucy moved her hand away so Gemma missed and caught her thigh instead.

"Oh fuck!" Gemma crossed her legs tighter and rolled backward out of the circle. "This game is hard."

Femi's phone beeped and he snatched it swiftly off the ground.

"I've got a text! 'Lovers—tonight, to celebrate the end of Bombshell Week, we're going to skip the rankings and host a partnering ceremony instead. Anyone not chosen to be in a partnership at the end of the ceremony tonight will be going home.'"

Freddie's phone beeped.

"'There is, however, going to be a twist.'"

The pause at the end was ominous, nerve-wracking, and Cas thought Freddie had left it there of his own accord, but then Lucy's phone beeped.

"'After the partnerships have been decided, you will get the opportunity to save one of the bombshells that wasn't picked for a couple. Choose wisely. #SeeYouTonight #BombsAway.'"

The Bombshell Week partnership ceremony was the most complicated of the entire summer. The men and women stood opposite one another, bombshells and original lovers together on each side, and, one by one, only original lovers got text messages signaling their turn to announce their intentions. The bombshells could only hope to be picked.

If both lovers decided to stick together, they stayed partnered up for the week. If, however, one of the lovers decided to re-partner with a bombshell, while their partner remained faithful, then the dumped lover had to leave the villa. An emotional double whammy if there ever was one.

Sienna's phone beeped first, and after a deep breath, she took one step forward.

"I'd like to partner up with this boy because, from the very first moment I met him, I knew there was something about him. As he and I grew closer and our friendship developed, I knew that I had feelings I couldn't deny.

"Being partnered up with him this last week has been a dream—I know we're going to be together the rest of our time in the villa and I can't wait to see what we do together when we're on the outside." Sienna's tone softened then, and it was clear that, despite the fact they were all standing around, to her, it was just her and Femi. "My feelings for you grow stronger each and every day. And I'm so excited to see what the future brings. I have a feeling that, with you, it's going to be incredibly bright."

Femi reached up and swiped at his cheeks, and Cas felt her own eyes start welling up. This was everything he deserved, everything they both deserved, and she wanted this for them so badly she could taste it.

This show had turned her into a such a melt, it was unbelievable.

"So, the person I would like to partner up with, of course, is . . . Femi."

Femi was supposed to confirm that he, too, would like to partner up with Sienna, but he didn't bother. The moment Sienna finished speaking, he ran, closing the distance in half a second before sweeping Sienna up in his arms. She laughed brightly, her arms wrapping around his neck as he lifted her into the air and pulled her in for a kiss. And they kept kissing until Femi's phone beeped from his back pocket.

"All right," Femi said, and Cas couldn't help but laugh at the look on his face, all frustrated and lovesick. "I want to partner with Sienna, too. Clearly."

And then Femi made a point of pulling Sienna back in for another kiss. Cas hooted and cheered with the rest of them, pumping her fist into the air, and Sienna laughed as she pulled away and buried her face in his neck.

One by one, phones beeped.

Tia and Reece chose to stay partnered up.

Leo went with bombshell Lucy.

Delilah's phone pinged next, and she took a deep breath, a smile growing across her face by degrees.

"I've only known this boy for a short time, but I've really loved the time we've spent together so far. Our start was a little . . . dramatic . . . to say the least, but I'm grateful every day that he decided to take a chance on me. That he saw the same potential in our connection that I did." With each word, Delilah's words grew more confident, her attention more and more firmly planted on Charlie. Charlie, though, was avoiding her gaze, looking everywhere but at Delilah, and Cas had a sinking feeling in her stomach. "So, the boy I'd like to partner up with is . . . Charlie."

After a long, lingering look, Charlie cleared his throat, his gaze dropping to the grass. "Um, I'd actually like to partner up with Rita."

Cas had seen it a million times on-screen, people deciding that they were going to choose someone else right in front of their partner's face, and it had always been sad. But seeing Delilah get rejected in real time was painful. Awful, actually.

Delilah's knees bent, like she was going to buckle, but Ada caught her round the elbow, turning her in for a hug instead.

"It's okay, babe," Ada said, brushing Delilah's hair back off her shoulder. "It's okay."

Delilah drew in a thick, wet gasp. "He doesn't—" She picked her head up off Ada's shoulder and pointed at Charlie, now standing in the middle with Rita beside him. "Fuck you, Charlie."

"I'm really sorry, I—"

Cas held her hand up at him. "She doesn't need to hear that right now."

"But I *am* sorry."

"Okay," Cas snapped. "Save it. Go sit down." She jerked her head forcefully toward the bench, and though Charlie glared at her for a long moment, he did as she said.

Delilah turned, wiping tears off her cheeks, toward Cas. "Thanks."

"'Course."

Delilah drew in a deep, trembling breath before she stepped back from Ada, still wiping tears off her face. "I'm going to . . ." She pointed at the stairs in the vague direction of the villa. "I can't be here right now."

"Do you want me to walk you up?" Ada asked. Cas knew she would get in trouble for leaving in the middle of the ceremony, but Ada didn't seem to care. She took a few steps forward, hand outstretched, ready to go, but Delilah shook her head, her gaze sliding from Ada to Cas for the briefest moment.

"No, that's okay. Stay here and get your partner."

Delilah pulled her in for another quick hug before walking off up the stairs. The entire villa was silent for a few long minutes, enough that everyone was shifting uncomfortably, waiting for a signal from production about what was to be done next.

Cas's phone beeped.

And immediately, her heart was in her throat.

Okay.

She started, at first, staring at the ground. "I've decided to partner up with this person because I can't imagine my time in here without them."

Slowly, she raised her gaze, scanning the couples on the bench, letting herself soak in her friends' smiles, urging her on.

"I have a hard time opening up, as I'm sure you've all realized"—a few laughs bubbled up, and Cas smiled to herself—"but this person makes me feel like it's the easiest thing in the world."

Finally, *finally,* Cas let her eyes find Ada's. Her brown eyes were swimming with emotion, and the happiness in them made Cas feel like she couldn't catch her breath. God, her hands were shaking. She tried to steady them by smoothing them over her dress.

"Getting to know you has been the highlight of my time here. It was unexpected, for sure, but, in you, I feel like I've found someone I can be myself with. You make me want to be brave, make it okay for me to be vulnerable. We walked in together, and now, I'm really hoping that, in a few weeks' time, we'll be able to walk out together."

Cas took a deep breath and let a smile fill her face. This was the easy part.

"The person I'd like to partner up with is . . . Ada."

The shouts reverberated around the villa, though Femi, Sienna, and Freddie were the loudest by far.

Ada laughed and dipped her head, her bright red hair falling to hide her expression. She brought her hand up to her eyes, like she thought she would disappear if she covered as many centimeters of her face as possible. Cas was sure her own face was going to crack, but that was nothing compared to when Ada looked at her. When their eyes met, it felt like it was the only thing tethering her to the earth.

"I'd like to partner up with you, too, Cas."

Nothing, not for the rest of Cas's life, would compare to that moment.

It was a short walk over to the bench together, but it seemed like slow motion. The twinkling of the lights, Ada's smile, everyone screaming and applauding, Cas felt like she'd stepped out of her life and into a movie.

Leo's phone beeped as soon as Cas and Ada sat down on his right. He tapped Ada on the shoulder and grinned at her before grabbing his phone from his back pocket and reading the message.

"'Lovers. Congratulations on another successful partnering ceremony. Now, it's time for you to choose one more lover to stay with you this summer.'"

Reece's phone.

"'With your partner, you must agree on one bombshell to remain in the villa. In two minutes, you will cast your vote in front of the rest of the villa. Everyone not chosen will be asked to leave the villa tonight.'"

They all glanced at one another for a few seconds, measuring one another up, before turning to their partners. Cas tipped her head toward Ada, lowering her voice to a near whisper.

"I feel like we should keep Freddie."

"No, yeah, me, too," Ada said, nodding. "He's so sweet."

"And I feel like he's integrated into the villa really well?"

"Definitely. He and Femi are already besties."

"Okay"—Cas rested her hand on Ada's thigh—"so we're decided."

It still felt novel that she could do this, that she could just touch Ada like this.

Ada put her hand on top of Cas's. "Decided."

This, though, turned out to be the easiest part of the night. With three votes, Freddie was invited to stay in the villa, but just as he made his way over to the bench, his phone beeped.

"'Freddie—congratulations on being selected to remain in the villa. Now you have a difficult decision to make.'"

He looked up at them, his face pale, and laughed awkwardly. "Oh fuck."

He didn't move, just waited opposite the fire pit, holding the phone in his hands like it was a detonator. After a few seconds, his phone beeped again.

"'Freddie, you must choose one couple to leave the villa tonight. Any of the couples sitting in front of you are eligible to be eliminated. You have one minute to make your decision. Good luck.' *Good luck*—are you fucking serious?" Freddie scraped his hand through his hair.

"Okay." Freddie exhaled hard, his eyes skipping over each of the couples on the bench in turn. "This is a really tough decision. I have enjoyed getting to know each and every one of you and I wish you all the most success in your partnerships. But . . ." He let that linger there for a second, his gaze drifting off as he collected his thoughts.

"There are definitely some couples here who are stronger than others. And if I'm thinking about who has to stay, it has to be the people that I see have a strong connection and a lot of potential on the outside. So, that being said . . ." He drew in a deep breath.

"Charlie and Rita, I'd have to choose you."

THEY'D BARELY FINISHED saying goodbye to everyone when someone's phone dinged.

The tension in Cas's body immediately ratcheted up to eleven. This was the worst thing about this show, she decided, how it swung you from complete calm, peace, straight to the edge of a cliff and left you dangling there.

It was going to give her heart problems later in life, for sure.

"'Lovers!'" Femi's voice was practically vibrating with laughter. "'The retreat is officially open—choose one lucky couple to spend the night together now.' Cas and Ada!"

Femi'd barely finished reading the text before he was shouting out their names, jumping up and down, his whole face lit up with a smile. The joy Femi exuded, the love he so clearly had for them . . . it was a type of unquestionable friendship Cas had only ever known in Skye and Aisha, and they'd been friends for years.

"Cas and Ada!"

The entire villa rang out with shouts of their names, and

Ada's cheeks flushed the softest, most gorgeous shade of pink Cas had ever seen. Cas had barely caught sight of it, though, before Ada dipped her head forward and buried herself into Cas's neck.

Cas had to focus every single ounce of her energy on the fact that there were about ten thousand cameras on them to keep from melting into a puddle right then and there. Even still, all she could think about was the way Ada's hair was sliding over her shoulders and the heat of Ada's breath against her neck.

It was a good thing they were going to the retreat then, because already Cas felt like she would climb out of her own skin if it meant she got to be closer to her.

"We have to go pick out your outfits," Sienna said. She grabbed Ada by the forearm, pulling her backward. Ada caught Cas's hand as she stumbled back, dragging her along with them.

"Uh, no!" Femi grabbed Cas's hand, separating her from Ada. "You have to get ready separately."

"It needs to be a surprise," Sienna agreed.

"But"—Cas reached for Ada's hand again, only to have Ada marched a few steps farther away—"all my clothes are in the change room."

"I'll get your clothes," Femi said, looping his arm through Cas's. "Tell me what you want and I'll bring options."

~~~

The door to the retreat was hidden along the back side of the villa, tucked away behind a wall of shrubs that was intended to keep people from being able to peek into the windows when someone was inside (and also intended to hide the dozen cameras that spied on people while they were in the back garden). It looked largely the same as in every prior season, but there were always subtle differences, especially because they were in a different house each year.

Cas felt strangely nervous as she and Ada walked down the garden path, carrying their clothes, toothbrushes, and hairbrushes in their hands for their overnight. It was almost like they were spending the night away together on holiday, rather than just going to a different area of the villa. Once they were inside, though, they were going to be locked in, and nothing, barring fire or medical disaster, was going to allow them out again until morning.

Not that Cas was complaining.

They would still have some cameras on them for about the first hour or so while they were in there, but production had explained at the start of the summer that cameras in the retreat turned off for the night. The retreat was the one place where the lovers could be genuinely, blissfully alone.

Cas couldn't wait to spend some actual private time with Ada. And, yes, it was partially because she wanted to get Ada under the duvet and see what she looked like with absolutely nothing on, wanted to hear the way that Ada exhaled when she was close, wanted to feel Ada shaking underneath her fingers, but it was also . . .

Cas wanted to simply *be* with her. To lie in bed, tucked together, hearing nothing else but the sound of their own breath. She wanted to feel what it was like to spend time with Ada and Ada alone.

Ada smiled back at Cas over her shoulder as they approached the door, and even though the entire villa was behind them, laughing and cheering them on to what they were probably convinced was going to be a night of raucous sex, in that moment, it was only Ada. Only her smile and the way the fairy lights were reflecting in her gorgeous brown eyes.

"Ready?" Ada pressed her palm to the door, her fingers flexing just the slightest bit, like she was having to stop herself from pushing it open immediately.

Cas nodded, her own smile taking over her face, before she grinned back at everyone following them.

"All right, bye, guys!"

"Bye!"

Femi ran up and grabbed Cas in a hug, squeezing her hard enough that Cas could nearly feel the air pressing out of her lungs.

"Have fun. You deserve it," he whispered.

When Femi stepped away, a few others stepped forward in turns—Sienna pulled them both into quick hugs, Freddie grabbed Cas and Ada both round the shoulders at once and pulled them in together. It was like they were disappearing from the villa forever, and it made Cas want to laugh and, god, cry all at once.

"You guys act like we're going off to war," Ada said, rolling her eyes lightly at them as Freddie released them both, their bodies springing apart.

"Well, I don't know what you're going to get up to in there," Freddie said.

Sienna immediately slapped his chest. "Don't be gross."

"Oh no." The apples of Freddie's cheeks flushed pink. "I didn't mean— I meant that, like, they could sneak you out onto

a date or something once you're in there. You could be gone
for hours!"

Cas laughed and gestured down at her outfit. "I doubt
they'd send us anywhere looking like this."

It was barely more than the bikinis that she wore on a day-
to-day basis, but the outfit she had Femi grab for her tonight
felt even more revealing somehow. It was a simple two-piece
set, a camisole top with scalloped lace around her breasts and
a pair of tiny shorts with lace trim that, as she walked, tended
to ride up so her arse cheeks poked out underneath. It wasn't
exactly conservative, especially when compared to some of her
bikinis, but it felt daring, wearing this in front of everyone,
knowing full well that she'd chosen it with the intention of
having Ada find her attractive.

That she'd been putting it on thinking about Ada taking it
off her.

She had a few other things tucked away inside the clothes
she was holding in her arms, and she was very, very glad that
she'd kept those things to herself. She wanted to keep this just
for herself. Wanted to keep this just between them.

With a few final goodbyes, Ada finally turned back and
pushed the door open. Everyone cheered as they closed the
door, and Cas grinned as she heard Sienna start admonishing
them all.

"All right, leave them alone." Leo kept cheering, but then
there was a muffled grunt and a scuffling outside the door,
and, eventually, everything went silent.

"Wow. It's so quiet . . . I never realized how loud they
all are."

Cas turned to find Ada, her arms folded across her middle, cradling her clothes. Her expression was wide with curiosity, her lips parted just slightly as she stared round at the pink and red explosion of a room they were currently standing in.

The walls themselves were white like the rest of the villa, but nearly every inch of wall space was taken up by some piece of furniture or art in shades of red. The wardrobes along the back wall were painted a dark shade of red, the armchair in the corner was red with a light pink accent pillow, the neon sign above it—this one, a pair of lips with a heart-shaped lollipop hanging off the tongue—was red. Every single thing was red.

It was like Christian Grey's red room, come to life.

The focal point of the room, though, was of course the enormous round bed. It had a plush fabric headboard in the shape of a heart and was covered in a crisp white duvet that was a brilliant shock against the red headboard, the throw pillows, and the matching throw along the edge. There was a bucket of champagne sitting beside it and, surrounded by rose petals, an envelope with a massive heart sticker on the back.

Ada turned to Cas, her eyes wide. "I think they bought every piece of red furniture in Europe and put it in this room."

Cas laughed. "Without question."

There was a thick tension in the air, something physical that Cas felt pressing against her chest. She had spent hours, days, weeks with Ada, but this, now . . .

Cas had been in situations like this dozens of times. In bedrooms with people, the moment rife with potential. In every single one of those scenarios, Cas had known exactly how to behave. Had only felt excitement or anticipation. The thrill of the moment, of having someone's body on hers, more than enough to satisfy.

Here, though.

Despite how similar this situation felt, there was something very different about it this time. Something real that she hadn't felt in too many years.

It was vulnerability. That's what Aisha would have called it.

It was scary, feeling that potential when you were with someone who mattered. But it was also probably what was making Cas's heart squeeze in her chest, and her legs press together in a desperate attempt to relieve the tension.

Cas sat down on the end of the bed and grabbed the envelope, her finger slicing open the seal as Ada started making her way around the room, opening every drawer and door she could get her hands on.

"'Cas and Ada,'" Cas read. "'Welcome to the retreat. Cameras will go off approximately thirty minutes after you've entered the room. The neon light will switch off as your signal that filming has ended. You are welcome to use anything in the space, including the hot tub on the back patio. Enjoy your time, xoxo *Hot Summer* Production.'" She set the note down on the bed. "I didn't bring a bikini. Did you know there was a hot tub?"

Ada hummed absently, her fingers trailing along the edge of the chest of drawers opposite the bed. She was clearly too preoccupied to care about a hot tub.

"What are you looking for?"

"I don't know." Ada tilted her entire body to the side so she could peer into the wardrobe. "What if there's something really cool hidden in here?"

"There isn't." Cas leaned back onto her hands, her eyes skimming the long line of Ada's legs, the curve of her bum. "The best you've got in here is the drawer under the bed."

She tapped said drawer with her heel, and something rolled over inside. And, oh god, she knew *exactly* what that was.

"That's a drawer?!"

Ada practically ran over to the bed and tugged the drawer open. Cas lifted her legs just in time, swinging them off to the side so that she didn't get thrown off the bed with Ada's enthusiasm.

Ada started cackling as soon as she looked inside.

"Holy shit, it's, like, a sex shop in here."

She wasn't lying.

There were handcuffs, feathers, riding crops, blindfolds, and different sexy outfits. Ada dropped to her knees and reached into the drawer, pulling more things toward her.

Edible underwear.

Candy bikini.

Body paint.

There weren't any vibrators or anything that Cas would have actually found interesting—it was probably too much of an expense, and after all, it was easier to replace or sanitize a set of handcuffs than it was a whole fucking vibrator—but the sight of everything else Ada had found laid out in a neat row inside the drawer was still enough to make Cas's cheeks heat.

Yes, she knew what was expected of them the moment they

walked through the door of the retreat, but it didn't make the reality of this moment any less, well . . .

"That's quite the collection," Cas said. She had never sounded more middle class than she did in that moment, and she wanted to go stick her head into the hot tub on the back patio and drown herself.

Ada laughed softly, though she sounded less amused and more like she was lost in thought. "It is. Though, I can think of a few things that I'd add."

"Can you?"

Ada hummed and slid her hand up along the outside of Cas's calf.

"I've been thinking about you all day," Ada said softly.

Cas felt like she was going to pass out. She *needed* to remember that they were on television right now.

And that as much as she wanted to slide off this bed onto the floor and tear Ada's shorts off and—

Cas reached out, her fingers nearly trembling, and threaded her hands through the ends of Ada's hair. It was so soft, the way it flowed over Cas's fingers like water. Everything about Ada was velvet smooth—her hair, her curves, her smile, her laugh. It was hard to be sharp, to be the most pointed version of herself when Cas was around someone like that. Someone who made her want to go easy.

"We don't have to do anything, you know," Cas said. She was twirling the end of Ada's hair between her fingers, trying to stay focused despite the fact that Ada was sliding her hand up along the outside of Cas's thigh. "Just because we're in this room—"

"I know." Ada pressed up onto her knees, sliding forward so that they were practically chest to chest now. If Cas took a deep enough breath, her breasts would brush up against the side of Ada's arm.

And, suddenly, Cas was met with an urgent need to take the deepest breath of her life.

"No, I know." Cas sounded hoarse. "I just wanted to say because, like"—she gestured around at the room—"I feel like there's a lot of pressure to, you know, *do stuff,*" god, she was *twelve*, "because we're in this room."

Ada either didn't notice or didn't care about the fact that Cas was actively regressing in front of her. She just smirked, the right corner of her mouth raising ever so slightly. "You mean because everyone's going to be asking us what we did first thing tomorrow morning?"

Cas let out a shaky laugh. "Yeah."

She had never been this uncool in her entire life.

She would have turned and run right now if she wasn't so desperately turned on. If she wasn't waiting, *waiting,* for Ada to touch her.

"I don't mind that people are going to ask tomorrow," Ada said. Her tone was casual, but there was something searing about her eyes when they found Cas's. Something that burned right through Cas's skin and shot straight to her core. "I still want to have a good time tonight."

"Oh yeah?"

"Mm-hmm." Ada shifted forward, and there was absolutely no mistaking her intentions now. She trailed her finger up along Cas's biceps, tracing the threads of ink along her skin, almost like she was sketching out the designs, though Cas knew better. The look in Ada's eyes made it clear that this was all a calculated step toward what she was really after.

"I've been thinking about this for a long time," Ada admitted. She said it casually, like she wasn't lighting fires up and down Cas's body. "What it would be like."

"Have you?"

She was desperate. So fucking weak for this woman.

Ada nodded. "I know we're going to have to wait until they switch these cameras off, but . . ." She brushed a few strands of Cas's hair off her shoulder, leaned forward, and pressed a kiss right at the start of her collarbone. Everything she wasn't saying lingered in the air between them and though Cas was desperate to know exactly what Ada had in mind, she understood the need for subtlety.

Cas hummed in acknowledgment, her hand sliding to the outside of Ada's thigh. Her tiny shorts had ridden up over her hips, exposing every single inch of her thighs, and that, already, was enough to make Cas combust.

Cas slid forward, her hand slipping along the outside of Ada's thigh, and finally, *finally*, kissed her.

The spark was immediate. They'd been here before, but the fact that they were alone, that there was no one to interrupt, made everything feel instantly intense. Ada drew in a deep breath as Cas swept her tongue along her lower lip, and Cas couldn't help her smile, couldn't help but graze her teeth along Ada's lip.

Ada groaned and her hair tumbled over her shoulders as she tipped her head back. Cas followed the strands with her gaze, her fingers moving automatically toward the nape of Ada's neck, gathering in the hair there. She would never get enough of this feeling, the way that Ada's hair felt in her hands. The tick of Ada's pulse against Cas's forearm. The curve of Ada's thigh under her hand.

Ada pulled back just far enough to press her forehead to Cas's. "Do you want to drink some of that champagne and stare at that light until it goes out?"

Cas barked a laugh and, in one smooth motion, leaned over to grab the bottle from the ice bucket.

ABOUT TWENTY MINUTES later, the neon light switched off and Ada exhaled, her relief palpable. She caught Cas's lips in a kiss, wrapping her arms around Cas's neck and bringing her down with her as she fell back onto the pillow.

"Eager," Cas said.

"A little." Ada slid her hands up Cas's shirt, her palms splaying wide over Cas's stomach.

A little.

Cas pressed a kiss to Ada's throat, dragging her tongue down across the ridge of her collarbone. Ada shuddered, and Cas grazed her teeth along the skin there, delighting in the way it made Ada press closer to her.

"Fuck." It was barely a whisper, but Cas still felt every single letter on her skin.

The heat of their breath, their bodies, clouded Cas's mind so Cas felt like she was seeing everything through a fog. The haze laid heavy on her eyelids, dragging her under as she skirted her hands across every inch of Ada that she could touch. Cas skimmed over Ada's breasts, passing just over her nipples and skirting away as Ada pressed harder, searching for a pressure that Cas was not yet ready to give.

Ada huffed, frustrated, as Cas's fingertips danced over her ribs, and she hid her smile on Ada's neck.

"What?" Cas whispered.

"You know what," Ada whispered back.

"I don't," Cas said. She did.

Cas fingered the elastic on Ada's underwear. They were thin, barely there, but they were going to taunt Cas in her dreams.

Ada groaned, tipping her hips toward Cas's hand. Cas chuckled softly into her neck.

"Shhh." She trailed her fingers lower. "They're going to hear us."

The retreat was close enough to the garden that if anyone was still out there, and it was likely since they probably hadn't been corralled into bed yet, it was more than possible that they could be heard. Reece and Freddie, in particular, loved a late-night workout and could very well be at the gym right now.

"I'm not a quiet person," Ada admitted.

Cas pulled Ada's underwear to the side, still close but not quite touching. Ada was practically panting underneath her.

"As soon as we get out of here," Cas whispered, her lips brushing up against Ada's ear, "I'm going to make you fucking scream."

As she said it, Cas swiped her fingers through Ada's folds, biting back a moan at the feeling. She was dripping, gloriously wet, and Cas couldn't wait to get her mouth on her.

She whispered all of this into Ada's ear as her fingers found

Ada's clit. Cas pressed her lips to Ada's pulse as she swirled her fingers once, twice, in an experimental circle.

"Cas." The sound of Ada moaning her name was beyond all Cas's wildest dreams. "Cas, I—"

Cas traced her tongue along the length of Ada's throat and swirled her fingers again, groaning as Ada's hands tightened on her.

"Fuck, Ada." Cas kissed her pulse point, the shell of her ear. "You're so wet."

"You're killing me," Ada said. She shifted her legs, pressed up into the space between them to grind against Cas's hand. "I need—"

Cas moved her fingers in a series of swift circles, and Ada bit back another moan as she pulled Cas's mouth to hers. Her kiss was hot, desperate, full of all the things she couldn't say, and it was making Cas feel lightheaded.

Cas caught Ada's lower lip in between her teeth and Ada groaned again.

"I need your mouth on me."

She didn't need to ask twice.

Cas pressed a swift kiss to Ada's lips before sliding down her body, dropping kisses along her throat, her collarbone, as she slid her hands up underneath Ada's shirt. Ada reached to tug her shirt up, the action restless, frustrated.

Cas exhaled hard. Hoping. "Do you want to take your shirt off?"

Cas had no sooner asked the question than Ada sat up just enough to fully tear her shirt off over her head. Her breasts were round, full, her blush-pink nipples hard, already, in the chill of the air conditioner. Cas wanted to trace them with her tongue, her teeth.

The dim light cast shadows across the dips and curves of Ada's body, her movement casting more as she writhed. This was all going to Cas's head. She drew her fingertips along the line of freckles on Ada's breastbone, reveled in the way Ada lifted up to prolong the contact.

"Mm-hmm."

Cas hid her smile against Ada's skin, kissing a line down the center of her chest, across her left breast, pausing just long enough to let her breath fan across Ada's nipple before switching to the right.

Ada groaned softly, still frustrated, and Cas let Ada see her smile this time.

"You're not as funny as you think you are," Ada said. She was clearly trying for an angry voice but was nowhere near managing it.

"On the contrary," Cas said, leaning forward and, very softly, tracing a circle around Ada's right nipple with her tongue. Ada arched up into her, her breath catching, and Cas's smile was so unbearably smug. "I think I'm very funny."

Truth be told, she wasn't all that interested in being funny at the minute. She was too busy paying attention to Ada's soft exhales, the twist of her fingers in the sheets, the sounds she made as Cas kissed and sucked and scraped her teeth against her nipples. Each new sound was a discovery, one Cas was going to store in her memory for the rest of time.

Cas hooked her hands in the sides of Ada's shorts and, making every possible attempt to steady her breathing, looked up and caught Ada's eyes.

"Okay?"

Ada nodded, and without another moment's hesitation, Cas pulled her shorts off.

Cas had already known that Ada was beautiful. Could have, if she were a writer, written a thousand very pathetic, very gay poems about it.

But Ada naked with her legs spread, hands already in Cas's hair and tugging her forward, was another level altogether. She could write epics about this Ada.

Cas nudged Ada's right thigh up higher, turning and placing kisses along the soft skin there. Ada's breaths became shorter, sharper, with each kiss closer to her center, and though Cas was tempted to drag it out, she was too desperate to know what other sounds she could get Ada to make.

Cas pressed a kiss at the very apex of her thighs and then hovered there, breath coming in waves, and flicked her gaze up. Ada's fingers tightened in her hair as soon as they made eye contact.

"Cas."

Cas held Ada's gaze as she leaned forward and, as slowly as she could manage, traced her tongue, just once, over the length of her. Ada's entire body tensed, and Cas moved her hand to Ada's thigh to stop her crushing her head. Not that she would have minded Ada's thighs crushing her to death, but she had a few more things she'd like to do first.

"Christ, Ada." Cas sucked her clit and Ada's entire body arched off the bed.

There was nothing better in the entire world than the sight of Ada coming undone above her. The way she writhed underneath Cas's mouth, the sound of her soft, breathy moans, it was too much for Cas to handle, too much for her to process all at once.

Every pass of Cas's tongue was an experiment, a test to see what she liked, what she loved, what made it seem like Ada was half a second away from combusting.

Cas watched as Ada traced her hand across her stomach, memorized the way that Ada touched her own body so she could replicate it later. She traced the curve of her breast, the edge of her nipple, and as she watched, Cas started tracing her own fingers along the inside of Ada's thigh, creating twin sensations. She tried to follow Ada's movements, sliding her hand closer as Ada brushed her fingertips over her nipple, backing off as she skimmed the edge of her breast again, so that, finally, when Ada gave her nipple the slightest pinch, Cas slid the very tip of her index finger inside her.

"I'm— Fuck, Cas, I'm—"

Ada exhaled sharply again, her free hand tangling in Cas's hair.

It was so unbearably sexy, watching Ada like this. Watching her moving closer and closer to the edge. Her rolling breaths, the tightening of her fingers in Cas's hair, the restless motion of her legs against the sheets. Every centimeter of Ada's body was alive, electric, and it was addictive, knowing that she was causing this.

Cas slid another finger inside her and, after one more pass of her tongue, sucked gently on Ada's clit.

The response was immediate. Ada exhaled shakily and, thighs trembling, fingers tightening in Cas's hair, she fell apart.

Cas hummed against her as Ada rode out her orgasm,

moving with the waves of Ada's hips for one moment, two, before Ada moved her hand to the back of Cas's head.

"Come here."

Ada pulled Cas up to the top of their bed, their bodies locking together as Ada's mouth found hers. Cas slid her thigh between Ada's legs, pressed forward, and Ada groaned, tightening her hands on Cas's waist.

"Fuck." Ada pulled back, breathed as Cas kissed her cheek, her neck, her throat.

"Cas . . ." Ada pressed her hands into Cas's hips. "Get on your back."

Cas had never been one for taking orders in bed, but *Christ*. She'd do anything Ada asked of her if she said it in that voice.

It took half a second for Cas to lie down, but Cas was soon on her back, panting in anticipation. She reached for Ada as she settled over her, tried to pull her down for a kiss, but Ada swerved her at the last minute and kissed the inside of her wrist instead before leaning over and switching off the lights. And, now that the sun had gone down, the bedroom was plunged into darkness.

"You're so gorgeous," Ada said. She leaned forward, hair spilling across Cas's chest, and kissed Cas's shoulder, collarbone, hollow of her throat. Cas's heart rate accelerated with each pass of Ada's lips over her skin. Ada never stayed anywhere too long—she kissed her breast through her top, the heat of her breath and the brush of the fabric against her skin intoxicating. She drew her fingers along the edge of her shirt, her shorts, pressed kisses down the center of her stomach.

"Cas." Ada whispered it into Cas's skin, her breath raising

goose bumps across Cas's stomach before her lips (and then, *god*, her tongue) swiped them away.

With only the emergency lights on, it was nearly impossible to see Ada properly. In the dark, Cas felt like she couldn't get a handle on where Ada was, on what, exactly, she was doing, where she was going to go next. Cas couldn't read her expression, couldn't see her planning her next step, and it left every bit of her on edge, waiting, anticipating.

Only the brush of Ada's fingers against her skin gave Cas any clue where she was going next. She hooked her fingers in Cas's shorts, a question, and immediately slid them off Cas's legs when Cas moaned her assent.

"You've got to be quiet," Ada said. Her tone was an admonishment, but there was a smile on her lips when she kissed her way up Cas's thighs.

"I can't." She couldn't. Every breath felt like one step closer to combustion. Like she couldn't possibly contain everything within herself anymore.

"You have to try," Ada said. She skimmed her hand up over Cas's stomach, teased the underside of her breast.

"Everyone's got to be in bed by now," Cas said, and Ada laughed, her hot breath nearly sending Cas over the edge.

Ada pressed a kiss at the apex of Cas's thighs and Cas threaded her fingers through Ada's hair. "Fuck."

There was no mistaking the smile on Ada's lips then, but it only held Cas's attention for about half a second because Ada then ran her tongue over the length of her, groaning all the way.

"God, Cas." Ada hooked her hands underneath Cas's hips,

pulling her hard so she slid a few inches down the bed. "You taste so fucking good."

She tried for a joke—"Thanks, I . . ."—but it died so quickly on her lips it might as well have never existed.

Cas liked it when Ada swirled her tongue in circles over her clit, but when Ada slipped one, two fingers inside, when she teased that spot inside her that made her bite her lip to keep from moaning too loudly? She loved it, fucking loved it, and she would have given anything to stay suspended in this moment for the rest of eternity.

It had seemed, at first, that Ada was going to tease her, drive her out of her mind, but now that she was between Cas's thighs, she seemed to have a singular focus. The suddenness of the switch, from her earlier languid movements to these targeted, precise brushes of her lips, made Cas feel like she was running behind her body trying to catch up, trying to get a handle on the sensation before it overwhelmed her.

Ada, though, was not interested in letting Cas get control of herself.

Ada skimmed her free hand up over Cas's stomach, her fingers brushing against Cas's breast. It was soft, barely there at first, but when Cas arched up into Ada's hand, Ada took the hint and rolled Cas's nipple between her fingers.

"Fuck. Ada, I—" Ada pressed harder against that spot inside her and Cas would swear she was levitating. "There, yes."

Ada hummed in confirmation, spending sparks along the length of Cas's body. The tension in her gut ratcheted higher and higher, each bit of suction, each press of her fingers driving Cas closer and closer to the edge. Cas was trembling, sliding, and when Ada had to move her hand from her breast to pin Cas's hips to the bed, Cas groaned softly in desperation.

This was something they needed to explore at some point. Ada pinning her down, Cas, trapped, unable to move—

"Oh fuck." Her orgasm almost took her by surprise, and Cas tightened her hand in Ada's hair as she rode it out. Cas's hips were straining against Ada's arm, trying for more friction, and though Ada held her fast for a few seconds, she loosened her hold as Cas came down.

Ada moved back slowly. Trailed her tongue in small circles, placed gentle kisses as she moved to Cas's thighs. She lingered for a few seconds before wiping her forearm across her mouth and climbing over Cas's body again.

"You," Ada said, dropping a quick kiss to her lips, "are unreal."

Ada leaned down and kissed her again, her hair falling into a curtain around them.

The taste of herself on Ada's lips went immediately to Cas's head. She wrapped her arms around Ada's neck, pressing their bodies together, delighting in the feeling of their sweaty, overheated skin sliding together. Ada caught Cas's lower lip between hers, tugging lightly, and Cas exhaled hard as she deepened the kiss.

Cas was no stranger to *after*, had been in this situation more times than she could count, but she had never wanted to linger in this moment. She was normally quick to tuck and run, to roll out of bed without a second thought and barely a goodbye, but Cas would stay in this moment for a lifetime if she could. Would lie here, just kissing, for decades if Ada would let her.

Ada kissed Cas once more before, smiling, she rolled onto her back. They just lay there breathing for a long second, the air ice cold against Cas's overheated skin.

"I can't wait until we get home," Ada said. "I want to do that about a thousand more times."

Cas expected to feel a spark of fear course through her chest at Ada's words, but, instead, there was just a surprising, quiet thrill. Excitement at the prospect of doing this again, doing this every day, with Ada when they got home in a few weeks' time.

"You'll have to take me to dinner first," Cas said, turning and grinning.

Ada laughed and nestled into Cas's side, her arm falling easily over Cas's waist.

"I guess that could be arranged."

It was such a sweet gesture. Trusting. Easy. As always with Ada. It blew Cas's mind that she could just sink into these moments without a second thought, that she could just let herself *be*. It made Cas want to be. To trust.

Cas kissed the top of Ada's head and closed her eyes.

THE NEXT MORNING, Cas woke up to the sun on her face.

She'd thought they'd closed the curtains the night before, but now Cas saw that there was a tiny sliver of window visible at the far edge. Perfectly positioned to cast a stream of light directly into her eyes.

She groaned softly, arching her spine, and turned her head away from the light. Only to bump her nose into Ada's forehead.

Ada was lying on her side in the exact same spot they'd fallen asleep last night. Her arm was draped over Cas's waist, fingers lying on her hip and face hidden in Cas's hair.

Ada drew in a breath and then her fingers flexed very lightly on Cas's stomach. She burrowed her face deeper into Cas's neck, and Cas exhaled a laugh as she reached up and brushed Ada's hair off her shoulders.

"Good morning."

"Morning."

"Why are you so happy?"

Cas shrugged, though she could probably think of a few reasons. "Femi's not jumping on me for once."

Ada snorted. "He's saving all his jumps up for when they kick us out of here."

"Great. I'm dead, then. Especially now that he's got Freddie in on it with him."

All this past week, they'd taken turns dive-bombing Cas's bed, apparently intent on causing so much seismic disruption on her mattress that she bounce off the thing entirely.

Ada patted Cas's stomach. "It was nice knowing you."

Cas frowned. Or tried to. "I'd say the same if you weren't throwing me to the wolves."

Ada laughed and hooked her leg over Cas's, pulling her closer. "Oh, please. Dramageddon."

"Not dramageddon," Cas said. She rolled onto her side, slid her leg farther through Ada's, pressing against her center. "I could die. This is serious."

She was really trying for serious here, but her smile kept betraying her.

"You seem really worried." Ada brushed a stray piece of hair off Cas's cheek. "How can I help get your mind off it?"

"I don't know." Cas slid her arms around Ada's waist, pulling her close. "I'm just so devastated."

Ada laughed and rolled her eyes before pressing forward and quickly giving Cas a chaste kiss. "You're so dramatic, I swear."

Ada rolled onto her back, and Cas buried her face in her neck.

"I'm not."

"You are." Ada brushed her fingers through Cas's hair. It

was so soothing, this simple gesture, and Cas felt her eyes fall closed again.

"Maybe a little," she agreed. She'd never live it down at home—she'd been evading this exact charge for years—but she supposed there was no denying it really.

Neither of them said anything for a few long minutes. Cas, eyes closed, nose in Ada's neck, was perfectly content to stay here for as long as the production team would let them, but she knew they were probably on borrowed time. She didn't know what hour it was, didn't know if anyone else was already awake outside, but she could feel herself trying to catalog this moment, track as many of the details as she could and store them in her mind.

It felt fleeting. Like the moment she opened her eyes, it might cease to exist altogether.

"I was thinking about the ceremony last night," Ada said quietly. She was still staring at the ceiling, but Cas thought she saw her peek at her out of the corner of her eye.

"What about it?"

Ada started tracing her fingers absently along the duvet. "What would we do if we got separated? Like, if they wanted to make one of us leave?"

"I'd pick you up at Heathrow," Cas said. If it was going to be one of them, they both knew it would be her going first. It should have made her anxious—the Friday contract still there, in the back of her mind, but she felt . . . at peace with it.

Cas didn't know how much longer they had in the retreat, how much longer they'd be free of the cameras, but if there was a moment to talk to Ada about her contract, it was this one. Here, away from prying eyes, she might be able to get away with it, but even as she thought it, she felt the clauses of the NDA digging into her.

Yes, she was forbidden from saying anything, but maybe they wouldn't find out. Maybe her microphone was off, maybe Ada was really good at keeping secrets, maybe . . .

No matter how much she tried to think through it, though, there was no way Cas could figure out how to tell Ada without getting herself sued.

Maybe they could talk about it when they left. When they were shut in Cas's room at home, no cameras or recording devices in sight.

"The height of romance," Ada said, laughing. "You must really like me."

"I do," Cas admitted. Her voice nearly cracked, nearly revealed just how much she meant those words, but she wrestled back a bit of control at the last second.

Though maybe she hadn't if the way Ada's features immediately softened was to be believed.

Ada spread her fingers over Cas's ribs, raising goose bumps across Cas's exposed skin. Cas shivered, and the smile on Ada's lips widened, became that saucy, powerful little smirk Cas was already in love with.

In like with. *In like with.*

"I really like you, too," Ada said. She then went quiet for a moment, her expression contemplative.

"You know," she said, gaze flicking down to watch the progress of her fingers as they traced up and down Cas's forearm, "if they send you out of here, I'd leave with you."

"Would you?"

It was reckless and vulnerable, asking that question.

"Yeah," Ada whispered softly. Cas leaned forward and pressed her forehead against Ada's, desperate for one last moment of contact. One last press of Ada's skin against hers. "I'm not going to stay here if you're not here."

Cas laughed. "You might. What if you get a better offer?"

Ada pinched Cas's hip. "I already have the best one."

Cas leaned down and pressed another kiss to Ada's lips, a firm press that led to another, softer, lingering pass.

"They could always try to make you stay. Imagine Chloe emerging from the beach hut, full of righteous fury. She'd try to drag you back by the hair."

"Maybe I'd like that."

Cas laughed again. "If I'd known you were into hair pulling, we could've had a lot more fun last night."

"I had plenty of fun," Ada said. Her cheeks were pink, but her words were sure.

"I did, too," Cas said.

"It'll be nice to be out of here, though. The villa," Ada clarified, "not the retreat."

"Yeah." As she said it, Cas could almost see it. The pair of them walking out of the villa together, hand in hand. Sitting next to each other on the flight home. Kicking her bedroom door closed, half their clothes already on the floor. Taking Ada to her favorite coffee shop down the street, walking along the canal with her, kissing her under the streetlamps on their way home.

In three weeks' time, it would all happen. They just needed to last three more weeks.

Ada turned to look at her, tilting her head back a little so she could make eye contact. "Isn't it wild to think, like, we didn't know each other at all five weeks ago. And now the idea of being apart is so sad."

"I guess that's what happens when you're trapped together," Cas said.

"It's more than just that, though—"

One of their phones beeped from the bedside table and Cas swore before snuggling back into Ada's neck.

Ada laughed. "I don't think that's going to work."

As though determined to prove her point, the phone beeped again.

"All right." Ada slid her arms from around Cas and, resisting Cas's attempts to pull her back into bed, rolled over to grab her phone.

"'Cas and Ada, we hope you enjoyed your evening in the retreat. Please gather your things and return to the villa.'" Ada scanned the next message and then looked back at Cas, wide grin on her face. "The second text says, 'The lovers have a little surprise for when you return.'"

"Oh god."

"What do you think it is?"

"Knowing them? It could be anything."

～～～

They thought they were ready—had spent the better part of ten minutes batting ideas back and forth as they got dressed and gathered their things—but nothing prepared them for what they were greeted with when they stepped outside.

There was a trail of fake rose petals all along the pavement that led from the retreat to the kitchen, and as they rounded the corner, Cas saw that they'd set up quite the display. There was a huge array of breakfast options on the island and a handmade sign proclaiming *Cas and Ada 4 Life* hanging from the ceiling. It was absurd, and Cas had no idea where they got the supplies from, but it was the best thing she had ever seen.

Freddie hooted as soon as he saw them. "There are our lovebirds!"

Cas rolled her eyes and held her middle finger up at him, unable to hold back her grin.

THE HIGH LASTED all the way through to the next afternoon when the fifth week's rankings were announced. Ada was at Cas's side the moment Freddie finished reading the announcement text, winding her fingers through Cas's.

"How are you feeling?"

"Okay," Cas said. And she was. She'd long come to terms with the fact that she was in the bottom of the rankings and was, in all likelihood, going to remain that way for the rest of her time in the villa.

She didn't need to be well-liked anymore. Ada liked her. Sienna and Femi and Tia and Freddie liked her. That was enough.

The television was already on when everyone entered the lounge, and without speaking, they took their seats on the sofa. It was nice, for once, sitting on this couch without the constant worrying about where she was going to rank, to be here without feeling overwhelmed by the result.

She was curious, sure, but it was less stressful. And thank

god, because she'd had more than her fair share of cortisol this summer.

As always, they started with the women first.

Leo's phone beeped. "'In first place this week, we have Sienna.'"

Then Femi's phone beeped.

"'And the second most popular girl this week . . . Ada.'"

Reece was up next, and though Cas heard the text he read out, it took a second for the words to click.

"'The third most popular girl this week is . . . Cas.'"

Cas saw Ada turn to look at her out of the corner of her eye, felt the extra pressure she used to squeeze Cas's hand.

She was in the top three. Top three. After *weeks* spent languishing in the bottom.

Ada leaned over and kissed Cas's cheek, whispered "Well done" in her ear, but all Cas could think about was the fact that she'd more or less rocketed up through the rankings in the last two weeks.

Two weeks ago, this would have been her dream. It was exactly what she was hoping for, enough of an improvement to make getting to the finals feel all the more achievable. Now, though, she couldn't help but wonder if this success was tied up in her relationship with Ada, if it was only *because* of her relationship with Ada.

After weeks of not clicking with the public, there was no other clear reason for the shift. It wasn't as if she had a sudden personality change. Given that same-sex couples were few and far between, she appreciated the show of support the ranking clearly indicated, but the idea that she was only doing better because she happened to be in this partnership, and that *that* might be what saved her? It made Cas feel sticky and uncomfortable.

For the first time since she'd arrived, Tia dropped into the bottom half of the rankings, and Lucy, surprising no one, was last, but she took it on the chin.

"Oh well," Lucy said, sliding into Leo's side. "Hard to compete with you ladies."

There was a short round of applause before the girls started getting notifications for the boys' rankings. Femi was consistent in the first spot, but the real surprise was Freddie, who came in at number two. It was an enormous jump for such a short time in the villa, but it was clear by how well he got on with everyone that the viewers could see he was a standout. Reece had dropped to third, likely because of a small argument he and Tia had earlier in the week but then squashed, which left Leo for last.

Cas felt like she was in a bit of a haze as they all filtered out to the back garden. She grabbed one of her two permitted glasses of prosecco off the kitchen island and, without waiting for anyone else, took a large sip on her way down to the pool deck.

The outdoor lights had switched on while they'd been inside, and the reflection of them shining in the pool was one of Cas's favorite views here. There was something almost magical about it, the navy blue sky, the sparks of light throughout the back garden, the whisper of the breeze through the trees.

Cas sat down heavily on the end of one of the deck chairs, pressing her knees together in an effort to keep the cameras from being able to see up her too-short skirt, and took another drink.

She wasn't upset exactly. Part of her was actually quite happy with where she'd ended up, happy that, after weeks, she'd finally managed to get herself into the position she'd been hoping for since the beginning. And given Ada's placement, it was almost a sure thing that they'd be in the finale at this point.

But there was something undeniably sticky about the reality of the situation—the fact that it was probably less Cas herself and more the relationships she'd fostered that had led to this reversal in her fortunes.

She knew that was part of her initial strategy—she wanted that friendship couple, wanted good connections—but she hadn't expected to care so much about the people in the villa. Hadn't expected to feel so guilty about using those relationships, manipulating them to get something she wanted.

Everyone was buzzing around up in the kitchen, conversation lively as they poured prosecco, celebrated their spots, enjoyed clearing this latest hurdle. This was the last ranking until the public vote at the end of the next week, the final vote before they were in the *Hot Summer* finale. They knew they wouldn't all last that long—Cas thought that most of them who weren't in a stable partnership, like Freddie, weren't expecting to make it to the final three—but there was a rush around it all the same. At being this close to going home, to testing out their relationships in the real world.

Or, if you were Cas, being one step closer to fulfilling her contractual obligations.

She could have just let herself get swept up in the connection she had with Ada and enjoy the very real benefits in terms of her popularity, but it felt gross, thinking about that side of things. Thinking about their relationship as something that had a kind of payout. A cold, calculated transaction.

She preferred thinking about it like she had in the peach orchard: beautiful, untarnished, with untold amounts of promise.

She was staring out at the horizon, sipping away at her prosecco, when someone came and sat down beside her. Cas knew who it was without looking, and, all at once, Cas felt something settle in her chest.

"Hey." Ada's voice was soft, a perfect match to the moment. "Are you okay? You disappeared kind of quickly."

"Yeah." Cas twirled her cup around in her hands, watched as a leaf floated down off a nearby tree and landed in the pool. "I was just feeling weird about the rankings."

"Were you hoping to be higher?" There was no judgment in Ada's voice. How she managed it, Cas would never know.

"God, no. I was shocked I was third."

"I'm not." Cas looked at her, surprised, but Ada's expression was even. "You've been more yourself recently. I feel like you're so much more relaxed than you were at the start of the summer."

"I don't feel any different," Cas said, but Ada was already shaking her head.

"You're not different, exactly, but you're just . . . you feel less tense, you know? Less aware of the cameras all the time."

Cas's brows pinched. "What do you mean?"

"In the first week or two, it seemed like you were always so afraid of saying the wrong thing or doing the wrong thing. I always wondered if maybe it came from all your knowledge of the show or something," Ada said, and it was that exactly. It was scary how well Ada knew her without Cas even having to say anything.

"I think maybe you were just thinking too hard about it," Ada continued. "It seems like you've stopped thinking so much."

"But what if people only like me because I'm partnered up with you?" Cas didn't quite know what she was asking Ada to say, if she was hoping for a confirmation or a denial, but she needed these feelings in her chest to go away.

"People are going to rank us for whatever inane reason, we can't control that." Ada said it so simply, like it wasn't the cause of so much of Cas's turmoil at the minute. "But I don't think that's why things changed for you. Really, I don't." She took Cas's hand, squeezed it like she was trying to press the words into Cas's skin. "The public is just starting to see the real you, Cas. And I know that's probably stressing you out, but it's okay to let them see you."

And, god, how prophetic those words would end up being.

#HotSummer—Live Updates

@tiffstuff: I'm so obsessed with cada like you don't understand

@dayla14: what are the odds of them uhauling the second this show is over

@tiffstuff: alksdjf pls there are no odds its 100%

@charleybee: did you hear that rumor about Cas though???

@tiffstuff: . . . What rumor?

@ciarap1246: uhh . . . did everyone know that Cas worked for a dating company?

> **Link:** dailypost.co.uk/entertainment/ hotsummer/11july . . .

> **What you don't know about the lovers!**

@isobelleking: I thought she said she was a party planner???

@ciarap1246: did you read the article? She works for Friday. It was on her Instagram bio, but she took it out when she went on the show. There were a few people talking about it a few weeks ago

@isobelleking: okay but like . . . how does her being there for her company make any difference?

@anjalimarx: well it's weird that she lied about it either way. everyone else shared their actual jobs

@isobelleking: no I get that part, but like . . . why would she lie?

@anjalimarx: fuckin weird right

@caracoven: are there any internet sleuths out here who can investigate???

@nowenthings: what are we looking for

@beannnews: evidence that something weird is going on probably

@somehowl: . . . what about confirmation that there's a contract AND an NDA involved?

@milianarogers: I'm a reporter with the Daily Post—can I DM you to talk about this?

THEIR SEVENTH MONDAY in the villa started like every other week.

Femi and Freddie brought around coffee and smoothies as the girls got out of bed. The five of them lay in a beanbag circle on the grass—Femi, Sienna, Ada, Cas, and Freddie—their feet in the center as they played yet another game Freddie had invented that was allegedly football-adjacent but, really, just ended with them all having bruised shins and ankles. Ada slathered on coat after coat of sun cream and still, somehow, ended up a little pink across the bridge of her nose.

It had been a while since someone had gotten an afternoon text, so Cas wasn't necessarily surprised when Tia's phone beeped from across the garden. She was sure the public was getting desperately bored, watching them messing about all day, and the producers needed to do something to keep the viewers engaged. She wasn't thrilled at the idea of having to get up, though, or do anything other than lie here until it was time to get ready for the party that evening.

"'Lovers!'" Tia's voice was so full of glee that it was almost impossible to understand her. "'Today, you're going to play the headline game!'"

"Oh my god!" Lucy's shout was probably heard across the whole of Cyprus. "I've been waiting for this!"

She was jumping up and down. Literally jumping. Hands clutched to her chest and everything, like someone just told her she'd won the lottery.

Cas didn't have the slightest idea why Lucy was excited. Every time the show ran this challenge, they always picked the worst possible headlines. You might get a hint at public opinion based on whatever gossip magazine they pulled from, but most often, the headlines focused on tiny tidbits about the relationships from "third-party" sources. Random second cousins or grade school neighbors had intimate insight, and then suddenly every relationship in the villa was tested. Secrets were revealed and bonds between partners—and, in some cases, even friends—were shattered all in a matter of minutes. A few years ago, an entire cheating scandal had been revealed in the middle of this exact challenge and it ended in one girl deciding to leave the villa entirely. People still quoted her exit speech online.

Cas would bet almost anything that they were going to have a surprise partnership ceremony tonight, too. Really cap off the evening in style.

"'Remember,'" Tia said, her tone extra provocative, "'whenever we read the headlines . . . things are not always as they seem. #TellTheTruth #WhosOnTop?'"

After a quick get-ready session in the bathroom, everyone ran down to the competition ring, the stones kicking up and scratching at the back of Cas's calves as they jogged over.

There wasn't much set up there today—just a few podiums and a board with something on it that, from a distance, Cas couldn't quite make out. It was better than seeing a rotating array of obstacle courses, but also a little more nerve-wracking when Cas considered the fact that there were cards up there with some (probably) very harsh and very public opinions.

"'Lovers—the boys will be competing against the girls in today's challenge, Fishing for the Goss. You will choose an envelope out of a fishbowl.'" Leo held up the fishbowl and gave it a shake, and the sound of the envelopes scratching against the glass was strangely menacing. "'Read out the headline inside the envelope and then kiss the person that you think the headline is about. If you're right, your team gets a point. The team with the most points at the end of the competition wins a seventies disco!'"

Everyone cheered, some of them genuinely, and Leo flashed a bright grin.

"Everyone ready to play?"

They all cheered louder, this time more excitedly, and after a short pause, Lucy's phone beeped, signaling that she should go first. She bounded forward and shoved her entire arm into the fishbowl.

"'*Hot Summer*'s *blank* had real feelings for one of the bombshells—they should have partnered up!'"

"Oh huh." Lucy twirled the card between her fingers as she walked over to the boys. She studied each of them as she moved down the line, swooping in on Femi and Leo like she was going to kiss them before turning on her heel and grabbing Freddie's face.

"Whoa!" Reece swerved, barely avoiding getting knocked

into as Freddie stumbled backward. It didn't make sense—Freddie *was* one of the bombshells—but maybe Lucy had just been looking for an excuse to get a kiss in?

Lucy grinned and wiped her mouth as she stepped back, barely bothering to spare a glance for Leo as she flipped open her envelope.

REECE

Cas's jaw actually dropped.

Tia whipped her head round, expression incredulous. "Does that say 'Reece'?"

Sienna's jaw dropped. "What the hell?"

Tia ran her tongue along her teeth, her eyes lasers as they swung round and found Reece. He looked like he was melting into the decking, desperate as he mouthed, *We'll talk later,* but Tia just waved him off.

Freddie's phone beeped next, and he plunged his hand into the bowl, coming up with a few envelopes stuck between his fingers. He held them up, sealed, and turned back to the boys.

"Which one do you think? One, two, or three?"

He indicated each with a nod of the head, and the boys burst out in a flurry of shouts. It didn't sound to Cas like they'd all agreed on any envelope in particular, but Freddie made an executive decision. "Three it is, then," he said, before chucking the other two back into the bowl.

"'*Hot Summer* fans convinced that *Freddie* and *blank* should get together!'" He hummed theatrically before making his way over to the girls. "I have a sneaking suspicion about who this one could be . . ." he said, throwing an overdramatic wink Cas's way.

As he stopped in front of Cas, he flicked his gaze toward Ada. "You all right if I kiss your girl? You know she's all yours."

Ada laughed, spots of pink blooming on her cheeks. "It's a game, go ahead."

Freddie leaned down and placed a swift, chaste kiss on Cas's lips, swerving to place another one on her forehead before straightening up. "Okay," he said, waving the envelope in the air, "let's see who we've got . . ."

The boys started stomping their feet making the entire platform shake with the force of their makeshift drum roll.

Freddie opened the envelope and, sure enough:

CAS

"Yes!" Freddie jumped and punched the air before sprinting back to the boys. They swarmed around him as they reached him, all jumping and chanting like they'd just been told they'd won half a million pounds each.

"All right," Sienna shouted, rolling her eyes. "It's my turn, you idiots."

Cas hadn't even heard Sienna's phone beep in all the shouting. She made her way over to the bowl while the boys straightened themselves out and grabbed one of the envelopes off the top.

"'Fans think *blank* will bag the hundred-thousand-pound prize now that he's coupled up with his dream girl.'"

Sienna didn't even hesitate. She walked straight to Femi,

his smile growing with each step she took toward him so he was all teeth by the time she reached him.

Their kiss was slow by comparison to the others, savored, and Femi seemed unwilling to let Sienna go as she pulled back a few seconds later to open the envelope. He kept his arms around her waist, his fingers toying with the tie on her bikini top as she unfolded the paper.

FEMI

Cas and Ada immediately applauded, and Freddie, to Femi's right, wrapped his arm around Femi's shoulders and gave him a little shake.

"You're taking us all out when you win, Fem," Freddie said.

"I don't care if we win," Femi said. He was smiling, laughing with them, but he only had eyes for Sienna. "I've got what I need."

Leo was up next, and now that Sienna had tied the score, he seemed to take his role extra seriously. He swirled his hand around in the fishbowl, pretending to choose a few envelopes with intentional slowness so, after about half a second, they were all shouting at him.

"Leo!"

"Hurry up, mate!"

"Come on!"

Leo just laughed, but his expression quickly sobered as he finally selected an envelope from the bowl. He took a deep breath before he read it out, his tone grave. "'*Blank* is on *Hot Summer* for a promotion! She's not there for love at *all!*'"

As soon as Cas heard it, she felt her stomach drop.

Oh god.

Oh *god*.

Leo didn't even bother looking at the girls. He walked straight across the deck, stuffing the card into his pocket as he went, and Cas thought he was going to know it was her, somehow read it on her face, but he took Lucy's face in his hands. The kiss was quick and his movements were short as he pulled the card out of his back pocket.

Cas would have done anything, anything in the entire world, to keep him from opening that card.

CAS

Everyone on the platform was staring at her, mouths open in disbelief. This was the worst offense anyone could commit on this show. It never ended well for people who seemed to just be there for the money, but the idea that she was intentionally put there, that she could have been manipulating things the whole time, was the worst-case scenario Cas had feared since Robert and the Friday team even suggested this crazy scheme.

Cas felt for all of the lovers, but there were frankly only four she truly cared about, and they were all staring at her like they'd never seen her before. They were trying to make sense of her now, trying to put together a new picture of her in their heads, understand who she was and what her actions meant in light of this possible news. She hated it, how clearly stunned they were, but she could talk with them later.

Cas saved her biggest fear for last, the one she was dreading most of all. She pushed every single ounce of will out into the universe begging it, *someone,* to make everything okay. To make Ada at the very least willing to hear her out.

But the look on Ada's face.

It was shock and anger and disappointment and hurt all rolled into one. She was staring at Cas as if she'd never seen her before, like the woman standing in front of her now wasn't the same one she'd been sharing a bed with for the last week. Or, worse, like she was, but Ada didn't ever want to see her again.

The anger Cas could deal with, but the hurt? The disappointment? The rejection? Cas didn't know if they could recover from that.

Ada took a step back, almost stumbling in her haste, and Cas reached out for her.

"No, Ada, I— *Please,* let me explain."

Ada opened her mouth, paused, then closed it again before shaking her head. "I need a second."

And Ada ducked underneath the rope and started up the hill without so much as glancing back.

Cas's phone beeped a second later.

> Cas—please report to the beach hut
> immediately.

CAS'S FOOTSTEPS WERE loud on the tile, echoing in the otherwise silent villa. This was the worst possible time for them to bring her into the beach hut—she hadn't had time to talk to Ada, to Femi, to anyone, but the producers had to talk to her *now?*

She'd run after Ada, her trainers slipping on the stones on the hill, but Ada hadn't been anywhere. She'd shouted her name, desperate, her brain running over a thousand possible things—maybe she'd left, maybe she was preemptively packing Cas's suitcase—none of which made her feel any better.

The door of the beach hut fell shut with a thud as Cas dropped into the circular chair.

She'd just opened her mouth to say hello when the speaker crackled, and though the producers always sounded busy, there was something particularly distracted in Chloe's voice today. "Thanks for coming so quickly, Cas. We've got a lot to talk about."

"Yeah." Cas shifted in her seat. "What are we doing about this?"

"Obviously, the production team was aware of the circumstances that brought you onto this show," Chloe said. It sounded like she was riffling through a stack of fifteen thousand sheets of paper on the other end. "But we've always known there was a possibility that the situation could become public knowledge, and now that that's happened, it changes things for us."

Cas frowned. "In what way?"

"We don't think it makes sense for you to continue on *Hot Summer*."

Everything froze.

"What do you mean?" She tried for a laugh. At the very least, it might make her stop feeling like she was choking. "Surely, you can't be kicking me off for this."

It wasn't right. Cas never said anything, never broke any terms of her contract. Production had arranged the deal with Robert and Friday, had negotiated the agreement for weeks. *They'd* done this—and, yes, she was part of it, but just as a chess piece, not the instigator. But to force her to leave was to act like she'd gotten into this on her own. Like she'd tricked them into thinking she was a regular contestant when, lo and behold, she'd been sneakily having marketing meetings the entire time.

She always knew in the back of her mind that the show could, and would, do whatever they liked. If the public had voted her off, or she hadn't been selected for a couple, or anything like that, they would have sent her home no problem because, per her contract, there were absolutely no guarantees for her safety. But for them to remove her? For them to send her home, outside of an elimination, felt like a punishment, especially because she'd done nothing wrong.

"Unfortunately," Chloe said, her tone detached and disinterested, "the public narrative has become that you've been planted on this show as a marketing ploy."

"How could they even know that? I didn't tell anyone."

Chloe hummed noncommittally. "However the information got out there is not our concern. But I can—"

"So you're not worried about how or why someone leaked sensitive information to the press, something that could be very damaging to your show, my company, and me personally?"

"No." There was the sound of a pen clicking on the other end and then the very distinct scrawling of said pen over a clipboard. "Rather, what we are focused on right now is maintaining our viewers' trust and commitment to our programming. And, from the start, this has been the contingency plan should this ever come to pass."

"What? To throw me under the bus?"

"It was part of your original contract, Cas. Page nine, if memory serves. We are entirely within our rights to remove you from the show for any reason including, but not limited to, public discussion of the Friday/*Hot Summer* agreement."

"And how long have you known that this was going to happen? It obviously was planned, since you guys built it into the challenge."

Because it wasn't enough, apparently, to throw her out. They'd had to embarrass her in front of Ada, her friends, the entire damn country, and make sure that this contingency plan of theirs stuck.

"Things started spiraling on social media within the last week. We've been keeping an eye on it."

"But it would've gone away if they never got any evidence.

It could *still* go away if you don't give it any credence—acting on it like this basically confirms it."

"We aren't tying ourselves to a sinking ship," Chloe said simply. They were harsh words delivered with an unrivaled ease. "We have to protect our interests."

"You can't do this." Cas was begging. "Regardless of what brought me here, I've more than proven that my motives now are completely genuine."

"Have you?" The skepticism in Chloe's voice was an ice-cold knife straight to Cas's gut.

"Yes." She knew she sounded desperate, but she didn't care. "Everything I ever said to Ada I meant. You can't let it end this way. My feelings for her are real."

Feelings that were so big, Cas could feel them swelling in her chest, blocking her throat. If this news had broken weeks ago, sure she would have been humiliated and annoyed at the PR control she'd have to do at work, but she would have left. But now, at the idea of leaving Ada behind . . . at leaving Femi and Sienna, and Freddie.

But maybe there was still hope for them. Ada had said, that morning in the retreat, that if Cas had to leave, she'd follow her out. Yes, Ada was definitely pissed off right now, but they'd both said they could see a future together. They'd made plans for what things could look like on the outside. They trusted each other.

It was that small promise that settled the anxiety clawing at Cas's chest. She and Ada would need to talk before they left—Ada deserved a full explanation long ago, and Cas would make sure she'd get one now, but then they'd be isolated in a hotel room until they flew back to London. They'd have hours and hours to talk, hours that weren't going to be filmed and broadcast for everyone in the country to see.

Chloe might not have believed that Cas's feelings were real, but people were going to think whatever they wanted. It didn't matter if she, or the other producers, or, hell, even the entire British viewing public, knew or cared about the reality of her relationship with Ada.

The only person Cas needed to convince was Ada. And, given a little bit of time on their own, she was certain that she could explain everything.

"Am I going to get time to talk to everyone before I have to leave? They deserve the truth."

"You're going to gather everyone at the fire pit," Chloe said. "And you're going to tell them you've decided to leave—"

"But I haven't. *You've* decided I'm leaving."

"We don't need to go into the details." Chloe's words were the audible version of a dismissive hand wave. "You're to say that you've decided to leave and you've loved your time here, you'll see them on the outside, et cetera."

"Should I say the 'et cetera' part?"

"No." In any other situation, Cas would have found it amusing that Chloe took her sarcasm seriously. "But under no circumstances can you go into the details of the arrangement or say this is a removal. It must be framed like it was your decision to leave."

"Why?" If she was going to leave because of a lie, she didn't want to double down at the last moment, she wanted to leave having told the truth. At least as much of it as she thought she could tell anyway. "I think I should get the chance to explain what's happening to my friends."

"In case you've forgotten, you signed an NDA. And refusal to follow these guidelines could mean serious legal trouble for you."

"I could explain it to them off camera," Cas insisted. "They've already heard about the deal through the headline, surely there's a little flexibility—"

"There isn't," Chloe said firmly. "You follow these guidelines or you leave right now without saying goodbye."

There was silence between them for a few long beats, and though Cas had half a mind to wait it out, she also just really, really wanted to get this over with.

Cas sighed. "Fine. Whatever you want."

~~~

Everyone was in the kitchen when Cas walked outside. She could hear them whispering, their voices hushed as though worried Cas would hear them when she was back in the beach hut. At the sound of the door falling closed behind her, the kitchen fell abruptly silent, and sure enough, all eight of her roommates were standing in the kitchen, eyes trained on the floor when she rounded the corner.

"Hey, everyone." Cas's voice cracked in the middle of "everyone," and she swallowed, started again. She needed to at least pretend she had some dignity. "Can we go to the fire pit, please?"

She expected some sort of reaction—confusion, maybe surprise—but the most she got was a very slight twitch of the eyebrow from Femi when their eyes met.

Ada was the last to leave the kitchen. She sat, her gaze trained on the countertop while everyone else filed out around her. The moment they were alone, Ada finally looked at her, her lips parting with an inhale, and Cas felt herself teetering on the edge, desperate for Ada to say something, anything, that would make her feel less anxious about what she was going to have to do now.

Ada pushed back her chair and walked toward the fire pit, and Cas watched her go, feet frozen to the spot.

Cas waited until Ada had nearly reached the others before following, looking and feeling like a woman walking the gangplank. There was a persistent voice in the back of her mind telling her to pick her head up, to throw her shoulders back, to show them (who *them* were, Cas wasn't a hundred percent sure) that she wasn't affected by this, but that's what had gotten her into this mess in the first place.

Maybe it was time to wear her heart on her sleeve. At least a little bit.

Everyone was sitting on the bench around the fire pit when Cas arrived, their expressions ranging from emotionless to incredibly pissed off. It wasn't the sort of supportive crowd you wanted when you were about to be thrown to the wolves, but Cas understood. What really got her was Ada, who looked like she'd rather Cas fling herself over the hedge than say a word.

Cas swung her arms behind her back, knotting her fingers together to keep from fidgeting with them too much while she was talking. "I've decided that it's time for me to go."

There were a few slight eyebrow raises, some clear side glances, but no gasps. No shock or demands that she stay, or at least think about it.

"It's clear, after the headline today, that I'll just be a distraction, and I don't want to be in the way of everyone else finding happiness here." Cas re-knotted her fingers together. Wearing your heart on your sleeve was one thing, but her heart was about to come out of her mouth. "I can't speak to whether the rumors are true or not, and trust me, I wish I could tell you everything."

It was probably skirting a little too close to her NDA, but whatever. Chloe could sue her. Or edit it out.

"There's a lot going on behind the scenes that I can't talk about. But I've already found what I'm looking for here anyway. I don't need to stay."

Cas was pleading. Pleading with Ada to see that when she said she found what she was looking for, she meant *her*, not some stupid thing that her boss had sent her in for. She'd found happiness, real happiness, and with someone just a few tube stops away, someone she could have met at any of the pubs, any of the clubs, but, somehow, had just never happened to bump into until now.

It was almost making her misty eyed just thinking about it. The *fate* of it all.

But Ada was staring at the ground, shoulders stiff, arms crossed, and the anxiety swirling in Cas's stomach reached new heights. This was not the expression she'd been hoping for.

"So, yeah." Cas let her hands move from behind her back, though she almost immediately clasped them together in front of her again. "This is goodbye."

No one moved for so long that Cas had half a mind to repeat herself. To shout, *Did you hear me?! I'm leaving!*

Instead, every single pair of eyes was trained on Ada, waiting to see what she'd do. Cas had already assumed that they'd all been talking about her when she'd come out into the kitchen, but it was clear, now, that some sort of game plan had been decided. Ada shook her head so imperceptibly that Cas would have missed it if she weren't watching, and everyone noticeably exhaled before getting to their feet.

Lucy was the first one to reach Cas's side, and though she tried for a sad expression, she didn't look even remotely upset.

"I'm really sorry you're going, Cas," Lucy said. She put her hand on Cas's forearm. "But maybe it's for the best."

Everyone else at least had the decency not to swipe at what was left of her dignity as they said goodbye. Reece made a half second's worth of eye contact and muttered goodbye, Tia tried adding that she would miss her and a placating tap on the arm.

"Bye, Cas." Despite the speed of the hug and the way that Sienna wouldn't quite meet her eyes, there was a sadness to the words as she whispered them into Cas's ear.

Freddie could barely make eye contact as he approached, head down, eyes trained on the decking. He gave her a hug goodbye, his hands twitching on her back once, twice, like he was thinking about squeezing her harder, but then he stepped away and walked off without saying anything else.

Femi was where it was really going to hurt.

His expression was soft as he approached her, a warm island in a sea of cold indifference. He wrapped his arms around her without a moment's hesitation, this hug slower, more intentional. "I'm going to miss you."

Cas felt her heart climb up into her throat, and she tried her best to swallow it down.

"You should've told me," Femi said. He wasn't chastising

her, but she felt the disappointment in his voice anyway. "I wouldn't've told anyone."

She squeezed him tighter, pressing him to her like he was the only thing tethering her to the ground. It was ridiculous—she'd only known him six weeks—but he had become one of her best friends and she was going to miss him. She was going to miss the way he sang around the villa; the perfect cups of iced coffee he made her, Sienna, and Ada every morning; his ridiculous laughter at the stupidest of jokes; even the damn jumping on the bed.

All at once, Cas felt the wave crash over her.

She was going to miss the routine she'd built in this house. The people she'd built it with.

"I couldn't," Cas said. "My contract—I couldn't."

"There were ways you could have told me," Femi said. "I wouldn't've judged you."

"Oh yeah right, you would have been fine if I told you that I 'wasn't really here for love'?"

Femi shook his head. "I'm not an idiot, Cas. I know a lot of people don't come on here for that. I'm your friend, you could've trusted me." Cas opened her mouth to argue, but Femi shook his head. "And whether you came here for love or not, we both know you found it. No matter what comes next, remember that."

He stated it so plainly. So baldly. And Cas clung to the words, to the truth of them—*what came next* was going to be incredibly hard, but at least she was stepping out of this villa with this feeling.

Femi gave her one more deep squeeze and whispered, "We'll leave you two alone. To say goodbye."

His words were ominous, especially when coupled with the way Ada still wasn't quite looking at her. And she knew it then, felt in her bones what was about to happen.

"Bye, Fem," Cas said. She squeezed his forearms before dropping her hands down by her sides.

Femi smiled at her one last time, his whole expression sad, before walking past her into the grass. Cas looked over her shoulder, and by this point everyone had gone. She appreciated that they were letting her and Ada have this conversation alone. That they were being given one last minute alone.

Cas swallowed hard. "Hey." Cas almost laughed at herself, the awkwardness in her voice. "Can I— Can we talk?"

Ada nodded silently, her eyes not quite meeting Cas's, but, instead, trained on something just past her left ear.

"I—" Seeing Ada like this, still completely unable to make eye contact, still folded in on herself, was making Cas a little desperate. She needed Ada to understand.

She needed Ada to forgive her.

"Ada, I am so, so sorry."

She shifted her weight forward, thinking of taking a step closer to Ada, but decided against it. As much as she wanted to, she wanted Ada to come to her. Wanted Ada to want her in her space again.

Ada nodded in acknowledgment. "I know you are, Cas."

Okay, that was something.

Not . . . a lot, granted. But it was something.

And she wanted to tell Ada everything, could feel the whole story there, waiting to be said, but the reminder of Chloe's threat about her NDA was there, echoing in her ears, strangling her. It had been annoying, not being able to tell anyone else, but it was infuriating, having to walk this line with Ada.

"I can't tell you everything right now, but I *will*. I just need you to trust me when I say that my feelings for you have always been genuine.

"I didn't come on this show expecting to meet anyone like you. I didn't think that they'd have anyone here who would make sense for me or would make me, like—" She pressed her hand to her chest. How could she describe the way that Ada made her feel? The way Ada made her heart race and her entire body feel like it was vibrating, constantly, with energy?

"I didn't plan for you. But then that first day you stepped out of the Jeep and . . ."

Cas shook her head, and Ada finally, *finally,* met her gaze.

Cas hoped there would be warmth in Ada's eyes. Understanding. The memory of the two of them arriving at the villa together could not be this one-sided, could not have been the moment that only Cas realized the connection between them.

Instead, her gaze was cold. Hard.

"I don't know if I believe that."

The words were a knife to the chest.

Cas felt herself desperately trying to deflate, but she refused to let herself give in to it. Not yet.

"I know you're angry with me," Cas said, "but—you *have* to trust me. There's so much more going on here than I can explain right now."

"But I don't trust you. I don't know how you could expect me to trust you when you've been lying this entire time."

"I only lied about what first brought me here," Cas said. "Everything after it was the truth."

"But it wasn't." Ada practically spat the words. "You said you'd never used a dating app and you fucking worked for one. You said you were a party planner. You said you didn't know what the next step was in your career when, the whole time, you've known *exactly* where you're headed the minute you're out of here."

And it was true. She fucking hated it, but it was true. She had lied, but the truth was tangled up with every single fib. But how could she untangle it here, in front of these cameras, the NDA hanging like an ax over her head?

"You lied to me over and over again, and now you expect me to just forget that?"

"I just need you to believe me when I say that there's more to this story. There are things I can't tell you here, but if we leave together now, we can talk about them. *Please.*"

Ada was quiet for a long moment. "I'm not going to leave with you. And I don't want to see you again on the outside."

Cas's heart couldn't break any more. It was already ground down into dust, blowing about in her chest. But Ada's *no* was the final straw. She felt the walls start going back up, could feel herself retreating, away from this moment, away from this woman, away from this villa and everyone watching her and everyone knowing that she'd shown her raw, emotional under-belly on this stupid show for someone who, again, would do nothing but disappoint her.

Would do nothing but abandon her at the first opportunity.

Cas huffed angrily, swiping her hair back off her face. "I

can't believe I stood there, in front of all of them, and told them that I'd found what I was looking for. That I was *happy*."

"It's hard to believe you were actually looking for anything," Ada snapped. "You came here for *work*. That's it. You said it yourself!"

"That was my initial reason, yes," Cas said. "But that isn't what kept me here!"

"Right." Ada laughed sarcastically. "But how am I supposed to believe that when partnering up with me is *exactly* what kept you here?"

It was a low blow and they both knew it. Ada's expression twitched, just enough to give her away, but she didn't take it back. Didn't apologize.

Cas half laughed, the sound hard and bitter. "I don't need the reminder that I'm now universally hated, thanks."

"I'm sure you'll manage on the outside," Ada said. She wasn't looking at Cas, but staring at something over her left shoulder. "I'm sure you'll get more than enough opportunities and payouts to make you forget all about it."

Cas, furious, opened her mouth to reply when the Voice of God sparked to life behind them.

"Cas, please come pack your bags. It's time to leave the villa."

Before Cas could move, before she could even say anything, Ada stalked off without saying goodbye.

THEY KEPT HER in a hotel for fifty-six hours.

Cas was alone, barred from leaving under any circumstances (unless, they were quick to reassure her, the hotel caught fire, in which case, she was perfectly free to leave).

In any other scenario, lounging in a bed all day and ordering free room service would have been a luxury, but here, isolated in this tiny room unable to talk to anyone . . .

It was a fucking nightmare.

She hadn't been given her phone back yet, which, while annoying, was probably for the best. Cas knew herself well enough to know that she had self-destructive tendencies at the best of times, and she didn't need the *Hot Summer* team to help her along in that regard.

There'd be plenty of time for her to obsess over whatever people were saying about her online in a few days.

They put her on a late-night flight back to London on Wednesday, sneaking her back into the country like you might sneak someone your parents disapproved of into your bedroom. Cas only half believed the producers when they told her the flight timing was a move to protect her. The paps, whatever amount of them there would be, were expecting her to fly out the next morning. But privately, Cas also thought they'd scheduled it like this to torture her; there was something exquisitely painful in spending the entire day being anxious about her flight—and what might come after it.

Just in case, though, she still pulled her hair up into a ponytail and tucked it into a baseball cap. That hat, paired with the most enormous sunglasses she owned, and Cas was convinced she was invisible.

The flight back to London was easy enough, in part because the *Hot Summer* team arranged for her to get picked up at Luton rather than having to sort out the train as a final way to avoid any press.

The driver popped his gum in way of greeting as she settled into the back seat. "Camden, yeah?"

Cas shifted in her seat. The leather was warm and sticking to the backs of her thighs. As much as she appreciated a good full-circle moment, she really could've done without this one. "Mm-hmm."

"Nice. Oh, and . . ." He held something back over the seats, and Cas realized with a jolt that it was her phone. "Chloe gave me this to give to you. There's a cord you can use to charge up down there." He pointed at the floor, and sure enough, there was a bright white cord curled up against the dark gray carpet.

"Cheers." Cas had barely bent down to grab said cord when the driver jolted the car forward, nearly sending Cas's forehead into the center console.

She let her phone charge peacefully on her lap for the first few minutes of her journey, debating just leaving it off entirely. But then, apparently now juiced up enough to have a mind of its own, it switched back on.

It was suspiciously, dangerously silent for six and a half minutes until, finally, the notifications started swarming in. Her email notifications were in the hundreds, every single one of her social media accounts exploded, and WhatsApp was just . . . It'd probably be easier to delete it than try to get a handle on all the messages.

She should have turned off her social media notifications before she'd left for the show, saved herself the trouble, but, truth be told, she hadn't thought that far ahead. The emails and texts she'd anticipated, and, okay, she knew people were probably going to be on her social media, especially if Aisha and Skye were as successful running it as they'd promised they would be, but nothing had prepared her to leave in a haze of scandal. No amount of muting or blocking would have saved her from the avalanche in her mentions.

The least she could do now was turn off push notifications, but she had to check all her apps once to clear the horrible red circles off her screen.

Twitter—792
Instagram—834
TikTok—904

The numbers themselves were wild—enormously large, especially compared to her usual social media activity—but the comments people had felt the need to tag her in . . .

@casmorgan is a fucking SNAKE for real

I can't believe @casmorgan really led actual
goddess @adahall on THIS ENTIRE TIME

fuck @casmorgan and @hotsummer for bringing
her on this year

Her DMs, too, were an absolute nightmare.

And she was an idiot for clicking into them in the first
place, but she couldn't seem to help herself.

There were hundreds of messages.

And if she thought the things that people were saying
about her in public were bad . . . it was nothing compared to
what was waiting in her inbox. But, even so, one could only be
told they're a horrible person who doesn't deserve love, or actively have death wished upon them, so many times before it
started to lose all meaning.

Cas was just about to lock her phone when she noticed an
exchange at the very bottom of her inbox and she felt her heart
stop.

ADA HALL

It wouldn't have really been Ada—her phone was still
locked up somewhere like Cas's had been—but this was her
friends, who had access to her accounts. And they'd been talking to Cas's friends.

The stupidest thing Cas could do right now would be to
click on that thread.

So, naturally, she did so immediately.

There were loads of messages there, usually exchanged as the show was airing, but there was a clear and pretty constant stream of communication. Cas couldn't sit here and read them all—she wasn't going to let herself—but she could . . . skim.

Cas Morgan: I know what they made it seem like in that challenge, but I swear to you, Cas was all in with Ada. I could see it on her face

Ada Hall: I . . . look, I want to believe you, but Ada is crushed. And Cas didn't say anything! There were so many opportunities that she could have spoken up

Cas Morgan: she signed an NDA before she left—she joined HS for a work thing, yes, but I know her feelings for Ada were real

Cas Morgan: she hasn't looked at anyone like that in years

Ada Hall: Have you spoken to her?

Cas Morgan: no not yet—she's supposed to be coming home tomorrow

Ada Hall: hmm

Ada Hall: ok. I want to believe you but . . .

Cas Morgan: I know. But trust me, we'll clear all this up as soon as she gets home. I'll get Cas to reach out to you or something

Cas Morgan: please just talk to Ada. Try and see if
she'd be open to a convo w Cas

Ada Hall: . . . ok

Cas didn't know if that was a great idea, all things considered. Didn't know if it was even worth it.

Ada's friends were making it seem like Ada was all in, like
she was *crushed*, but through the screen, they might have
missed the pure hatred in Ada's eyes when she'd looked at her
back in the villa. Ada hadn't listened, hadn't cared about Cas
enough to believe her.

Angry or not, if Ada'd meant it when she said that she
wanted to be with Cas, she should have given Cas the benefit
of the doubt. Trusted her.

Especially when Cas had put so much trust in her.

Cas scrolled through the rest of the messages, but the earlier ones were hard to read. They'd started a spreadsheet, apparently, trying to find her and Ada a flat (Cas would never
look at that spreadsheet, no matter how much they paid her),
they were celebrating when Cas and Ada had kissed for the
first time outside of a challenge. They thought Cas and Ada
had chemistry. Talked about how they could see it on their
faces.

It was one thing when people inside the villa told Cas that
she obviously had feelings for Ada. When Femi and Sienna
and Freddie made a point to outright say or subtly suggest that
there were feelings there. But for her friends, for Ada's friends,
the people who knew them best in the world to see it?

It made Cas feel like her heart was breaking all over again.

Because, even if there had been something between her and Ada, the fact remained that it was over now. She was alone—she'd flown back alone, was in this car alone, and Ada had had the opportunity to come back with her, to let Cas explain, make amends, but she'd shut the door on that. Forever, as far as Cas was concerned.

In spite of her best efforts to get a handle on herself, Cas felt her emotions ratcheting higher and higher as they approached her flat. It was emotional, seeing these places that were so familiar to her. She hadn't even been gone that long, but each one she passed—the Turkish restaurant on the corner, the pub, the big Sainsbury's—was a reminder that she wasn't in Cyprus anymore. That the moment she stepped out of this car, she was going to be severed from the show entirely.

It was so frustrating, that separation, but also the fact that part of her wished she was back there at all. This show had observed and exploited and manipulated her and here she was, wishing that—

She bit the inside of her lip. Squeezed her phone just to feel something.

If the emotions were powerful driving into Camden, they were overwhelming as they turned down her road. When she spotted the Georgian terraced house, the windows in their top-floor flat thrown open, curtains fluttering in the breeze.

The moment she saw Aisha and Skye, Cas burst into tears.

She hadn't meant to, was actually mortified that it had happened, but the sight of them there, arms outstretched, faces sad . . . Everything sitting just underneath the surface had bubbled over so quickly that Cas didn't have any hope of retaining it.

"Oh, babe."

Aisha was the first to move, Skye about half a second behind. They were so familiar, but it had been so long it was almost nostalgic, seeing them again, smelling Skye's cologne and Aisha's hand cream, feeling their arms around her again. Aisha's arms were around Cas's shoulders, Skye's were around her middle, and they crushed Cas to them as they whispered over and over that it was okay. That they loved her. That they had her.

Cas dropped her bag on the ground with a heavy thud and wrapped her arms around them both, clinging to them like they were in the middle of a vast, bottomless ocean.

They stood in the entry for a long time before, finally, Cas pulled away, wiping her face with her sleeve. "Thanks."

"We missed you," Skye said. They grabbed Cas's bag off the ground and stepped back so Cas could kick off her shoes.

"We really did," Aisha agreed. "How was the flight?"

They both seemed to be walking on glass, sticking to the easiest topics while Cas got through the door. She knew it wouldn't last—Cas might get away with it for a while with Skye, but Aisha was going to let her have it as soon as she thought Cas could handle it—but she appreciated the game of pretend they were all playing.

"Okay." Cas started shuffling down the corridor and Skye and Aisha followed.

"We left your door open," Aisha said, "so it didn't get musty."

"And we gave it a refresh last night," Skye said. They flung Cas's suitcase onto her bed, and now that she was looking, it did look nice in here. Nicer than Cas had left it.

Her pillows had been recently fluffed and the throws she normally had balled at the end of her bed were now artfully draped over her white duvet, the patterns layered so they looked intentional rather than random selections Cas had picked up over the years. Her desk, too, had been dusted, and the assortment of cups and mugs that nearly always lived there or on her bedside table was gone.

"I see you remembered to water my plants," Cas said, nodding toward the collection around her room.

Skye nodded. "I knew you'd kill us if we didn't, so we set up a rotation."

Cas's lips twitched with a smile. "Really?"

Aisha nodded and dropped down into the round wicker chair Cas had in the corner near the window. "It started with passive-aggressively putting the watering can into each other's rooms, but we upgraded to a magnet for the menu board in the kitchen a few weeks ago."

Cas huffed a laugh before moving over to the bed. She intended to open her suitcase, to start unpacking, because the faster she washed the villa off everything, the better. It was easier thought than done, though, because her hands froze on the back of the case.

They were all silent for a few seconds before Skye cleared their throat. "I'll go make tea."

Skye walked off down the corridor, and Cas counted their footsteps before taking a deep breath and, unable to come up with any more reasons not to, unzipped her suitcase.

Aisha watched as Cas flipped open the lid, stopped to stare at the things she'd shoved inside.

"Do you want help?"

Cas shook her head, still just looking at the contents.

Aisha let her process silently for a few seconds before she got quietly to her feet, walked over, and sat down on the other side of Cas's bed.

"So, obviously you're upset," Aisha said. She lifted a handful of clothes off the top and dropped them to the floor.

"What gave you that impression?"

"It's a mystery, for sure."

Cas took out her toiletries bag and set it on her nightstand.

"I mean, yeah, I'm not *thrilled*." She grabbed her trainers and one of her pairs of sandals and threw them toward her wardrobe. "But I'll get over it."

"Will you?"

Aisha's expression was too intense. Too earnest. Cas couldn't look at her, just more shoes onto the floor.

"Look, I'm not saying this to upset you, and I'm sure Skye will kill me—"

"Why will I kill you?" Skye walked in, three mugs of tea balancing between their fingers.

"She's about to confront me about something," Cas said, walking over and grabbing the most precarious mug from Skye's hands.

"There are treats in my pocket," Skye said, nodding at the kangaroo pocket on the front of their hoodie. Cas reached inside as Skye handed Aisha her tea and pulled out an entire packet of ginger biscuits.

Cas raised an eyebrow. "Do we need the whole pack?"

"We probably need two if Aish is confronting you already," Skye said. They plucked the biscuits from Cas's hand, took one for themself before handing one to Cas.

"I just feel like we should get it out of the way," Aisha said, accepting her own biscuit from Skye. "There's no point dancing around it when we're all thinking about it anyway."

"Okay, but we didn't need to bombard her the moment she walked in," Skye said.

"Yeah, but—"

"Guys." Cas held up her free hand. "It's fine. You're right anyway, I'm sure. You usually are."

Aisha flashed Skye a smug smile before dunking her biscuit into her tea. "See."

Skye rolled their eyes. "Anyway, what were you going to say that was going to make me kill you?"

"Just—" Despite her earlier confidence, Aisha seemed a little nervous now. Like she wasn't entirely certain she wanted to say what she was going to say next. "You were really happy with Ada. And I know"—she held her hand up before Cas could even start protesting—"I know, but when she comes back, I really think you need to talk to her."

Cas set her mug down and started tossing clothes out of her suitcase and onto the bed. "There's no point. She made it pretty clear she doesn't want to talk to me."

"It was the heat of the moment," Aisha said. "You both were angry."

"I wasn't angry; I was upset." Her voice cracked on the last word, and she swiftly took a drink of tea to cover it. "I wanted to explain, but she wasn't listening."

"So you decided to run away."

"Aisha—" Skye said, but Cas shook her head.

"I had to leave. They were literally kicking me out the door."

"No, I'm not talking about then. I'm talking about now."

Cas crossed her arms. "How am I running away now?"

"You're already refusing to talk to her when she gets out of the villa. You're the one closing the door."

Skye sighed heavily but, apparently, was going to let this conversation run its course, because they grabbed Cas's toiletries bag and started unpacking it in silence.

"I'm not—" It was actually outrageous, the suggestion. "I'm not *running away*. She doesn't want anything to do with me. You saw it." She pointed angrily out the door, toward the lounge where their television sat. "You heard what she said to me."

"Look." Aisha put her hand on top of Cas's, and though Cas, in her frustration, wanted to pull away, she knew that it came from a kind place. "I'm not trying to piss you off, I just wanted to circumvent all the doom and gloom I know you're about to get up to in this room. Remind you that you've got another option."

It was almost rude, the fact that Aisha knew exactly what she'd been planning on doing the second she finished unpacking.

Cas sighed and sat down on the end of her bed, scooting back so she was half leaning up against her pillows.

"It doesn't really seem like an option, talking to someone who doesn't want to talk to me anymore."

"Only because you're afraid."

"I'm not—"

Aisha held up her hand. "You are. And I know you don't like to hear that or believe that, but you're terrified that Ada refusing to leave the villa with you is the same thing as Saoirse fucking off back home."

As much as Cas wanted to reject the suggestion, there was

no point denying it. She was afraid. Had been since the moment Saoirse had walked out on her.

She'd avoided relationships for years because she was too afraid of the consequences, and now the first time she opened up to someone, it happened again.

"She said she'd come with me if I left." Cas tucked her feet up underneath her, careful to balance her tea on her knee. "She didn't. It's simple."

"You have to see it from her perspective," Aisha said gently. "She thought you never actually cared about her."

"Ada didn't stay behind because she wanted to," Skye added quietly. They'd been so quiet, just listening, that Cas had almost forgotten they were there. "You could see it in her face, her heart was *broken*."

Cas laughed bitterly. "Yeah, well, how do you think I feel?"

In spite of herself, she felt a few tears leak out of the corners of her eyes, and she swiped away at them with her sleeve.

"Like hell?" Aisha guessed, and Cas laughed.

"Yeah, pretty much."

"Look." Aisha slid across the duvet and put her hand on Cas's thigh. "I'm not saying you need to pick yourself up right now. Wallow for a few days. A week, hell." She squeezed Cas's leg and gave her a bracing smile. "But figure out what you're going to do. Even if you don't want to get back together with her, you can't just leave this forever."

"Especially because you're going to have to see her at the reunion," Skye added.

Cas hadn't even thought about that. She groaned and fell back onto the pillows, careful not to slosh her tea.

"Great," Aisha said, "you killed her."

32

CAS TOOK ONLY one part of Aisha's advice seriously at first—she wallowed.

She didn't watch *Hot Summer*, didn't go online, barely even looked outside. She put her phone, her whole life, in metaphorical rice. If she didn't turn it on or look at it or even think about it, then maybe all the poison would get sucked out.

It was wishful thinking, and she knew it, but she'd rather engage in a bit of delusion than face up to the reality of her situation. Especially in those first few days.

Eventually, she mustered up the courage to drag her laptop off her desk and, after wiping the dust off it, switched it on. She was tempted to check her social media, but she forced herself, instead, to just log on to her work email.

Only to find twelve hundred emails sitting in her inbox.

"Jesus fucking Christ." Cas scrolled through her emails, glancing at the subject lines, deleting any that looked suspiciously hateful without even bothering to read them. Far fewer people than she expected had found her work email—a relief, to be sure, but it also made her nervous for the state of her DMs.

She'd just finished scrolling through her email when her inbox pinged with a notification and Cas swiftly jumped back to the top.

From: Robert Doding
Subject: Meeting—Wednesday, 7 August, 11 A.M.

Cas sighed. "Great."
Just what she needed. Another meeting with Robert.

Dear Cas,

I sent you a message via WhatsApp, but it doesn't appear to have delivered. Assuming you still have your phone off, so thought I'd try here. Please come in on Wednesday the 7th at 11 A.M.—I'd like to have a quick chat with you about next steps.

Hope you enjoyed your time off in Cyprus.

See you then,
Robert

Her time *off?*
Cas took a screenshot of the email and pasted it into her group chat with Aisha and Skye:

Cas: HE HOPES I ENJOYED MY TIME OFF!!!!!

Cas: TIME!!!! OFF!!!!!!!!!!!

Skye: . . . you're kidding

Aisha: be SO ffr

It was the first time since she'd come home that Cas was frustrated about something other than her collapsing personal life.

When she exclaimed as much in the group chat, Skye sent a stream of leaf and sparkle emojis.

Skye: Nature is healing

~~~

Cas felt like she blinked and found herself at Wednesday morning, staring at herself in the mirror as she put the last few touches on her eyeliner. She probably didn't need to get all dressed up, probably could have just rolled in, dead eyed and sallow skinned and made Robert confront the reality of her *time off,* but Cas needed to feel like she had something under her control.

Again, delusion. But for a good cause.

She hadn't missed the Northern line—the smell, the sound, the crowd of people who didn't have the slightest idea how to queue for the train—but she felt herself settle into her routine more or less automatically as she made her way through the station. It was a little scary how quickly her body remembered, how, even after nearly two months away, she was able to fall back into her routine like it was the most natural thing in the world. And, because the number one rule of London commuting was to avoid making eye contact at all costs, she made it through without a single person recognizing her.

Jana was sitting behind the desk as always when the lift opened at the office, and she smiled as Cas walked into the lobby.

"Good morning, Cas. You're looking tan."

"Ha. Thanks." Cas unearthed her badge from her crossbody and tapped it on the card reader. "It's the best thing I got this summer."

It wasn't true, she knew it as soon as she said it, but it was too late to take the words back now. Too hurtful to acknowledge what her real favorite part of the summer was.

Jana laughed and shook her head, her fingers clicking away on her keyboard. "You never change."

Robert was sitting behind his desk when Cas walked into his office, fingers hunting and pecking across the keyboard. Cas scanned the view of the city over his shoulder, the sun shining off the buildings in the distance, the glitter of the Thames. It was beautiful here, the exact kind of view she'd been hoping for in an office of her own.

Robert hit ENTER and looked up, his face immediately blossoming into a smile. "Cas. Welcome back. I hope you had a nice summer."

It took a lot of energy not to laugh directly in his face. She sat down, gripped the arms of the chair instead.

"Well, it was nice up until the end, obviously."

"I can imagine," Robert said. "That's part of why I wanted to talk to you today."

This could go one of several ways—he could surprise her and, for once, be genuinely helpful. He could give her some useless advice. He could encourage her to go on Instagram Live or something and "set the record straight." Anything, realistically, could come out of Robert's mouth.

"I got an email from Chloe. They're not happy with how the partnership turned out this year."

"Well, yeah, I'm not exactly thrilled with them, either." Cas should have tried for a more genuine tone, but her ability to contain herself had gone completely out the window. "They pinned this entire situation on me. They still haven't taken responsibility for it."

"You can't have expected them to publicly acknowledge the contract," Robert said. "There's a lot riding on this for them— they don't want people questioning the legitimacy of the show they're running."

"But we're okay with people questioning *my* legitimacy? My intentions?"

"From their perspective," Robert said, "it's better if the damage is contained to one person rather than across the brand as a whole. And, I have to say, it makes sense."

"I—I wasn't even the one who said anything. I understand damage control, but this wasn't on me."

"Regardless of who's at fault, someone has to take the fall. And, unfortunately, you're the person closest to the situation."

Cas couldn't keep the disdain out of her voice. "This is unbelievable. I was only there because *you* asked me to be."

After all the years she'd given this place—all the late nights and long hours and last-minute event plans that got dumped on her head—they weren't willing to fight for her. To take responsibility for the situation that they put her in.

"I mean, ultimately, you did agree. And, I think, given the state of your relationship with *Hot Summer* and your public position at the minute, it would be best if we held off on installing you in your new role for a few months."

Cas felt like an anvil had been dropped on her head. "What?"

"A large part of the position is the ability to make connections with these brands," Robert said, and from his tone of voice, you might have thought he was talking to a child. "Someone smack in the middle of a public scandal like this isn't going to be able to do that effectively, and we need to get this office off the ground. We're going to set George in charge in the interim, but you should be okay to take over by the beginning of next year, as long as everything has passed."

Cas really didn't like how many conditionals there were in that sentence.

And to be replaced by George of all people? He was one of the least organized, most annoying people in events.

"So I *should* be able to take over *if* everything has been sorted?" She was livid and didn't bother hiding it. "And how's everything supposed to get sorted if you all aren't addressing it publicly?"

"That seems to be the best way to navigate these kinds of situations," Robert said. He wasn't making eye contact now, instead staring at something on his computer screen. "If you don't address it publicly, either, it should just go away."

"So then the entire public will just forever think I tried to game the system to trick people into sponsoring me or whatever the hell they're saying about me."

"Does it really matter if they don't know the truth?" Robert asked. "As long as the people in your real life know your intentions?"

He probably hadn't meant to, but his words were eerily reminiscent of the things Ada used to tell her in the early rankings. That they knew her, they loved her. That she didn't need to take public opinion into account because the people who really mattered understood.

But in this case, the people who really mattered *didn't* understand. She couldn't leave this unaddressed. Couldn't move forward until she fixed things.

Robert seemed to take her silence as assent, because he just carried on talking. "Like I said, we'll circle back on this in a few months' time. You should be more than able to go back into events in the meantime."

Events. Fucking *events*.

"Well, if we're not going to take this seriously . . ." Cas unclipped her badge from her jeans loop and tossed it onto Robert's desk. "I quit."

~~~

Cas was almost giddy as she walked out of the building. Giddy in that uncontrollable kind of way, like she was so overwhelmed by her feelings that she couldn't sit still. She didn't have anywhere to go, didn't have anything to do, but she needed to walk. Get this energy out of her system.

One of the best parts of having an events job was that she didn't have a desk to clean out. She could just throw her badge on the desk and walk out, as if she were in some kind of film and this was the dramatic moment. But it felt strange, too, that she could leave this place she'd worked at for half a decade without having to pack a box or even so much as pick up her mug from the staff kitchen.

Even when she'd had no plans to leave Friday, she'd clearly been careful to avoid making any actual connections to the place. Setting down any roots.

A theme in her life up until recently, apparently.

She'd just got to the nearest corner when her phone started vibrating in her pocket. *Robert.* Cas ignored it, ignored it again when he called three seconds later, and finally just switched it off vibrate altogether.

Robert could keep calling her. She wasn't going to answer. She didn't owe him anything anymore.

It was an exhilarating thought, but also a really fucking terrifying one.

As the adrenaline started to wear off, the terror began to take over and Cas needed to go somewhere, anywhere, to just sit down. Get her head together. There was a park not too far away from her office building—her old office building—and she found her way back there easily enough.

It wasn't a large park; it was little more than a few basketball courts, a fairly large bit of grass, and some benches, but it would do. One of the great benefits of city living: She could sit on any bench and freak out about the state of her life without causing a scene.

She chose one of the benches at the far end of the park under the shade of one of the large trees, and pulled her phone out of her pocket as she sat down. There were a few people playing basketball on the courts at the end of the square, and Cas listened to the squeak of their trainers on the pavement, their shouts of laughter as one of them missed a shot.

She had seven MISSED CALL notifications from Robert. Cas didn't even consider them for half a second before she swiped and erased them from her home screen.

Cas's phone lit up again, this time, thankfully, with a message from Aisha.

> **Aisha:** I know you're still in a place about
> this and I cannot vouch for the source
> because I don't think anyone should be
> spending this kind of time editing you BUT

Aisha had attached a link below and, though the preview hadn't loaded, Aisha's description of it was enough for Cas to worry. What could Aisha possibly have sent that involved some sort of viewer edit?

Her browser took a few seconds to load the link, and when it did, she felt her heart start hammering in her chest again.

> **@toffeetay:** Cas and Ada are the Cutest Couple
> in #HotSummer History, You Guys are Just Haters:
> A Thread

There were more than a dozen posts in the thread, and each and every one was a picture or a GIF of Cas and Ada. Cas looking at Ada as they got out of their Jeeps on the first day. Cas getting a smudge of ice cream off the corner of Ada's lip. Ada diving into Cas's bed in one of the early weeks, Cas and Ada laughing on the striped pool float, Ada throwing a pair of socks at Cas's head when she was complaining way too loudly about being cold. Ada kissing Cas in the orchard.

It had been easy to convince herself in the days since she left Cyprus that everything with Ada had been her invention. That her experience of their relationship didn't match up with reality. But seeing it now playing out again in front of her, even in these highlights, it was impossible to ignore the real chemistry between them.

Impossible not to see the real love in Cas's eyes as she looked at Ada.

Cas watched the last GIF—Ada kissing her good night on their last night together in the villa—before she clicked back into WhatsApp.

> **Cas:** Is that what you guys were all seeing???
>
> **Aisha:** YES
>
> **Aisha:** do you see what we were saying now?
>
> **Cas:** Yeah, actually, I do
>
> **Aisha:** so . . . what are you going to do about it?

There was really only one thing she could do now, wasn't there?

> **Cas:** I'm going to stop running away

#HotSummer—Live Updates

> **@topsyturvey:** this reunion better be good or i stg
>
> **@sprinkleofsparkles:** don't know why you have hope they've been terrible for the last 3yrs

@topsyturvey: 😭😭😭 then why tf do we keep watching

@sprinkleofsparkles: we hate ourselves.

@zoeybug: ok but they have to bring Cas back for the reunion

@pixelpenguin: honestly they probably won't

@SaraSays: yeah they literally dropped her as quickly as humanly possible

@infinitescroll: @HotSummer bring Cas back—we need to hear her side

@taliatells: 💀💀💀 you actually think that's going to work

@averyart: no but seriously they just sent Cas off, we DO need to hear from her

@hypernautical: bring Cas back for the Hot Summer reunion!!! #HotSummer @HotSummer

@farahfinesse: there's literally no point in watching if they don't bring Cas back

@retroretorgrade: should we boycott???

@HotSummer ✓: Ready for the reunion, lovers? We have a few special surprises lined up . . . 👀

FROM HER VANTAGE point in the corner, Cas could see no fewer than a dozen people running around backstage.

She couldn't see the soundstage from where she was sitting, but she could hear the crowd—the laughter, the conversation, the shuffling as people got to their seats. They were all anxiously awaiting the reunion, hoping, probably, that the drama that would unfold would be worth the time it had taken them to come into Central London on a Friday night.

If Cas weren't waiting in the wings, planning to surprise most everyone there, she would have bet that this reunion would have been just as boring and pointless as all the other reunions for the last decade.

Cas didn't know who knew, beyond the production staff, that she was going to be there. It should have been a foregone conclusion—she was on the show for almost the entire summer, she shouldn't have to fight to be on the reunion—but with the way she'd left, Chloe had insisted time and time again that there would be a lot of pushback if the audience even *thought* they were going to see her face at the reunion.

Cas still didn't know why Chloe had caved in the end, but having got her way, she wasn't going to question it.

Cas was assuming, too, that they hadn't told the lovers that she was attending, probably in the hopes of some dramatic reaction shots, but it put her in an awkward situation over the past week. Once everyone else returned home, she had debated reaching out directly to her friends over DM to apologize. She wanted them to know how sorry she was, and to give them a heads-up that she planned to clarify a few things at the reunion.

Uncertain of how they'd react, she'd decided against it, but just barely. She was still arguing with herself about it now as she sat there, tucked away in the corner, turning her phone over in her hands.

She'd done everything she could to make herself feel ready for tonight. Skye had helped her reach out to brands on social media and, after a couple of promising DMs back and forth, had sourced a dress for the night. It was white (*Perfect if you're trying to convince everyone you're innocent,* Aisha had said) with a slit so high that Cas had had to buy special underwear for the occasion. The top had corset detail and fit Cas like a second skin.

It wasn't the most comfortable dress to sit in, but it looked gorgeous when she was up on her feet.

"There's no way Ada will be able to take her eyes off you," Skye had said as they were helping get Cas ready for the night.

It was a pipe dream, probably, this idea that Ada would be transfixed by her, but it was one Cas had clung to in the car on the way to the studio.

Now Cas tried her best not to smooth her sweaty hands

along the dress, instead running them along the leather jacket she'd slung over the back of her chair.

The producers were still running around a few minutes later when the lights in the studio went up, and on the screen a few meters away, Cas saw Mila walk onto the stage in a gorgeous skintight black dress with a maze of cutouts. She hit her mark on the stage and posed for a long minute, hands on her hips, just beaming at the camera before she finally started speaking.

"Welcome to the *Hot Summer* reunion. I'm Mila Sexton, and I'm so excited that you're all able to be here tonight!" Mila held for applause, grinning at the camera as the audience cheered. "We have some big surprises in store for you tonight, but first, let's start with a look back at our summer in Cyprus."

They cut to a long montage of all the best moments from the villa, and Cas felt surprisingly nostalgic as she watched. She expected she'd be cut from the footage given the way she left, but she kept catching glimpses of herself—she was there in the arrival section, in the background during the obstacle course event, they showed Ada grinding on her during the nurse challenge. She saw, for the first time, clips from Rita and Charlie's hot air balloon date, Sienna and Femi's dinner on the beach at Aphrodite's Rock, and, of course, the two of them winning it all at the finale. It was bizarre, seeing these moments, many of which she'd lived through, from another perspective, outside of the context of her own memory.

When the montage was over, Mila busied herself with talking to some of the lovers who had spent the least amount of time in the villa—Maddison was up first, and, for someone eliminated in the first week, she was all laughs and smiles in her bright pink dress. Lexi was brought up in the middle of Maddison's interview, and the two of them shared a heartfelt reunion that drew a strong round of applause from the audience. Reece and Tia gave their interview and though there was a bit of suspicious distance between them on the sofa, they both denied that anything was wrong when Mila asked about it.

Although Cas definitely noticed that Tia's hand twitched away from Reece's on the walk back to their seats.

"Now"—Mila's voice was lower, more intense—"we want to talk about one of the most dramatic and controversial moments of the summer."

Cas's heart started hammering in her throat. This was it.

She could do it. She was nervous as hell, but she could do it.

"In order to start us off"—Cas expected to see a cameraperson approach her, but was surprised, instead, to see the camera moving through the tables where the lovers were sat—"let's talk to Ada. Ada, would you mind coming up onstage?"

Suddenly, Ada was there on the screen and she was gorgeous. *God,* she was gorgeous, in a one-shoulder, royal blue, figure-hugging full-length dress that popped against her freckled skin. Her face was highlighted to the heavens, and combined with her dark smoky eye and subtle pink lip, she looked like a siren ready to drag Cas straight into the sea.

Cas was up on her feet before her better judgment could take over. Was out in the wings, at the corner of the soundstage before her brain caught up with her feet.

This was a terrible idea. She should wait until she was called. Until Ada said her piece. Because maybe Ada didn't want to hear from her, maybe Ada was *glad* that Cas was out of her life.

But she was already halfway out now and some of the audience had clocked her.

"Oh my god, is that *Cas*?"

"Cas is here?"

The whispers seemed to carry through the audience, down to the lovers' tables, to Mila on the stage. Cas stood there, still frozen in the corner, but she saw Freddie stand up, neck craning, his eyes blowing wide when he spotted her standing there. He turned around and shouted something—Cas couldn't hear what—but Femi stood up next, his eyes immediately locking on Cas's.

And, thank god, his whole face brightened.

He smiled and waved, and immediately started tapping Sienna on the shoulder. She stood, and though her own smile was more guarded, it was there.

And that was all Cas needed to see to know that she was doing the right thing.

"Wait." Cas wasn't sure if her mic was on, but if it wasn't, she was certain they were hitting all the buttons to make sure it was as she spoke. "Before you talk to Ada, I have a few things I need to say."

Mila only stumbled for a second, but she recovered quickly.

"Cas Morgan, everyone." She gestured toward Cas, inviting her onstage, and the crowd applauded. There were a few scattered boos—to be expected—but it was far less than she would have thought. Most people were probably too stunned to see her there to work out how to respond appropriately, but, whatever.

Cas moved as quickly across the soundstage as her towering heels and dangerously high slit would allow. Mila extended her hand to help Cas clear the step onto the stage, and as Cas turned to sit on the neon pink couch, her eyes immediately found Ada at the other end.

Her mouth was hanging open with surprise, but her expression was guarded. Uncertain. She didn't look angry to see Cas, more like she wasn't quite sure what to do about it yet.

And, you know what? Cas would take it.

"So, Cas," Mila said, settling into her own chair, this one neon blue. "You said you had a few things to say."

She knew she needed to be careful, but she had spent hours combing through her NDA with her friends to figure out exactly where the lines were. She ran through the list of permissible things again in her head and took a deep breath.

"Everyone knows that I left the show in week seven and, as it's since come out on social media that I used to work for Friday, a dating app—"

Mila sat up a little straighter. "'Used to'?"

She was walking a very thin line here and made sure to choose her words carefully. "I left after it became clear that we had very different perspectives on how to address this."

Mila nodded slowly, her fingers drifting, almost subconsciously, toward her earpiece. Cas could only imagine the things the producers were saying now that Cas was a little too close to throwing them under the bus.

"Anyway, Friday had entered into an agreement with *Hot*

Summer because they're interested in building connections with broadcast programs." She had never been more grateful for the Twitter sleuths than she was in this moment; she never would have been able to say this publicly if they hadn't already uncovered it and released it. "I can't confirm behind-the-scenes conversations for legal reasons I'm sure people can understand, but I wanted to set the record straight. As much as I can."

"What do you think is unclear?"

"People seemed to think that my goal remained the same throughout the summer. That the *only* reason I was still in the villa was because of an agreement between production and my former employer. That I was manipulating Ada somehow in order to stay until the finale." Cas could feel the audience watching her, but she refused to take her eyes off Ada. She was only speaking to Ada anyway. Only cared what Ada thought about what she had to say.

"What other reason could you possibly have?" Mila asked.

"My relationships. I made real, hopefully lifelong friends in the villa." She looked to them now, Femi and Freddie beaming at her, Sienna, still reserved, but growing a little warmer. "They're people I never would have met on the outside, and after spending hours and hours with them, they became some of my best friends. It broke my heart to leave without getting to explain everything fully to them, and I hope they know that the minute they're ready to talk about it, I'm ready to tell them everything."

"You're already forgiven!" Freddie shouted, and Cas couldn't help the laugh that bubbled out of her. A matching laugh rippled through the audience, and as Cas looked, she saw more and more people who seemed open to what she was saying.

"More than anything, though," she said, turning back to Mila, "it was my feelings for Ada that motivated me. I think anyone who watched me with Ada knows that the minute I saw her, everything became genuine for me. I was never manipulating her, all of that was real. Terrifyingly real."

Cas let her eyes find Ada again, and she tried to put every single emotion she'd ever felt into her gaze. To make Ada really feel, really understand, just how much Cas meant what she was saying.

"I know I said it on the show a few times, but I really struggle with opening up, with being vulnerable. And when I went on *Hot Summer*, I didn't think that was going to change. But the more I got to know Ada, and the more I fell for her, the more I wanted to tell her. The more I needed her to know me. It wasn't about trying to stay on the show longer or get better rankings. I don't know if you remember, but when my rankings started to improve, I actually freaked out. I didn't want Ada to think that that was the only reason I was opening up to her and exploring our connection."

Cas took a deep breath before she continued. "I won't lie, the truth of the situation is really messy," she said, turning back to Mila. "It's complicated, and I know it's easy to boil it all down to the idea that 'I was just there for work and none of the connections were real,' but from the moment I got there, it was instantly more layered than that."

"Why do you think so many viewers were so quick to believe the narrative, though?" Mila asked.

"I recognize that my own comfort on the show changed and shifted over time, and that may have looked suspicious to people. Part of that is just the way in which I open up, but I think when my own company and *Hot Summer* didn't bother to contradict any growing rumors, I think it spoke volumes to people." This was outright combative of her and she knew it. "They allowed people to believe a version of events that suited them, even if it made me out to be someone I'm not. Even if it made my relationships appear false."

Mila's mouth opened to say something, but Cas barreled on. Refused to let herself be contradicted.

"And I think—you know, as someone who's watched this show every summer—we see people every year who are obviously only there because they want the brand deals at the end of it. I think that makes viewers skeptical of people's motivations. And, after all, you don't know me, what reason would you have to believe me when I say that, yeah, I wasn't there for love originally, but I ended up staying because of it? It's easier to believe the lie you're being sold when the truth isn't nearly as dramatic."

This was the last bit. The hardest bit. She caught Ada's eyes again, and in that moment, there was no one else in the entire world.

"I didn't go on *Hot Summer* to find someone, but I did. I found someone who changed me for life, and I don't say this to pressure you, Ada, but I need you to know the truth. If you want to be friends, if you never want to talk to me again, it's whatever you want. But it was never about deceiving you—I was always, am still, head over heels for you."

"Well," Mila said, clapping her hands together. The sound snapped Cas to attention, and her head whipped around. Her smile was tight and Cas was preparing to get unceremoniously chucked offstage when Mila said, "Since we're making dramatic declarations to Ada right now, there's one more person who I'd like to bring out before we hear from Ada herself."

As soon as Mila said it, Cas knew who was going to be walking out onto the stage, but she still couldn't believe it. Couldn't believe that, after all this time, after everything he'd said and done, that they'd bring him out right now.

The boos were so loud that Cas didn't hear when Mila said his name. Mila gestured toward the opposite wing, and in spite of herself, Cas looked over to see Brad walking out. His blond hair was slicked back, he was wearing a too-tight baby blue button-up shirt tucked into gray trousers, and he walked out like he was holding the world in his hands; clearly production had been planning to bring him out this entire time. Even after the show had ended, they just wanted to twist them all around for maximum drama. Cas jumped up before he could even approach the stage—they would get a picture of her sharing a stage with Brad over her dead body.

Only to freeze after about five steps when Ada shouted her name.

"Cas." Ada looked pointedly at the camera now barely a meter from her face. "Meet me outside?"

Cas didn't even hesitate before tearing her microphone off and handing it to the producer standing, slack-jawed, staring at her, and fucking hell, Ada smiled.

Ada didn't even spare a glance for Brad on the stage before she walked out to meet Cas in the wings.

ADA CALLED A car the moment they stepped onto the pavement.

"I feel like we need to get out of here," Ada said, rocking back and forth on her heels, arms crossed in an attempt to stay warm. It was unseasonably cold for mid-August, but especially so after weeks spent in Cypriot sun. "I keep thinking they're going to bust out this door any second and drag us back into the studio."

"I wouldn't be surprised." Cas pulled off her leather jacket and draped it across Ada's shoulders, and Ada smiled gratefully at her.

"Aren't you cold?"

"No," Cas lied, and she immediately shivered, giving herself away.

Ada rolled her eyes, a smile tugging at the corners of her lips, and though she didn't return Cas's jacket, she did step into Cas's side, let her share a bit of body heat.

They stood there, the silence genuinely awkward for the

first time since they'd met. A car horn beeped a few streets away, there was an ambulance off in the distance, and it was strange, seeing Ada in this context, out in the real world.

"Can you believe they brought Brad out?" Ada said. She was scowling at the office building opposite them, the traffic signal lights reflected in the glass. "What the fuck were they expecting?"

"You to forgive him, I guess."

"Right." Ada kicked a pebble with her shoe and they both watched as it bounced into the road. "He called me a fucking whore on national television. He can choke."

A black sedan pulled up outside the studio, the red lights flashing bright against the pavement. Ada stepped forward to check the number plate before opening the back door.

"Who are you here for?"

"Ada?"

"Okay, cool." Ada stepped back and held the door, gesturing for Cas to go in first. "That's us."

Neither of them spoke as they drove. The traffic of Central London was stop-and-go until they hit about Whitechapel, then it thinned out, albeit slightly, as they continued east. Ada's flat was in Mile End, just off Regent's Canal, and she added a tip to her drive request as they stepped out onto the pavement.

Ada was carrying a small bag, little more than the size of her palm, but she just managed to stuff her phone inside after removing her key.

"We're upstairs," Ada said quietly, bending to grab the mail out of the basket inside the door. She stuffed it under her arm as she unlocked her flat door and they made their way upstairs.

"My flatmates are out," Ada said. She grabbed the banister

at the top of the stairs, using it to balance as she took off her heels.

"What are your flatmates' names?" Cas asked. She set her shoes along the wall near the piles of trainers just inside the door.

"Shan and Elsie." Ada tossed the mail onto the small side table before sliding out of Cas's jacket. She half extended her arm like she was going to hand it back to Cas before she froze. "Do you . . . Are you cold?"

When Cas shook her head, Ada hung the jacket on the hooks over the shoe rack.

It was so awkward, almost unbearably so. Even in the best of circumstances, Cas knew that it would likely be a bit weird, being in each other's actual houses after so long in the villa together. Getting used to all the idiosyncrasies of each other's actual lives. Cas and Ada had the added bonus of not even knowing what they were to each other at this point.

Cas didn't know if things were okay or if she needed to brace herself for another emotional sucker punch.

"I'm going to run to my room and put my shoes away," Ada said, breaking the silence. "You can take a seat. Make yourself comfortable."

Ada switched on a lamp in the living room as she disappeared farther into the flat, the creak of a door the only thing announcing that she'd reached her destination. Cas hesitated for a moment longer before she took a deep breath.

"You're fine," she whispered to herself. "Just go sit down."

Ada's living room was small, but about what Cas would have expected for a flat in Central London, and certainly no smaller than her own. They had a gray L-shaped sofa and a collection of furniture that was just mix-match enough to feel intentionally eclectic. They had a white-tiled end table with a wavy iron lamp on the side closest to the door, the pink shade diffusing the light so it gave a soft glow to the room. The coffee table was reclaimed wood and iron, and in the center, there was a plant in a mirrorball planter that reflected the lamplight around the room so tiny rainbows shot across the walls. They had a small shelf with some art hanging above the sofa, a few more plants and a smaller cement lamp on the window ledge over the radiator. There were stacks of books and board games in the corner, a pile of Switch games under the television stand. It was the kind of place that Cas would have gladly spent hours of her life.

She'd just sat down on the edge of the sofa when Ada walked back out of her bedroom, and Cas immediately hopped to her feet again.

"No, no, sit down," Ada said, waving her down. "Can I get you some tea? Water?"

"You don't have to do that," Cas said automatically, but Ada just shot her a look.

"I'm having tea. So if you want some, it's really no trouble."

"Well, if you're having some." A cup of tea would actually be nice right now. Would give her something to do with her hands.

Ada returned a few minutes later, perfectly prepared cups of tea in hand. She passed one to Cas before taking a seat, her own mug cradled in her lap.

"Thanks," Cas said, wrapping her hands around the mug. The tea was warm against her palms, and the first sip soothed the nerves jangling about in her chest.

Neither of them said anything for a few long moments. Cas kept her gaze trained on the coffee table, keen to avoid staring at Ada, but all the time, she could feel Ada's gaze on her.

After a long minute, Ada cleared her throat. "So that was a surprise."

Cas exhaled a laugh, another huge chunk of tension falling off her shoulders.

"They weren't going to let me come to the reunion at first," she said. She took another sip of tea before setting it on her knee, the heat against her skin a reminder to stay focused.

"I can't imagine they were keen to have you there given what you said tonight," Ada said. She let that sit there for a second before she added, "I'm glad you were there, though."

The relief in Cas's chest was immediate. Overwhelming. Like she'd just come to the surface after a long time underwater and was taking her first deep breath.

"I hated that I couldn't tell you," Cas said. "There were so many times that it was on the tip of my tongue and I had to stop myself at the last second."

"Would you have told me if we weren't on camera all the time?"

"I thought about telling you in the retreat," Cas admitted. "But I'd signed an NDA. I didn't even know what I was allowed to say at that point."

Ada hummed, didn't say anything. Took a sip of her tea.

"In a way," Cas said, turning the mug around in her hands, "it was for the best that the news broke online. That I wasn't the one to reveal it. I spent a *lot* of time rereading that agreement when I got home—since it became public knowledge at no fault of my own, it's really freed up how much I can talk about."

"So what exactly was the goal, then? I haven't been reading any of it online."

"Some of this is still technically covered by the NDA," Cas said, "so I can tell you, but—"

"If it'll get you into trouble, I don't want you to feel like you have to tell me," Ada said, but Cas was already shaking her head.

"No, I want to be completely honest with you," she said. "I just wanted you to know that not *everything* is public knowledge, so it just has to stay between us."

Ada nodded, and Cas took a deep breath.

Where to begin?

She took Ada back to the very beginning—her first meeting with Robert, the division Friday was planning on opening, her tragic years spent in pub basements getting sweated on by strangers.

"I'd been applying to every single internal opportunity that came up for the last, like, four years, but every single time I was passed up for someone with less experience because Robert 'couldn't bear' to lose me in events. When this opportunity dropped into my lap, I think I would've done just about anything to make it a reality."

"I can see that," Ada said, and then her cheeks went pink. "Sorry. I didn't mean that in, like, a shitty way. I just meant that I can imagine. I probably would've, too."

"I was so obsessed with how I appeared that first week," Cas said. "I was constantly thinking about how they were filming shots, what I was saying, what I was doing . . . It was overwhelming. And then we got the rankings and I was in last place, and it was like someone had punched me right in the chest."

"Everything you'd done hadn't worked. People didn't like you."

"Exactly," Cas said. "But then you came to find me that night and you told me that it didn't matter what they thought. That you all, well, loved me anyway." The word was heavy on Cas's tongue, weighted with all the potential they'd probably lost. "And, I don't know. I still wanted the job and to make it to the finale to get it, but over time, I cared more about you guys. I wanted my friends in the villa to actually like me for me. To care about me because of who I was, rather than some social strategy."

"It wasn't about the job anymore."

Cas nodded. "Sometimes, I genuinely forgot why I was on the show. And it wasn't until the rankings after our night together that I realized what I'd gotten myself into," Cas said. "When I got third, I panicked. I knew we'd have to talk about Friday and the partnership eventually, and I was certain you'd think I was just using you to get ahead. My feelings were never anything but genuine, but I don't know . . ." She pressed her palms into her mug, let the heat sear into her skin. "I thought I'd at least be able to tell you on my own terms. I was terrified of what you might think."

Neither of them needed to say what happened next. All of Cas's worst nightmares had come true. Her relationship with Ada looked like nothing more than a game play. And Ada believed it.

Cas had opened up to someone for the first time in years and the entire thing blew up in her face.

"So the agreement was that you get to the finale?" Ada asked.

Cas nodded. "Finalists always have their pick of brand endorsements. My boss wasn't naïve enough to think I could win, but making it that far would open a lot of doors we could then leverage for the new division he was setting up."

"Hmm, okay." Ada took a slow, considered sip of her tea before leaning forward and setting the mug on the coffee table. "So you up there tonight," Ada said thoughtfully. "Was that some sort of . . . grand gesture?"

"More or less."

They were quiet for a beat, and then, slowly, Ada slid a few inches across the sofa. She wasn't anywhere near to touching Cas, but she was almost as close as they had been in the back of the car.

"I think it was really brave of you, you know. Coming on to the reunion when you knew the audience would probably be against you."

"I just needed to tell you the truth. I didn't want you to feel like I was trying to pressure you into saying anything to me because we were on camera, but I didn't think there was another opportunity I would get to tell you."

"I didn't feel like that. I was glad that you said something," Ada said. She stared down at her lap for a long beat. "I'd been thinking about reaching out to you, actually."

"Were you?"

Ada nodded. "I don't know if they ended up putting it on air, but Femi talked to me."

"Did he?"

"I don't know if I was in the place to hear it at the time. I just said that you could have been honest with me, no matter what, was still stomping my foot, frustrated, you know." She waved her hand. "But it really settled over me as the week wore on. I was barely sleeping by the time we got to the end."

Cas almost wished she had watched the rest of the show now. If only because she'd driven herself mad thinking that Ada hadn't been missing her at all.

"Really?"

"I should have left with you," Ada said quietly. "I hate that I let you walk out that door alone."

"I thought you'd given up on me," Cas admitted. She was staring at her distorted reflection in the mirrorball, begging the tears in the corners of her eyes not to fall. "You're . . . you're the first person I've let in in a really long time. I wasn't lying when I said that you made me feel safe being vulnerable again. I know why you didn't leave with me, but it was really awful, walking out of there on my own."

Ada reached over then and threaded her fingers through Cas's. It was a simple gesture, nothing they hadn't done a thousand times before, but it felt like everything was finally clicking into place.

"I'm sorry," Ada said quietly, and Cas squeezed her hand.

"I'm sorry, too."

They sat there for a long minute, just holding hands, listening to the muffled sounds of the cars on the road outside.

"Do you think we'll be able to move on?" Cas asked finally. She was still staring at the mirrorball, as though it would make the words any easier to say. "I'll be nothing but honest. If we can forgive each other and want to start again or pick up where we left off. Or even just figure out what our relationship looks like now. No more keeping anything from each other, I promise."

"I can forgive you," Ada whispered. "I already had, really."

Cas looked up and met Ada's gaze. The pink light softened her features, but the intensity in her eyes still felt dark. Tantalizing.

"I really, *really* like you," Cas said. She was laying her heart bare, setting it out there, ready for the taking, and just crossing her fingers that Ada didn't leave her out to dry.

Tentatively, Ada moved one hand to Cas's thigh, and the heat of her palm seemed to sear through the fabric of Cas's dress. "I really, *really* like you, too."

And without a moment's hesitation, Cas leaned forward and kissed her.

Ada's response was immediate. Her free hand slid to the back of Cas's neck, crushing her closer, and it was heady, the way that Ada wanted her. How she wore it so plainly on her sleeve, didn't try to hide it or disguise it or pretend it was anything other than the raw, intense feeling that it was.

It felt like no time had passed at all, like nothing had ever come between them. It was as easy as it always was kissing Ada, but now, without a dozen cameras watching them?

It was going to be way too easy for Cas to lose herself here.

"Do you . . ." Ada's breath caught as Cas pressed a kiss to her jaw, her throat. "Do you want to go to my room?"

Oh, thank *god*.

ADA'S BEDROOM WAS at the far end of the flat, on its own behind the kitchen and the bathroom. It overlooked the garden, and the door squeaked just a little when Ada pushed it open.

The minute they stepped inside, Cas started scanning the space, trying to take it all in.

"This looks exactly like what I would have expected," Cas said.

"What do you mean?"

"Like, this just feels *right*, looking at it and knowing you."

The room was an explosion of plants and color, with soft hand-knit touches that added additional warmth. She had fairy lights twisted around the curtain rod and woven in the book-shelf in the corner, and though they were off at the minute, Ada's room would be remarkably cozy if they were switched on.

"Thanks. It took me forever to get it looking how I wanted it."

Ada sat down on the edge of her bed and reached back to

unzip her dress. The fabric loosened across her chest, the single strap sliding forward so she could slip her arm free.

And suddenly Cas's mouth was dry.

"This dress was cute," Ada said, "but, hell, so tight." She wasn't wearing a bra, just nipple pasties that she promptly peeled off and, as Cas saw when Ada shimmied the dress down over her hips, high-waisted nude underwear.

She leaned over, draped her dress along the stools at the end of her bed, and Cas took a step forward into the room.

"Can I . . . ?"

Ada's eyes were on Cas as she reached up and took her simple gold hoops out of her ears. She set them in a small dish on her bedside table, and with a nod, she leaned back onto her hands, her body stretching long and languid.

And she knew, she knew what she was doing to Cas. Letting Cas see the way her body moved, trace the lines of her in the light from the streetlamp streaming in through the window. This was everything, *everything*, Cas wanted when they'd been in the villa.

Ada sat up as she reached her, her hands sliding up to the base of Cas's neck as Cas leaned down and kissed her. Cas couldn't touch enough of her. She trailed her fingers over Ada's collarbone, down the curve of her shoulder, along the dips and curves of her waist.

"Cas." Her name was a whisper on Ada's breath, and it sent a shiver down her spine in the best way. Cas brushed her thumb over Ada's nipple, and Ada bit her lip, her breathing picking up as Cas dropped to her knees in front of her.

The rug was soft, thankfully, against her knees. Cas leaned forward and pressed a kiss, two, to Ada's stomach, her fingers rolling softly over Ada's nipple as she moved. She put her free hand on Ada's thigh, and pushed her legs apart in a single, swift motion. Ada drew in a sharp breath, her fingers moving, in anticipation, to Cas's hair.

"You're gorgeous," Cas said, her palm sliding over Ada's thigh, pushing her leg up onto the bed. She was glistening wet and Cas felt like she could already taste her, the memory of her, on her tongue.

Cas wanted to tease her—to tease herself—but it was impossible when Ada was spread out in front of her like that.

Still, she forced herself to move slowly, to linger, before she trailed her tongue over Ada's clit.

Ada's fingers tightened in Cas's hair and she groaned, her hips arching immediately off the bed. Cas went in again, slow, gentle circles at first, each one drawing a breathy moan out of Ada's mouth.

"That feels so good," Ada said. She moved one of her hands to her breast, her fingers rolling over her nipple.

Cas sucked her clit lightly, and Ada moaned again, louder this time. She kept the suction light for a minute, alternating between drawing slow, languid circles on Ada's clit, before she increased the pressure. Ada's leg scrambled along the edge of the bed before hooking over Cas's shoulders, pressing her closer, and Cas exhaled hard, the sensation sending a shiver through Ada.

Ada's entire body went stiff as Cas moved to curl her fingers inside her and her back arched up off the bed. She trembled, her fingers loosening in Cas's hair as her hands flew to her breasts, pinching and kneading as she rode out her orgasm.

Cas didn't dare move, didn't dare stop, just slowed and

eased her suction as Ada came down. She drew her tongue in lazy circles over Ada's clit before she leaned back onto her heels.

"Could you go again? Do you want to use a vibrator?"

Ada was nodding before Cas even finished asking.

"In the drawer." Ada was panting. It looked like she tried to push herself up onto her elbows but, ultimately, decided she didn't have the energy and pointed vaguely in the direction of her bedside table.

Cas went to open the drawer, but it got stuck at half a centimeter.

"Uh, Ada."

"You have to jiggle it," Ada said. She picked up one hand and wiggled it back and forth to demonstrate. "It's never really opened properly, but I got it for free and it's cute, so I'm just dealing with it."

It was typical Ada, seeing the good in slightly broken things. Cas wiggled the drawer and it popped open, suddenly sliding out several inches.

The drawer was deep, and behind the remotes and jars of face and lip mask and ChapSticks, there was a small pouch with a few condoms sticking out and a larger zipped pouch. Cas grabbed the zippered pouch and set it on the end of the bed. Ada pressed up onto her forearms and watched as Cas unzipped the bag, and, one by one, pulled out her vibrator options.

"That one is so good," she said, nodding at the suction vibrator Cas set on the duvet. There was a bright pink bullet, a light blue teardrop-shaped vibrator, but her eyes brightened as Cas took out the yellow, curved vibrator with what looked like a small tennis ball stuck to the end. "But oh, that one. Use that one."

Cas didn't need to be told twice. She threw the other vibrators back into the bag and, after hastily zipping it up, returned it to the drawer and closed it with her hip.

"I'm going to wash it quickly," she said, getting to her feet.

"There's cleaner in the cabinet under the sink," Ada said. She fell back onto the bed, her arms splaying wide. And like that, spread out, still sopping wet, Cas wanted to forget the vibrator altogether, wrap her arms around Ada's hips, and bury her face between Ada's thighs for the rest of the evening.

Cas was glad none of Ada's housemates were home as she ran out of Ada's bedroom, brandishing a vibrator on her way to the bathroom. She washed it quickly with the silicone cleanser underneath the sink and, after taking care to pat it dry, practically ran back to the bedroom.

Ada was trailing her fingers over her body as Cas walked in, her touch casual, light. She had been tracing her fingers over her nipple when Cas first walked through the door but, as Cas made her way to the bed, her fingers traveled down over her stomach before drifting in between her legs. Cas watched, her breath tight, as Ada's fingers tripped over her clit. She moaned softly at the first bit of contact and dragged her right leg up onto the bed.

"Do you have it?" Ada's voice was broken by soft exhales. "You can use it while I do this. That'll be really nice."

Cas switched the vibrator on and Ada moaned quietly at the sound.

"Just tease it first, but it should be— I might ask for more, but tease me for a second first, okay?"

"Okay."

Cas traced the round vibrator head along Ada's left thigh, delighting in the way Ada's entire body shuddered. Her leg twitched higher onto the bed, and Cas slid the vibrator up her thigh.

"Cas." Ada's fingers were slick, wet. "Cas, please."

Cas dipped the head of the vibrator inside and, just as Ada arched to try and take it deeper, Cas pulled it away. Ada groaned, her fingers picking up speed.

"Fuck."

Cas teased her again, before, on the third time, she slid the vibrator fully inside. Ada immediately moaned, her voice loud, carrying, and it went right to Cas's head.

"Oh fuck." Ada's fingers tripped. "Up a little bit, I— Yes, yes, right there. Just back and forth really small right there."

Cas could do that. She would happily do anything that Ada asked her to right now.

She barely moved it more than a centimeter, but each small thrust dragged a deep moan from Ada. She felt each moan viscerally, and she pressed her own thighs together to try to soothe some of her own need, before she leaned forward and started trailing kisses along the inside of Ada's thighs.

Thighs that were trembling under Cas's lips.

"Cas, I'm—" Ada moved her free hand to her breast, started rolling her nipple in between her fingers. Cas thrust the vibrator again, and Ada's entire body briefly went rigid before she lifted herself up off the bed. "Fuck, fuck, fuck."

Cas continued to move the vibrator as Ada settled before finally pulling it away and switching it off. She'd just set it on the bedside table when Ada grabbed Cas by the shoulders and dragged her up onto the bed, moving until they were lying in the center.

Cas's body landed on Ada's with a heavy thump, and she laughed roughly as she picked some of her weight up onto her arm.

"Eager?"

"Yes." Ada barely got the word out before Cas was kissing her, pressing her hips desperately against Ada's, trying for any little bit of friction she could get. Her dress had long since ridden up around her waist, but it wasn't enough. She needed more of her skin touching Ada's, needed to feel the press of their bodies together.

Almost as though she was reading her mind, Ada's fingers found the zipper on the back of Cas's dress and slashed it open, her fingers immediately tracing the exposed skin of Cas's back.

Cas pressed her knees into the bed, sitting up just enough to start pulling the dress up over her head. The corset top was tight, but after some maneuvering she got it off and threw it back over her shoulder without a second thought, especially once Ada sat up and took one of Cas's nipples into her mouth.

"Oh god." Cas threaded her fingers through Ada's hair, holding her there. She rolled her other nipple between her fingers, a moan slipping out from her lips as Ada's free hand started tracing down her belly.

Cas knew where she was going, could feel the anticipation building. She wasn't quite naked yet, but the minimalist underwear she'd had to wear with the dress made her feel like she was.

"What is this?" Ada traced the top of Cas's underwear, her fingers trying to slide underneath.

"Strapless," Cas said. She was breathless, barely explaining. "No lines. And the slit, you know."

Ada nodded, dazed. "How do you . . . ?"

"Just peel them off." Cas reached back and unstuck the back from the base of her spine, sliding it back over her bum. Ada peeled the front section off and managed to remove them completely and throw them onto the floor in the vague direction of Cas's dress.

Ada's fingers were between Cas's thighs before she could even catch her breath.

"You're soaking wet," Ada said, her voice thick with want, and Cas whimpered as Ada's fingers brushed, just once, over her clit.

"It's really fucking hot watching you come," Cas said. She was trying to keep her hips still, trying to let Ada lead, but she was desperate for contact. Desperate for Ada's fingers inside her. She reached up and rolled her nipple between her fingers, and at the movement, Ada leaned forward again and kissed Cas's breast, blowing gently until her nipple formed a hard peak.

"Ada." Cas rocked her hips, pressing down so she was very nearly grinding against Ada's thigh. Ada circled her tongue over Cas's nipple before, finally, drawing a deep, intentional circle over Cas's clit.

"Fuck." Cas wrapped one arm around Ada's shoulders, her hips lifting up, like she was trying to evade the sensation. Ada's hand followed her, her fingers persistent, slow, torturously good. But she needed more, needed the pressure inside her to ebb.

"Put your fingers inside me," Cas said. "Please, I—"

She was usually not one to beg, but something about Ada made everything in Cas fall apart.

Ada, luckily, didn't feel the need to tease her. She curled two fingers inside without hesitation, and Cas slid her free hand down to roll frantic circles over her clit as Ada fucked her with her fingers. Her thrusts were slow, deliberate, and with each one, Cas got closer and closer to the edge.

Ada slipped a third finger inside and that, finally, was what did it. Her entire body trembled, her arm tightening around Ada's shoulders like it was the only thing tethering her to the bed. Cas rode her fingers, the circles she was drawing on her clit loose and sloppy, until her orgasm passed, slowing her hips as her body settled.

Ada trailed her fingers up over Cas's clit as she moved her hand away, making a point to lick them clean.

"You're a dream," Cas said. She took Ada's cheeks in her hands and kissed her, slow, steady, savoring. She could taste herself on Ada's tongue, and it was a heady combination.

"Go again?"

Cas shook her head and slid off Ada's lap, her legs trembling a little bit too much to safely support her weight. "I just need to lie here for a second. Get my breath back."

Her skin was hot, sweaty, her hair was sticking to the back of her neck. She shifted her hair off her skin, but it was so short, it didn't move far enough to provide her with any real relief.

Ada slid over to the opposite side of the bed and fell back onto her pillow, Cas lying down beside her. As soon as Cas was settled, Ada rolled onto her side.

"It's a thousand degrees in here," Ada said. She was more speaking to the ceiling, but Cas nodded. Every single inch of her felt warm and sweaty.

"I'm going to open the window, hold on." Ada rolled away and walked quickly to her windows. She reached behind the curtains, and after a few seconds, Cas heard the distant sounds of traffic a few streets away.

Ada collapsed back onto the bed. She didn't curl into Cas's side again, but took her hand instead, her eyes falling closed as the breeze fluttered into the room. Neither of them spoke—it was just their breath, the brush of the curtains on the floor, the sounds of the cars out on the road—and Cas had never felt more at ease.

She'd been in these moments hundreds of times, these "afters," when they were both sated, but every time before, Cas had been keen to put her clothes back on. To go home, to forget, entirely, the person she'd just spent the last few hours with.

Cas could have lingered in this moment forever. Could have spent the rest of her life, here, in this bed, with Ada holding her hand.

Ada slung one arm around Cas's waist, her fingers trailing over the tattoos on Cas's right arm.

"I really like these." Ada traced the outline of the lion on Cas's biceps before moving to the triangle at the back of her elbow. It wasn't a cohesive sleeve, but she'd added so many one-offs to her arm over the years that it was steadily becoming one.

"I'm going to add another one." Cas twisted her arm and pointed at the blank space on the inside, just above her elbow. "A little heart right here."

"Your heart on your sleeve," Ada said.

"I—" Cas felt her cheeks heat. "Yeah. I thought it was fitting given . . . recent events." She squeezed Ada's arm, and Ada's eyes brightened.

"That's the gayest thing you've ever said."

Cas laughed and nudged Ada's side. "Shut up."

"It's cute, though," Ada said. "When are you getting it done?"

"Appointment's in a couple of weeks."

She'd scheduled it a few days before the reunion, determined, no matter what, to commemorate her time in the villa. Her time with Ada. Even if things hadn't worked out, she knew that Ada had changed her irrevocably.

It was a little scary, even now, but she knew it was for the best. And it was worth remembering that.

"Do you think your artist would be willing to pencil me in, too? I want one."

"Now this is the gayest thing *you've* ever said," Cas said, grinning.

"Shut up," Ada said, but Cas couldn't stop smiling.

"And here, I thought your perfume would be enough. Now you need a matching tattoo with your villa girlfriend."

Ada turned to look at Cas, their faces a few inches apart. "If you were my villa girlfriend, you'd take me on that tarot card, pasta-making, walking date."

Cas laughed and tightened her hold on Ada's shoulders, rolling onto her side so she could press their bodies together.

"We can go tomorrow if you want. I'm very, *very* free from now until the end of time."

Ada buried her face into Cas's neck, pressed a kiss to her pulse point. "Perfect."

EPILOGUE

ONE YEAR LATER

"DO YOU THINK I could spend the rest of the ride on my knees?" Cas was already shifting up in her seat as she asked. "My arse is going to be so red and sweaty if I don't stop sitting on this leather."

The media company driver, Jeremi, laughed and rolled his eyes at her in the rearview.

"You're more than welcome, but if I have to hit the brakes suddenly and you go flying, that's your problem."

Cas snorted. "I'm sure they'll eventually find someone to replace me."

Jeremi grinned at her in the mirror. "Bold of you to assume they don't have a queue of replacements already lined up. There's a whole new *Hot Summer* cast that'll be out of the villa in a week. You're not the only one that can chat shit about reality TV."

Cas held her middle finger up at him. "Fuck off."

Cas's phone pinged from the seat—a sound that still gave her flashbacks to her time in the villa—and she looked down. She expected to see her producer's name since they'd been in near constant touch after she and Ada had signed the collaboration deal with Boom Media last month, but was delighted to see Ada's name there instead.

Ada: here yet?

Cas couldn't stop the smile that filled her face as she replied.

Cas: no not yet

Cas: we're on the way

Cas: I'm going to have a red arse in the pictures because this leather is literally a million degrees

Cas stared at their conversation until **typing** appeared underneath Ada's name. After a few seconds, Ada replied.

Ada: jesus christ what is wrong with you how is your arse always red

Cas: Alskjdf it's not my fault stop blaming me

Ada: 😶😶😶

Ada: right. It's not your fault for wearing the shortest shorts money can buy and then getting in a leather-lined car

Cas: a;skdjf shut up, you loved these shorts last I checked

Ada: correction, I loved taking them OFF. I
couldn't care less about the shorts
themselves

Cas: tell that to the way your jaw dropped
when you saw me in them

Ada: . . .

Ada: well it's not my fault you have
excellent thighs

Cas laughed out loud and typed out a quick reply (I do don't I? See you soon x) before clicking into her email.

She'd read through the plan for today approximately fifteen thousand times, but every time she thought about the pending photo shoot and recording session, she was convinced that there was something she was going to miss or forget about. It was a feeling she was too familiar with after years of event planning, the way the rush of panic never seemed to really ebb.

It was a good thing that Cas apparently found all the cortisol exciting.

It's just promo shots and then we're recording the first episode, Tatum, her producer, had said in their latest response to Cas's panic about some detail or another. Nothing to stress about. Just bring yourself, good questions, and a smile!

Cas tried to remind herself to relax as the car trundled down Hackney Road toward the studio. They were planning on taking a couple of pictures in the studio itself—her and Ada in their podcast chairs, dramatic poses with the mics, etc.—before walking down to London Fields and grabbing some lifestyle photos in the park. Their photographer had a vision, apparently, "Very Dalí-esque, if you're down for it," and Cas didn't quite know what he meant by that, but she was more than willing to roll with the punches these days.

Ada was already waiting outside when Jeremi pulled up to the studio, and she immediately bounded over to the car and practically tore the door off the hinges.

"Hi." She kissed Cas full on the mouth, hardly concerned with the fact that Cas was in the process of falling out of the car door. "I missed you."

"I missed *you*."

Ada had been in Berlin all week working on expanding her most recent stationery collection, a collaboration with a European paper goods brand. They'd spoken every night, but their flat had been dreadfully quiet without her. Their cat, Tarot, a recent addition, had kept Cas company in the interim, but it was still far too lonely, rolling around their flat without Ada around.

It was all very gay and pathetic if Aisha was to be believed. And Aisha was, as usual, to be believed.

"Did you get everything sorted?" Cas asked, waving goodbye to Jeremi and climbing out of the car. Ada sighed heavily, and Cas laughed. "Oh no."

"No, it's fine, there's just a lot that still needs sorting out, so I'll probably have to go back in a few weeks. But I'm excited to be here today."

"I'm excited, too," Cas agreed. "It's about time we finally stopped talking about the first episode and actually filmed the thing."

There had been a surprising amount to figure out in the month since Cas and Ada had signed on with this latest opportunity. They'd needed a podcast name, a calendar of guests, a laundry list of sponsorships they'd then had to record. They'd known, without a doubt, who their first guests were going to be, but their calendars were packed these days, so they'd been nearly impossible to pin down. Still, Cas and Ada would never have started with anyone else.

"What time are Sienna and Femi supposed to get here?"

"Half one." Cas resisted the urge to pull out her phone again and confirm. "We'll be taking pictures right up until they arrive."

They crossed the pavement, hand in hand, pausing on the doorstep so that Cas could rummage around in her bag for her ID card. Ada just watched, expression amused, as Cas pulled out her wallet, a USB stick, a ChapStick, and no ID.

"And how many questions do you have planned about Femi and the ring he hasn't yet bought?"

Cas barked a laugh. "Only about a dozen."

Femi had shown up on their doorstep six months ago, soaking wet from the rain, and told them that *I know it's early, okay, but I want to propose to Sienna and is that crazy? Am I going to freak her out? And what kind of ring should I get?*

Cas and Ada had talked him off the ledge, if only barely, and Cas had taken to pestering him about it ever since.

"He just needs to do it," Ada said, watching Cas's continued struggle. "When you know, you know."

She checked one more pocket and, finally, unearthed her ID card.

"Does that mean I should just do it, then?" Cas asked. She

raised an eyebrow, a somewhat successful attempt at making her very serious comment seem humorous.

Ada pressed her lips together, a failed effort to contain her smile. "Are you thinking about it?"

"Only every day."

"Me, too."

It wasn't going to happen today. Probably wasn't going to happen for a while. But the promise of this, of forever, was making Cas giddy.

Cas leaned in, her lips a breath away from Ada's. "I love you."

Cas felt more than saw Ada's smile. "I love you, too." Ada kissed her once, twice, before she pulled back, eyes bright. "Now, let's go before Tatum kills us for being late because we were making out."

"Again," Cas added, and Ada laughed.

"Exactly."

Together, they opened the door and crossed the threshold, the late morning sun on their backs. And if you asked Cas, it felt like the perfect way to take their next step forward.

ACKNOWLEDGMENTS

Me from several years ago was convinced that writing a second book would be easier than writing a first. That, having cleared many of the initial hurdles, I would have a little more confidence, a little more of an idea of what a completed book looked like before it made its way into the world. Unfortunately, that is exactly what made writing this book so difficult.

Writing a book from scratch after spending so much time perfecting a late-stage manuscript was an enormous challenge, and I'm eternally grateful to everyone who not only made this process bearable but made it enjoyable. To everyone who reminded me that I can, in fact, write a book.

Thank you to my wonderful agent, Jill Marr, for her continued and much-needed support. I appreciate you always, but especially in your enthusiastic responses to my random emails about book ideas I've had while desperately avoiding sorting out the plot issues in *Hot Summer*. Thank you, too, to the entire team over at SDLA—I'm grateful to each and every one of you. You work tirelessly to support your authors, and I'm grateful to be among them.

Thank you to my out-of-this-world editor, Gaby Mongelli—getting to work on this book from the very start with you was a dream. We started with an idea we both couldn't stop giggling about and, together, made it into a book I'm proud of. I can't thank you enough for the calls, the emails, and the ideas that helped me turn this from a mess of words into a love story that makes my heart soar.

Thank you to Ashley Di Dio, my lovely editor: We brought this book over the finish line together, and I'm so grateful for you.

The team at Putnam, too, is beyond—Brittany Bergman, Erin Byrne, Emily Mileham, Maija Baldauf, Lorie Pagnozzi, Alison Cnockaert, Madeline Hopkins, Alice Dalrymple, Megha Jain, Emily Leopold, Molly Pieper, Nicole Biton, Bianca Mestiza, Anthony Ramondo, Sanny Chiu. Thank you all for everything you've done and will do to bring this book into the world. *Hot Summer* wouldn't be what it is without you, and I'm eternally thankful.

Thank you to the outstanding team across the pond at Michael Joseph, but particularly my brilliant UK editor, Hannah Smith. I'm grateful every day that we get to work together.

Thank you to my fellow writers, my friends: Annie Abel, KT Hoffman, Jenny Howe, Courtney Kae, Alexandra Kiley. I love talking shop with you guys and screaming about how brilliant your books are. Thank you to the wider romance community, too—I am inspired every day by the love stories you write, talk about, celebrate. There are way too many writers to thank here, but know that your words have meant the world to me.

I'd also like to thank all the other artists and creators who helped me find space to breathe this year. Thank you to Carly Rae Jepsen, Niall Horan, David Bisbal, and Taylor Swift for making the music that was my soundtrack over the last year. Thank you, Pally, for your piano renditions of the *Stardew Valley* soundtrack, and to every single person on YouTube who made hours-long compilations of gaming music that I used to write this book. Mike's Mic, mila tequila, Plumbella, Friendly Space Ninja: Thanks for making videos that provided much-needed breaks and gut-busting laughs. I know how much work it takes to make things, and I am grateful to all these people for their time and creative energy. It kept me going.

Enormous thank-you to my friends and family. The people I love more than anything else in the world. Thank you for your incredible support and for always knowing exactly when I need a laugh or a random story or a care package full of Kraft Mac & Cheese and Pop-Tarts.

Thanks to my dad, as always, for his unending support. Dad, your random phone calls about the Idaho news were a much-needed distraction from my spiralling about this book. I appreciate each and every time you asked me about it and, though I know you've never watched *Love Island* properly in your life, I love that you were excited anyway. I'm sorry it's not the sequel to *Wanderlust* that you're after, but trust me, this is a much better second book.

Thanks to my sisters, Hannah and Megan. I love you both so much. I miss you every day and have cherished every moment we've gotten to spend together this year. Thank you for sending me hauls of everything (even the silly things), for

FaceTiming me at random, and for coming up with increasingly complex plans for what we'll do if/when One Direction finally goes on a reunion tour. Hopefully this year is the year.

Thank you to my amazing friends: Ashley, Beks, Eloise, Mallory, Sam, Sarah, Serena. I'm terrible at replying to texts, but I love you. Thank you to Aqsa—our after-school chats bring me so much joy, especially after a difficult day. I'm eternally grateful for our friendship.

Thank you to my best friends, Eli and Vanessa. I miss you constantly and can't believe that we've now been friends for ten years. TEN YEARS . . . and we've lived in the same time zone for two of them. You guys are my perpetual reminder that love and friendship aren't determined by distance or country but, instead, by the time you give and the dedication you show to one another.

And even though they can't read, thank you to the pets I love—Waffle and Muffin and Petey. Waffle, you've brought so much happiness into our house and I'm so glad we adopted you. I love your fluffy tummy, twitchy tail, and annoyed little meows when I don't get up to feed you fast enough. Muffin and Petey, I love getting pictures of you from across the ocean and I can't wait to give you a big hug (that you'll probably hate) and sooo many toys.

And, of course, to Emmet. I love you beyond words and cannot even begin to tell you how much I love watching you grow up into the amazing person you are and are becoming. Thank you for always being willing to enter into "I write or I have to buy you V-bucks" deals with me and for letting me borrow your gaming headphones so I could focus. Thanks for letting me sit in your room while you designed your Minecraft builds and enduring my severe lack of knowledge as you asked me questions about what you should do—getting out of my room and away from my writing desk was very necessary, so thank you for letting me pester you and sorry for not understanding anything about Minecraft. Thank you, too, for indulging and engaging in my *Hunger Games* obsession—it was a much-needed distraction from all the ways I wasn't writing this book and I think made us both very creative last spring. Or, at the very least, it gave us something to talk about endlessly, even if most of my comments boiled down to, "Do I want a sugar cube? *Yes*."

And finally: Thank you to everyone who read *Wanderlust*— your joy over a story that had consumed several years of my life brought me so much happiness . . . I can't even begin to describe it. You've changed my life and made one of my biggest dreams come true. I hope that you enjoyed *Hot Summer* and that you found Cas and Ada as delightful as I did. I hope that I get to write many more books for you and that, together, we can follow more and more people along their journeys to find love.

DISCUSSION QUESTIONS

1. What is your favorite reality dating show, and why? What did you find similar or different about that show and the fictional dating show *Hot Summer*?

2. If you could create a reality dating show, what would it be called? What would be the rules? Would you participate, and if so, what would your one-line introduction be?

3. Why do you think Cas is drawn to Ada, and vice versa? What makes their connection special?

4. Which contestant on *Hot Summer* do you think you'd be most attracted to or develop a romantic connection to in real life, and why? Which contestant do you think you're most like, and why?

5. Have you ever encountered (or dated) a "Brad" type of person in real life? If so, how did that go? If you were in Cas's position, how would you have handled interacting with him?

6. What was your favorite scene in the novel, and why?

7. Do you think Cas would have developed the same friendships and relationships from the villa if she'd met the contestants in the real world? Why or why not?

8. Entering the show, Cas had a particular view on dating and relationships—to keep it light and fun, no commitment. Have you ever experienced heartbreak in previous relationships, and if so, how did it color your views on dating? What is your viewpoint on relationships and love now?

9. Do you think Cas should have told Ada the truth about why she was on *Hot Summer* when they were in the retreat room? Why or why not? What would you have done?

10. What were your thoughts on the ending of the book?

ELLE EVERHART is the author of *Wanderlust* and *Hot Summer*. She is a secondary English teacher in East London, and when she's not writing or teaching, she's hanging out with her son and obsessing over the worst shows on television.

VISIT ELLE EVERHART ONLINE

elleeverhart.com

🐦 📷 ElleEverhart